SESSIONS

Therapy For the Soul

A Novel by

PAZ LÓPEZ

Sessions Therapy for the Soul

First Edition English: March 13, 2025

Copyright © 2025 by Paz López (Marcela Paz Maldonado)

Registered in the Library of Congress, March 13, 2025.

ISBN: 979-8-218-64883-1 (Paperback)
ISBN: 978-1-645-16312-1 (Digital Version)

© Published by Paz López (Marcela Paz Maldonado).
© Cover design by 3DSmartDesigns.
© Translated and Edited by Renée Maldonado.

Dedication

To my husband, the love of my life, who has stood by me for so many years with unwavering support. You held me up when I felt like falling, patiently waiting for me to take the leap and bring my stories, reflections, experiences, and dreams to life on paper. Your belief in me has been my strength, and for that, I am forever grateful.

To my daughters, who have shown me the beauty of life and who, every day, remind me that dreams can come true. Through you, I see a reflection of my greatest joys and my most precious hopes fulfilled.

To my grandchildren, both those here now and those yet to come, the expansion of my heart and soul. You are the future I cherish and the light that keeps my dreams alive.

To my dear friend Wendy, who, many years ago, told me, "You can do it," and never stopped believing in me. Your unconditional support has been a guiding star in my journey.

Finally, to anyone reading this: never forget that dreams don't come true unless you dare to try.

With all my heart,
Paz Lopez

Contents

Prologue

This is the story of Dennis, a young woman tormented by events and situations that, due to her short existence, she has not yet been able to understand. However, these are the very things she will have to battle for a long time before finding the balance her life needs. The search for answers to all her questions will lead her to discover a reality different from the one she knows, but time and her virtues will make her realize that her destiny was always the same.

The loss of her parents will mark the beginning of a chain of events that will show her a different path—one that feels hostile to her at first, not knowing that this very path, in the future, will be the one that brings back the peace and harmony she has always longed for.

She will have to deal with pain and misunderstandings that will steal the smile from her face. But Dennis's heart is much bigger, and it will not harbor hatred or resentment, which will make her understand that she was not born to hate, especially not the one who was the love of her life.

Life will present Dennis with difficult and extreme situations. Little by little, she will discover her purpose in life, and her charisma will make her a beloved person among all those who come to know her. Dennis will always be remembered and admired by those around her.

She will meet people who will take an important place in her life and heart—people she will come to love as much, or even more, than those who are no longer by her side. In the end, they will become the family that life has given her in return for her love and dedication.

CHAPTER 1

The First Step

The waiting room was full of people, which was precisely what Dennis had wanted to avoid, only now it was impossible to go back. She had made the effort and was already there, now she just needed to wait. After all, she could not let all the extra energy it took for her to decide to find someone to help her deal with the difficult problem on her hands in vain.

Dennis raised her head and looked around the room for an empty seat so she could sit down. She knew she could not hold everyone's eyes—she needed to quickly find a place to sit so she could disappear from the sight of others. Conveniently, a lady who was right next to the entrance door was called, as it was her turn, and she quickly left, leaving behind a vacant chair. Dennis didn't waste any more time looking and swiftly sat down. She just wanted to stop catching everyone's attention. She felt that everyone was looking at her which made her very uncomfortable.

Once seated, she braced herself for the long wait since the room was full of patients. As she began to look around, slowly and carefully, she watched everything, as was habit with Dennis. Suddenly her eyes stopped at the opposite corner of the waiting room. There, she saw a small table next to a water dispenser, and on the table, there were glasses and other supplies to make coffee. She thought about getting up for a coffee in order to make the waiting more bearable, but at the same time, she was struck by the idea that, if she did so, someone would take her seat leaving her standing again, and for who knows how much longer. With that, she dismissed the possibility of coffee.

The minutes began to pass quickly and the clock that hung over the patient care window already read five o'clock. Dennis checked the time with the watch on her left hand, and yes, it was five in the afternoon, an hour later than when her appointment had been schedule. To make sure she was right, Dennis opened her bag in search of a small white card, which had been sent to her by mail, confirming the date and time of her appointment. The card did, in fact, have her scheduled for four in the afternoon that Thursday, yet it was already five.

She knew there were surely other patients before her, and that the queue was reason for such a delay. Suddenly, her attention was drawn to a loud bang, caused by a blonde woman who was leaving the doctor's office. It was so strong that the lithographs that were hanging on the wall trembled and lost their perfect alignment, leaving them all crooked. The woman kept talking, and the tone of her voice implied that she was very upset. She was heard saying a couple of insulting words as she crossed the hall and picked up her bag and umbrella which were hanging on the hook next to the entrance door. Dennis wondered, what could have angered that woman so much that she would react like that?

Outside, the afternoon was gray and sad and, although it had stopped raining, the sky continued to look menacing. That morning, weather reports had said that the chances of rain were less than 30 percent, yet it had rained almost all day. But who could believe meteorologists? They were almost never right about anything.

The girl behind the window looked like she was busy, but you could also tell that she was tired. Every time the phone rang, she slammed her fist on the table and grumbled. The tone of her voice made clear that she was very irritated, and after a while, she had lost her good manners since she no longer used a polite greeting, as was customary, whenever she answered the phone. Dennis thought that perhaps it would have to do directly with the fact that, for some reason she didn't know, the appointments of the consultation were not running on time which made the patients upset, in turn taking their anger out on the receptionist.

No one dared to get up, or even move, after the angry blonde left. The room plunged into a long silence. Still, time continued to progress, Dennis becoming a little impatient. She wanted to see who the next patient would be, who would get up from their seat to enter the doctor's office, but still, no one had come out to call for anyone.

The medical office was home to three doctors: a traumatologist, a cardiologist and a deaf mute—that being a psychologist (Dennis thought all psychologists were deaf mutes since they never bothered to listen or say much). Seeing that more time had passed and with no signs to indicate they'd be calling the next patient, Dennis thought about getting up and going to ask the receptionist directly when it would finally be her turn. She knew she there was a chance they would dismiss her and tell her to go bother someone else, but she got up anyways. At the very moment Dennis stood up, she heard her name. The receptionist had called her. She gestured with her hand, beckoning her to the window. Dennis picked up her bag and walked over to the receptionist.

Dennis was a little intimidated by the receptionist, thinking that she would explode and take it out on her person, but decided not to indulge in that fantasy, instead opting to listen to what the woman had to say. She hoped she wasn't going to tell her that something had changed regarding her appointment and that she would have to stay there, sitting, who knows for how much longer.

Already at the window, the receptionist spoke in a low voice and normal tone.

"The doctor will see you now, please follow me."

Dennis felt something interesting, a shiver running through her body, and as the girl walked around the small reception to show her the way, she noticed the tears in the receptionist's eyes. She had been crying. Dennis felt an immense sadness emanating from the woman and, when she opened the door indicating where to enter, Dennis took her hand, deciding to tell her that everything would be fine. The woman's face twisted slightly as she spoke: "Come in and have a seat, the doctor will be here shortly."

Dennis looked at her and nodded, not saying a word. Her eyes scanned the room, watching everything as she walked slowly towards a small area furnished with two armchairs, a small table, and a floor lamp. Something told her she would be sitting there. As her gaze went from left to right, very slowly and carefully, leaving nothing behind, she looked at pictures on the wall. Shelves also lined the walls with only a few books, a choice Dennis noted as purely decorative. The books were probably the works of unknown doctors, those whom nobody remembered anymore, but who once did something that made them important or famous. Just like the lawyers who put out legislation and penal codes, volumes and volumes of them, now caked with years of dust; books that are never opened and even less often read.

She then found herself facing the doctor's desk. A large and wide table, evidently treated with care, it was noticeable that it was just recently polished as it shone with that special shine that only a rich oil could possibly give. Dennis also noticed that everything was very well organized (too much for her taste), a stark contrast to the rest of the things in the room.

The left side of the table housed a small lamp and a tiny, miserable house plant, the kind that grew in glass bottles. The placement of the plant was deliberate, the lamp being its only light source. The only other things on the desk were a notebook and a glass of water, nothing else. The remainder of the space was dedicated to showcasing the plain, exposed surface of the table.

Conversely, the rest of the room had congested walls with shelves full of things stored without care, placed there purposely with no intention to use them. On the right side of the room, a door revealed an attached space. The connected room emanated an air of clarity, distinct from the messy space which Dennis was currently standing in.

The room was dark, with a lone lamp illuminating the space in the absence of natural light. There was a window behind the desk, however it was covered by thick curtains, the kind that are designed to block out all light. It seemed important, if not intentional, that the place maintain a dim light.

Dennis continued to explore the rest of the new space, leaving the door of the previous room behind her. The walls were bare, empty, nothing hanging, cluttering, or congesting the space. There were also two armchairs, just like the ones she had seen in the first room. Once Dennis had finished scouring the place with her eyes, she made her way back to the first set of chairs with nothing left to do but wait for the doctor to come and the interrogation to begin. She seemed to have only bad experiences in the past with these types of doctors, so the thought of having to start therapy again started her stomach up in knots.

Once seated, she noticed a frame on the wall behind the armchair in front of her, a diploma which read: "Rona Michaels, Bachelor of Psychology, University of Buffalo, New York State"

Dennis, upon receiving this new information, felt shocked. *The doctor is a woman? I was sure he was a man!* Dennis thought to herself, a little confused.

As she settled in the armchair, she set her handbag on the floor. She had no other place to put it and thus opted to rest it up against the leg of the chair. Silence quickly filled the room, the minutes slowly passing. It had been at least ten minutes of complete silence before Dennis finally heard a noise which came from a neighboring room. It was the sound of a closing window, the kind that is made when you need to push down hard to get it to close. The glass shook from the force.

That noise alerted Dennis that the doctor was in the next room, and that she had been with the window open, enjoying the daylight and fresh air, unlike her, stuck in the gloom with the most suffocating silence as her only company, so very bored after so much waiting. It was already six o'clock in the afternoon, two hours later than when her appointment had been scheduled for.

CHAPTER 2

Remembering The Pain

The door suddenly creaked, pulling Dennis out of her thoughts. It was the doctor who had finally decided to treat her. Dennis felt a little confused, as when she had prepared to see Dr. Michaels, she expected a man, but now that she had the doctor in front of her, she realized that she guessed wrong, as the doctor was actually a woman.

The doctor made her entrance into the room after having made Dennis wait a long time and, without giving her any preparation, she presented herself to Dennis. It was all the same to her; she was a psychologist and would certainly treat Dennis as such.

Dennis thought to herself: in addition to all the previous waiting, she would also have to pay for time the doctor had wasted. It seemed quite unfair and perhaps even unethical since she had arrived on time.

Dr. Michaels first approached her desk, and without turning to look at the patient sitting there waiting for her, she took the glass of water and drank it. Then, she picked up her notebook and pencil and turned. She walked slowly, taking down some kind of note in it without looking up until she stopped right next to Dennis.

Dr. Michaels finally spoke:

"Hello," said the woman. "Good afternoon, I'm Dr. Michaels. You must be Dennis, right?" She down without waiting for Dennis to answer. Dennis nodded.

Dennis began to prepare in her mind, not knowing what the next thing the doctor would ask her could be, although she had practiced for some possible questions, such as those she thought would be infallible. *Why are you here?* and *What problem do you have?* And several other questions that, according to her, were likely to come up.

The doctor, already sitting in her chair in front of Dennis, watched her silently. She didn't ask any questions or make any gestures—she almost didn't breathe. Dennis was still waiting for the doctor to ask her first question, but it seemed that she was in no hurry to do so, even though it was already well past the time of her visit.

Dennis' hands were beginning to sweat, accompanied by a full-body flush which was reflected in a show of restlessness evidenced from her face to her feet—which did not stop moving, of course—which she believed to be completely inconspicuous. Dennis was already very tired of waiting. She was distraught and ready to run out of there any minute.

Dennis looked around everywhere while waiting for the doctor to ask the first question to start the session, but she made sure to keep her gaze from meeting the doctor's. As the room was rather dark, one would be able to look around without drawing much attention to themself. Minutes passed and still time felt frozen. No one was talking and Dennis, even if she wanted to, didn't know what to say, as the doctor *hadn't asked her anything yet*. How or where to start was the big question.

The heat that emanated from her hands brought up some memories. It reminded her of the time when she was so worried while waiting for Mark. It must've been a little over two years ago now. She was at the airport. It was packed with people and there was a lot of noise both from the people and from the airplanes on the tarmac outside. She remembered feeling extremely nervous. *I hadn't seen him for five years, amazing how the time had passed.* She had thousands of questions and doubts then as well. *How would it feel to see him again?* She wondered with her eyes glued to door at the fourth gate. She still hadn't seen him.

As the crowd pushed past her on all sides, she tried to keep her eyes focused on that door.

During the conversations prior to his arrival, Mark had told Dennis not to remember him as he was, that he had changed, that his hair no longer had those curls that she had always loved. Mark's hair was something Dennis always admired. That golden, curly hair, full of life and radiance, had always been something that attracted Dennis and put a smile on her face, always pulling deep sighs from her lips.

Of course, Mark had lost more than the divine hair he once had in his youth. He had also lost a leg. That was the reason why he returned home. At least, that's what Mark told Dennis in one of his phone calls, in which there had not been much talk because they were always accompanied by long silences. Every time he called, Dennis instantly pressed for information through questions, the kind of which Mark couldn't answer yet. Thus, the conversation always seemed to fall flat "*We'll talk about it soon,*" Mark would tell her.

Mark and Dennis had been in a relationship for what seemed like forever. They had shared so many things together that it was impossible to think of seeing them apart.

But Mark left. He left her without any explanation. Rather, he didn't even tell her that he was leaving her; Mark didn't say anything. He left, breaking her heart and leaving a deep void in her soul, something that was very difficult for Dennis to overcome.

Eventually, long after his unexplained departure, Dennis received news from him that he had joined the Navy and would be off traveling for a while, and, if it weren't for that accident, Dennis probably would never have seen him again.

Her pupils grew wider than thought possible when she finally saw him. There he was! It was real, there Mark was right before her eyes. He was much thinner since the last time he saw him. He also looked taller, although that was probably because of the weight loss and drastic change in hairstyle. It looked as if his head had been shaved just a few hours ago. There was no stubble or visible hair growth, but none of this mattered to her. For Dennis, she felt like she was coming back to life after having been lost for so many years.

She couldn't believe it; she was looking at him head-on and she couldn't feel any anger at him. She had loved him so much that she had no words to describe what he meant to her. At the same time, he had also caused her some of the greatest pains of her life next to the loss of her beloved parents. Mark was everything—her past, present, and future. They shared dreams and had made hundreds of plans together, all of which were destroyed the day he left.

Underneath his jacket, he wore a sporty, black turtleneck paired with jeans. She noticed he had very little difficulty walking. It was amazing how well he looked given that Mark had spent the last 8 months in rehab. But, of course, those months allowed him a strong recovery. That's what he had told her in his phone calls, which, although there had not been many, were enough to inform Dennis of the terrible accident he had been in. Still, after all this time, he returned home to her.

Agitated she began to scream: *Mark, Mark here, over here!* Jumping onto her tiptoes and beckoning with her hands. She could be seen very clearly; at that point it was difficult to go unnoticed. Mark raised his hand, nodding, and walked towards her. They hugged each other as tightly as they could, any harder and they would have melted into each other's skin. Seconds became minutes, and minutes stretched into more. It seemed that there had never been any distance. Could it be that they had never stopped loving each other? Mark was back, and that was the only thing Dennis cared about at the time.

In the consultation

A slight hoarseness was heard as the doctor cleared her throat, pulling Dennis out of her thoughts. The doctor swallowed and wet her lips taking a sip of water. She didn't say a word, opting to continue to watch Dennis. Dennis didn't know what to do; she had already lost track of time, caught up in remembering her painful experiences. Reliving her reunion with Mark, he who had been the greatest—perhaps only—love of her life, after whom she had decided not to love anyone else, proved to be quite the distraction.

Worried about how much time had passed, she searched for an opportunity to look at her watch. Unfortunately, Dennis always wore her watch with the dial on her forearm, which made it impossible for her to see what time it was without having to raise her arm to look. This would undoubtedly expose Dennis for her impatience, as she was very eager to get out of there.

At one point she couldn't take it anymore and moved carefully, using the greatest dexterity to change the position of her legs. She managed to rearrange herself in the armchair, which, luckily, was comfortable. It had a good backrest. Without it, it would have been impossible to spend so much time sitting there and doing nothing.

After that attempt at comfort, she raised her arm and delicately turned it over, leaving her forearm exposed that white sphere on her wrist now visible. She looked to how the hands were positioned, and they indicated that it was already a quarter past seven in the afternoon. It had been more than an hour since the receptionist had called her into the doctor's office, and three since she was originally supposed to have her appointment. Even though Dennis had arrived at her appointment ten minutes early—as she always did in order to ensure she wouldn't be late and that she'd have enough time to compose herself—nothing had gone according to plan.

Surprised by how quickly the afternoon had passed, she leaned over to pick up her bag. To follow, she looked at the doctor and spoke in a subtle voice.

"I'm sorry but must leave, I have a prior commitment and I can't be late."

"Don't worry, no problem, Dennis," she responded immediately. "I think we're off to a good start, don't you? See you next Thursday at the same time?"

Dennis, caught between confused and amazed, already moving towards the exit door, replied:

"Yes, for sure, on Thursday at the same time."

What was she saying? She realized that she had signed her own death sentence by confirming that she would return next week!

How could she have done that, having already spent more than three hours in tremendous agony, getting tired of sitting, waiting, and having barely spoken to the doctor? Her confirmation implied that she thought the doctor was a rather good doctor. On top of everything else, the doctor had thought they had a good start because of it. What "start" was she talking about? Dennis felt very confused. She just wanted to get out of there as fast as she could—and that's what she did.

As she left the room, she noticed that there were no patients left in the waiting room and that the receptionist had left. Quickly, she walked to the door, opened it, and walked out. She hurried across the street to the parking lot where her car was waiting for her, opened the door, put the key in the ignition, and left.

CHAPTER 3

The Importance... Move On

Dennis' week went by at its usual fast pace. By the following morning, her initial and peculiar encounter with her new therapist had slipped from her thoughts, and as the week drew to a close, even the prospect of their next session had faded from memory. Her life seemed to always be caught on the edge of restlessness, a constant back-and-forth rhythm leaving little room for personal pursuits. In the absence of close family ties, her social development seemed to be stunted, leading to a scarcity of friends or romantic connections. This inadvertently directed her focus towards her work, effectively deterring intrusive thoughts and unanswered questions.

The familiarity of being overburdened accompanied Dennis in the role she'd assumed. Navigating the realm of advertising agency management had been an unexpected opportunity, almost as if plucked from a daydream. It bore the hallmarks of a once-in-a-lifetime chance, a feat she regarded with much contentment. The allure of the potential for success and recognition had exerted a powerful pull, an aspiration that her persistent effort and commitment had begun to crystallize into reality.

An astute and responsible individual, Dennis willingly embraced challenges, regardless of their complexity. The passage of time had her on the precipice of her thirties, prompting reflective contemplation. Echoes of past plans she'd shared with Mark occasionally surfaced, although the disparities between then and now tempered her introspection. Preferring not to linger, Dennis poured her energies into her work, her forte and comfort zone.

While exercise wasn't a fervent pursuit for Dennis, she remained in admirable physical shape, albeit perhaps leaner than she'd prefer—a possible consequence of work-induced stress. And not to be overlooked, there were ongoing concerns that weighed heavily on her mind, evolving into persistent anxieties that blurred the line between normal apprehension and genuine distress.

In recent years, Dennis' life had witnessed remarkable transformations. Her ascent from a mere assistant to department head was marked by whispers of skepticism and conjecture, with some insinuating ambiguous "favors" for her superior as the catalyst for her swift progression.

In truth, the agency operated without a conventional hierarchical structure. Rather, it was guided by the vision of two remarkable women who stood as its proprietors. These two sisters, now seasoned with age, had nurtured a dream from their early days, resolute to manifest it into reality. They invested their utmost into the company, which held a significance surpassing that of a mere advertising agency—it was a labor of personal devotion. Through unwavering dedication over the years, their endeavor had blossomed into one of the city's most esteemed and renowned agencies.

The defining hallmark of the Harrison sisters was their unwavering support for women's advancement. Their philanthropic efforts were primarily channeled towards initiatives that championed the well-being of children and young women. Rooted in their own struggles, having lost their parents at a tender age, the sisters had confronted adversity head-on, leaving them orphaned and with just each other for family. This history served as the driving force behind their formidable undertakings, echoing the sentiment that resilience could surmount any obstacle. Their firsthand familiarity with sacrifice and hardship lent a poignant authenticity to their efforts, resonating particularly with young women aspiring to transcend the limitations fate had dealt them.

Dennis, akin to many other determined young women, had taken a path marked by arduous sacrifices to simply complete her high school education. The aspiration of attending college had seemed a distant dream, almost unattainable. It was around this time that the Harrison Scholarship emerged, opening doors of possibility for a select cohort of determined women annually.

Renowned within its sphere, the Harrison Scholarship was an esteemed accolade. The agency, each year, meticulously chose ten recipients based on their academic and professional profiles. This scholarship entailed the annual coverage of tuition expenses, with potential employment opportunities unfolding in the future. Naturally, it came with certain prerequisites, encompassing active participation in agency activities and devoting time to volunteer endeavors aligned with the Harrison advertising agency's charitable endeavors. Moreover, maintaining a commendable academic performance was of paramount importance—a non-negotiable the agency upheld rigorously.

Dennis' journey intertwined with the agency during a communal project where she participated in social initiatives. These ventures were emblematic of the agency's ethos, bridging their dual objectives of amassing funds for the annual scholarships they bestowed while concurrently spearheading community engagement initiatives. Although over two years had since elapsed, Dennis vividly recalled this moment— an interval marked by diligence, activities, trials, and, at times, a tinge of melancholy.

Some time ago

During her undergrad years, Dennis gained a positive academic reputation, motivated her ultimate goal: getting her degree. She was exceptional in all of her classes, but she needed an extra year to finish due to a few subjects. She was almost there, just a few months away from graduating, but sometimes she felt like it that day would never come.

With fewer classes to worry about, Dennis could dedicate more time to part-time jobs that helped her make ends meet. However, this particular year was tough. Her financial situation had become much more complicated causing her to lose her biggest financial support. She couldn't renew her student loans because she hadn't graduated on time like she was supposed to. Despite her efforts, she couldn't do anything to fight this rule.

She managed to balance her work and late-night study sessions, but she had hit a wall of exhaustion. She kept pushing forward, not thinking too much about the financial problems that burdened her until they became impossible to ignore. She didn't know how she'd pay for the rest of her schooling. Thankfully, Dennis held onto a belief that things would work out somehow—her motto had always been *"something will happen."* And something did happen. A turning point came, and her circumstances changed for the better.

During her college years, Dennis formed a strong friendship with her advertising instructor, which led to numerous internships in the field throughout her studies. The instructor, affectionately called Tammy, though her real name was Mary, had a discreet persona and didn't reveal much about her personal life.

Tammy possessed a charismatic and kind-hearted nature, always eager to lend a hand to those in need. Although Dennis initially attended college part-time due to financial constraints, her dedication to moving forward didn't go unnoticed by Tammy. Their student-teacher relationship developed and grew over time.

In recent years, Dennis not only assisted Tammy's classes but also took on projects within Tammy's work at the Harrison advertising agency. Tammy's dual role as an educator and a publicist allowed Dennis to witness the practical application of advertising concepts, strengthening her admiration for Tammy's profession.

Despite her admiration, Dennis often felt overwhelmed by financial and psychological challenges. Balancing assistantships, part-time jobs, and academic demands took a toll. However, these part-time jobs did provide some much-needed extra income, which helped her manage minor expenses while relying on student loans as her primary support.

During her final semester of school, Tammy approached Dennis with an opportunity to assist with a significant agency project. This project involved a presentation with various agencies participating, coordinated by the Harrison advertising agency. This annual event had become a tradition for the agency and required meticulous planning and execution. Dennis readily accepted, as saying no to Tammy was never an option.

In that particular year, Tammy found herself honored to represent the agency and contribute her insights to the event. However, recognizing the need for additional support, she immediately thought of Dennis. The event revolved around fundraising for annual scholarships, a cause dear to the agency's owners, Eileen and Mary Harrison, who were expected to attend.

While Dennis hadn't interacted with the agency's owners personally and their recognition wasn't her primary focus, she held a deep respect for Tammy. Demonstrating her ability to handle the pressures of practical work and keen to impress Tammy, Dennis eagerly embraced the opportunity to contribute and ensure the success of the presentation.

Remembering the day of the event

Everything was prepared and very well organized so that the event went perfectly. "*To trust Dennis was to expect perfect results,*" Tammy said.

The evening commenced with a series of presentations highlighting ecological and multicultural projects, eliciting applause from the audience. As is common with such gatherings, there were varying reactions. Some expressed disapproval towards the explored ideas, while others maintained a serious countenance, showing reserved enthusiasm for the proceedings.

The initial segment of the event transpired swiftly, aligning with the schedule outlined in the day's program. Dennis remained steadfast in her position from the event's commencement, her determination to witness her esteemed teacher Tammy's presentation unwavering.

The intermission arrived, prompting attendees to step outside for a breather and partake in refreshments. The cocktail lounge, conveniently located in the main lobby, had been thoughtfully arranged with an assortment of appetizers and canapé pastries. Both participants and event guests indulged in the offerings. Overheard conversations resonated with positive assessments of the evening and the intriguing nature of the presented projects. Curiosity buzzed in anticipation of the unveiling of the Harrison agency's project.

As previously announced, Tammy's presentation was slated to be followed immediately by the keynote address from the day's special guest, a distinguished historian. On this occasion, the agency's proposal centered on the restoration of an antiquated bookstore, acquired through a city auction. With the acquisition of this significant building, the Harrison agency initiated a public tender to solicit a range of ideas, including those from within the agency's own ranks. The responsibility for this project had been entrusted to Tammy, who had devoted considerable hours to its development. Dennis, collaborating closely with Tammy, played an integral role in shaping this initiative.

Dennis had played a pivotal role in orchestrating Tammy's entire presentation, affording her a comprehensive understanding of its content. Aware of the substantial commitment Tammy had dedicated to this fresh challenge, Dennis recognized it as an opportunity to garner recognition and acclaim after years of tireless effort. Though Dennis didn't anticipate personal recognition, the realization that she possessed the skillset necessary to spearhead a project of this caliber bolstered her self-assurance.

Tammy's fervor for the project was palpable. This chance was indeed exceptional; the project had been entrusted entirely to her stewardship. A favorable reception would signify the green light for its execution, marking a notable milestone in her career trajectory. While direct conversations about these matters between Dennis and Tammy were scarce, Tammy consistently acknowledged Dennis's aptitude for the field. This manifested in her commendations for Dennis's role as an assistant in both classes and various projects, affirming her capacity and potential in the profession.

That afternoon, the day of the event

Hours before the event, Dennis engaged in a conversation with her teacher, Tammy, sensing a subtle shift in her demeanor. Unable to pinpoint the exact issue, Dennis inquired gently:

"Tammy, everything okay?" she asked.

"It's nothing, just some nerves perhaps, nothing serious," Tammy responded.

"Don't worry, you're going to do great!" Dennis reassured her.

Tammy nodded, her attention focused on arranging pamphlets at the lobby entrance. Her voice carried across the distance.

"You're probably right. I'm likely just tired, I didn't sleep much last night. But tomorrow I'm going to rest all day," Dennis smiled and replied.

"I hope you can! You certainly deserve it. It's also likely I won't be able to make it to class, so you'll need to be in good shape to handle things without me. I have an important commitment I need to attend," Dennis concluded.

Having arrived early to organize preparations, Dennis had been observing Tammy for a while. She had distinctly noticed a faint, luminous white light encircling Tammy. This phenomenon had been a part of Dennis's reality for several years, originating from an incident that tragically claimed her parents' lives. As a result, this had become a deeply private and guarded matter, undisclosed to anyone.

The exact nature of these luminous occurrences that appeared beside people, or even near her, remained a mystery to Dennis. Nonetheless, she did acknowledge their presence. Troubled by the notion that these lights might be a sort of personal curse, she grappled with the worry that they could somehow trigger unfortunate events for those she held dear—painful experiences she had endured in the past with loved ones.

Dennis's intuition hinted at something amiss that afternoon, sparking her repeated contemplation about the implications of the luminous glow enveloping Tammy. Despite a strong inclination to approach Tammy and share her observation, Dennis chose to proceed with the day as usual. This wasn't due to a lack of concern, but rather a learned caution from previous instances where her well-intentioned comments had inadvertently caused distress. Thus, she decided to remain silent, recognizing the complexity of the matter.

The subject was intricate, often dismissed by skeptics due to its lack of scientific grounding. Dennis herself struggled to comprehend the phenomenon, making it even more challenging to broach with others. Understanding the potential consequences, Dennis opted to prioritize her financial concerns regarding her education. Dwelling on the uncertainty surrounding Tammy seemed impractical, especially considering the improbable nature of the situation.

Focusing on impending bank-related tasks became Dennis's priority. Recognizing the urgency of her situation, she scheduled a visit to the bank on Monday to explore options for negotiating her credit. Given the circumstances, she anticipated missing school, coinciding with Tammy's class hours.

The event continued

The intermission's musical interlude yielded to a speaker's announcement, signaling the return to seats for the event's second half and concluding segment. Amid the crowd's return to their positions, Dennis found herself seated off to the side, close to the central podium. However, a lingering unease tugged at her, as she hadn't spotted Tammy since before the event commenced. Wondering where Tammy might be, the nagging feeling churned in her stomach.

One of the Harrison agency representatives stepped up to the microphone, expressing gratitude to the attendees and emphasizing the dual purpose of the event: both a platform for presentations and a fundraiser for scholarships. She encouraged guests to contribute their donations to the designated person.

Following this introduction, the stage was given to the special guest speaker. Utilizing visual aids projected on the large screen, she recounted the history of the old bookstore, underscoring its significance for the city. She highlighted the agency's acquisition of the property through a public tender, aiming to restore and repurpose it in a way that honored its historical value while benefiting the community.

With her presentation concluded, she extended a gracious invitation to the upcoming Harrison agency presentation. However, when the agency representative called for Tammy to take the stage, an unexpected silence hung in the air. The absence of Tammy left a void on the platform. Suddenly, another agency staff member hurriedly approached Dennis, urging her to follow. Puzzled, Dennis complied and hurriedly left the room, guided by the agency staff member.

Their destination was an office space located at the rear of the building. Filled with trepidation, Dennis entered the room, only to come face to face with Mary Harrison—the owner of the Harrison agency and one of the Harrison sisters.

CHAPTER 4

Feelings of Guilt

Intrigue and fright were killing Dennis inside. The crowd did not stop their arguing until she raised her voice to ask a question.

"What's going on," she asked. "Where is Tammy?"

There was a lull in the commotion until Mary Harrison broke the silence. She spoke to her in a very soft but clear voice: "Excuse me, do I remember correctly that you are Tammy's assistant?"

"Well, we need you to help us continue with the event and take over the part of the presentation that was supposed to be Tammy's."

"What happened to Tammy," Dennis asked, surprised. "Where is she?"

Dennis was very upset. She still couldn't seem to understand a single thing that was going on.

Once again, the silence returned, but it was less overwhelming this time. One of Tammy's colleagues approached Dennis with important information.

"She was taken to the hospital," they began. "Tammy wasn't feeling well. I noticed she looked very emaciated when I saw her at the beginning of the event. I was there the moment she fainted. Luckily, we were able to call the paramedics quickly and Tammy had finally regained consciousness by the time they arrived, but they still decided it was best to take her to the hospital for further examinations."

Dennis brought her hands to her head, overwhelmed by guilt. She couldn't believe what had happened. She berated herself for not taking action when she should have seen it coming. Her heart pounded, and she couldn't express her true emotions to anyone. A deep sadness engulfed her as she realized the bright light she had seen near Tammy was some kind of warning. She wanted to curse, scream, and cry, but she couldn't—not in front of these strangers who wouldn't understand her. Dennis was quiet for a moment before speaking up again.

"Why do you want me to speak on her behalf," she questioned. "I have no idea what she intended to talk about. What's more, I don't even have the details of what Tammy had planned. I understand that it's important to find someone to cover for her, but I don't know enough about this."

Mary raised her hand and rested it on Dennis' shoulder before speaking.

"I was there when Tammy was taken away by the ambulance," she started. "She came to just before the paramedics were able to take her away. Right before being carted into the ambulance, she specifically requested that you take her place, mentioning you by name. She assured us that you would know exactly what to do."

"That's why we have called you here," Mary concluded. "What do you say?"

Dennis' face was pale. It was just as she always told herself—even challenging events are worth the risk. And without further ado, she steadied herself to provide her response.

"Yes," Dennis started, trying to sound sure of herself. "Of course, I will help. But I have no idea what Tammy had in mind for her speech, so, if you want me to speak, I will be giving my own speech. I've seen

Tammy's work up close, but I don't think I'd be able to execute it the same way. I can try to lay out my version of the project if you think that will be a good idea."

Mrs. Harrison met Dennis' gaze and simply stated, "I appreciate your honesty and your ability to speak your mind. Well then, go ahead." She continued, remarking that Tammy had often spoken highly of her as a bright student with a promising future. Despite the less-than-ideal circumstances of their meeting, Mrs. Harrison expressed genuine happiness at the opportunity to connect. Concluding her words, she shook Dennis' hand, accompanied by a warm smile on her face.

Dennis confidently approached the podium, effortlessly claiming it as her own. She commenced by extending a sincere apology to Tammy, publicly conveying her well wishes for a swift recovery. Without delay, Dennis delved into a remarkable portrayal of a project that instantly captivated the entire audience, including Mary and Eileen Harrison, who attentively observed her from the back row, discreetly positioned behind the rest of the spectators.

Naturally, Dennis never once divulged her lack of knowledge regarding the project at hand; quite the contrary. Her words cascaded with remarkable fluency, and her entire presentation portrayed her as an ardent expert on the subject matter. Her enthusiasm and unwavering confidence elevated her status, as she generously attributed all credit as the originator of this concept to her beloved teacher and mentor, Tammy.

Each and every one of those present applauded, including the Harrison sisters, who were still amazed at what they had just witnessed.

* * *

Dennis stayed behind, clearing up the items left on the tables near the entrance even after everyone else had gone. She knew it wasn't her job, but she felt guilty leaving everything scattered, including the pamphlets. She imagined that if Tammy had been there, she would have taken care of it. Dennis had a sense of responsibility not only for her own actions but sometimes for others as well. She wondered who would handle things the next day if Tammy wasn't around.

Dennis suddenly heard voices coming from one of the nearby rooms. It was Mary and Eileen Harrison, leaving one of the offices and heading towards the exit, right where Dennis was. When Mary spotted Dennis still cleaning up after the guests who had left, she smiled and said, "Why are you still here? It's time to go home! Leave that; someone will take care of it tomorrow. I'll make sure someone from the office comes and picks up everything left behind."

Dennis offered a polite smile, opting not to interject and nodded while shaking her head to acknowledge their words. She maintained her composure until she was certain that they had left the building. Once outside, their driver awaited them, opening the passenger door of their old, yet well-maintained Rolls-Royce—an exquisite vehicle that exuded elegance and radiance, clearly possessing ample life left in it, evident even from a distance.

Startled, Dennis jumped in alarm as sudden knocks on one of the entrance doors caught her off guard. It was the chauffeur for the Harrison sisters, gesturing for Dennis to approach. Curious, she went over to investigate. The driver relayed a message from the Harrison sisters, saying, "Miss, they are waiting for you in the car right now. Mrs. Harrison insists on taking you home."

Dennis was already getting ready to leave, so she didn't hesitate for a moment. During this time, Dennis primarily relied on public transportation, which could be more challenging at night due to the reduced frequency of service. Naturally, Dennis was very grateful for such an opportunity.

Dennis grabbed her coat and bag, exiting the building. Shortly after, the driver steered onto the main highway, leaving the bustling downtown area behind. As the glass partition between the front and rear cabins lowered, the driver, in a casual yet professional tone, asked, "Where would the lady like to go?"

Eileen, one of the sisters, interjected, addressing the driver.

"First," she started. "Let's head to the café in Plaza Madrid, and then we'll drop Dennis off at her house. A comforting cup of coffee sounds perfect after this eventful evening, wouldn't you agree, Dennis?" The three women exchanged smiles, in mutual agreement that a coffee break would be most fitting.

In the following hour, they laughed, conversed, and connected as if they had been lifelong friends. Dennis savored those moments, momentarily forgetting that if Tammy had been present and in good health, she wouldn't have been in this situation. She didn't dwell on it, perhaps intentionally. Time flew by swiftly, and before she knew it, Dennis found herself stepping out of the car and bidding farewell to the Harrison sisters at around eleven-thirty at night. The sisters continued their journey to a neighboring town, where their private residence was located.

The weekend flew by, and Monday arrived swiftly. Dennis decided to spend the day visiting different banks, diligently completing student loan applications that would cover the expenses of her final semester at school. As the morning progressed, she frequently called the hospital to inquire about Tammy's condition. Dennis planned to visit Tammy after she finished her paperwork, aware that this morning was very likely already busy as Tammy's family were probably visiting. She didn't know Tammy's family all too well and decided it was best to avoid interrupting their time with her. *I'll go,* she contemplated, *but I'll just leave the flowers and stay for no more than five minutes.*

Around four o'clock in the afternoon, Dennis entered the hospital room where Tammy was located. Following the nurse's directions, she walked down the chilly corridor and turned the knob to find Tammy lying on a bed in a somber and still room. Dennis could sense the prevailing sense of fragility in the atmosphere. Tammy was alone, without any company. It appeared that the previous visitors had already left, yet it was certain that one of her daughters or perhaps her husband would return later to stay with her through the night. During such crucial times, she wouldn't be left alone.

Dennis felt relieved that there were no other people accompanying Tammy. She wasn't sure how she would handle the emotions of Tammy's relatives, so it was easier not to interrupt the gathering. This personal sentiment was special to Dennis, considering her own solitude and deep respect for Tammy. Upon entering, she saw Tammy lying there, visibly weakened. Tammy's face lit up with happiness as she reached out, welcoming Dennis with open arms for a hug.

In a feeble voice, Tammy broke the silence.

"Dennis, I can't thank you enough for coming through for me. My trust in you has only grown stronger," Tammy said, while attempting to reposition herself on a small chair beside the bed. Nearby, a machine monitored her vital signs and regulated the intravenous fluids connected to her arm.

Dennis looked serious as she urged Tammy not to talk about the issue at that time. She emphasized the need for rest, considering Tammy's fragile health. The truth was that Tammy's condition remained critical, as the nurse had mentioned at the pavilion entrance, though the nurse didn't provide specific details about her dear friend and teacher's condition.

After some time, the nurse arrived and administered a sedative into the intravenous drip that was connected to Tammy. Gradually, Dennis observed Tammy drifting off to sleep. As she sat by her side, Dennis noticed the presence of other visitors in the room. The familiar white lights, visible only to her, reappeared, moving leisurely from one corner to another. Dennis discerned four lights, albeit not as radiant as the one she had witnessed levitating beside Tammy on Friday.

Curiously, Dennis didn't experience fear; it had become almost customary to see and sense these lights. It was as if she knew that someone was always present with her, even though she couldn't explain it or confide in anyone. This had become a part of her daily private life. Often, she felt puzzled, questioning the reality of these lights and why she was the sole observer. She also found herself wondering about their purpose in relation to her existence.

Observing Tammy's peaceful and undisturbed slumber for a while, Dennis silently exited the room, leaving her in the comforting embrace of her sleep and the calming presence of those subdued white lights, which appeared to have settled down as Tammy dozed off.

Dennis struggled to explain her feelings toward the lights. Sometimes she blamed them for her misfortunes, but most of the time, their presence brought her a sense of companionship and inner calm. However, she often found it challenging to reconcile these emotions, as she couldn't share them with anyone.

CHAPTER 5

Relief

Back to reality

Tuesday, Wednesday, and finally Thursday arrived, the days seemingly passing by in a blur. From early morning, Dennis was aware that her appointment with the psychiatrist was scheduled for that afternoon. She couldn't help but anticipate the hours that would elapse between waiting for the appointment and the actual session with her new psychiatrist. Determined not to endure another prolonged wait like the previous week, Dennis made up her mind that if the doctor, or whatever their name was, failed to initiate the session with questions, she would take the initiative herself. After all, she was paying for the session, right?

The traffic was chaotic, with heavy congestion and a seemingly immobile line of cars. Some impatient drivers resorted to honking their horns, urging the vehicle in front to move faster. However, there was no use getting worked up over it. The bridge these drivers were supposed to cross was raised so that boats could pass through the bay. Until the boats finished crossing, the bridge wouldn't descend, and Dennis realized that stressing over this situation was futile. She estimated that the traffic wouldn't start moving for at least another twenty minutes.

"Why is it that I always seem to arrive at the bridge when it's raised?" Dennis muttered to herself in frustration. "There must be something I'm missing. This can't be mere coincidence!"

In truth, it had become somewhat of a peculiar pattern. Crossing the bridge to the city seemed to coincide with the bridge being raised for passing boats. Although there wasn't a fixed schedule for boat crossings, Dennis found herself waiting fifteen to twenty minutes almost every time. It was odd, and she often pondered why it happened, but she couldn't provide a definite answer. It seemed to be an unusual coincidence, as she crossed at different times each occasion. The reality was that Dennis frequently encountered strange and challenging situations, so this was just one of many, and likely not the last.

As she waited for the ships to finish passing and the bridge to descend, allowing traffic to resume, Dennis settled into the familiar routine of patient waiting. It had become almost customary for her to reach into her bag and retrieve a notebook that she always carried with her, along with a pencil.

Dennis's notebook served no specific purpose; she would jot down single words or make random doodles—whatever came to mind. It was a calming activity, almost like entering a trance. This routine had become almost automatic for her. If the wait lasted more than five minutes, she would retrieve her notebook and occupy herself with scribbling on the blank pages. However, Dennis rarely reviewed what she had written; she simply stopped when the break was over. She would close the notebook and only open it again during another similar moment of forced waiting, preferably when she was alone. This way, she didn't feel the need to explain or justify her actions, as she herself hadn't fully grasped the reason behind them yet.

This time was no exception. Dennis strained her eyes to catch sight of the sign in the middle of the bridge, indicating how much longer the bridge would remain closed before traffic could proceed and continue toward the city. Turning off the engine and leaving the keys on the passenger seat, she stepped out of the car and walked along the car's front until reaching the right sidewalk. Shielding her eyes from the sun, she saw that there were still 16 minutes remaining. Dennis couldn't help but smile and think, "With this free time, I could even take a nap." With a content expression, she returned to her car.

She rolled down the car windows, allowing the cool breeze from outside to waft in. Without much thought, Dennis reached into her bag and retrieved her notebook. Closing her eyes, she began to write, somehow managing to stay within the lines despite her eyes being shut. It was a mysterious process, but when she closed her eyes, she felt a sense of relaxation that enabled her to write.

Most of the things she wrote didn't make sense. Not only because she never read them, but also because she didn't understand them, at least not yet. The blaring of car horns broke her out of the trance she had slipped into. With regained consciousness and clarity, she composed herself and started the car. Raising her hand in a gesture to the honking drivers behind her, she urged them to stop rushing and honking impatiently.

The bridge had already consumed twenty minutes of the additional half-hour buffer time that Dennis had allotted for unexpected delays. However, it seemed that this time, that extra anticipation wouldn't be of much use, as she would still arrive later than planned.

Dennis felt less concerned and somewhat disheartened, recalling her experience from the previous week. Who would want to arrive on time for an appointment only to endure such a lengthy wait? She pondered these questions, finding immediate answers that required little contemplation.

The remainder of the journey was swift, and within ten minutes, she reached the parking lot in front of the doctor's office, or whatever it was called. At the office entrance, Dennis delicately opened the door, hoping not to draw attention. However, a bell chimed, alerting everyone present and making her entrance conspicuous. *Oh no! Where did this little chime come from? It wasn't here last week,* Dennis silently wondered.

Approaching the reception window, she noticed that the previous girl was absent, replaced by a slightly older, kindly lady who attended to her with gentleness, collecting her information. The receptionist informed her that the doctor would see her later. The term "later" triggered thoughts of the previous week, a frustrating waste of time that lingered in Dennis' mind.

The waiting room appeared sparsely occupied this time, with only three seats taken. Dennis felt a sense of relief as she settled in, removing her light jacket. She decided to make herself a cup of coffee, intending to enjoy it while seated near the window in an unoccupied chair. However, she had barely taken the first sip when she heard her name being called.

"Miss Russel," the receptionist's delicate voice called out.

"Yes, that's me," Dennis responded. She set the coffee aside and walked toward the window, where the lady sitting there began to speak.

"The doctor will see you now," the receptionist informed politely. "Do you know where her office is?" The receptionist stood up and gestured for Dennis to follow, guiding her toward the doctor's office. "It's the first door in front of you," the receptionist added, maintaining eye contact with Dennis.

Without further delay, Dennis returned to her seat to retrieve her jacket and bag, then followed the receptionist's instructions toward the doctor's office. The door was slightly ajar, and without pausing to survey her surroundings like she had the previous week, Dennis walked straight to the chair she had occupied before. She sat down, placing her belongings beside her and holding onto her coffee, which provided some comfort. At least she had something to occupy herself with this time, reflecting on the long wait from the previous week, Dennis thought.

To Dennis's astonishment, this time the wait was brief, and the doctor entered the room without letting even five minutes pass. The creaking of the door alerted Dennis, and just like before, the doctor first went to her desk, took a sip of water, picked up her notebook and pencil, and took a seat in front of Dennis.

"Hi, Dennis," the doctor greeted in a friendly manner, catching Dennis completely off guard. "How have you been?"

"Well," Dennis began, her response carrying a tense tone due to the unexpected interaction. She hadn't rehearsed the possible questions and answers the doctor could pose, as she had done for her previous appointment. In that moment, Dennis felt a lack of preparedness, unsure of how to advocate for herself.

Without leaving much time for Dennis to react, the doctor immediately asked her another question. However, Dennis's mind had wandered, preoccupied with thoughts of what hadn't happened, leaving her distracted and lacking control over her thoughts. As a result, she couldn't fully grasp the doctor's question or comprehend what was being asked.

"Well," Dennis responded suddenly, reacting belatedly to what Dr. Michaels was asking her. "I don't really know. I believe I have a severe case of insomnia, but the doctor thinks there might be an underlying factor preventing me from sleeping. That's why they suggested trying therapy since medications haven't been effective."

Dennis took a moment to catch her breath, realizing that she hadn't noticed the doctor's actual question. She had responded in a way she thought was appropriate, assuming the question was about why she was there. However, it turned out that the doctor had asked something different.

Realizing her mistake, Dennis felt a sense of embarrassment. It was evident that Dr. Michaels had actually asked her about the weather, not something related to her personal struggles. The doctor looked at her for a few moments, speaking calmly to reassure her.

"I see that you have been preparing your answers, but let me assure you, Dennis, that I am not here to judge or criticize you. My intention is simply to listen and offer you my help. You don't have to come if you don't want to, but I assure you that after sharing your thoughts, you will feel better."

Feeling uncomfortable with the misunderstanding, Dennis took a sip of her coffee and apologized sincerely. "I'm very sorry," she began. "And yes, the weather has improved. I enjoy the warm breeze, especially when I have the chance to step out of the office, which doesn't happen often these days. I genuinely apologize for giving the impression that I had rehearsed my answers or that I didn't value your time. The truth is, sometimes I struggle to find the right words to express myself. I had thought... never mind, that's all."

Shifting the conversation, Dennis continued to open up to Dr. Michaels, sharing her experiences and concerns. "I don't know what's happening to me. Most days, my mind is constantly racing, and I find it difficult to stop thinking. I'm always occupied, even with my eyes closed, and recently, I've been getting very little sleep. Time seems to fly by, and the hours feel too short when I'm working. When I get home, I can't seem to stop. There's an inner drive compelling me to keep doing more. My projects have consumed my life and space, and it's hard for anyone to understand. Even I struggle to comprehend why I can't find rest or relaxation at any point. But please understand, it's not that I dislike my job. On the contrary, work is my life."

"In addition, I've unintentionally lost weight, and my doctor suggested seeking help from a psychologist to address other personal issues or aspects of my life. According to my doctor, my physical health is fine," Dennis continued, sharing her concerns about her well-being.

Dennis continued to share her story, emptying everything she had kept inside. In those moments, she felt a growing sense of confidence, finding solace in opening up to Dr. Michaels.

CHAPTER 6

The Lights

Expressing herself to the doctor had provided a much-needed release for Dennis. It was a conversation she had been longing for, as she rarely spoke about her innermost thoughts and feelings with anyone. Opening up to Dr. Michaels had already made her feel significantly better. As she observed the doctor making notes, a question arose in Dennis' mind, prompting her to ask.

"Do you think it's something serious? Why is it that I can't find the rest that normal people do?" Dennis's voice carried a hint of anxiety, reflecting her desperation to find answers to her problems quickly.

Dr. Michaels responded calmly, reassuring Dennis. "Calm down, Dennis. We'll take it step by step. I want you to tell me about yourself. What do you do? Do you enjoy your work? What plans do you have for the future? Share with me in the way that feels easiest for you. Please take your time and continue at your own pace."

Taking a deep breath, Dennis gathered herself and decided to resume her story, feeling a slight nervousness as she delved into personal matters. Sharing her experiences and thoughts in such depth was unfamiliar territory for her, but she recognized the importance of opening up to the doctor in order to better understand herself.

It felt like an extensive list as Dennis recounted all the things she did in her life. When Dr. Michaels asked if she enjoyed these activities, Dennis thought to herself, "Of course." As for her plans, she had once had them, and they had brought purpose and light to her life. However, everything had suddenly crumbled, and she found herself rarely thinking about those plans anymore. Instead, she sought solace in her work, the one stable and reliable aspect of her life. Dennis proceeded to share with Dr. Michaels the events that had caused her life to unravel.

After Mark's unexplained departure, her life shattered once again, leaving her with no anchor or reason to hold onto. The journey to stability had been a painful one, and whenever she attempted to make new plans, a sense of impending doom loomed over her, preventing her from escaping the anguish she had grown to associate with her ambitions.

Soon, Dennis reached the part of her story where she described the loss of her parents at a young age. This event, which remained unexplained, had left a void in her heart. She missed her parents deeply, remembering them every day and wondering why they had left her alone. However, it was the loss of Mark that had impacted her the most. Together, they had built a new life, dreams, and a future to fight for. Yet, once again, an unexplained event shattered her world, forcing her into solitude as a means of surviving the immense pain.

With each revelation, Dennis gradually opened up to Dr. Michaels, sharing the profound impact of these experiences on her life and her struggle to find a sense of stability and purpose amidst the pain.

When Dennis paused, Dr. Michaels continued their conversation.

"Dennis," she asked, her gaze focused intently on her patient. "What is it that no one can understand? What is it that eludes comprehension?" Dr. Michaels spoke in a tone tinged with intrigue.

Dennis hesitated, unsure of how to articulate her thoughts. Those fleeting words she had mentioned earlier were the ones she wanted to avoid, but she knew she had to share them. She shifted her gaze nervously, considering how best to convey her experiences without being dismissed as crazy.

With a deep breath, Dennis began to speak, her words hesitant and filled with trepidation.

"At times, I don't know what happens to me. It's like I lose touch with reality, although it's not a constant occurrence," Dennis confessed, her anxiety palpable.

Dr. Michaels listened attentively, her professional demeanor offering reassurance.

"Is this something that happens frequently?" Dr. Michaels inquired. "Many individuals with insomnia often experience fatigue due to the lack of restorative sleep their bodies require."

Dennis nodded, acknowledging the connection between her sleep troubles and her altered perception of reality. The conversation with Dr. Michaels was unveiling a deeper layer of her experiences, one that she had previously hesitated to discuss.

Dr. Michaels made additional notes in her notebook before posing another question to Dennis.

"Do you recall when you first experienced these episodes?" the doctor asked, prompting Dennis to reflect.

Dennis responded promptly, eager to provide insight.

"I remember the initial experience, but at that time, I didn't understand what was happening. What I can't recall is when I realized it was becoming a problem. Can I try to explain?" Dennis sought to organize her thoughts and convey them in a way that Dr. Michaels would comprehend.

"Of course, take your time. Tell me what you remember," Dr. Michaels encouraged.

"On the day of the terrible accident when my parents passed away, I was with them," Dennis shared, her voice growing somber. Pausing briefly, she continued, "I don't remember the details clearly, only fragmented images. But I know I was filled with an overwhelming sense of something extraordinary. I saw numerous bright orbs, like floating spheres, both inside and outside the car. They varied in size and color, with white orbs being predominant. The others stood out due to their vibrant hues. Following the accident, the doctor at the time attributed my perception to a head injury. However, as time has passed, I've come to question whether that explanation fully captures what truly occurred."

Dr. Michaels listened attentively; her curiosity piqued by Dennis' account.

Dr. Michaels posed a question, intrigued by Dennis' perspective. "Dennis, what do you believe happened?"

Dennis responded with a touch of irony in her voice, "I'm not entirely sure, but I know that the lights I saw were not merely a result of a head injury. If it were just a bruise, it should have healed by now, shouldn't it?"

Perplexed, Dr. Michaels inquired, "Are you suggesting that you still see the lights?"

Dennis hesitated briefly before summoning the courage to admit the truth. "Yes, I still see them, and it's something I can't share with anyone. That's the most disheartening part."

Curious, Dr. Michaels probed further. "Why is it that you feel unable to confide in others, Dennis?"

"Because I've had experiences in the past where mentioning these lights resulted in me being treated as mentally unstable. If I hadn't made the decision to keep it to myself, I might have ended up confined in a psychiatric facility," Dennis explained, her voice tinged with sadness.

44

Dr. Michaels nodded in understanding. "I see. What else do you recall, Dennis?"

Dennis delved into her memories, painting fragmented images for the doctor. "In certain memories, I see my father lifting me into his arms and carrying me away from the car we were traveling in. Then I remember my mother draping a blanket over me, covering my head and protecting me from potential harm."

The doctor, still scribbling in her notes, inquired about the condition of Dennis' parents in those images. "How do you perceive your parents in these memories? Are they unharmed, or do you see them injured?"

Dennis noticed the doctor's momentary interruption but continued to share her experiences. "After the accident, I believe I regained consciousness after being unconscious for several days. When I woke up, my aunt was the only one with me," Dennis explained.

Dr. Michaels returned to her seat and leaned forward, urging Dennis to keep sharing. "Please, go on. What do you remember after waking up?"

Dennis took a deep breath and continued, "I remember feeling disoriented and in pain. My aunt tried to comfort me and assured me that everything would be alright. She explained that my parents had passed away in the accident, but she was there to take care of me."

The doctor maintained her focused attention, encouraging Dennis to express herself freely. "And what about the lights, Dennis? Did you continue to see them after waking up?"

Dennis nodded, a mix of relief and apprehension washing over her. "Yes, the lights were still there. They didn't vanish. In fact, they seemed even more vibrant and numerous. I couldn't understand why I was the only one seeing them. It was both fascinating and unsettling."

Dr. Michaels scribbled down notes, capturing the details Dennis shared. "Can you describe these lights further? How did they behave, and how did they make you feel?"

Dennis thought for a moment, recalling the ethereal nature of the lights. "They appeared like floating bubbles or transparent spheres. Each one emitted its own radiant light from within. They moved with a sense of restlessness, traversing the space around me. Witnessing their movements was captivating, yet it also stirred up a sense of curiosity and intrigue within me."

The doctor briefly excused herself, walked to her desk to take a sip of water, and returned to her chair, signaling for Dennis to continue. "Please, Dennis, share any other significant details or feelings you recall regarding the lights."

Dennis leaned forward, her voice filled with a mixture of hope and uncertainty. "Doctor, those lights have been a constant presence in my life ever since. I have questioned their purpose and significance. I have yearned to find someone who could understand and shed light on this peculiar phenomenon. It's something deeply personal that I've never shared before."

Dr. Michaels nodded empathetically, assuring Dennis that her experiences were valid. "Thank you for opening up, Dennis. I believe it takes great courage to share such personal encounters. I'm here to listen and help you make sense of these experiences. Together, we will explore the significance of the lights and their impact on your life."

"When did you learn about your parents' passing?"

Dennis began to explain, "I believe I already had an inkling. You see, when the doctors visited me, their demeanor was unusually affectionate, and they chose their words delicately."

"Did their behavior give you an indication that you were about to receive bad news?" the doctor chimed in.

"No," Dennis replied with a slightly elevated tone. "It was the presence of lights that made me grasp the reality of their absence. Those lights, they were with me, and that's when I understood they would no longer be by my side."

"Tell me, Dennis, which doctors examined you after the accident? Did anyone assess your eyes for potential damage to the optic nerve?"

"Well, I believe there were several doctors involved. Everyone wanted to examine me, and numerous tests were conducted. Strangely enough, they couldn't explain how I emerged unscathed, without a single scratch. Furthermore, the paramedics discovered me on the side of the road, draped in a blanket—the very same one my mother used to cover me. I know it wasn't a mere dream, despite what many claim. It was real because I saw her with my own eyes. She kissed me on the forehead before joining Dad in the car. They held hands and vanished into the illuminated bushes, surrounded by countless bright spheres." Dennis lowered her head, let out a sigh, and continued speaking.

"However, nobody believed me. Everyone dismissed it as a figment of the accident," her voice began to tremble.

"Tell me, Dennis," Dr. Michaels began, "now that you've grown older and many years have passed since the accident, how do you experience these visual anomalies?"

Dennis lifted her gaze and searched Dr. Michaels' eyes, seeking a signal that would guide her. Should she divulge more about the subject or halt her story to avoid making a misstep? Just like with previous doctors, they had attributed Dennis's visions to the head injury sustained during the accident. Countless modern X-rays and MRIs had been conducted to detect any potential brain damage, but they yielded no results. Gradually, Dennis came to realize that no one would ever believe her. Consequently, she had grown reluctant to share these personal experiences with others—until now, as she found herself once again seated in front of Dr. Michaels.

Unexpectedly, in the corner of the room, on the right side, almost obscured by Dr. Michaels, one of those spheres materialized. It floated gently, modestly sized, emitting a subdued glow as if intentionally trying to evade notice. However, Dennis immediately perceived its presence.

Believing that the appearance of this sphere held the answer to her question, Dennis confronted the doctor.

"What distinguishes seeing something unexplainable from seeing nothing at all? Does perceiving things that others cannot make me mentally unstable, at the very least? Or would suppressing these experiences render them insignificant? Dr. Michaels, what do you think?" Dennis asked, her voice filled with fervor.

It was a complex moment, where roles seemed to have reversed momentarily—Dennis appeared to be leading the therapy instead of the doctor. However, Dr. Michaels reacted swiftly and reassured her.

"No, Dennis, it's not about that. I don't believe you're imbalanced or crazy. I believe there's much more to explore in order to understand why you're experiencing these sensations."

Time had flown by quickly, perhaps too quickly for Dennis. She had only just begun to release the tremendous burden concealed beneath her cheerful and seemingly ordinary demeanor, and the therapy sessions never seemed long enough to share everything she needed to.

She understood that eventually, she would have to confront the intricate complexities of her life. Yet, her fear of not being believed had kept her silent all these years. Whenever she recollected her past experiences, she realized that they would forever remain fragmented within her, as nobody had truly comprehended them.

But now, things were different. She felt an urgent need to express herself, even though she feared that once she had bared it all, she wouldn't know how to reconcile and integrate those experiences within herself again.

"Dennis, by opening up and sharing your emotions and innermost thoughts, you've taken a significant step. Although I don't want to end the session abruptly, I think we've accomplished enough for today. Do you feel comfortable pausing here?" the doctor asked, carefully observing Dennis.

Dennis nodded, albeit with some uncertainty about whether this was truly what she desired. She rose from her chair, gathered her belongings, and bid farewell to the doctor. As she approached the door, she inquired, "Same day, same time?"

"Yes, Dennis. I'll see you next week," Dr. Michaels replied.

CHAPTER 7

Tammy

That afternoon, Dennis left the consultation feeling even more confused. She decided to avoid diving into such a personal topic, as it only led to more unanswerable questions and added to her stress. She was searching for answers that could bring peace of mind and ease the discomfort caused by these experiences.

Luckily, her session was shorter than the previous week's, and there was less waiting time to see the doctor. With time to spare, Dennis went for a coffee at her favorite spot, a cozy café. The café had a second level with tables overlooking the street, arranged along a narrow corridor. Each table accommodated only two people and was separated by a small partition with a hanging lamp. There were a total of ten small tables.

From the outside, the café looked appealing, resembling a shopfront rather than a regular café. The small string lights on the window added a warm and festive touch, creating a hint of mystery when the place was empty. However, when the café was full, it transported visitors' imagination to the streets of Paris in the olden days.

Dennis found solace in that place, often seeking refuge there whenever she grappled with problems. The last table at the end of the corridor seemed to await her, almost always empty, as if reserved for her arrival. Seated there, she would order the largest cappuccino the café offered, generously topped with extra foam. She observed people passing by on many occasions, and at times, tears welled up as she experienced feelings of sadness and isolation. Yet, in these moments, the luminous spheres would manifest in the vicinity. Bizarre? Undoubtedly.

Dennis had discerned a pattern—these spheres of light materialized whenever she confronted sorrow, complexity, or matters concerning her own being. These ethereal orbs materialized in various locations; at times, they materialized right before her eyes, while on other occasions, they glided through walls or hovered near certain individuals. It was as though these luminous manifestations responded to an unseen beckoning, remaining steadfastly present by her side.

Uncertainty shrouded the purpose of these light spheres and whether they provided a shield of protection or not. However, the impact of their presence was undeniable. A profound sensation enveloped Dennis when they appeared. Expressing this sentiment was challenging, for there were instances when she wished these spheres would remain absent altogether. Yet, more often than not, they conferred a sense of constant companionship. They brought forward a feeling that someone, or something, was always close by—a vigilant listener to her thoughts and a sharer of her emotions.

The conflict stemmed, in part, from the odd existence of these luminous spheres. Being unable to share the remarkable encounters or express her experiences had coerced her into self-imposed isolation. She felt confined within an imaginary cell, severed from the freedom of open expression. Her connection with a world that couldn't fathom her encounters left her adrift, struggling to comprehend her plight.

As she sipped at her impressive cappuccino, her gaze wandered to the sidewalk beyond the glass. A woman stood there, accompanied by one of these spheres. The woman appeared relatively young, perhaps in her early fifties. The sphere of light danced alongside her, tracing erratic paths from side to side and top to bottom. Abruptly, the woman crossed the street toward the café, and the luminous sphere mirrored her movements. Dennis briefly lost sight of them, triggering thoughts of Tammy.

Tammy, her cherished mentor, was more of a friend to her than anything else. Her hospital visit had left her in distress—unforeseen illness had eclipsed her well-being. Cancer had taken hold of Tammy. This pivotal moment proved to be a turning point in Dennis' life, although she only fully comprehended its impact later on.

Back to when Tammy was sick

It had been just a few weeks since Tammy's release from the hospital, her return to normal classes and routines. But for Dennis, things weren't quite the same. She couldn't help but watch Tammy closely, sensing the need for a genuine conversation. She struggled to find the right words, not wanting to burden Tammy with her concern yet yearning to be there for her.

Dennis had observed the luminous spheres around Tammy before—whenever they appeared, people tended to leave or, in some cases, pass away. But she was hesitant to intrude upon Tammy's privacy, respecting the changes she'd embraced since resuming her regular life. Tammy had grown quieter, more reserved, a shift Dennis had clearly noticed.

On a particular afternoon, after one of her classes had concluded, Dennis spotted Tammy engrossed in grading papers at her desk. Gathering courage, Dennis approached and initiated a conversation.

"After you're done, would you join me for a coffee?" Dennis asked, hoping for acceptance. Before any excuses could arise, she hurriedly added, "It won't take long, I promise."

Tammy met Dennis' eyes, seeing a masked expression that concealed concern beneath an attempted smile. To Dennis' relief, Tammy agreed. The two women left the university, making their way to Dennis' favorite spot, Café Italia, just around the corner.

Once settled on the cafe's second floor with their coffees, Dennis pondered how to initiate the conversation. However, before she could find the right words, Tammy spoke abruptly, divulging, "I have cancer." The statement hung in the air, stark and unfiltered. Dennis reached out, holding Tammy's hands in a comforting gesture.

"How are you feeling about this?" Dennis asked, her query straightforward. It made sense in her mind, echoing previous instances involving the light spheres and people she knew.

Tammy hesitated, meeting Dennis' gaze. "I'm still coming to terms with it. Difficult times lie ahead, and my family knows. I couldn't face this without their support. I've made a decision," she declared resolutely. "I'll step back from work and focus on recovery. Even if I don't fully succeed, I'll have more time with my family. It's the right choice. After years of worrying about leaving my husband alone, this presents a serious dilemma. My children have their lives, but him... I can't simply leave him behind."

Tammy's words resonated with conviction. There were no tears, no overwhelming sorrow—just unwavering determination. Dennis felt her own eyes moisten, attempting to avoid Tammy's gaze, though it proved impossible.

"Don't be sad for me. I've lived a fulfilling life—a life with a loving family and husband. I have no regrets," Tammy reassured, her tone steady and calming.

As Tammy spoke, her resolve clear, Dennis couldn't help but observe a radiant aura enveloping her. The familiar light spheres appeared, encircling Tammy, seemingly detached from her being. Gradually, they multiplied, filling the space with their gentle luminescence. Dennis fought to keep her attention on Tammy, intent on listening, yet the spectacle of the spheres captivated her gaze.

Tammy opened up about facing the potential end of her journey, and Dennis acknowledged the ethereal beauty of the spheres gracing their surroundings. This was a unique and poignant moment, one that Dennis would always hold dear. However, amidst this, a seed of doubt sprouted in her mind. Tammy's calm acceptance of whatever lay ahead raised questions: Were the spheres somehow linked to misfortune, guiding their futures, or perhaps even a harbinger of things to come? Dennis found herself wondering.

Dennis hadn't dared to ask Tammy before, but this instance felt different. It was one of the few times she felt personally connected to someone facing a significant departure. Memories of her parents' loss surfaced, a time when she believed her visions were merely products of head injuries, as the doctors had asserted throughout countless sessions.

By the time Mark, her childhood friend, had passed away, Dennis had grown older and had come to associate the light spheres with sorrow. Their presence around Mark had foretold tragedy, a realization that had solidified her suspicion. However, at that point, she hadn't yet comprehended their purpose, or maybe she'd chosen not to understand. The orbs symbolized the sadness left behind by his departure.

Back at the café with Tammy

As Dennis watched the luminous spheres dance, her mind raced. Could it be her? Was she somehow linked to the misfortune that befell these people? She forcefully quashed these troubling thoughts.

Tammy, though appearing content on the surface, carried a weight of pain within. Nonetheless, she had made a decision to reveal her plans not only for her own remaining time but also for Dennis.

"Listen closely, Dennis. I've chosen you as my successor. I'll talk to the agency to give you a chance," Tammy declared with unwavering resolve.

"I'm certain you'll excel and face any challenges that come your way. I have no doubt," she added.

Dennis was momentarily stunned, caught off guard by the abrupt turn of events. Lost in her thoughts, she hadn't anticipated this discussion. Struggling to collect herself, she questioned, "What? What do you mean, Tammy?"

"I just told you. You'll be taking over for me!" Tammy affirmed.

"At the school?" Dennis sought clarification. "But how? I'm not ready yet."

"No, not at the university," Tammy clarified. "I'm talking about the agency."

Dennis' mind whirled. "Tammy, what are you saying? How could I... No! You'll recover, you'll return! This is just a temporary setback!"

"Dennis," Tammy responded sternly, a rare seriousness in her tone. "You're not hearing me. I won't be returning, period. I'm leaving both my school and agency positions for good."

"Tammy, let's not discuss this now," Dennis choked back her emotions. "Please, I know you're resolute in your decisions, but this is your life, your career. You can't just end it."

"How else can I handle this?" Tammy's voice quivered, a touch of desperation creeping in. "I'm doing my best with the situation I'm facing. Do you want me to ignore the reality of my situation and keep living in denial? Tell me, Dennis, you've known me—what should I do?"

Tears welled up, emotions ran high, and hands clenched tightly. Two distinct worlds converged, two women at different junctures—one embarking on a new chapter, the other grappling with the end of her earthly journey.

In the days following Tammy's revelation of her plans, the Harrison sisters arranged for a personal interview with Dennis, just as Tammy had foreseen. Although Dennis remained somewhat uncertain, she agreed to attend the agency meeting and hear the offer presented by the owners.

A solid foundation existed for this opportunity. Both Eileen and Mary vividly remembered Dennis' remarkable actions during the company event, when Tammy's illness was first evident. Dennis' capable handling of the situation had showcased her potential to champion the company's endeavors. This had a significant impact, particularly after they heard the impressive ideas she had proposed for the ongoing project.

The interview itself proved enjoyable, with the conversation centering around the project proposals for the company's sponsored contest. The participants and their ambitious designs were discussed, reflecting the culmination of ninety days from the event where Tammy had been taken to the hospital.

During the interview, Eileen made a single comment about Tammy's situation, expressing their reluctance for Dennis to simply replace her. They understood the depth of Tammy's suffering and admired her wise decision to prioritize family time. The sisters recognized the need for someone with the talent and motivation akin to Tammy's. Dennis had received strong recommendations that positioned her well to step into Tammy's shoes. It was clear that she had played a pivotal role in the agency's heart—the driving force behind their great ideas and projects.

In response, Dennis confidently stood up, addressing Eileen and Mary. "Ladies, believe me when I say that while this opportunity arises from a serious situation, it is also a dream come true for me. I have consistently dedicated myself to giving my best, and this time will be no exception. I do want to clarify that I'm not perfect and I anticipate making mistakes, which is why I ask for your patience. But I also want you to understand that I'm not here to replace Tammy. What I can promise you is my commitment to learning quickly and giving my utmost effort. I will learn and adapt swiftly, that I assure you."

Approaching them to shake hands, Dennis found both sisters extending their arms for a warm hug—a symbolic gesture that marked Dennis' official welcome to the company. With this embrace, a bond of friendship commenced, one that would strengthen over time.

Thus began a new chapter in Dennis' life, initiated in a manner she hadn't anticipated, catalyzed by Tammy's illness. Within just under two months, Dennis found herself seated behind a desk once occupied by Tammy, surrounded by folders and documents demanding her full attention. Despite the undeniable weight of responsibility and the sheer volume of work, Dennis found herself captivated. This realm was her ideal sanctuary, a world that would consume her time and prevent her from dwelling on her own concerns or wandering aimlessly in her thoughts.

This role, in essence, saved her life—a lifeline and a pursuit she embraced wholeheartedly. Every day, she threw herself into the tasks at hand, armed with the passion to excel and to contribute her very best.

CHAPTER 8

Lucas

"Excuse me," a voice shattered the silence, jolting Dennis from her reverie. "We'll be closing soon. Is everything alright?"

One of the café workers had approached Dennis, concerned by her prolonged trance. The barista, a young man who had often seen Dennis at the café, had been struck by her deep absorption. "A long time" was an understatement; she had been lost in thought for hours. In fact, he had observed her presence throughout his rounds where he cleaned and tidied up around the café. He had even taken the initiative to replenish her drink earlier, a gesture she had thanked him for, though her demeanor hinted at a disconnection from reality.

Lucas, the barista, had been quietly observing Dennis during her visits. He felt a unique connection to her from the very first day he saw her. This sentiment urged him to attend to her needs during these absent moments, making sure she continued to order something to avoid the cafe's owners requesting her departure. Lucas was well aware of the unspoken rules about lingering around the café without purchasing and how that could draw unwanted attention.

Naturally, Lucas found himself drawn to her, his feelings guiding him to look out for her during her episodes of detachment. Despite his shyness, he paid for her coffees as a way to care for her, though he hadn't yet mustered the courage to approach her when she was fully present. Lucas was a unique individual, with his own journey of growth ahead. He had his own quirks and had learned to trust those instinctual feelings that stirred within him, recognizing them as indicators of something special. His attraction to Dennis had led him to dream of a time when he could engage with her directly.

Dennis attempted to reorient herself, but everything seemed to unfold in slow motion. The hours had slipped away, and the café was preparing to close. Midnight was approaching, judging by her calculations. How had so much time passed without her noticing? And how could she remain so oblivious to the activities around her at this late hour?

This is what she feared: these lapses in time where she lost track of her surroundings and her own actions. It was precisely this lack of control over herself that had driven her to seek help.

Dennis looked up at Lucas, a mixture of embarrassment and bewilderment on her face. "I'm so sorry," she began, her voice tinged with regret. "I completely lost track of time."

Taking a moment to survey her surroundings, Dennis sensed a faint flicker of familiarity. She continued, her tone marked by curiosity, "Do we know each other? Your face seems very familiar to me. Please forgive my absentmindedness. I'm genuinely sorry for overstaying my welcome here; I don't know what else to say."

Lucas reassured her with a friendly smile and a gentle wave of his hands. "No worries, it can happen to anyone. And, well, in a way, we do know each other," he replied with a hint of amusement. "You see, every time you come in, I'm the one who serves you that giant cappuccino...

Luke," he paused momentarily, contemplating whether to continue before gathering his courage to do so.

Dennis looked intrigued, prompting Lucas to continue, "I'm also the one who brings you the additional coffees."

Confusion and a touch of irritation crossed Dennis' face. "Additional coffees? What do you mean? How? When?" she inquired, her brows furrowing as she navigated the unfamiliar situation.

"As I mentioned, it's just that when you visit the café, you tend to stay for a while. And on certain occasions, while I'm doing my rounds, I notice you here, alone, for an extended period," Lucas explained. "I've asked if you're okay, assuming there might be an issue. But then, I didn't know what to make of it. It was like you were present but not entirely. I hope I'm making sense."

Pausing, Lucas continued, his tone sincere, "The truth is, I didn't want to disturb you. The first time I approached you and offered you an additional cappuccino, do you remember? You accepted, and since then, whenever you're here alone, during my rounds, I check in on you and ask if everything's alright. You always answer affirmatively, even though it's quite evident that your mind is elsewhere. So, to avoid interrupting you, I bring you another coffee. It's a way to ensure that you're not bothered and that you're free to stay here as long as you'd like without the owners raising any concerns."

Lucas felt a sense of relief after finally sharing this information. He had been contemplating how to convey this for months, and now he had taken the step he had been avoiding. The surprise in Dennis' eyes was matched by the expression of astonishment on her face. It was an extreme revelation—an unexpected layer to her detachment from the present. Not only did she lose herself in her thoughts, but now she discovered that someone was discreetly looking out for her to prevent disruption. What was happening to her? As a wave of shame and humiliation engulfed her, she rose to leave, her emotions weighing heavily upon her.

Dennis hurried down the stairs with a swiftness borne of both embarrassment and distress. She didn't utter a farewell or cast a backward glance; she simply left the café that night, her cheeks wet with the most intense sense of humiliation she had ever encountered. Tears streamed down her face, and she allowed them to flow freely, a physical manifestation of the overwhelming emotions welling up inside her. What she felt was a profound need to vent her pent-up frustration, to release it in a torrent of words or cries.

As the night dragged on and the sunrise began to peek through her windows, Dennis lay in bed, her mind consumed by thoughts. The tears had ceased, having been expended over hours of unrelentingly deep thought. Unable to find solace in slumber, she mulled over the young barista's revelations, each word etching deeper into her consciousness. Amidst the silence of her room, she grappled with an urge, a compulsion to scream—to vocalize the frustration that she kept bottled up for so long.

Words flowed from her lips, unbidden and raw, as if her anguish had finally found a channel to escape. The tears streamed anew, a torrent of emotion, reminiscent of her childhood cries for her parents. The sheets clenched in her fists bore witness to the forceful release of her pent-up feelings, her grip a testament to the storm raging within her. Yet, as if prompted by an unseen force, a sudden stillness overcame her, a paralysis that halted her sobs. Her attention was drawn to the corner of the room where a sphere of light emerged, growing in size and brilliance with every passing moment.

Unlike any before it, this sphere was grander, more luminous, emanating a resplendent blue that evoked the serene seas she had glimpsed on screens. But beneath the surface of that mesmerizing blue, a kaleidoscope of colors intermingled—turquoise, green, gold, and a deep, entrancing purple. It was a sight beyond description, an experience so surreal that only firsthand witnessing could encapsulate its essence.

Her tears dried in an instant, replaced by awe as her gaze remained transfixed on the breathtaking spectacle. Slowly, Dennis raised herself, propping her upper body against the headboard of her bed. From this vantage point, she beheld the sphere of light, which now hovered nearer, casting an incandescent glow that illuminated the room. Its radiance was all-encompassing, a luminosity so intense that it brought forth the vividness of the colors emanating from within.

In her recollection, the sphere resembled a mirrored disco ball of yesteryears, refracting brilliant flashes across the room. Breath held, Dennis mustered the courage to address the enigmatic presence before her:

"Who are you? What do you want from me?" The question hung in the air, waiting for an answer that never came.

A torrent of questions poured forth from Dennis' lips, each word dripping with anguish and frustration, as if she hoped to pry open the locked gates of understanding. "I don't understand! Why do they follow me? Why do those who come close to me suffer? Is it because I care for them? Why? Is this a form of punishment? Why can't I understand the reasons behind all the tragedy in my life?" The weight of her inquiries hung in the air, a plea for answers to the mysteries that had relentlessly haunted her existence.

And then, silence. The grand sphere, serene and unwavering, began to rotate almost imperceptibly, triggering the emergence of more luminous entities. These orbs of light entered from every direction, passing through walls and windows, ascending from the floor and descending from the ceiling. They bathed the room in a golden-white brilliance, as if each orb was a messenger, joining a grand assembly.

The lights danced in harmony, their movements an intricate ballet of luminescence, a symphony of radiance that enveloped her in serenity.

Amidst the ethereal dance, Dennis felt her tensions ebb away, replaced by a sensation of calmness and lightness. With rapt attention, she observed the celestial choreography, entranced by the celestial display that had eclipsed the bounds of her room, creating a realm of radiant splendor.

In a moment of disoriented desperation, an odd notion invaded Dennis' thoughts like an intruder breaking into a sanctuary. "Could this be a dream? Am I going crazy?" The words spilled out of her mouth in a mix of confusion and distress, the fabric of reality unraveling at the edges. The need to confirm her own existence gripped her tightly; she pressed her hands against her arms, her face, needing the tactile reassurance of reality.

Summoning the courage to stand, Dennis slowly maneuvered herself to the edge of the bed, her movements cautious, as if any sudden action might shatter the fragile illusion around her. The ethereal lights pulsed and moved, encircling her, dancing in response to her every gesture, except for the largest orb which held its position steadfastly. The curiosity and disbelief etched onto her face deepened, morphing into a mix of awe and skepticism.

As she took tentative steps forward, the lights intensified their choreography, speeding up and enveloping her in their luminous embrace. A palpable energy tingled across her skin, as if static electricity was coursing through her veins. The wind picked up, whipping her hair and clothes in a frenzy, yet her astonishment and fascination outweighed any sense of fear.

No one will believe this! Dennis thought to herself as she continued watching, perplexed by event unfolding before her.

Dennis extended her arms, feeling the sensation of the lights brushing against her like a gentle caress. The whirlwind of color and radiance reached its crescendo, culminating in a resplendent golden ray that engulfed the room. And then, in a blink of an eye, it all vanished. The lights, the wind, the overwhelming spectacle – all reduced to a tiny point of brilliance that winked out of existence, leaving nothing but a deafening silence in its wake.

Alone in the room once more, Dennis was left to grapple with the remnants of an experience that defied description. She stared at the emptiness that now enveloped her, her heart racing, her mind reeling, and a profound sense of wonder and uncertainty intertwining within her. It was an encounter she knew she could never share, an enigma destined to remain within the confines of her own consciousness.

CHAPTER 9

Rona's Experience

Several weeks had passed since the remarkable encounter with the spheres of light. During this time, she had been occupied with office matters and work challenges. The incident at Café Italia that day had left her unsettled. These factors weighed heavily on her, causing daily unease and prompting changes to her sessions with Dr. Michaels. While she hadn't considered giving up on therapy entirely, she recognized the need to address the turmoil within her mind—an internal storm fueled by unshared experiences.

The mystery of the lights remained complex; she was uncertain about their origin and significance, which troubled her greatly.

Thursday had come around again, and she found herself reluctant to attend the session with Dr. Michaels. She had already canceled multiple times in the past weeks for various reasons. The question of its worth lingered—she believed therapy wouldn't alleviate her challenges or ease her daily life. She conveyed this sentiment to her doctor when he proposed therapy as a beneficial avenue to understand her feelings of overwhelm and confusion.

Meanwhile, she had been engrossed in the agency's projects, finding fulfillment in seeing her ideas realized. Moreover, she was nearing the completion of her career thesis, bringing her closer to her aspiration of becoming a publicist. This goal was among many dreams she held. Despite grappling with existential conflicts and emotional hardships, Dennis remained ordinary, like everyone else, with dreams that were often concealed yet undoubtedly present.

Recent days had rekindled memories of the young man from *Café Italia*. Despite the past embarrassment, she yearned for the café's cappuccinos, which she hadn't ordered again since the incident. There was simply no replacement for the exceptional cappuccinos at *Café Italia*.

Dennis understood that she would eventually need to address that issue. However, she hadn't contemplated the specifics of how she'd approach it. Would she return to the café? Perhaps wait for him to leave? Regardless, she felt compelled to reconnect with the young man, to express gratitude for his kind gesture. There was also the matter of settling her account; he had generously covered numerous coffees. Amidst everything, she faced another small predicament: she couldn't recall his name.

As she worked diligently in her office, taking care of pending projects that required review, an unexpected noise disrupted her focus. Glancing around, she searched for the source, but her workspace appeared undisturbed. Deciding to investigate, she stood and approached the door, hoping to find a clue in the corridor. Surprisingly, everything seemed in order outside—just a few individuals passing by.

Returning to her chair and facing her computer, she noticed her agenda's reminder for the afternoon appointment with Dr. Michaels. With only two hours remaining, she realized she was conveniently close to the doctor's office. Even so, a part of her leaned toward skipping the session this time.

The weight of not having preemptively canceled the appointment gnawed at her. She held herself to high standards when it came to commitments, valuing others' time. Driven by this ethic, she concluded that she should attend, albeit reluctantly, acknowledging that it might feel like wasted time.

She wrapped up a couple of tasks and assessed the time, estimating how long it would take to reach the doctor's office on foot. The weather was pleasant, and she figured walking could provide a welcome distraction, easing the internal pressures she was grappling with.

And so, she made the choice—walking would be her course of action.

In the prelude to the medical consultation

Her appointed time arrived, and she found herself in the waiting area, joining the few individuals present—much like the previous week. This time, a different receptionist greeted her. She was just as nice as the last receptionist she had seen. The receptionist assured her that the wait would be brief, just five minutes, leaving Dennis with little opportunity to become comfortable in her seat. Opting instead to stand, she directed her gaze out the window. From her vantage point, she observed a portion of the river beyond the parking lot that lay in front of the medical office.

Once inside the consultation

"Hello, Dennis. How have you been?" Dr. Michaels spoke as she took her seat, already waiting for her patient by the time Dennis entered the office.

Slightly taken aback, Dennis responded, "Um, well, I'm not sure. I've been facing some issues." Dennis hesitated briefly before walking over to the chair and settling in front of the doctor. "I mean, I do have problems, but I'm not sure how to make myself feel better."

"We have plenty of time today for you to share your concerns with me, I assure you that," the doctor reassured, her words echoing as Dennis situated herself.

Already seated, Dennis caught the implication and nodded in understanding. Truthfully, she wasn't in the mood to dive into a conversation; she felt overwhelmed about where to even begin.

To break the initial tension, the doctor posed a question without delay. "Dennis, in our previous session, you mentioned these peculiar visions. Perhaps we could start there. Can you try to explain how you feel when one of these visions appears to you?"

Dennis met the doctor's gaze, momentarily grappling with the question. It was as though she hadn't fully comprehended the depth of what was being asked, though in reality, she understood all too well. She simply hadn't anticipated this line of inquiry. Dr. Michaels maintained her direct approach.

"Consider this, Dennis: when you see something out of the ordinary, what's your initial emotion? Do you feel anxious? Afraid? Maybe even threatened?" Dr. Michaels probed.

In an unexpected impulse, Dennis responded, "No, not at all. It's more of a distinct feeling. It's become almost routine—I'm not scared of them. These visions tend to show up when I'm feeling isolated or distressed."

"So, if these experiences don't bring about negative emotions or a sense of pressure, why do you perceive them as problematic?" The doctor inquired.

"I'm not really sure. Sometimes I wish others could understand me, but it feels like no one can grasp what's happening to me," Dennis voiced.

"Do you believe it's necessary for others to understand, Dennis?"

"Why wouldn't it be?" Dennis responded with a hint of frustration.

"But, when these visions aren't something, others have experienced, do you think it's realistic to expect them to perceive it from your perspective?" Dr. Michaels probed further.

Dennis took a breath and paused, contemplating for a moment. "Well, not really. Not everyone has gone through something like losing their parents in an accident."

"So, are you suggesting that these visions somehow caused the accident that resulted in the loss of your parents?" Dr. Michaels clarified.

"No, that's not what I meant. I'm saying that not everyone has experiences like mine, and I don't think these visions caused or resulted from the accident."

"Dennis, you're misunderstanding me. I'm not implying the visions caused the accident. I mean that significant life events, like the accident, can act as turning points, revealing vulnerabilities within us. There are fleeting moments that change us profoundly. Sometimes, it's just a split second that prompts someone to make an undesirable decision, like taking their own life or becoming an alcoholic. These pivotal instances shape our lives, even if we don't fully grasp them at the time. You might not recall experiencing these visions before the accident, but that doesn't mean they weren't there. It's possible that the accident became a pivotal moment, drawing your focus away from other things and onto the situation."

The doctor shifted her posture, folding her hands in her lap. "Certain junctures expose us, where our mind opens up without the usual layers of defense. Those moments when you're solely attuned to your inner voice—they're intimate and emerge from instances of extreme pain or joy. Such moments lead us to confront our utmost vulnerability."

"Are you suggesting that these visions stem from my inner voice?" Dennis inquired with a tremor in her voice.

"No, Dennis," the doctor replied in a composed manner. "I'm conveying that only a select few can delve into the depths of their being and, from that place, open themselves to connections with other entities."

Dennis was at a loss for words. Uncertain whether to ask for further clarification, she grappled with comprehending what the doctor had just stated. Other beings? What did that mean?

Dennis remained silent, her facial expression mirroring her deep confusion.

"Dennis, I believe it's time for you to recognize that you're not unbalanced or ill. As you've pointed out, these presences haven't caused you harm. I believe your confusion stems from a lack of understanding rather than anything else. I suggest you allow yourself the chance to consider this as something new and different—a concept that can develop within you just like any other idea. You should take the time to understand, assess, accept, and most importantly, embrace it. I don't want you to be afraid, Dennis. There's no reason for fear. What you're experiencing isn't a result of mental instability or the accident. It's something far greater than what can be easily comprehended."

Dr. Michaels's tone shifted as she continued speaking to Dennis, her gaze transforming with a distinct luminosity in her eyes.

"Allow me to share something from my own life so you can gain a better understanding. Years ago, I lost my son in a mountain accident— an event that shattered me completely. My faith and my strength crumbled, leaving me utterly desolate. My anguish was so all-encompassing that I lost sight of anything beyond my pain. I rejected assistance and had no desire to keep living. Even my family distanced themselves from me. During my darkest hours, I decided to take my own life by taking a lethal dose of medicine. In what I thought would be my last moments, I wrote a letter to my family, and something astounding occurred. To my astonishment, I found myself in the company of someone—an individual by my side.

"Beside me sat a strange, important looking man who gently rested his hand on my shoulder. Surprised, I racked my brain—how had he come to be here? What was his purpose? Is some kind of hallucination from an overdose? Maybe I had already died. He addressed my thoughts, assuring me to remain composed, explaining that my pain would fade once I learned the truth: my son wasn't gone. Just as you hear me recount this, he told me that my son was not gone. Hurt and shocked, I treated him with skepticism, yet he held knowledge beyond my own. Extending his hand, he helped me up from where I was sitting and, instinctively, I followed his lead.

"We walked a few steps, eventually stopping before a wall that faced the exterior of the house. In a matter of seconds, an astonishing sight unfolded before me. A cloud-like formation appeared on the wall, gradually revealing a pathway. It emitted a warm, golden glow reminiscent of a sunset, accompanied by a gentle breeze that instilled an indescribable tranquility. I lacked the words to express my awe, yet my feet moved alongside his, almost as if I were floating. The gentle breeze, the beautiful trees, flowers, and grass enveloped us. The sky was so beautiful with the sun casting everything in a resplendent golden hue. We continued along this path until we arrived at a garden which was brimming with hydrangeas and lilies, their colors more extraordinary than imagination itself.

"The man who accompanied me invited me to sit with him at a bench nestled among the flora and trees. As I sat, time seemed to lose its meaning, my attention wholly consumed by the enchanting picture before me. It was only when a golden, circular light floated toward me that I snapped back to the present. I stood, surprise enveloping me as the light approached. In a fleeting moment, the radiance dissolved, revealing a figure before me.

"My son! There he stood, his smile radiating as he gently grasped my hands. Words were unnecessary—we communicated silently through our connection. He gestured around him, conveying that this place was now his abode, where he'd await my eventual arrival. I embraced him, sensing the rhythm of his heart—a pulse that affirmed his vitality. Alive, albeit not in the human form, he existed within this realm we shared, a truth that encompassed everything to me.

"The following day, I awoke, still alive, of course, in my own room. However, something had shifted. The pain that had held me captive was gone, replaced solely by serenity. From that day on, everything within me transformed—everything! A period of questioning ensued, followed by moments of profound unrest. Although I still missed my son, little by little, with each reinforcement of this newfound peace and acceptance, I found unwavering support from those who weren't ordinary individuals but rather extraordinary ones.

"As time passed, I recognized a more potent reason for my continued existence, one that guided me to the path I tread today—sharing my experience with people like you, Dennis. You are undoubtedly unique, destined for a mission of love, a mission to both give and receive, to stand as a beacon for others in need. And there are many who need you, myself included. You possess a gift, an exceptional quality that sets you apart from others. Though it may not be comprehended or embraced by everyone, it remains a fundamental part of you, a lesson to be accepted and integrated into your being."

The doctor eventually wrapped up, finally concluding her very personal story. This unexpected revelation left Dennis feeling a bit overwhelmed. Dr. Michaels' voice kept spinning in her mind like a broken record, repeating over and over again. There was a lot for her to process, and many attempts to make sense of all that the doctor had disclosed would be needed to truly digest everything she learned. Her heart raced, thoughts piled up, and she briefly wondered if it might all be a confusing dream. After leaving her appointment, she walked and walked, lost in thought, until she found herself in front of *Café Italia*. Glancing inside, she spotted the barista working behind the counter, brewing coffee as usual. Then it hit her—yes, she remembered his introduction: *"My name is Lucas."* A smile spread across her face, a sign that her thoughts were finally coming together.

CHAPTER 10

Dennis and Lucas

Feeling something other than stress was a welcome change for Dennis. It had been a while since she had smiled so genuinely.

Upon entering the café, she joined the line to place her order. Her attention was drawn to the menu, a sizable board adorned with colorful chalk drawings showcasing the day's featured coffee and its accompanying snack. Dennis was taken aback by how well-executed the drawings were and how the vibrant colors caught her eye—something she hadn't really noticed before. Her gaze swept the café, instinctively looking behind the counter for something. Confusion settled in as she thought, *Where did he go? I could've sworn I just saw him.* She was searching for Lucas.

"What would the lady like to drink?" a voice from behind the counter inquired. As Dennis began to place her order, another voice intervened, responding on her behalf from the opposite end of the counter.

"A double cappuccino with chocolate and extra foam!" the voice chimed in. "Coming right up!" It was Luke! He had been observing her from where the baristas prepare the orders.

Dennis glanced up, her cheeks warming slightly. Lucas' face lit up with a broad smile as he approached Dennis, handing her the order ticket.

After settling the payment, she moved to the end of the counter designated for waiting customers. With a clear view before her, Dennis began to notice details that often escaped her during her routine visits. The café itself possessed a distinctive character, adorned with local artwork hanging on the walls. Standing there, she also realized that many of the windows inside weren't actual windows; instead, they were realistic paintings. It became evident that these were paintings when it dawned on her that real windows would reveal the mural outside the coffee shop—a view only accessible through the second-floor windows.

She thought to herself, *Who could have done all that beautiful work?* There wasn't much that stood out, but it served to confirm her impression. Yet, something else caught her attention—Lucas. She observed him intently, though she could only see his back as he worked on brewing coffee. He appeared taller than she remembered from the previous night. Clearly, there was more to him than her memories and images could capture; they were akin to fleeting glimpses of the sun, recognizable but never quite clear. As Lucas finished his tasks and placed the coffee on the counter, he offered a friendly smile, to which she responded with gratitude.

"Thank you, Lucas," she smiled back.

This marked the first time she had directly engaged with him, consciously initiating a conversation and addressing him by name. It was a departure from her usual approach, which was mostly transactional and distant. Taking her coffee, she headed up the stairs to the second floor. However, upon reaching the first step, a sense of uncertainty arose, prompting her to pause and contemplate whether she should proceed.

A peculiar sentiment enveloped her, compelling her to pause and reflect. Glancing back, there was nothing remarkable—people in line, a girl tidying the floor, and the woman tending the counter, along with Lucas crafting coffees—all appeared normal.

Undeterred, she continued up the stairs, relieved to find her favorite spot unoccupied. There was no one else upstairs aside from a quiet couple sitting a few tables away from her own. With cautious steps, she approached the table, placed her bag down, set the cappuccino on the surface, and settled into her seat, a contented smile playing on her lips.

For a while, she simply gazed out of the large windows. Dennis observed the pedestrians passing along the sidewalk across the street, the stores adorned with decorations illuminated by small lights in every stained-glass window and even in the sidewalk trees. The trees had shed their leaves, signaling the imminent arrival of the holiday season. These festivities brought a profound sadness that had become almost routine for her. Years of practicing the same patterns, evading anything that might lead her toward happiness due to a pervasive fear of losing it all.

She allowed a few minutes to pass before she started to take small sips from her coffee. Hot beverages weren't her forte; she preferred letting them cool naturally before consuming. Gradually, she felt more at ease, attempting to piece together the events of that afternoon—specifically, her session with Dr. Michaels. It was a subject she had been avoiding, as its enormity warranted careful consideration. She aimed to revisit each of the doctor's words, ensuring she had comprehended them correctly.

Even now, it all seemed surreal. Dennis occasionally touched her hands to verify she was indeed awake and not trapped in a dream. Thoughts swirled within her, maintaining their place in her mind with a sense of awe. She struggled to believe what she had been told. She entertained the notion that perhaps her mind had concocted it all.

For the longest time she had wished for someone who could truly grasp her experiences. Yet was it conceivable that her psychiatrist had shared such profound insights? Had she finally found someone who could relate on some level? A person to whom she could finally unburden herself about the occurrences she had kept locked within? Wasn't that what she had wished for fervently? Strangely, however, she didn't feel a sense of fulfillment; instead, her mind was teeming with more questions than ever before.

The recurring thought echoed in her mind, eliciting an indescribable sensation. Dr. Michaels' words kept reverberating: *"My son is not dead."* Those words held immense power and intensity. Coupled with the entirety of the narrative, they propelled her toward a fresh wave of unease. It was as if the understanding she had yearned for was now on her doorstep, prompting an almost immediate question to emerge:

Will I see my parents again?

Her eyes welled up for a brief moment, threatening to overflow, but an unexpected occurrence curbed the impulse, holding back the tears from cascading freely.

Up on the second floor, Lucas had ascended to ensure the tables were tidy and chairs properly arranged. As he busied himself, tidying up and attending to minor debris on the floor, the couple who occupied a nearby table began to gather their belongings, preparing to leave. This time, Dennis had spent just about forty minutes seated there, keeping track of time.

The departing couple exited the scene, prompting Lucas to subtly approach their table. With a quick clean-up and rearrangement, he restored order. In a slightly playful manner, and perhaps attempting to make his presence known, Lucas pivoted and directed his gaze toward Dennis. Often lost in thought or daydreaming, Dennis was typically distant, mentally preoccupied or journeying away from her immediate surroundings. However, this instance found her keenly present and attentive to his actions.

As Dennis climbed up to the second floor earlier, she had resolved not to let herself drift away or lose focus, determined to remain grounded. She observed Lucas intently, this time able to append another descriptor to the characteristics she had noted before—Lucas was also slender, boasting light brown hair and a sun-kissed complexion. It led her to ponder whether Lucas might have European roots, possibly of Italian or Spanish descent.

Meeting Dennis' gaze caught Lucas off guard, generating a touch of embarrassment. He didn't wish to come across as intrusive or bothersome, but he found himself standing before her, lost for words. In a slightly uncertain manner, Lucas managed to articulate, "Oh, excuse me, I didn't think..." His voice trailed off, leaving a silence that he hastened to fill, "What I meant is: do you need anything else?" His eyes averted Dennis' gaze as he concluded his sentence.

However, Dennis was in no hurry to withdraw her gaze; instead, a faint smile graced her lips. "I'm fine, and yes, I'm still here," she replied, her smile lingering. "Thank you for your concern. I won't be staying much longer today, so don't feel obligated to keep an eye on me. I'll finish my coffee and head home."

Lucas felt a flutter of nervousness at her words, his hands rubbing together as an instinctual response to discomfort. He hastily assured her, "Oh, no, it's nothing! Please don't think it bothers me." A smile accompanied his words, attempting to convey his sincerity. He turned away and began moving toward the staircase, mustering a sideways glance in Dennis' direction, though she was outside his immediate field of view.

A mere moment later, a voice carried to him: "Wait, Luke? I have something to ask you." Surprised, he pivoted to find Dennis standing, her gaze locked onto him.

"Actually," Dennis began, surprising herself, "I was wondering if you'd be up for taking a break one of these days. I'd like to return the favor and treat you to a coffee. What do you think?"

Even as the words left her mouth, Dennis couldn't believe what she had just said to Lucas. She had always kept personal commitments at arm's length, but this time, the words flowed effortlessly. Now all she had to do was wait for Lucas' response.

For Lucas, the unexpected request required a bit more thought than usual. Firstly, he wasn't entirely sure if he had understood correctly. Secondly, the words didn't come as easily as he had hoped. It was something he hadn't anticipated, even though Dennis was someone he thought about quite often.

"Yeah, sure, why not?" Lucas replied, a bit short of words but earnest in his response. He mustered the courage to make plans, albeit of a friendly nature. After all, friendships had to start somewhere.

Dennis' smile radiated gratitude as she confirmed they could meet up for lunch on Sunday around one o'clock in the afternoon. They decided on a nice promenade at the bay park, replete with charming restaurants and souvenir shops. A leisurely walk was on the agenda, and the expansive park offered them ample space for strolling and conversing. There was no denying that Dennis and Lucas had plenty to talk about.

Heading back to her company's parking lot, where her car had been parked since the morning, Dennis reflected on everything. A new sensation seemed to accompany her—a lightness that was difficult to put into words. Perhaps it was the result of making plans with Lucas. Regardless of the cause, she felt a newfound buoyancy, a sense of release that allowed her to breathe more freely.

As she ascended to the third level of the parking structure, where her car was situated, Dennis took out her keys from her bag and pressed the remote control to activate the lights and unlock the doors. It was a habitual action, but this time, something caught her eye. Small orbs of light were hovering around her car, an unusual sight that immediately altered her expression. An uncertain feeling crept in—something didn't seem right. Could it be that these orbs were celebrating her newfound positivity? Dennis wasn't sure, but she felt an inkling that these glowing spheres held a deeper significance.

Pacing with a quickened stride, Dennis neared her car only to realize that the glowing orbs weren't hovering around her vehicle, but rather around the one parked two spaces away. This realization didn't bring her any solace; if anything, it heightened her unease. Recognizing whose car it was only intensified her concern. The orbs seemed to confirm that something was amiss.

The car belonged to a fellow employee at the company. He was known for working late hours, and lately, he'd been grappling with numerous difficulties, including his wife's illness. The ongoing struggles in his personal life mirrored what Dennis often sensed when she saw these lights. Her intuition had a track record of being on point, which left her feeling both frustrated and helpless. She wished she could do more for others, but often found herself at a loss.

However, there was a shift in Dennis' response this time. She didn't cry or become frustrated. Instead, she simply observed, allowing her gaze to linger on the orbs for a moment before turning her attention back to her own car. She started the engine and drove away without any tumultuous emotions. It occurred to her that perhaps the first step toward effective assistance was acknowledging and accepting both herself and the experiences that came with her unique perspective. Was this insight what Dr. Michaels had been trying to convey to her all along?

CHAPTER 11

Uncertainty

Part One

The previous day had been unusually intense, unlike anything Dennis had ever experienced. Despite the unexpected twists and turns, it was Friday, and her duties at the office awaited. Far from being displeased, she actually found some comfort in the routine. Yet, that morning, an inexplicable heaviness lingered in her chest, its cause elusive and troubling.

Amidst a typical project, a faint breeze brushed against her back, prompting her to search for its source. Finding nothing to explain the sensation, she rose from her chair, seeking the simple solace of a glass of water. As she moved through the office, a sense of absence washed over her. Despite the usual hustle around her, everything felt strangely detached. Dennis moved with a heightened awareness, her steps deliberate, as if to affirm her own presence. A passing colleague's concern, "Are you okay?"—mistaking her intentional movements for a stumble— was met with a nod and a reassuring smile from Dennis. She continued on, fully aware of her surroundings, dispelling any notion of being lost in thought or daydream.

Yet, an unease persisted. She pondered whether this disquietude was linked to the mysterious lights she had seen near her coworker's car the previous night. Driven by a need to understand, Dennis impulsively gathered a stack of papers and headed to the design area, hoping to find the coworker in question. There, amidst the familiar bustle of creativity, she found her colleague, seemingly unaffected by any oddity. Dennis hesitated, realizing any inquiry would seem intrusive, if not downright absurd. What could she possibly ask? About his wife? The thought alone felt reckless. With no clear reason to engage, she retreated to her desk, leaving her curiosity unspoken and her disquiet momentarily shelved.

Pondering the potential connection between the mysterious lights she'd seen near her coworker's car and her current unease, Dennis acted impulsively, grabbing a stack of papers and heading to the design area to look for her colleague. Upon finding them working as usual, with nothing amiss, she hesitated to approach. The questions she might have asked seemed too personal, too intrusive, so she retreated to her office without engaging.

As lunchtime neared, Dennis wrapped up some pending tasks and decided to take her break. She sometimes ate in the company cafeteria, but on this day, she sought the tranquility of the small garden behind the building. This space, rarely frequented by others due to the smoking ban, offered her a sense of peace.

Dennis had a routine of calling Tammy, a habit she worried might seem overbearing to Tammy's family. Despite her concerns of being intrusive, she limited her visits to Saturdays, opting instead for daily calls under various pretexts, leveraging her new job as a reason to reach out. Dennis's intention was to mask her deep concern for Tammy, who had yet to fully grasp Dennis's reliance on her presence and support through this new chapter in her life. The conversation often circled back to the company, a topic Tammy wished to distance herself from, but Dennis would take those chances to gently reminded her of the promise to stand by her through this new opportunity.

Dennis went to great lengths to keep Tammy engaged and active, witnessing her struggle with the side effects of chemotherapy over the past few months. As Tammy neared the end of her treatment, she adhered to a regimen of eight chemotherapy sessions, spaced three weeks apart, tailored specifically for her situation. The first week post-treatment was always the most challenging, the second showed improvement, and by the third, Tammy began to regain her strength, ready to face the next round.

Dennis observed Tammy's struggle with the side effects of chemotherapy, a treatment regimen of eight sessions spaced three weeks apart. Despite the grueling cycle, Tammy's prognosis was positive, buoyed by supportive therapies and a significant reduction in cancer markers. This progress filled Dennis with hope, despite the ominous feeling the mysterious lights had instilled in her. They were a chilling reminder of her fears, yet she chose to focus on hope, embracing optimism over pessimism, much like anyone clinging to the possibility of a brighter future.

In Tammy's family, the grasp of her illness and its severity was elusive. Despite understanding the diagnosis, the reality of cancer hadn't fully sunk in. Her children were baffled and distressed, their confusion manifesting as anger and resentment towards the divine. Her husband retreated into silence, overwhelmed by the uncertainty and unable to process their altered future. He was haunted by thoughts of their plans and dreams, struggling to understand what they might have done to deserve such a fate. His mind was a battleground of futile speculations, not realizing that his introspection distanced him further from Tammy.

She frequently found herself lost in thought, *What about the plans we made together? The future we planned, side by side?* Grappling with the harsh reality of their situation, she struggled to comprehend what they might have done to deserve such a trial. Her mind was a whirlwind of relentless, tormenting thoughts, often fixating on the possibility that they had made a mistake somewhere along the line. She dwelled on what that mistake could be—there had to be *something*—not realizing that these hours of introspection were time spent away from her closest friend. It was time she would never get back. Eventually, she would come to recognize the folly of her ways.

On that particular day, Dennis opted for a light lunch—a salad and a soft drink—and found solace under an old plum tree outside the building, offering both shade and a perfect spot for her break. Settling down, she was about to indulge in her meal when she decided to call Tammy, anticipating a heartfelt conversation.

However, the phone just rang unanswered, stirring a flutter of concern in Dennis's heart. She reassured herself, imagining Tammy might be preoccupied or resting. Despite her attempts to stay calm, the uncharacteristic silence from Tammy's end troubled her deeply. "Perhaps I'm overthinking it," Dennis murmured, trying to shake off her worries.

Unable to focus on her meal, she only sipped her soda, her gaze fixed on the phone, counting the seconds that stretched into infinity. After ten minutes, she discarded her untouched salad, her appetite lost to growing anxiety. She tried calling again, but the persistent ringing only led to voicemail, amplifying her distress. A torrent of questions flooded her mind—*where could Tammy be, what could have happened, why was there no answer this time?*

After ending the call without a response, Dennis knew she had to reach out to Tammy's husband. Despite her hesitation, feeling like an intrusion into Tammy's family life—a boundary she had always respected—she couldn't shake off the concern. Tammy had always kept her family matters separate, and Dennis respected that boundary, even if she occasionally felt a pang of jealousy. She admired Tammy greatly and felt that Tammy's children didn't fully appreciate the wonderful person their mother was.

Dennis's longing for her own parents, gone too soon, might have clouded her judgment. She saw Tammy as the kind of dynamic, caring person she wished her mother could have been. But deep down, Dennis knew that it wasn't fair to place Tammy in the role of a mother figure in her life. Their bond was special, akin to sisterhood, even if it wasn't the maternal connection Dennis sometimes fantasized about.

Sitting under the shade in the garden, Dennis gathered her courage and dialed Tammy's husband's number. The phone rang, tightening a knot in her throat, until she was interrupted—not by a voice on the line, but by an office colleague in person, informing her of an urgent message waiting on her office call receiver. With a heavy sense of premonition about Tammy's wellbeing, Dennis rushed back to the office, opting for the stairs in a frantic bid to save precious seconds.

Reaching her office on the sixth floor, trying to appear composed despite the urgency, Dennis navigated the familiar corridors. She burst into her office, quickly closing the door behind her. The call receiver blinked ominously with a new message. Knowing she couldn't delay the inevitable, Dennis took a deep breath, picked up the headset, and braced herself to listen to the awaited message.

The message was from Tammy's youngest daughter, her voice filled with sorrow. She relayed that her mother had taken ill and was now at the clinic. Although Tammy had somewhat recovered, she had insisted on contacting Dennis. The news brought tears to Dennis's eyes, prompting her to replay the message multiple times, each playback a reminder of the gravity of the situation.

Amid her emotional turmoil, there was a knock at the door. It was the secretary of Mrs. Mary Harrison, with a message that Mrs. Harrison wished to see her immediately. Dennis, though not in shock, was visibly distressed, a mix of emotions that she felt uniquely hers. She composed herself quickly and informed the secretary she would be there shortly, who in turn relayed the message back to Mrs. Harrison.

Attempting to wipe away the tears and mask her sorrow proved futile; Dennis's face betrayed her pain. She knocked and was promptly granted entry by the secretary. Dennis briefly sat in the anteroom of Mrs. Harrison's office, awaiting her turn to be announced.

"You can go in now," the secretary indicated.

"Thank you," Dennis responded, gathering her strength as she approached the door.

"How are you, Dennis?" inquired Mrs. Harrison upon her entrance.

Dennis, wrestling with her emotions, pondered how best to reply, keen on not revealing the depth of her sorrow. Mrs. Harrison then shared that Tammy had experienced a significant health scare but was currently stable, having managed to overcome the immediate crisis. The family, understandably, had been deeply alarmed by the turn of events.

"Dennis," Mrs. Harrison continued, pausing for a moment before adding, "I thought you should know that you're welcome to take the rest of the day off to visit Tammy at the clinic if you'd like. Actually, I'm heading that way myself shortly after I handle a pending matter."

"Would you like to come with me?" Mrs. Harrison offered.

Without hesitation, Dennis agreed, and as they wrapped up their immediate tasks, Mrs. Harrison's driver was ready in the parking lot to transport them to the clinic.

Upon their arrival at Tammy's private room, the weight of the situation was palpable. The room was crowded with relatives, enveloped in a heavy silence that spoke volumes of the emotions swirling through the air. Conversations were hushed, faces etched with concern and despair.

Inside, only Tammy's husband was with her. Mrs. Harrison gently knocked on the partially open door and asked, "May we come in?" extending her arm to Dennis, guiding them both inside.

The expression on Tammy's husband's face was distant, perhaps a testament to the pain he was enduring, leaving him seemingly in a daze.

The two women offered their greetings to him as Tammy rested, unconscious and visibly worn from the medication. The room was arranged with two chairs to the left of the bed, beneath a large window, while on the right, a medical device monitored Tammy's vital signs and administered her medication intravenously, making the left side the only accessible area.

Unlike typical hospital rooms, this private space was warmly decorated, offering a sense of harmony and comfort. The decor was delicate and soothing, making the room feel more like a bedroom in a home than a clinical setting.

Tammy's husband exchanged a few words with Mary and attempted to engage Dennis, but she was overwhelmed, unable to speak with the lump in her throat. After some time, Dennis chose to step outside, allowing the family a moment of privacy. Unbeknownst to many, it was the Harrison Foundation that had ensured Tammy received the best possible medical attention.

The Harrison Foundation was steadfast in its commitment to aiding those in need, providing support to individuals facing hardships without seeking public recognition. Their efforts were typically carried out quietly, without any desire for accolades. In Tammy's case, however, the situation was exceptional. Mary Harrison ensured that Tammy received the best possible care and accommodations available, a testament to the foundation's dedication and Mary's personal involvement.

As time wore on, Dennis and Mary remained by Tammy's side, though she was unaware of their presence, her condition unchanged.

Eventually, the duty nurse informed them it was time to allow Tammy some rest. While it felt as if they were being asked to leave, they understood the importance of giving patients space, a principle respected in any clinical setting.

They retreated to the waiting area, mingling with other visitors and occasionally engaging with Tammy's family members. Later in the afternoon, the attending doctor arrived to check on Tammy, accompanied by her husband into the room.

After their consultation, the doctor and Tammy's husband emerged, prompting Mary to swiftly approach the doctor for a private conversation. They moved to a quieter spot near the nurses' station, visible to Dennis as she sat pondering in the waiting area. She couldn't help but wonder about the nature of their discussion, curious about the information being exchanged.

Time passed, and Mary decided it was time for her to leave, assuring Tammy's husband she would remain in contact. Throughout the day, family members came and went, while Dennis stayed quietly in her corner, observing and reflecting in silence.

"Dennis," Mary said, reaching out to her, "would you like to come with me? It might be good for us to get some rest. Tammy is stable and doing fine, so there's no need for too much worry."

Dennis looked at her, almost in a trance, then stood up and followed without a word. She didn't glance at anyone else or bid farewell; her spirits were notably low. The two women got into the car that had been waiting for several hours. Mary instructed the driver to start driving. When the driver inquired about their destination, Mary's response was uncertain. "I don't know yet," she admitted. "Just take us away from here." The car then headed onto the highway, direction unknown.

They drove in silence until the vehicle slowed before a set of imposing iron gates which gradually swung open. Dennis, coming to her senses, inquired, "Where are we? I'm sorry, I didn't give any directions on where to stop. How silly of me—I've been so distracted."

However, the car continued at a slow pace along a driveway lined with perfectly aligned gray stone cobblestones and majestic pines, illuminated intermittently by soft lights that only partially lit the path winding uphill.

"Oh, don't worry, Dennis," Mary reassured her. "The driver took a detour and brought us to my place. We thought some company might do you good right now. Plus, the doctor will keep me updated on any emergencies, so we can head to the clinic immediately if needed. What do you think? If you'd prefer, I can have the driver take you home. It's no trouble at all, but I'd love for you to join me for dinner first!"

Dennis managed a smile, mirrored by Mary's own.

The car traveled about a quarter of a mile before arriving in front of a grand residence, an English mansion styled in the distinctive Tudor architecture. The front boasted many windows, dimly lit, casting a somewhat somber, yet imposing presence. Despite the property's vastness, it had an air of faded grandeur. Dennis and Mary exited the car and descended a small set of cobblestone steps to the entrance, where a woman welcomed them inside.

"Please, make yourself at home," Mary encouraged as they entered her home.

"Thank you," Dennis responded, her gaze wandering over her surroundings.

"Dinner will be ready soon," Mary mentioned, excusing herself momentarily. "I'll be right back."

Dennis offered a polite nod, taking the opportunity to truly appreciate the grandeur around her. The house was a testament to elegant and tasteful decor, striking a balance between simplicity and refinement rather than opulence. The charm of the space was enhanced by numerous floral arrangements placed near the windows and a cozy seating area by the fireplace. The flooring caught Dennis's attention—a splendid dark, reddish mahogany that spoke of age and beauty. The welcoming lady who had opened the door for them kindly pointed out the location of the restrooms, should Dennis wish to freshen up before dinner, a gesture Dennis found thoughtful.

CHAPTER 12

Uncertainty

Part Two

D ennis moved towards the fireplace area, intending to sit and wait for Mary, but her attention was captured by some photographs on the mantle. Among the images of Eileen and Mary, she was surprised to find Tammy featured prominently. Not just a single photo, but around six, chronicling different stages of their lives together. Dennis was immediately curious about the nature of Tammy's relationship with the Harrison sisters. The presence of Tammy in these photographs, especially one where she appeared notably younger, possibly during school years, raised questions about the depth and origin of their connection. This revelation was unexpected for Dennis, who had never delved into the private lives of Tammy, Mary, and Eileen, yet she couldn't help but be struck by the evident joy shared among the three women in the photos.

Dennis knew little about their personal histories, as Tammy had been reticent about her life outside work, sharing only sparing, vague details about her activities at the agency and university. This moment of discovery underscored Tammy's guarded nature regarding her personal affairs.

When Mary returned, she approached Dennis to lead her to the dining room. Located adjacent to the staircase on the first floor, to the right of the entrance, the dining area was elegantly appointed. The walls were adorned with delicate wallpaper featuring a rose pattern with an antique finish. At the heart of the room, a hemispherical window opened up to a garden that overlooked the mansion's back courtyard, adding a serene backdrop. The table, small and refined, was set for four, suggesting intimacy rather than grandeur, covered with a pink lace tablecloth. Additional chairs were positioned near the window, offering a cozy arrangement, while a swinging door on the opposite side provided access to the kitchen.

The dinner was a welcome treat for Dennis, who hadn't eaten since the early hours of the day, and it was now well past six in the evening. After they finished their meal, the housekeeper announced she would prepare tea in the living room. Seizing the moment, both women proceeded there, continuing their amiable conversation which, up until now, hadn't entirely centered around Tammy. Yet, seated comfortably in the living room, the warmth of the fireplace nearby, Dennis found the perfect moment to inquire about the photographs she had noticed earlier on the mantle, sensing their significance to Mary.

"I noticed you've known Tammy for quite some time. She looked quite young in that photograph, didn't she?" Dennis asked, her curiosity piqued.

"Yes! That was taken on the day of her undergraduate graduation. It was indeed a wonderful day," Mary responded, catching the drift of Dennis's curiosity and elaborating further. "Tammy had been in fragile health and we were worried she might not graduate due to missing too many classes. But, as always, her determination saw her through," Mary concluded.

Dennis contemplated delving deeper into their connection, wondering about the roots of their close relationship and the evident depth of their care for Tammy. However, before she could voice these thoughts, Mary addressed the unspoken questions.

"Dennis," she began, anticipating Dennis's curiosity, "you're probably wondering about the presence of Tammy's photos here and our relationship with her. Well, I'm about to share something few people know—Tammy is my daughter! Not by birth, but she is my daughter in every sense that matters. Let me explain a bit for better understanding.

"Years ago, when we were just starting what would become our company, I met a woman facing many challenges, and I did my best to assist her, genuinely wanting to help. Then, she revealed she was pregnant and planning to put the baby up for adoption. At that time, I hadn't yet had the chance to start a family of my own, and her situation deeply moved me. I decided then that I wanted to be that child's adoptive mother. Things unfolded in such a way that the birth mother chose to relinquish all her rights to the baby, and so we proceeded.

"The adoption was finalized when Tammy was just a few months old, and from that moment, I raised her as my own, providing her with all the love and care I had to offer. When she turned 13, we were blindsided by the diagnosis of a terrible illness. The news brought immense anguish to our family. We embarked on a journey through countless medical consultations, seeking a cure for the affliction that had befallen us, but the answer remained the same: Tammy's only hope was a bone marrow transplant from a biological relative.

"Breaking the news to Tammy that I wasn't her biological mother was heart-wrenching, and it was even harder to accept that, despite our financial means, we were powerless to help her. The diagnosis was childhood leukemia. I felt as if my world was collapsing and there was nothing I could do to prevent this calamity.

"In our desperation, we sought out Tammy's birth mother, about whom we knew very little. Our search revealed that she had led a solitary life, never having more children or marrying. This discovery, though sad, gave us a sliver of hope for assistance.

"Despite Tammy's initial resistance, we proceeded with the transplant. The wait for the outcome was agonizing but, after three long days, the doctors confirmed the transplant's success. Tammy had beaten the disease and could look forward to a future filled with dreams and possibilities. However, the ordeal had altered our relationship. An invisible barrier had arisen between us, changing the dynamic of our bond.

"As Tammy grew older, so did the distance between us. I began to believe that the revelation of her adoption contributed to her feeling detached, as if she didn't belong to our family name. There were many factors that might have influenced her feelings, including the painful revelations about her mother. It was a challenging period for both of us, witnessing her struggle with these revelations and feeling so powerless to help.

"When Tammy got accepted into college, I was puzzled by her decision not to go away, contrary to the dreams I had for her. She chose to stay local, and for a while, it seemed our relationship was on the mend. I initially thought her decision was about us, but I later discovered she was aiding her biological mother, who was pressuring her for money. Tammy felt a sense of obligation to her, crediting her with the 'miracle' of her life, despite the less-than-ideal circumstances surrounding their connection. That's when I made a pivotal mistake."

"Mistake?" Dennis interjected, fully engrossed in the unfolding narrative.

"Yes," Mary continued, "In my role as her mother, and driven by a desire to alleviate her burden, I offered money to the woman to leave Tammy alone. She accepted the money and vanished. But when the money was gone, she returned to Tammy, who then learned of my interference. This revelation infuriated her. She felt I was trying to sever their connection again, leading to immense pain and sorrow on my part, and ultimately, to our estrangement.

"Years later, Tammy unexpectedly appeared at my doorstep. The joy I felt at seeing her again was indescribable; my heart and thoughts had lingered on her throughout our time apart. Through numerous heartfelt discussions, we began to rebuild our relationship on a foundation of simplicity and transparency. Tammy needed time and something else for this new phase to succeed. She set a condition, one that, out of love for her, I readily accepted. Letting go of my pride, I was content just to have her back in my life, no matter what it took."

"What was the condition? If you don't mind my asking," Dennis inquired, eager to learn more.

Mary was ready to share the next chapter of her story.

"Well, during the years Tammy was apart from me, she attempted to build a relationship with her biological mother. It was in that period she met her now-husband, yet she chose not to disclose any of her past to him—not the fact that she was adopted, her illness, or anything she considered her past. Tammy had convinced herself to live with the narrative she had crafted, viewing her life with me as nothing more than charity. But that was far from the truth. I never gave her any reason to see my love as merely charitable; on the contrary, Tammy was the center of my world, my entire existence. And that hasn't changed; she remains my reason for living.

"Tammy led a modest, diligent life and continued to advance, retaining all the lessons from our travels and the cultures we experienced during our happiest times. In this new phase of our relationship, she wished for things to remain as they were back then, without any obligations. She began visiting me more frequently, trying to bridge the gap between us without any pressure. Accepting her terms was the only way I could ensure she remained a part of my life, to hear about her days, and to share in her life's moments. She was, and is, my daughter, regardless of any circumstances; she will always be my daughter."

"But did the relationship improve?" Dennis inquired, seeking clarity.

"Yes, our relationship did evolve. Tammy remained adamant about not accepting any form of aid from me, a wish I respected. We developed a friendship, and she grew into an admirable woman and professional, excelling in her studies and later joining the agency. She insisted on earning her way, refusing any advantages not born from her efforts. Although I've been present in her life, at her wedding, and during the birth of her children, I've had to content myself with being just a friend, a close friend," Mary explained, her voice tinged with emotion, betraying the tears she couldn't hold back.

Dennis listened intently to the story, moved by its depth and complexity. Tammy was indeed a formidable woman, marked by her resilience and a complex blend of emotions, sometimes directing her frustrations at those undeserving. Yet, as the saying goes, it's never too late for reconciliation and healing, as long as there's life, there's always hope.

The afternoon waned as the hours slipped by. Dennis had listened intently to every word shared by Mary, absorbing the significant impact Tammy had on the Harrison sisters, particularly regarding Dennis's introduction as her replacement. Yet, the situation was now set, leaving Dennis puzzled over Tammy's reluctance to see Mary's intentions as purely benevolent. How had Tammy missed the depth of Mary's maternal love?

Dennis possessed a unique ability among her many qualities: the capacity to empathize deeply with the emotions of others, and this scenario was no exception. She could sense the depth of pain and love in Mary's words. The greatest sacrifice Mary had offered was her boundless love and dedication, willing to give even her health for Tammy's sake, a testament to a love so profound it could only be likened to that of a mother.

Glancing at her watch, Dennis was startled by how late it had become, the engrossing conversation making time seem to vanish. Mary paused to call the clinic for an update on Tammy, reassuring Dennis before her departure that Tammy was stable and well-cared for, especially now that Dennis understood Mary's significant role in Tammy's life.

As Dennis prepared to leave, the driver awaited her. She turned to Mary with a question, "Mrs. Harrison, does Tammy's family know now? I mean, do they understand the whole story?" Mary responded, "It's unfortunate that it had to come to light under these circumstances, but yes, since Tammy's illness escalated, we've had to bring them into the fold so Tammy could accept our help. She has her children to fight for, which helped her see things more clearly and ultimately accept the support. Everything I have is also hers, and although I'm somewhat of a stranger to her children, I believe it won't take long for me to show them how much they mean to me. Time will reveal how things will unfold."

"Good evening, Dennis. Would you like me to pick you up tomorrow on my way to the clinic around ten?" Mary inquired.

"Yes, of course, I'll be waiting," Dennis responded, ready for the next day's visit.

Dennis took a moment for reflection, recognizing for the first time that her personal troubles paled in comparison to the profound sadness and turmoil in Mary's life. The struggles faced by Dr. Michaels with the loss of her son, and now Tammy's illness—the looming fear of leaving her family before mending unresolved issues—made her own concerns seem minor beside those of these remarkable women.

A new, deep emotion stirred within her, coupled with an intriguing realization that came to her just as she turned off her bedroom light, on the verge of sleep. She hadn't noticed the mysterious lights that usually accompanied her, not during her visit to the clinic, nor at Mary Harrison's house. The absence of these lights puzzled her; could their absence signify something positive? What could be the reason behind their disappearance? Questions flooded her mind as she sat up in bed and turned the light back on.

Pacing her room, then moving to the living room, she searched in vain. Though unsure how to articulate her desire for the lights, she found herself longing for their presence, just as they had appeared unbidden before. In a moment of vulnerability, she called out: "Please, I need help!" Her voice was shaky, tinged with fear.

Returning to her bedroom, Dennis collapsed onto her bed, staring at the ceiling, her mind racing with thoughts until sleep overtook her. That night, she slept undisturbed, not waking until seven the next morning.

Awakening on that Saturday, Dennis felt a change within herself, an inexplicable sense of calm and inner peace that was hard to describe but palpable in the air.

With ten minutes to ten, she got ready to meet Mary's transport for their visit to the clinic, as arranged the night before. The realization that Mary was the mother of her dearly regarded friend, Tammy, filled her with awe.

The atmosphere was charged with a newfound optimism as Mary shared her positive feelings with Dennis on their way to the clinic, a sentiment that buoyed both women. Upon arriving at Tammy's floor, they were met with a flurry of activity that sent their hearts racing, painting their faces with concern. Mary led the way with urgency, though the corridor to Tammy's room seemed to stretch interminably.

Reaching the entrance, Mary, with bated breath, nudged the door open, only to be rooted to the spot by what she saw. Dennis, trailing closely, bumped into Mary, who was frozen in the doorway. The collision nudged them both into the room.

"Oh, no!" Dennis exclaimed, trying to stabilize herself and Mary, reaching for a chair to regain balance, while Mary found support in Dennis's inadvertent guidance.

Their entrance first drew laughter from those inside, then concern, and finally, a room filled with joyful laughter, their initial awkwardness dissolving into a shared moment of relief and embarrassment.

What had stunned Mary was the sight of Tammy sitting up, vibrant and eating breakfast— a stark contrast to her condition just the day before. This transformation was nothing short of miraculous, catching Mary completely off guard.

Tammy, ever the spirited friend, greeted Dennis warmly, chiding her for the undue worry with a light-hearted rebuke. "Dennis! What a joy to see you, and how sorry I am that you've fretted over me. I've told you not to worry so much about what happens to me. Remember, I've got everything under control," she joked, her laughter infectious as she continued with her breakfast.

A broad smile illuminated Tammy's face, its warmth infectious, prompting smiles from everyone in the room—Dennis, Mary, Tammy's husband, the attending nurse, and one of Tammy's daughters.

After the shared laughter and joy, Tammy's husband mentioned he would step out to grab some breakfast for himself, now reassured by the additional company Tammy had. He carefully navigated past the visitors to exit the room, but not without warmly embracing Mary and planting a gentle kiss on her cheek, a gesture that visibly moved her.

Following him, Tammy's daughter exited the room, leaving the visitors with Tammy. The nurse, after adjusting the equipment Tammy was connected to, reminded everyone in a light-hearted manner not to overexcite Tammy, emphasizing the clinic's principle of rest.

Dennis moved closer to Tammy's bed, sitting down and gently taking her hand. "You don't know how happy I am to see you so much better. It's truly wonderful to see you this lively; it brings me immense joy," Dennis said, her eyes brimming with tears of happiness.

Mary, choosing to keep a respectful distance, positioned herself near the window. She wanted to ensure her presence didn't overwhelm Tammy, observing and listening from afar.

"Thank you, Dennis. I actually feel quite spirited today. I've regained some strength, and the nurse mentioned the doctor might visit earlier than planned because my blood cell count has improved. That's really good news," Tammy shared, her face alight with optimism.

Feeling a sudden urge for discretion, Dennis thought it might be best to leave Tammy and her family some space. With this in mind, she contemplated a tactful excuse to step out, aiming to provide them with more privacy.

"Did you know? I couldn't get the coffee machine to work today, something was off with it. Would it be okay if I pop down to the cafeteria for a bit to grab a coffee?" Dennis asked, to which Tammy enthusiastically responded, "Of course not! Go ahead, and if you find something tasty, bring me back a treat. I could really go for a cream cake right now." The three women shared a hearty laugh at the suggestion.

Thus, Dennis excused herself from the room, bound for the cafeteria under the pretext of needing coffee—a little white lie for a good cause.

Back in the room

Mary's eyes remained fixed on Tammy, and with Dennis momentarily gone, Tammy sensed the perfect moment to express something profound.

"Mom!" Tammy exclaimed, reaching out to Mary. "Come here, please."

It had been ages since Mary heard Tammy refer to her as 'mom', especially after the revelation that she was not her biological mother. Mary was momentarily stunned, questioning if she was hearing things or if her deep yearning for closeness had conjured up the words. But it was real, and Tammy called out to her again.

"Please, mom. Don't be so distant; I want you right here by my side," Tammy said with clarity and conviction, reaching out for Mary's hand.

To Mary, these words were a profound affirmation. She rose and approached Tammy's bedside. As she was about to sit, Tammy's hand clasped hers. Overwhelmed by emotion, Mary couldn't hold back her tears any longer, tears of joy and relief that had been pent up for too long, yearning for a moment of release.

Releasing Tammy's hand only to embrace her, Mary held her daughter with a tenderness that was mindful of her strength, their hug a silent exchange filled with years of unspoken love and reconciliation. This silent communion was only interrupted when Tammy's husband returned to the room with their youngest daughter and Dennis, who came bearing coffee.

Smiles adorned every face, a palpable sense of something extraordinary hanging in the air, a feeling that one had to be present to fully grasp.

CHAPTER 13

A New Friend...

That Saturday was one of the most memorable days Dennis had had in a long time.

When she returned to Tammy's room, she was greeted by smiles all around and, most notably, Tammy was holding Mary Harrison's hand. Dennis felt an overwhelming sense of belonging; she didn't feel out of place or overlooked but instead shared in the collective joy. It seemed Tammy was on the mend, showing signs of a miraculous recovery. Though not fully out of the woods yet, she was certainly heading towards something positive.

The vibrant conversations and warm atmosphere kept Dennis engrossed, but as the afternoon waned, she remembered her plans for the next day. She had promised Lucas to go out for lunch on Sunday, almost forgetting amid the day's happiness. Yet, there was still time, and considering the day's events, it felt like the perfect opportunity for some personal time. She was in high spirits, notably without witnessing any mysterious white lights.

That Sunday

The morning was beautiful, warm, and sunny—ideal for a stroll. Dennis chose a blue dress adorned with small white flowers, cinched at the waist, featuring a high collar and rolled-up sleeves, perfect for spring. She decided to pair it with a short-brimmed hat, long neglected in her closet, now rescued from its cobwebbed corner.

Driving to her rendezvous, Dennis felt a flutter of nerves but nothing that dampened her anticipation. It had been a while since she had been on a date, and she was slightly anxious about what to say or do. The radio played softly as she envisioned the approaching bay, almost smelling the sea breeze.

Crossing the bridge meant she was close to Bay Park, where the pair said they would meet up. On Sundays, boat traffic was minimal. This meant the bridge would likely lift only twice throughout the day, ensuring a smooth drive. Dennis parked under a tree's shade and set off to meet Lucas.

When she looked around, Dennis could see that Lucas was nowhere in sight. With just about five minutes to spare, she took a leisurely walk along the bay. The path was lined with benches and planters bursting with colorful petunias, complemented by colonial-style lampposts with hanging oil lamps, reminiscent of the early 1900s. This picturesque setting made Bay Park a magnet for tourists and locals alike.

The park stretched for two miles along the bay, its central tree-lined avenue splitting into two footpaths. To the right was a scenic seating area overlooking the water, offering views of the various boats on the water. On the opposite side, a promenade flanked by quaint shops and eateries paralleled the bay, housing unique tourist attractions, restaurants, cafes, bookstores, and shops selling souvenirs, pastries, and ice cream—the latter two being the park's best sellers.

The park was a hive of activity. There were people enjoying walks, shopping, and simply relishing the outdoor ambiance. Beyond the commercial zone lay green spaces that ventured inland into a wooded area, offering various walking trails. The beauty of the place, coupled with the fresh sea breeze, cultivated an air of leisure and exploration.

Amidst this idyllic scene, Dennis found herself nervously wondering where Lucas could be.

Deciding to return to the entrance in hopes that Lucas might be waiting there, she turned and made her way back. She thought she spotted someone familiar from a distance, but the sunlight reflecting off his face made it hard to be certain. Approaching, she realized it was indeed Lucas, though he appeared somewhat different.

"Lucas?" Dennis called out, seeking confirmation.

"Yeah," Lucas shouted back with a smile. "Hi! I've been waiting for you. I got here about five minutes ago."

"I got here a bit early and walked down to the bay looking for you," Dennis explained, her smile broadening. "When I realized you weren't there, I came back. And here you are!"

"Oh," Lucas started, concern in his voice. "I was under the impression we were meeting here at the entrance. I hope you haven't been waiting too long!"

"No, not at all," Dennis admitted, her smile persisting. "Just a few minutes. I must admit, I barely recognized you."

"Do I look that bad?" He joked.

"No, it's not that," Dennis clarified. "You just look different."

"Different? How so?"

"It's probably because I've only ever seen you in the café, wearing that black apron," Dennis explained, still smiling. "But really, it's nothing. Just me rambling."

"That's true," he replied, extending out his hand. "You've only seen me in my work attire. Allow me to introduce myself properly, then."

Dennis chuckled, playing along. "There's really no need."

But Lucas persisted, still holding his hand out. "Hello, my name is Lucas, Lucas Verdi."

"Hi, I'm Dennis Russell," Dennis responded, joining in the playful exchange. "Pleased to meet you!"

Their handshake cemented their official introduction, their laughter setting a cheerful tone for their outing. The two of them walked towards the park's interior, finding a bench by the bay where they sat, enjoying the gentle, warm breeze. The afternoon was shaping up to be perfect.

Lucas seemed taller than Dennis remembered from their previous encounters. He was dressed casually in light, pre-washed jeans and simple gray suede shoes. On top, he wore a blue and white striped button-up left open over a white polo. His hair also seemed different, contributing to his altered appearance. Dennis examined him curiously from head to toe, noting the distinct difference in his look.

The conversation flowed effortlessly, with Lucas proving to be an engaging companion. Dennis felt at ease, thoroughly enjoying the simplicity of the moment and the serene view of boats gliding through the bay. They touched on light topics, including work and the park's attractions, without delving too deeply into personal matters.

As it neared two in the afternoon, Lucas perked up with a suggestion. "Dennis, how would you like to go to lunch? Your choice: seafood or Italian? Both options are excellent here."

Dennis, having sampled both cuisines in this area before found it easy to make a decision.

"I think it's a perfect day for seafood," Dennis proposed. "Don't you agree?"

"Excellent choice! I'm in the mood for some delicious seafood myself," Lucas exclaimed, expressing his anticipation. "I'm hoping they'll have my favorite dish; it's been too long since I've treated myself."

"And what might that favorite dish be?" Dennis inquired with curiosity.

"I'll give you a hint: it's something you eat with chips," he responded, playfully miming a full stomach while rubbing his belly. "Ah, my appetite is getting the better of me."

With that, they rose from their bench and walked to the restaurant which was just a short jaunt away. Luckily, despite it being a busy Sunday, they were seated immediately. Their table was by a window in the main dining room, offering a splendid view of the park and bay framed by the trees lining the shore.

Lunch proved to be a delightful experience; they shared in laughter and joy. A welcome respite for Dennis, who reveled in the normalcy of the outing. It was a reprieve from her usual concerns, a moment of pure happiness. However, as she was about to learn, the afternoon was about to take startlingly unexpected turn.

As the two of them finished their meals, Dennis looked at Lucas with a playful glint in her eye. "Now, how about we head to the ice cream parlor for dessert?"

Lucas, ever ready for a sweet treat, responded eagerly. "Absolutely. I'm in the mood for some chocolate ice cream in a sugar cone. Oh, and topped with nuts, if they have them!"

* * *

You'll see, they have everything there, and their chocolate ice cream is one of my favorites. And what a coincidence—I like it with walnuts too." Dennis took it as a simple and innocent coincidence. Was it possible that Dennis was letting herself get carried away, failing to notice the deep affinity between them?

Once they both had their delicious ice creams in hand, they began to stroll leisurely through the park. They enjoyed a peaceful conversation until they reached a spot where they decided to sit and admire the bay. Suddenly, Lucas said something to Dennis that startled her:

"Dennis, I need to confess something to you," Lucas said.

Dennis looked at him, surprised and curious, trying to guess what he was about to reveal.

"Dennis, I'm sorry. I've been playing unfairly, and I don't want to keep doing it. It's just that..." Lucas paused, and Dennis immediately pressed him with urgency.

"But tell me, Lucas, what are you talking about?" Dennis was trying to piece together what he might mean, but the truth was, she had no idea what he was about to say.

"I've been trying to impress you all afternoon. I'm sorry, but I didn't want you to think I was boring or that you wouldn't want to go out with me again. But now I realize I've made things worse—I've really messed up."

"But Lucas, can you just tell me what you're talking about? I don't understand a word of it."

"Yes, I know, I know you don't understand." Lucas lowered his head and, rubbing his hands together, finally admitted:

"It's because, in trying to impress you, I've used something I shouldn't have—I've read your thoughts to figure out what you like."

Dennis started laughing, softly at first, but then she burst into loud laughter.

"Sure, I see—you can read my thoughts. Okay, tell me what I'm thinking right now!" Dennis replied playfully, assuming Lucas was joking. Just for fun, she thought of Mark, someone she hadn't thought about in a long time, someone who used to make her just as happy as she was feeling now—when they were together and she was his girlfriend.

"You're thinking about someone named Mark. I feel like he was, or still is, very close to your heart. Am I wrong?"

Dennis's smile faded, and her expression changed. Suddenly, everything going on between them froze in the air. It took her a few seconds to realize Lucas wasn't joking.

"How did you do that? How do you know that name? Please, explain yourself!" Dennis demanded, serious and a little confused—almost angry.

"I can't really explain it. But when I'm near someone I feel a special connection with, I can sense their thoughts—it's like I hear them in my head. It happens naturally. And even though I try to avoid it and never say anything, it doesn't mean it stops happening," Lucas explained.

He turned to sit sideways, facing Dennis directly. It was clear that he was now very nervous. Dennis looked him in the eye, thinking to herself: *Can you hear what I'm thinking right now?* She didn't say it aloud but waited for confirmation. It came instantly.

Lucas raised his gaze and, in a soft voice, said, "Yes, I can hear it too." He lowered his head, burying it in his hands as if realizing he'd made a mistake.

The truth was, Dennis was taken by surprise. Everything had seemed too perfect—so much so that it felt like the final note was needed to snap her back to reality.

Then something happened. It was like hearing someone talk, but no one was actually speaking. She was clearly hearing a voice in her head:

I knew I shouldn't have done it. I don't know why I thought this was a good idea, especially on a first date. What must she think of me now?

Dennis couldn't believe what she was hearing. She lifted her eyes to meet Lucas's gaze and said, "It's you, isn't it? But how can I hear you? This is incredible!"

It was no longer anger Dennis felt but amazement at what was happening.

"I can't believe I can somehow hear what you're thinking. How is this even possible?" Dennis was beyond surprised—she was stunned. Her mind was racing with questions, one after another. She wanted to ask so many things but didn't know where to start.

Lucas answered, this time speaking aloud:

"I know. It's hard even for me to understand this thing inside me, ever since I woke up."

"Woke up? What do you mean? Lucas, are you saying this started after you woke up? I'm not following."

Dennis's questions kept coming, swirling inside her head, but it wasn't until Lucas began to explain that she started to understand. Several years ago—he couldn't remember exactly how many—he had been in an accident that left him in a coma for a long time. His parents had even been told it was likely he would never wake up again. Eventually, they were faced with an impossible decision: to disconnect him from the machines keeping him alive.

When the moment finally came, when they had made their heartbreaking choice and were saying their final goodbyes, Lucas suddenly let out a deep, guttural cry and woke up. It was a miracle—one that nearly sent his parents into shock, though out of pure joy. They had braced themselves for the moment he would slip away forever, yet instead, against all odds, he had come back to life.

From the very moment he regained consciousness, Lucas knew something was different. Something was wrong. He could hear voices and thoughts inside his head that didn't belong to him. At first, he considered telling a doctor, maybe even a psychiatrist—but deep down, he knew they wouldn't understand. He had tried before, and the outcome had been far from positive.

It took time—more than he would have liked—before he could adjust to this peculiar "ability," if it could even be called that. His family struggled too; they had to come to terms with the fact that he wasn't the same person he had been before the accident. And neither was he. He had a long journey ahead of him, a path he had no choice but to walk if he wanted to understand why he had returned and what his purpose now was.

Little by little, Lucas began to accept this—his *gift*—though he still wasn't entirely convinced it was something good. He had managed to intervene in a few situations that would have otherwise ended badly, using his ability to help people in trouble. And as time passed, with the support of someone who had become more than just a friend, as well as a psychiatrist who encouraged him to see his gift as something *divine*, he slowly gained confidence in himself. Eventually, he decided he could try to live a normal life and reintegrate into the world.

It was not long after he started working at the café that Lucas first saw Dennis. His first impression was unclear—he couldn't explain why, but something about her caught his attention. He didn't know what it was, but he *felt* it. His heart reacted first, making a strange and undeniable connection with her.

For a long time, Lucas did nothing but observe her from afar each time she came into the café. He never tried to strike up a conversation, never made a move to interact. He kept his distance—not because he was shy, but because he didn't *want* to know her thoughts. He was certain there was something different about her, something special. And so, for months, he simply watched, keeping his silent vigil.

It wasn't until later that he began to notice something… *off* about her. Something in the way she carried herself, the way she would drift away, as though her mind had traveled somewhere far beyond the walls of the café. It was then that he decided to get closer, and in doing so, he saw that Dennis was unlike anyone else. But getting to know her wasn't easy—because Dennis would *disappear* for stretches of time, lost in some unknown place inside her mind, leaving only her body behind, sitting motionless at her usual table, a cup of coffee often left untouched in front of her.

Lucas wondered endlessly about these absences. More than once, he had tried approaching her, asking simple questions just to confirm that she was alright—but it was useless. She never answered. She only stared blankly into the distance, lost in something he couldn't see. And he understood—because he had lived through something similar himself. He felt an inexplicable need to protect her, almost as if he had become her silent *guardian* whenever she visited the café. He even started buying extra coffees for her, just to make sure the owners wouldn't mind how long she stayed.

More than once, he had tried to learn more about her, to understand the walls she had built around herself. But Dennis had mastered the art of keeping the outside world at bay—shutting everything *out*. Sometimes, after closing, he would climb the stairs to the second floor of the café and find the table where she had been sitting. He would walk over, sit down in her seat, and stare out at the same view she had. Trying to *see* what she saw. To *feel* whatever it was that pulled her away from reality. But all he ever found were more questions. Never answers.

Back to the present—on the day of the date

Dennis had so many questions, yet she didn't seem unsettled by his revelation. If anything, an unknown curiosity was awakening inside her—a new and strangely pleasant sensation. Despite everything, she was *enjoying* this moment with him, these extraordinary moments that she had almost forgotten were even possible.

There was so much still ahead of them. Shocking revelations, unexpected discoveries—like the fact that they had someone *very* special in common, a connection that would eventually lead them to understand why fate had brought them together.

But for now, in this moment, Dennis just wanted to keep smiling. To *be* here. To enjoy this unexpectedly wonderful date.

Time slipped away unnoticed, and at last, the moment came to bring their conversation to an end. And though she was left with confusion, surprise, and a whole array of strange and new emotions, there was one thing Dennis couldn't deny.

It was *fantastic*.

To have found someone like him.

Someone who understood her completely.

Someone who had been through the same things she had.

For the first time in what felt like forever, she wasn't alone.

There was *another* like her.

CHAPTER 14

The Stay and the Divine Plan

D ennis tossed and turned all night, unable to fall asleep. It wasn't until dawn that she finally managed to close her eyes, though she knew her alarm would wake her soon.

At 6:30 in the morning, the alarm clock rang as usual. Dennis stretched out her hand to hit the snooze button and stop the tormenting sound. With her eyes now open and her gaze fixed on the ceiling, she took a moment to enjoy the silence. She hesitated to get up, feeling that her daily routine might be different today.

As her mind became more alert, Dennis stayed in bed a while longer, ignoring the passing minutes. She had many things to do, but her thoughts kept returning to what she would say to Dr. Michaels that afternoon.

Almost six months had passed, and a lot had changed. Her life had transformed in many ways. She had opened up more in her sessions with Dr. Michaels and seen significant progress. She was more comfortable talking and asking fewer questions, a skill she was learning and practicing constantly. Dennis had come to believe that life's science was about accepting things as they came and acting based on needs rather than wants.

During this time, she had often spent time with her friend and mentor Tammy, who continued to fight cancer with all her strength. Tammy was determined to beat it, even though it remained a constant threat. Over time, Tammy had learned to see things differently, taking lessons from everything that happened. She had even re-established her relationship with her mother, which had greatly benefited both of them and the entire family.

Everyone was closer, including Tammy's husband, who was now more supportive than ever. Not only because of the fear of losing her, but because her thoughts were clearer and her fears had dissipated. Now, the focus was on being there for their family, especially since Mary Harrison had joined their family, bringing them joy.

Amid all the positive changes, Dennis couldn't ignore the importance of a very significant person in her life. Lucas was special, especially since he revealed his rare ability to her. From that moment, their relationship deepened into a meaningful bond that quickly grew in Dennis' heart.

Things at work were going well. There were always many projects, and the agency enjoyed great prestige, which made every employee proud. This seemed to be everything she had ever longed for. Sometimes she wondered if this was what people called happiness.

Through her sessions with Dr. Michaels, Dennis felt that she had grown, overcome some fears, and gained new insights. She had learned to view things from different perspectives and accept that each person's experiences were unique. This had opened her mind to the wisdom around her. Dr. Michaels sensed the change in Dennis and felt she could now extend a special offer to her.

Dennis was much better. The constant anxiety she once felt was gone, and she could sleep normally most nights. As a result, Dennis felt more in control of her life, even though she didn't have all the answers to her questions. The important thing was that she now had the tools to move forward and continue learning on her journey.

This was why Dr. Michaels wanted to invite Dennis to participate in a special program she was involved in. This program was new and different, and Dennis had not yet answered.

Volunteering at a hospital was not a difficult decision. It wasn't just any hospital, but a psychiatric hospital known for treating terminal mental disorders. The hospital's efforts to provide the best quality of life for these patients were remarkable.

The hospital, called "The Stay," was located on the outskirts of the city in a suburban area with nice neighborhoods and colonial haciendas. Before becoming a reality, the project had been a topic of interest among the city's residents. The city lacked a facility for treating patients with both mental problems and terminal illnesses, forcing residents to travel long distances for care. This led a prominent family to donate land, which included an old hacienda previously used as a hotel. The property was perfect for the clinic, providing ample space for many patients.

Since its opening, the hospital had benefited not only local residents but also patients from surrounding areas. It was the only place offering such specialized care. What began as a clinic grew into a well-known health institution, housing about forty adult patients and a few younger ones with full-time care. *The Stay's* primary focus was animal therapy, allowing patients to interact with horses, dogs, cats, and other animals.

The institution was funded by donations from generous individuals and doctors who donated their time. Initially, this was sufficient, but over time, funds dwindled, and the need for volunteers increased. Few people knew about the hospital's needs because it wasn't a common topic of conversation unless it directly affected someone.

The diffusion was poor; people did not talk about it spontaneously, and it was even more difficult to find people willing to volunteer their time. Only those with patients at *The Stay* offered the most volunteer time, helping with maintenance and other activities necessary for its proper functioning. Even the doctors who worked there helped during their free time. Some anonymous donors contributed financially, and their donations were, of course, well-received. Many people only learned about the place when it affected them personally, a blessing given that most people are never prepared for such tragic and traumatic situations.

Dr. Michaels was one of the doctors at *The Stay* and had been part of the staff since its inception. She not only cared for patients but also volunteered whenever she could. The doctor knew better than anyone how difficult the situation could be and always tried to recruit new volunteers, as she was doing with Dennis. She had explained the situation to Dennis and hoped she would join the dedicated team at *The Stay*.

Dennis still didn't fully understand what volunteering entailed; she only knew what the doctor had told her.

"Dennis, it would be fantastic if you could visit The Stay. *There, you would see everything I've told you about,"* Dr. Michaels *had said enthusiastically. But for Dennis, it was confusing, and she couldn't explain why it bothered her so much.*

"In the next session, you can tell me if you'll go on Saturday or not. I'll be there and can personally show you around. It will be a good experience, you'll see," the doctor added.

Dennis knew she could come up with many excuses to avoid it. She was genuinely busy, and saying no to the doctor's request wouldn't be a lie. But since learning about *The Stay*, she couldn't stop thinking about it. A strange feeling lingered, and for some reason, the memory of Mark was stronger than ever. The day would come when she had to give Dr. Michaels an answer, whether she liked it or not.

In those days, Dennis divided her time between visiting Tammy, having tea with Mary, and spending time with Lucas, whom she saw at least three to four times a week. Lucas always had plans for them, and Dennis enjoyed his company immensely. She knew where her feelings for him were headed, but she wasn't ready to face them yet. It wasn't a bad thing, but she needed to close a few chapters in her life before moving on.

The sessions with Dr. Michaels had helped her a lot. She now understood that the things of the past were not her fault or a punishment. Her life was beginning to make more sense, and she could simply enjoy the moments she was living. Her existence had become more pleasant since Lucas entered her life, without a doubt.

Dennis had no problem dealing with Lucas's rare ability; instead, she found it oddly enjoyable. Whenever they were together, she would check again that Lucas could hear her thoughts, and he would respond silently. This made her feel very special. Sometimes they walked down the street, talking in silence, which gave her a sense of security she couldn't explain but found pleasant.

Dennis was so tired when she got home that she hadn't paid much attention to other things happening around her. She no longer stopped by Café Italia but went to different places with Lucas. They went to movies, concerts, out to eat, or just for walks. Time with Lucas was precious. Her life had changed visibly; the glow in her eyes said it all. She was happier and more attentive to everything and everyone.

However, Dennis had a pending matter that she kept postponing. Every day she thought about it and knew she had to address it soon to close that chapter in her life. It was about Mark, her ex-boyfriend, who had left her without a word. She felt it was time to reason that it might not be Mark who needed to say the final words but her. Now that she understood things better, she believed that something had driven him away, possibly even frightened him. For a long time, she had avoided questioning whose fault it was, thinking bad things only happened to her.

But now, after much reflection, she saw it might have been part of a higher plan, beyond her understanding at the time.

Unfortunately, Dennis's feelings were deeply tied to that relationship. She had suffered for years from Mark's abandonment, without understanding the reason for such a cruel action. After so many years together, future plans, sorrows, and joys, he suddenly left, disappearing in the most unusual act of cruelty. She could never understand it and had only learned to survive with that sorrow in her soul, along with other feelings that tormented her daily for a long time.

Now that she felt something new blossoming with Lucas, she knew she needed to talk to Mark. Although Mark hadn't sought her out since their last encounter, she felt she needed to find him to truly close that chapter in her life. But she knew nothing about him, where he was, or what he might be doing. The last she had heard was that he had left the city. It was something she would have to think about. She couldn't move forward without first putting an end to that relationship. But where to start? Where to look for him? That was the big question.

* * *

As she had predicted, staying in bed for those extra minutes threw off her entire schedule that morning. She got ready in a hurry and left without drinking her coffee, the one thing that gave her so much pleasure every morning. By the time she reached the bridge, it was already up, so she would have to wait another 20 minutes to finally cross into the city. In the past, such situations would have made her very nervous, causing her to mentally escape from any situation she couldn't control. But that morning was different. Despite everything, she was not nervous, even though she knew she was late.

While working at her desk, making some changes to a project nearing completion, she noticed something that shook her to her core. "But how is this possible," she cried out in surprise. "How could I have worked on this project all this time and not realized it?"

Dennis was looking at the projections of a remodel right in front of her. It was a shared group effort on which she had been managing revisions for weeks. She had even gone to meet with the people in charge to suggest changes in the advertising campaign.

"This must be part of the *Divine Plan* Dr. Michaels mentioned," Dennis exclaimed loudly, not worrying that others might hear her. "There is no other explanation." She was so astonished that she couldn't decide if she was more surprised by the fact that she hadn't noticed what she was working on or by the supposed reality of her so-called *Divine Plan*.

Dennis quickly moved to print the information sheet for the project, which included a small map of the location. It was amazing to think that she had been working on this project for weeks and only just realized it. "The timing, the placement—it's incredible," Dennis spoke loudly. "It's happening to me, and I can't believe it. I have to tell Lucas as soon as possible."

With the sheet in hand, she sat down and reread the title to confirm her discovery: *Recovery Campaign,* The Stay, *Stage II.* This was what had shaken her—it was indeed the project for the psychiatric hospital Dr. Michaels had told her about, now in its second stage, expanding the facility to accommodate more patients.

Now, several other questions crowded her mind. Since this project was one of the company's philanthropic endeavors, Dennis recalled the day Mary had told her this project was special. Mary had said something along the lines of, "I want everything to be excellent and go as quickly as possible. We want to get many donations, and it depends on us to make the project a success. They have put all their confidence in us to achieve this new pavilion." Those were Mrs. Harrison's words that day.

Dennis stood with the information in her hand and walked around the office, trying to clear her mind. On one hand, it seemed to her that this was exactly what she had been trying to incorporate into her life— this new philosophy of the *Divine Plan*, where things happen as they are meant to. But on the other hand, she wondered about the Harrison sisters' relationship with this place. Was there some other connection she was missing, perhaps between the doctor and someone else?

A twinge of fear tugged at her just then, all of her anxiety flooding back to her for a brief moment. *Is it possible that all this is the product of some manipulation unknown to me?* Now a tremendous doubt had taken root in her mind, although Dennis actually had no legitimate reason for thinking like that. Her thoughts were trying to create something almost sinister, a perfect reason for saying no to Dr. Michaels' request that afternoon.

The day progressed, and Dennis took the sheet with her to ask the doctor if she was aware of such a coincidence.

5:30 pm

To buy herself some time, Dennis had moved her appointment to the last available hour, 5:30, helped her to prepare for her incoming session. The doctor's secretary approached Dennis and informed her that the doctor was ready. Dennis greeted the doctor as usual, and they exchanged pleasantries about their week. Unable to contain herself, Dennis abruptly asked about the doctor's involvement in the campaign. Her curiosity and anxiety were evident.

"Oh, yes! Something special did happen this week," Dennis said abruptly. "Aren't you wondering why it took me so long to notice?"

"What do you mean, Dennis? I don't understand," the doctor replied, still calm and composed.

"Well, I mean, you do know that my company is handling the recovery campaign for that place where you work," Dennis tried.

"Hmm," the doctor murmured. "No, Dennis, I had no idea! I knew the fundraising campaign would be ready soon, and as part of the committee, I could review it before it went public. But I had no idea that your company was involved. Don't you think that's a funny coincidence?"

Dennis remained silent, trying to restructure her thoughts. She had assumed the doctor knew, and by revealing this, she would expose some conspiracy. But before she could finish, the doctor interrupted.

"And tell me, Dennis," she said. "Will it be a good campaign? The institution desperately needs income for the new pavilion. They need money to start their pediatric program, build new rooms, start general renovations, and improve the stables to receive more animals."

It became clear to Dennis that there was no conspiracy, just a happy coincidence. Her fears were unfounded. She had been wrong.

The rest of Dennis's session went smoothly. She felt comfortable and talked more about her daily life, plans, and projects, which was a good sign. Most of the session was conducted by Dennis, indicating to Dr. Michaels that she was doing well and almost ready to move on.

Dennis gathered her things to leave, and Dr. Michaels extended her hand, saying, "See you soon, Dennis. I hope you have a good week."

"Thank you, the same to you," Dennis replied. She walked towards the exit, but as she grabbed the handle, she stopped, looked back, and asked, "What time should I be at *The Stay* on Saturday? And can I bring someone?"

"Wonderful, Dennis," the doctor smiled. "I didn't want to bother you with the question earlier, as you seemed surprised. But it's great that you want to visit. I usually arrive early in the morning and stay until the afternoon, so come at your convenience. Just ask for me at reception." The doctor paused before answering the second part of Dennis' question. "And yes," she started. "You absolutely can bring someone. Will it be Lucas? He knows his way around the facility pretty well, as he usually volunteers for us almost every Saturday."

Dennis's expression changed instantly, shocked and unsure of what to say. She knew that both she and Lucas had agreed to take things slowly and didn't have to share everything about their lives. However, there were now too many weird details pointing to *The Stay*. Why hadn't this common connection between them come to light before?

Dr. Michaels, noticing Dennis' puzzled expression, quickly responded. "I'm sorry, Dennis. Perhaps I shouldn't have assumed you knew that Lucas was my former patient. We've since become good friends. I apologize sincerely."

"And when did you find out that Lucas and I are friends?" Dennis asked, looking directly at her.

"I found out last Saturday at *The Stay*. During lunch, we ended up at the same table, and I mentioned how glad I was to see him so happy. That's when he showed me a photo of the two of you together on his phone. I assumed he would have told you right away. I'm not sure why he didn't," Dr. Michaels explained.

"I think I understand now," Dennis replied, trying to end the conversation there. "I remember he seemed eager to tell me something last Sunday. I guess I was too busy talking about myself to ask him about it. What a shame."

"Are you sure everything is okay?" Dr. Michaels asked sincerely. "I care deeply about our relationship. I thought it had evolved past patient-doctor, but I want to make sure I didn't cross a line."

"Yes, everything's fine," Dennis smiled, making toward the door. "Don't worry. I was just shocked about how I totally missed that Lucas also volunteers there. Seems like another coincidence. Could it be part of that *Divine Plan*?"

As she exited and walked towards her car, Dennis noticed a radiant orb of golden light hovering over it. It shimmered like liquid gold, reminiscent of something from a fantasy movie. Mesmerized, she cautiously approached, not wanting to miss a moment of this extraordinary sight. The orb remained still, emitting intense flashes of light against the backdrop of the evening darkness.

Glancing around, Dennis worried if others were witnessing the same phenomenon, but the street was quiet and dimly lit. As the darkness deepened, the orb suddenly shot off into the horizon at incredible speed.

Returning to her car, Dennis felt an unusual calmness wash over her, a sense that her choices were being affirmed by some higher presence. She felt reassured that she was on the right path and, more importantly, not alone.

CHAPTER 15

The Surprises Life Gives You...

Friday evening

Dennis arrived home from the office, her arms full of things she had accumulated throughout the week. None of them were urgent matters, but she needed to figure out what to do with it all. Among the items was a lovely card Lucas had given her, just as a small gift with no special occasion. The card read, *Just to have met you.* He had given it to her the afternoon they met for dinner to finalize plans for the next day. She had finally decided to go with Lucas to *The Stay* and spend the day there, deciding to get to know the place.

She didn't dwell on the fact that Lucas hadn't mentioned Dr. Michaels or her involvement with The Stay, even though he was normally open and truthful about things. It was possible he had wanted to tell her but never got the chance. Despite this, Dennis couldn't help but think about it, turning the reasons for this new coincidence over in her mind. She didn't lose sleep over it, but curiosity nagged at her.

Dennis relied heavily on her conversations with Dr. Michaels and trusted in what she called "The Divine Plan." She believed everything had a specific reason and that, eventually, she would understand it all.

In her thoughts, Dennis realized she hadn't shared much personal information with Lucas. Rather, she had skimmed over the details of her life without delving deeply. She knew that if she started to dig even a little, she would have a lot to tell—old sorrows would resurface, which was horrible just to imagine.

This new experience would be good for Dennis. For a long time, her world had been very limited, revolving around work and, before that, school. Her personal life had always been hidden away. To avoid worrying about why she had no people in her life, she had poured all her energy into school and work, leaving her personal life to the side.

But over time, her fears returned, making her life miserable and eventually leading her to seek help. Although she tried to cope on her own, she soon realized that help was more than necessary. She felt she was losing her sanity and didn't know where her life was headed.

Now, as things progressed, Dennis' life began to lighten, and daily problems took on a different color. She understood that in life, one must close chapters to move forward. She accepted the facts of past events and made every effort to give herself closure, especially with what haunted the back of her mind all day and night.

When Dennis learned that Mark was coming back, her heart rejoiced. When he called her to pick him up, she felt his homecoming as his return into her life. Her immense joy blinded her to the past and all the suffering she had faced. All she cared about was that he was back. That, and her devotion to him as he was the only man she had ever loved. She still missed him as much as, if not more than, the first day he left.

The two of them had been through so much together that it was difficult to find a reason for his abandonment that made sense. But the disappointment and pain of his departure were much greater the second time. She could do nothing to rectify the situation. Instead, he moved even farther away and, even after being so close, he did nothing to contact her, causing her even deeper grief and leaving her with many unanswered questions.

Eventually, she stopped loving him. But a big question in her mind remained: why had he left? This question tormented her, preventing her from living in peace or moving forward.

Already in her room

Dennis turned the lights off, threw herself onto the middle of her bed, and closed her eyes, trying to fall asleep. But something felt different, something that pulled her away from sleep. As soon as she closed her eyes, she saw a white light. It wasn't too bright, but it was definitely an orb, this time in her mind rather than in visible form. She was used to seeing them with her eyes open and had never experienced them any other way. That night, Dennis experienced something different.

She kept seeing the light whether her eyes were open or closed. She wondered, *could it be that I have fallen asleep and this is a dream?* It seemed strange because if it was a dream, it must have been a very special one. She could think and reason during this possible dream. If this was real, it would be incredible.

She decided to keep her eyes closed longer, letting the seconds pass. The light grew, taking up more space until almost all she could see was a white glow. A feeling of relaxation washed over her. She didn't want to open her eyes again. Instead, she waited patiently, watching as the light covered the span of her vision. After a while, everything was white with golden flashes. While Dennis kept her eyes closed, her mind watched the incredible, relaxing vision. Flashes of golden light appeared at the corners. She felt as if she was in front of a large concave screen that spanned her entire view.

She could move her pupils from side to side, exploring the vision. Suddenly, the flashes became more visible, shining like golden shooting stars. It was an unprecedented spectacle for Dennis.

In the center of this giant screen, a dot appeared. It seemed to approach and enlarge, resembling the silhouette of a person. The silhouette was amber and approaching her with great speed.

Dennis couldn't distinguish it well, but within seconds she saw it. Yes! As he got closer, she began to recognize the figure. Her heart raced, and she felt anxious. She could see flashes forming around the silhouette, dancing softly. She saw blue and green colors with intense golden rays, outlining the silhouette of this man.

Dennis told herself, "I can still think, but I know I must be dreaming." She thought it was wonderfully peculiar.

The man approached until he was in front of her face. Despite the vividness of the dream, she couldn't see his face well. His image moved like a hologram in one of those futuristic films. The man stretched out his hands, inviting Dennis to take his. She didn't hesitate and quickly extended her hands. When she touched him, she felt a special vibration that made her heart race. She felt she knew him. *Where do I know him from?* she wondered.

His gaze was tender and full of love. He communicated with her through thoughts she couldn't understand, but she knew were meant for her. After some time, he let go of her hands and began to walk away. She watched him until he became a dot on the white screen, full of beautiful, flashing golden stars.

The curtain of the internal screen began to close, and the white surface faded until there was nothing but blackness. Finally, she opened her eyes, lying in the middle of her bed as if nothing had happened.

Dennis sighed a couple of times, turned to her side, hugged her pillow, and thought, *I don't think it was a dream. I could feel it. It was real,*

I'm sure. She wondered, *who was that man? I feel I know him. I'm so sure I've seen him before.* As she pondered, her eyes grew heavy, leading her to sleep.

Dennis fell into a peaceful, uninterrupted sleep until the new dawn.

Morning came, and Dennis woke up calmly. She was in a state of incredible serenity, feeling that her plans to visit *The Stay* would undoubtedly turn into something good, something much awaited. She couldn't explain concretely how she felt but was looking forward to going to see *The Stay*.

Suddenly, she heard the sound of a car horn coming from outside. Dennis leaned out the window to wave to Lucas, who was waiting for her downstairs with his car running, parked at the entrance of her apartment building. They had decided to carpool and spend the day together. After visiting *The Stay*, they decided they would return to the city to see a movie or get coffee if they weren't too tired. Dennis loved making plans with Lucas because he always agreed with her on everything. It even seemed like he did it just to make her happy, which made her feel very seen, a nice after spending so much time alone.

Lucas was quite reserved with his thoughts, especially those concerning Dennis. But today, he had a strong feeling she would feel comfortable at *The Stay* and that they wouldn't need to leave earlier than planned. How did he know this? It wasn't hard to see that Dennis was a good person with noble motives, and such people naturally feel good after helping others in need. Lucas, although often not understanding how or why, was deeply moved by Dennis. Whenever he was around her, he was a slave to his inner instincts. It was like there was a little voice always telling him what to do or say. He even thought sometimes that another person lived inside his head, albeit a lazy one, since this inner voice never helped him with anything else.

The journey felt short, like the blink of an eye, and they were already at the entrance of *The Stay*. As they left the main road and took a bumpy dirt road to the entrance, the car raised a dusty cloud that lingered behind them. After about a mile, they parked in front of a large, old willow tree, which would provide perfect shade from the sun's heat.

Dennis got out of the car and walked to the right where there was an old wooden gate barely standing. But it was impossible not to be amazed by the sight before her: a spectacular valley, painted a beautiful emerald green with all shades of red in the tree foliage, and a clear blue sky without a single cloud. It was a spectacular late October, mid-autumn view.

They were on top of a small mountain, with most of the property spreading out from that point. On the right were barns where horses poked their heads out as if curious about the two newcomers. The grounds were filled with animals like dogs, chickens, and ducks. On the left was a large house with no visible end, facing an old English garden, or what was left of it. There were garden benches under leafy trees, and colorful flowers bordered the small shrubs along the path to the main entrance.

The house was in urgent need of repairs. Its windows, paint, and roof all screamed for attention. Yet, it was still an impressive three-story building, rare for its time since most buildings then had only two floors. The previous owners had used the space between the roof and the second floor for storage, but it had been converted into more bedrooms over time. The house had two extensions at the back, added later, but they were no longer sufficient for the number of people *The Stay* housed.

Dennis recalled the agency's proposed plans she had seen in her office the day she learned about the project. Looking from this specific point, she could see that if the project materialized, the result would be beautiful. She felt Lucas walking towards her.

"Isn't it wonderful? And you still haven't seen the best part!" Lucas exclaimed.

"What do you mean?" Dennis asked, intrigued.

"I mean you still haven't met the people who live here and the animals. They all have names and are very sweet. You'll see," Lucas added, his voice filled with excitement.

"Well, of course, I imagine everyone here must be very special. Even the animals," Dennis said cordially. "Lucas, tell me, what exactly do you do here?"

"Ah, you want to know how I spend my time here? It's simple: I do everything. When I get here in the mornings, I meet with others who've come to help and with those who live here in the dining room for breakfast and a chat. Then, we go to the help station, where there are always long lists of things that need attention, and we choose what we'll help with that day," Lucas explained with a proud smile and enthusiastic gesticulation.

"So you're not one of the patients?" Dennis asked.

"One of the first things we learn here is that there are no patients, only residents. While I do spend time with them, I am not one of them. We all try to spend time with at least one of the residents during our time here. The variation and rotation are good for them. Many of them never get visitors," Lucas added, a deep sorrow in his expression.

"No relatives?" Dennis asked, surprised.

"Unfortunately, no. Many residents are people forgotten by time, rejected by society, and excluded from the realities of others. But there are still kind souls in this bleak world," Lucas said.

After a few minutes, Lucas invited her to continue towards the entrance of the hacienda. They were finally going to sign in for that morning, which brought much anticipation for Dennis.

They knocked on the door, which triggered an intercom buzz. Both entered and walked a few steps to the first room, a small office where everyone checked in. They signed their names on a paper pinned to a bulletin board which read in big letters, *Sabbath Volunteers*. Dennis was surprised to see only a few names before theirs and immediately asked Lucas, "Are there no more volunteers today?"

"Help is scarce these days. Almost no one wants to give even a little of their time. Selfishness has taken over the soul of humanity," Lucas said with a strained smile. "But don't worry, I'm sure more will come later."

A friendly lady received them warmly, smiling as she told Lucas that breakfast was being served. He took Dennis' hand and led her down the hall, giving her a quick tour of the facility. The first room on the right was a large salon serving as a waiting room with old armchairs and worn curtains.

Across the hall was the doctors' office, the door closed. Lucas explained that they met there to talk and go about their business. The pair continued and found a large room with nice murals on the walls, serving as a common room where residents could watch TV or participate in fun activities. The room had many tables with four chairs each, clear windows letting in plenty of light, and a sizeable library full of books with comfortable sofas for reading.

They reached the end of the corridor and opened the door to the dining room. It was a huge hall with cathedral-like ceilings. The far end was rounded, with many windows showing the property grounds. Tables fit for eight or ten people were lined up in three rows, nine tables in total. The kitchen on the right side looked like a fast-food restaurant, with a long counter and display cases full of prepared meals. The aroma of fresh, strong coffee filled the air, just how Dennis liked it.

Lucas quickly entered and said, "Let's start setting the tables. Grab those trays at the end of the counter and distribute them on the tables." Dennis complied, watching the doors open and close continuously as more people arrived.

She didn't know if she was ashamed to be seen there or what, but for some reason she felt very shy. That was until a beautiful old lady approached her, took her hand gently, and said, "Good morning, you're a new face. Thank you for coming," before walking away to sit at one of the tables.

This broke the ice for Dennis, making her feel much more comfortable. Soon, she was all over the place, ensuring everyone had their breakfast. At one point, Lucas came over to check on her.

"How are you doing?" He asked.

"Fantastic! The people are very nice," she replied, advancing with a pitcher of juice towards a table where only a few children sat. They all seemed very happy; she couldn't see any symptoms of illness.

After a while, Dennis sat down to drink her coffee, looking out the window when she saw something—or rather, someone. She stood up almost immediately to get a better view, but the person had disappeared just as quickly. For a second, worry gnawed at her. But then Dr. Michaels entered the dining room and called out to Dennis from across the room.

"Good day, Dennis," she greeted. "It's great to see you here! I'm glad you could come. We all appreciate your service."

"Oh, it's nothing," Dennis replied quickly, her cheeks flushing. "Everyone here seems to be very nice people. There's nothing to thank me for."

The doctor sat for a moment at Dennis' table. Then, Lucas arrived, followed by others who quickly welcomed Dennis. In less than thirty minutes, she had gone from feeling like a stranger to being an active participant. She felt comfortable and at ease. When she left the dining room, another volunteer offered to finish showing her around the facility. When she returned, Lucas was waiting to accompany her to the stables, where they would prepare the horses for a group therapy session scheduled for that morning.

Dennis and Lucas left through the long corridor, crossed the property, and reached the stables. As they walked, Dennis turned to look back at the side where she had seemed to see someone. "Are you looking for something?" He asked, sensing her uneasiness.

"Nothing, nothing really," she answered.

"Are you sure it's nothing?" Lucas asked, taking her hand and looking into her eyes. "You know you can tell me if there's something you want to talk about?"

"Of course, I'm sure. Nothing's wrong. I just thought I saw someone I knew, but obviously, it wasn't," Dennis concluded.

"It'd be a funny coincidence if you found someone here," Lucas said.

"Why do you say that? What's so funny?" Dennis' voice was tinged with worry.

"It's just because we don't get many visitors or volunteers," Lucas said, continuing towards the stables. "It would be nice if you had a reason to continue giving your time here at *The Stay*."

The two of them moved to open the stables and bring the horses to the corrals. Dennis, despite having never been around horses before, was a natural, handling them without any problems.

After a while, she saw a group of people approaching from the large house. Two women in dark purple uniforms and four other people. Dennis assumed they were the ones coming to work with the horses.

One of the nurses approached Lucas and said, "We're missing a resident, but he'll be here soon. He's still inside."

"No problem, I'll get another horse ready for therapy. Who's missing?" Lucas asked.

"Mark," the nurse replied.

Dennis, hearing this name, turned quickly with wide eyes. Could they be talking about *her* Mark? She had thought her mind was playing tricks on her when she thought she recognized someone earlier.

But how could that be possible? It was impossible. Mark had left the city long ago, probably to another, in search of work or to get away from it all. At least, that's what she thought. She turned her attention back to her tasks but looked up from time to time to see if this Mark would appear.

She took to filling feed buckets to feed the birds. The chickens had already gathered around her, knowing the sound of the bucket meant food. She moved around, trailed by a following of chickens, ducks, and other small animals who were all waiting for their meals.

She thought about how large the barn was and all the things that were inside it. It was clear they needed a lot of help. Anyone could see that labor was scarce. Suddenly, she heard two men talking.

She put the bucket on the floor, which was quickly seized by the birds, and without leaving the barn, she peeked around the door's edge to find the owners of the voices. It didn't matter, though. One of the voices she heard was undoubtedly Mark's. Yes, the same Mark who had been her boyfriend, who had left her without an explanation, who had stolen her thoughts for countless nights. The one she wanted to find to close one more chapter and begin to rebuild her life.

And just what is he doing there? Dennis wondered, trying to find a quick answer to the thousands of thoughts firing in her mind.

CHAPTER 16

Life with Mark

Dennis was left alone at a very young age. A terrible car accident took the lives of her parents, whom she loved deeply. From that moment, Dennis' life was different, weighed down by a heavy burden and questions that always remained unanswered.

Her tragedy was different from most, or at least that's what she told herself. She always kept her past to herself, as people often thought she lost her mind after the accident. Dennis wasn't stupid and soon learned that it was in her best interest to stay quiet and say what others expected, even if it wasn't the truth. She had tried everything, but no one believed her.

Dennis lived with father's sister after being orphaned. While her aunt wasn't bad to her, she wasn't the best either. Her aunt was quite old and only cared that Dennis had a plate of food and a place to sleep. There was no affection or love from her aunt, and she accepted this from the moment she set foot in her house.

Dennis met Mark when she entered ninth grade. The pair went from friends, to close friends, to a couple. Theirs was a beautiful connection with incredible communication, and the two bonded over feeling alone in the world. They found the companionship they needed in each other.

Together, they dreamed and made plans, sharing everything including their futures. Soon, Dennis came to trust Mark with her life.

Mark felt great love for Dennis. His most important goals in life were to grow up quickly, get a job, and take Dennis away from her aunt's house. He wanted to start a family with her, putting an end to their sad and lonely lives.

His father was serving a prison sentence for a crime he committed too long ago for Mark to remember. Since his mother rarely spoke of his father, Mark knew very little about the man. He accepted this, understanding that his mother had done her best to make a life for the two of them after being left alone and helpless.

As Mark grew older, he stopped wondering about his father. He could barely remember the man, and figured it was best to keep it that way. Mark's mother left it all in the past and never talked about it again—why shouldn't he?

Mark knew that Dennis had lost her parents in an accident. Their parent trauma was something they bonded over. But Mark came to know much more than that. Over time, Dennis managed to open up and tell him every detail of her parents' untimely deaths, which was not only horrible and devastating but also logically inexplicable. For Dennis, talking about what had happened became forbidden, something no one could know. Mark came to understand and respect this, accepting the idea that his girlfriend was different. Special, even. She was able things that he often wished he could.

Dennis' only outlet was Mark, the only person she could confide in when she felt bad or had her visions. Although neither of them understood why these visions, they certainly felt better knowing they could talk to each other. Given the nature of what happened to Dennis, they decided to keep it private and not complicate their lives with more questions. From their understanding, it seemed that the lights only appeared in the threat of imminent danger, whether from illness or impending tragedy. It a secret thrill every time Dennis told Mark she had seen the lights. He would ask, "Where? Who will it be this time?"

Many times, they followed the lights and committed to repeatedly checking in on the person in question. In most cases, the lights would disappear, and no one would die. Those were the good moments. It took a long time to convince Dennis that the lights were not her doing, that she wasn't some harbinger of death. Mark reminded her of this every day, and most of the time, it worked. Still, some days nothing would work, and Dennis felt simply miserable.

The two of them grew up together, becoming independent adults' side by side. They planned to go to college together, seeking out scholarship programs for young married adults, despite not having taken that step yet. Dennis knew she had some money put away in a college fund for her, though she didn't know exactly how much. Her aunt had told her it would be enough for her education when the time came.

Eventually, they graduated from high school. Freshly eighteen, the two of them were ready to start their life together. Years of planning, dreams, and desires were so close to being realized. But then, Mark's mother got sick. Unable to support herself, Mark felt obligated to help her. Suddenly, their plans were shelved indefinitely.

One day, Dennis saw the lights again. She shut down, refusing to visit Mark's mother, terrified of the possibility that she might see something she didn't want to: that the lights were connected to her. She kept telling Mark, "No matter what you say, I'm not risking it!" She was consumed with dread, fearing that the lights would inevitably lead to her, and the very thought of something ill befalling Mark's mother was unbearable.

While she kept her distance, Mark's mother's condition got worse. The prognosis was not good. Mark had spent that whole summer by his mother's side and, by autumn, her days were numbered. Her condition continued like this until one day Mark arrived at the hospital to visit her, only to find out she had already passed away earlier that day.

This was a turning point in their relationship. Mark had always been calm and healthy, with no serious issues to worry about. But in the year that followed, his health deteriorated. He was tired and weak and caving in on himself. Mark told no one about his condition, figuring it was just the stress from school, work, and his mother's death catching up with him.

Meanwhile, Dennis had gotten a job in a warehouse, hoping the extra income would help their situation while tried to get ahold the money her parents had left her. Life insurance, disbursed as a result of the accident. However, like everything, this would take some time—weeks, months, maybe even longer.

And she was still living at her aunt's house. Though the woman was getting older, she always seemed to be doing well. It was something Dennis knew innately, something she felt every time she kissed her goodbye. It was one of those hunches where Dennis knew her aunt would be around for a long time, or at least that's what she thought.

Mark and Dennis made the effort to spend all their free time together in between their hectic schedules. One day, while Dennis was staying at Mark's house, she saw something that left her at a loss for words. A strange light had started to fill the room where they were. Since Mark was living alone now, Dennis made an effort to spend more time with him. They hadn't made plans to move in together yet because they weren't married yet, so she spent whatever time she could with him. Dennis also had her own affairs to manage—she needed to finish the insurance paperwork and collect her money.

Dennis couldn't feel comfortable at Mark's house after his mother passed away. She wasn't overly attached to the woman, but she had known her for a very long time. Mark's mother was quite the reserved woman, never known for being friendly or too involved in her son's life. Despite everything, Mark still loved his mother and missed her immensely. Being with Dennis made the pain more bearable, though.

One night, like any other, they were in the living room. Dennis had gone to the kitchen to get a drink. When she returned, she saw a bright light that was gone as fast as it came, making her question if she had really seen anything or if she was simply hallucinating. Hesitating, she sat down and told Mark.

"Y'know, I just saw something strange," she said.

"Strange? Like what? Where?" he answered.

Mark straightened up from his position on the sofa and turned to wait for Dennis' answer. She resisted but, given his insistence, continued on to tell him about the light. The night continued without major interruptions, the calm keeping for the next few days. That was, until Dennis saw something that left her mouth dry.

It was a Thursday night after work. She stopped at Mark's house to have dinner with him. When she entered, she saw him lying on the couch, seeming to have fallen asleep after a long day. She came over to him quietly and nudged him gently, confirming that he was, in fact, asleep. This wasn't unusual, but what Dennis saw next certainly was. Just as she raised a hand to stroke his hair tenderly, a flurry of orbs began to manifest.

First, it was only one, moving around the room with great speed. Then, the others showed up. Dennis tracked them with her eyes, confused and concerned. She stood next to the armchair where Mark slept, and from in front of her, along the wall, several more began to appear, filling the room in a matter of seconds.

They flew about everywhere, some very dim and others radiating light so bright that Dennis had to squint. Still standing there, she turned to follow one of them. Dennis felt an indescribable feeling, something that squeezed at her heart. Overwhelmed, she let out a surprised shout, waking

Mark. As he sat up, all the orbs vanished. Astonished, Mark asked, "What's wrong? When did you get here?"

"I just got in," Dennis answered, steeling her nerves.

Dennis took a moment to think things over and made a decision: she would not tell Mark what she had seen. She wanted to spare him the worry. For the rest of the night, Dennis was quiet and distant, stuck thinking about the meaning of the lights. From experience, it was clear that the lights were not good at all. Time passed, and she went home.

From that day forward, things got weird. The lights appeared more frequently, almost daily, and she kept her resolve to remain quiet about it. Weeks passed, and Mark piled on the work. The two of them hardly saw each other anymore, and whenever they did, it was always brief. Dennis believed these lights were her burden and she didn't want to see them anywhere near Mark, under any circumstances. She couldn't bear the thought that something bad could happen to Mark.

Finally, Dennis was able to finalize the insurance paperwork, and they deposited the money from her parents' life insurance policy to her bank account. It was enough to go to school, and maybe some other things. Elated, she called up Mark and set up date night for the two of them.

As soon as Dennis arrived at Marks, she noticed he was emaciated and looked unwell. Upon seeing how worse for wear he was, she immediately asked, "Do you feel okay?"

His heart was beating a thousand beats per minute, but he steadied himself and told her, "It's nothing, I'm fine."

"How is it nothing? Look at you," she responded, grumbling. "What's wrong? Aren't you going to tell me?"

"Don't worry," he answered, standing up from where he was seated. "It's just that I got the leftover bills from when my mom was sick and in the hospital in the mail today. They're asking for a lot of money that I don't have. I think I'll have to sell the house to finish paying them off. It looks like we're going to have to put our plans to move in together on hold until after I get this settled."

Dennis came over and hugged him. "I thought you were going to break up with me. We've been kind of distant lately."

"You know I love you with all my heart. I live for you," Mark replied.

That night, the two of them had dinner, and Dennis suggested using the money she'd received from the insurance company to pay off those debts so he wouldn't have to sell the house. Mark initially refused, but Dennis insisted. They spent that night and several others discussing the matter. Finally, two weeks later, Mark called Dennis and caved, promising to only use her money until his mother's house was sold.

Dennis was grateful that Mark accepted her offer. There was nothing in the world that made her think twice about what she was doing. Dennis not only loved Mark; she lived for him. He was her other half.

A week later, they were in Mark's living room, checking out places to rent. They decided to rent a small place while the house was sold, giving them time to prepare for university. It had been a good idea to take the time off to study. Everything had gone well, except for the loss of Mark's mom, of course.

At one point, though, Mark looked straight at her and took her hands in his, making Dennis shudder.

"What's going on?" She asked. "Is there something you need to tell me?"

Mark's eyes were glassy, as if he was about to cry, but he didn't shed a tear. He hugged her tightly, telling her he loved her and always would. Dennis was moved by the emotion in Mark's words, and as she reciprocated his embrace, she spotted the lights again. They were everywhere. *What are they doing here?* she wondered.

She thought for a moment about telling Mark about what she was seeing, but the idea quickly faded. Dennis concluded that it would cause too much worry—exactly why she hadn't told him before—so she said nothing. They sat there, embraced, enjoying the moment while the lights flew around the room, doing their thing.

Dennis eventually fell asleep on Mark's shoulder, and when she woke up the next morning, he had already left for work. She was overcome with a strange feeling, like emptiness. Something wasn't right, but she didn't know what it was until a couple of days later.

Dennis went about her usual morning routine. She went to work, and, in the afternoon, she found it strange that she hadn't received a single call from Mark. She decided to call him but only got his answering machine. After several attempts, she decided to stop calling, reasoning that she would see him soon since it was the weekend, and they always saw each other on weekends.

She usually stopped by Mark's house in the evenings, and they had dinner together. Some nights she stayed, some nights she didn't. But that night, she went straight home to her aunt since she had spent the past several days at Mark's house figuring out how to pay off his medical debt with her insurance money.

The bills were costly, and they were still looking for a place to rent. Dennis also had to be there to support her aunt in case she needed anything, regardless of her independent nature.

Dennis spent that whole afternoon trying to call Mark, but he still didn't answer and didn't even show up for dinner. The next morning, before leaving for work, she decided to stop by his house to make sure everything was okay. The door was locked, and no one answered when she knocked. She kept knocking, but no one came. Days passed, and there was still no word from him. She called the hospitals and the police, but no one found anything about him.

Time passed, and Dennis noticed the "For Sale" sign had been removed from Mark's house. *Someone must've bought it*, she thought, but no one ever moved in. She hoped the new owner would have information about Mark, but there was never anyone to ask.

Almost five months later, she received a letter from Mark. It didn't say much, except for that he was serving in the army and wouldn't return for some time. He suggested she continue her life and not to wait for him signed the letter at the bottom adding, "I promise I'll pay you back for the money I borrowed."

Dennis realized that that was it. It gave her a sick feeling that slowly tore at her insides. It was a pain she couldn't explain, something too hard to understand and even harder to accept. She was plunged into a depression for days, weeks. She didn't eat; she didn't want to live anymore. It seemed as if everything was stacked against her.

She suffered deeply, and the orbs of light were her only company. Day after day, they were there, listening to the curses Dennis shouted at them. She hated them, believing that those treacherous lights had once again robbed her of someone she loved. There was no comforting Dennis.

As time passed, Dennis decided it was time to continue with her life. She got up one morning and just moved on, locking away that painful part of her past along with everything else she had buried before. She kept going; without him, without her dreams, without those plans, with nothing inside. But she kept going.

From time to time, she thought about her parents and imagined they would want to see her become someone good. Knowing her aunt couldn't take care of her forever, she drew all her strength to push herself out of her slump, no matter how much it hurt.

It had now been more than six years since Mark disappeared out of thin air from Dennis' life. Though not entirely, because, over the years, he'd gone out of his way to leave a few notes for her. They were a far cry from letters—just a couple of words on a piece of paper that always left Dennis worse off that she'd been before. She tried to convince herself that he still loved her, but his meager attempts at reaching suggested otherwise.

She wondered why he kept insulting her that way. Wouldn't it be clear by now that she hated him? Didn't he realize she was repulsed by what he had done to her? And how could she not be hurt by the false hope each note had given her, convincing herself that Mark was returning? She had filled herself with delusions time and time again, only for him to vanish again each time without reason or explanation.

CHAPTER 17

The Reunion

Part One

In the barn

Dennis was stuck like a limpet on a rock to the barn door, peering through the small crack that that old door provided her. She was perfectly hidden, able to observe what was happening outside without anyone seeing her. Without a doubt, the voice she heard was Mark's, but she couldn't see his face. She could only see his back, and that was only if she craned her neck just so. She knew that someone would be looking for her sooner or later—she had been holed up in there for too long.

What should I do? She wondered, trying to will herself to think clearly. But the storm brewing in her head proved too strong to quell, and she was soon overcome with emotion.

She could hear them all talking laughing. It seemed that they all knew each other, the familiarity of friends evident in their tone. A few moments later, Dennis saw Lucas walk past, leading one of the horses to one of the outer corrals, passing by the others. One of the nurses was accompanying him.

Dennis had not yet seen his face; the man hadn't turned around. Her desperation to know if he was a ghost or truly Mark gnawed at her. With renewed energy and a touch of excitement, she left the barn.

Almost halfway to the corral, Lucas saw Dennis approaching. He spoke to her immediately.

"Where were you? Are you okay?"

"Yeah, I'm fine, but something has happened, I think..." Dennis trailed off, despite Lucas's persistent questions.

"What happened? Are you feeling okay?"

This time, Dennis didn't respond. She was stunned, eyes fixed on the corral. The man had finally turned around, revealing his face. It was Mark—the same Mark she loved, the one who had left her with no time to understand.

There he was, right in front of her, riding a horse led by a nurse. Dennis couldn't comprehend what was happening.

Why was he here? What was wrong with him? What did all this mean? A thousand questions exploded in her mind, and she only reacted when Lucas grabbed her arm. His voice sounded distant, like an echo. She felt faint, overwhelmed by emotion. *What should I do?* she wondered, but she had no answer.

Lucas helped her sit down and rushed to get a glass of water. Fortunately, there was a cooler nearby for the patients. He returned with a glass of water, his hand shaking as he held it out to her. Lucas felt the same way Dennis did—helpless. Kneeling in front of her, he said, "Is it really him? I'm sorry, I didn't know this would happen. I'm sorry you're going through this right now. I'm sure there's an explanation."

"What is he doing here?" Dennis asked, still shocked.

"Well, Mark is one of the residents here. He has been for a long time."

"But *why* is he living here?" Dennis asked, watching Mark from afar. He was still on the horse, circling the corral at a steady pace, seemingly in no hurry.

"Volunteers don't know why the residents are here; we just help them. But I can tell you that, from my experience, Mark is a good man. He's very quiet, almost never speaks, and has been very weak from his treatments."

"What treatments?" Dennis asked. "Please tell me, I need to know."

"As I said, they don't tell us much—but I know it's something serious. When he comes for his treatment, I can sense his pain. I think he's battling a terminal illness."

Dennis, recovering from her brief moment of overwhelming emotion, tried to focus on listening intently to Lucas. She couldn't take her eyes off Mark. She got up and walked to the edge of the corral, waiting for the horse to come around. She waited for Mark and the nurse to reach her before speaking.

"If you'd like, I can take it from here," she offered. "That's not a problem, is it?"

"Of course not!" The nurse smiled. She handed over the horse's lead.

Mark seemed absent, as if asleep. He paid no attention as someone else took the horse's reins. The lead, about seven feet long, allowed Dennis to walk freely in front of the horse without any issues.

Dennis counted her steps as she debated whether to speak. Although she feared his reaction, she had to try. She couldn't continue living with this anguish. Taking a deep breath, she spoke.

"Mark, do you know who I am?" Dennis turned to look at him, but had to repeat his name to get his attention. "Mark? Mark, look at me. Do you know who I am?"

This time, Mark reacted. He looked up as if waking from a dream, finally meeting Dennis's eyes. He seemed amazed and, clinging to the saddle, he managed to dismount with some effort. He walked nervously until he was finally face to face with her, his eyes and countenance reviving, even his cheeks gaining a bit of color. Gently, he brought his hands to Dennis' face and stroked her cheeks with his thumbs.

"Am I dreaming?" Mark asked, looking puzzled. "Are you just my imagination?"

"No, it's really me, Mark," Dennis said, not knowing how else to respond. Moments earlier, she felt she might explode, but now? Nothing. Her mind was completely blank.

It was as if time had frozen. Everything had come to a standstill; it was just her and him. Dennis could feel her own breath, the warmth of the blood running through Mark's hands as they caressed her face, and the silence which grew louder with each passing second. She could hear her heart pounding and her name being called in the distance.

"Dennis, Dennis!" Lucas had been calling her from the other side of the fence for a while, but to no avail. He felt compelled to get closer, aware of the significance of what Dennis was experiencing. He didn't intend to intrude on her thoughts, but he knew his own feelings were also at stake. Lucas knew who Mark was, or at least what he had meant to Dennis. However, he didn't know the whole story or everything she had been through with him. He also knew little about Mark's personal life, only that he lived there, wasn't a bad man, and suffered greatly—both from his illness and his solitude. Lucas only hoped to learn a little more about their shared history, praying that this wouldn't mean the end for either of them.

Lucas slowed his pace, giving Dennis time to hear him coming. He didn't want to interrupt but felt he had to. He began calling out to her in his mind, *Dennis, Dennis, please listen to me!* He repeated it over and over, but she was deaf to the world.

He sidled up to them and coughed as hard as he could, breaking the trance, they were in. Dennis, acting quickly, managed to remove Mark's hands from her face. She stepped back, as if to apologize to Lucas. Lucas wasn't sure exactly what was happening, but it was evident that something significant was unfolding, and he felt he owed his respect.

"Dennis, I see you know Mark," Lucas said, looking directly at Mark and trying to normalize the complicated situation. "What a coincidence, don't you think?"

"Yes, indeed," Dennis let out a small, almost imperceptible smile, which she quickly hid by lowering her face. "Mark and I actually go way back. It's a great surprise to find him here, in this place."

"It's incredible. I never thought I could see you here," Mark added, keeping his eyes on her. Mark already knew who Lucas was, but hadn't realized Dennis had arrived with him that day.

"Who'd have thought you'd find each other here? And on Dennis's first day as a volunteer," Lucas said, taking two more steps and placing his hand on Dennis's shoulder. "A volunteer just like me, since she came with me."

Was this Lucas' attempt at subtly letting Mark know there was something between them? Part of him worried he was fighting a battle he was already losing. Just in time, a nurse appeared to break up the tension.

"I'm glad you've met and are talking," she said. "But Mark needs to continue his therapy. You can catch up in an hour, during his downtime."

The nurse got to work, swiftly taking Mark's arm and leading him to the next corral. Just as he was being whisked away, Mark looked at Dennis and said, "I would love for us to continue this later."

"I'll be there," Dennis replied, watching him walk off. She turned and walked towards the barn, bringing both hands to her head. She looked very disturbed—and who wouldn't be? Suddenly seeing the man she had loved so much, who had abandoned her like she meant nothing to him, whom she'd grieved for so long. What would send anyone into a spiral.

Lucas followed her, hoping to find the right moment to interrupt, but he was afraid. He knew he had to navigate this moment with precise delicacy, so he decided to hold his tongue. Once in the barn, Dennis plopped down on one of the hay bales near the door. Lucas that she would have to look up and see him there sometime, silent and patient and dying inside. He said nothing.

"I know you must have questions," Dennis said, breaking the silence.

"Well," Lucas replied. "I don't know if it's my place to ask. If you want to tell me, I'm here."

"It's really a long story," Dennis sighed. "And I don't know if I can explain everything well enough, but I'll tell you this: Mark and I have known each other for a very long time. We grew up together. He was my boyfriend. We basically used to live together and had even planned our lives together. But, one day, out of the blue, he up and left me without saying a word.

"I tried to reach out to him. I made many attempts to rekindle some kind of connection, but they were always in vain. He'd left the country for some time, and I even picked him up at the airport when he came back, thinking it was a chance to reconnect, but I was wrong. Since then, I hadn't seen or heard from him. After a while, I found out he'd left the city again, gone without a word.

"A while back, I decided to cut him out of my life completely, to stop dwelling on the heartbreak. But some gut feeling kept urging me to find him and demand an explanation for why he did what he did. Of course, I couldn't find him anywhere. And look at how life is—life really gives you surprises. Just as I was starting to move on, I run into him here of all places."

"I understand," Lucas said, taking in Dennis' story. "This is obviously a tough situation for you. Do you still love him?"

"How should I know?" she said, on the brink of tears.

"I can feel the swell of your emotions and how fast your heart is beating. I think that means something. Or am I wrong?"

"No," Dennis relented. "Honestly, I don't think I ever *stopped* loving him. Mark was everything to me, but that's not what really matters. He hurt me deeply and left a darkness in me, full of uncertainty and thousands of questions. I haven't been able to live with or even begin to understand what happened between us. I always had this feeling that something terrible would take him away from me. I thought it was my fault and hated myself for a long time. But then I felt that there could've been something larger at play. But I could never get myself to sit with a reason."

"And what do you feel now, knowing that he is here?" Lucas asked softly, his voice almost trembling. It was clear that he was as affected as Dennis was. This situation turned his world upside down. How could he be with her, knowing she loved another?

"Well, I don't know," she shrugged. "I'm so confused. But I know I'll have to wait until I can talk to him later. I won't leave without getting answers. I've waited a long time for this, and although this is now how I thought this would happen, if this is my only chance, then so be it."

Dennis turned to Lucas, and she could see that he was on the verge of tears. He stayed quiet, gritting his teeth as he worried about what the future might hold.

Suddenly, Lucas remembered that he had brought Dennis to *The Stay* today. He was her ride. He would have to sit around and wait for her and drive her home, regardless of the outcome.

While Dennis sat silently on her hay bale, Lucas straightened himself out and told her he needed to get back to his work. He told her that she could back to the main building to wait for Mark there, that it would be more comfortable. But Dennis refused to leave, reasoning that the fresh air might better calm her nerves given the weight of the situation.

A couple of hours later, a nurse arrived with a message: Mark was in his room, ready to talk. Dennis didn't hesitate for a moment and stood up to leave immediately. As she walked, something shocked her, causing her to spin around. Lucas was looking back at her from afar, his words—*I'll be right here*—echoing in her mind.

She didn't say anything, just lowered her head as if nodding in acknowledgment and carried on. Her steps seemed to betray her, she somehow felt stuck in place while the front door seemed to only get farther and farther away.

Finally inside, a nurse offered directions, telling her to continue to the end of the corridor, past the dining hall, then to take a left and continue to the other end, where she would turn right. There, she would find the patient dorms. Mark's door was labeled *W-1*, because his last name was Wilson, and there were no other patients with last names that started with that letter. It might have been a unique system, but it seemed to get the job done.

Dennis walked very slowly, much like she once did on her way to her first session with Dr. Michaels. She was trying to get her thoughts in order, unsure if she would yell at him or break down into tears. But she knew one thing for a fact: she needed to talk to him, to finally answer all of her burning questions. Why had he left her like that, so coldly, without even so much as a goodbye?

When she got there, Mark's door was already ajar. A chill ran down her spine, shooting back up to her head. Taking a deep breath, she pushed the door open.

"Hello? May I come in?" Dennis asked as she pushed the door open wider.

"Of course," Mark replied from inside the room. "I'm in here."

As Dennis entered, she took in her surroundings. Mark's room was not very big, longer than it was wide. Directly across from the door, on the opposite wall, was a window, with a small armchair just below it. There was also a small table with a lamp and some books piled on it. She kept her vision trained on the wall opposite the entrance, eyes panning to the right; another chair followed, this one a desk chair, and a little further was another window.

The windows let in a lot of natural light. They were large and dressed with curtains that were drawn up on the sides. Her eyes eventually led her to the bedside table, and next to it a bed that was attached to the adjacent wall. Tucked in the opposite corner of the room was a small bathroom and a closet.

Dennis reached the end of the short corridor and her eyes searched for Mark, sweeping from left to right around the room and finally seeing him on the right, lying on the bed. He had several cushions stacked under his back so he was almost seated. He also had bandages covering part of his right forearm.

"Come closer," Mark beckoned. "Pull up a chair, please. I'd hug you if I had the energy, but I'm a little weak right now."

His words completely derailed her train of thought. Dennis took one look at him and forgot everything she had planned to say to him. Meekly, she made toward the desk chair and brought it next to the bed, promptly sitting down. Instinctively, she reached for his hand. Mark reciprocated the gesture.

A few seconds of silence passed where their gazes did not leave each other's eyes, a moment that they both could have lived in forever. But naturally, someone would have to break the silence, and Mark was the one who took the initiative.

"You're just as beautiful as I remember," he said, his words wrenching Dennis's sore and resentful heart. "You haven't changed at all. Your hair is longer, but your eyes...Your eyes have the same brightness as before."

She wanted to scream at him but, at the same time, she couldn't. She didn't have the courage. Her feelings for Mark went far beyond hatred or resentment. Her love for Mark was a feeling that had become part of her being. Dennis had grown up with him; Mark was part of her life and she couldn't forget him no matter how badly she wanted to. He had been her everything—her past, her present, and she thought for a long time that he was her future as well.

"Well, I'm older," she smiled and continued, "and yeah, my hair is longer. I like it this way." She didn't know what else to say to him, how to respond, or even how to bring up his state of health, which was what concerned her most at that time.

"I know what you're thinking," Mark said.

"Oh, yeah? What am I thinking?" She replied in a playful tone, trying to lighten the atmosphere.

"You're trying to piece together why I'm here, why I look this way, and probably deciding when to start throwing things at me so you can hurt me as deeply as I've hurt you," Mark said, his voice brittle, as if it was losing strength. But, in reality, he was beginning to let go of a pain he'd harbored for a very long time, something so immense that Dennis could not begin to imagine what it felt like.

"Yeah, you're right, I'd like to know why you're here," Dennis said, adjusting herself in her chair. She didn't want to move her hand from where it rested, but she needed to; her arm was going numb.

"Oh, my Dennis! If I could explain it all to you without having to relive so many painful memories, I would. But I'm not sure I can. Honestly, I just kept making mistake after mistake, and before I knew it, it was too late to undo the damage I had caused. Time has shown me how wrong I was to make that foolish decision that has haunted me ever since."

"What are you talking about?" Dennis said in a worried tone. "I don't understand what you're saying."

162

"I'm talking about leaving you!" Mark exclaimed. "Thinking I was doing what was best for you! I realize now just what a coward I was. It's only now that I understand."

"That's true, you acted like a coward, I won't deny that. If you didn't want to be with me anymore, you shouldn't have left the way you did. You should have told me. I might have understood. Sure, I would have been angry, and yes, I would have cried. But what I truly needed was an explanation..." She paused, collecting her thoughts, then corrected herself. "Actually, I've never stopped needing that explanation. For so long, I have dreamed of finding you and asking what I had done wrong, why you stopped loving me so suddenly. I have suffered so much thanks to you."

As she spoke, tears began to roll down her cheeks. Her emotions were too hot to hold back, now flowing freely, easing the tightness in her chest.

"Please don't cry," he said, bringing his hand to Dennis's cheek, trying to wipe away the tears he had caused. "You're going to make me cry."

Dennis instead broke down into a sob, unable to compose herself. She had waited so long to finally confront him, to tell him off, but now words failed her. Suddenly, the alarm clock on the bedside table went off. Mark quickly reached to silence it. Once quieted, he adjusted himself on the bed and swung his legs over, sitting on the edge.

He stretched out his arms and embraced her as tightly as his strength would allow. For several minutes, he held her, and gradually, her breathing became more regular, her tears and sobs subsiding. Dennis slowly pulled away from Mark's embrace, wiping her face with her hands. Mark offered her a tissue from his bedside table, which she accepted before angling away from him.

"Tell me," she demanded, her voice steadier now that she had shed her tears, ready at long last to hear the explanation she'd chased all these years. "I want to know everything you didn't tell. Everything since that day at the airport. Everything you were afraid to say, everything I deserved to know after all the love we had for each other. I need to know, and I won't leave until you tell me everything."

CHAPTER 18

The Reunion

Part Two

Mark's story began without any excuses or delay. The first thing he disclosed was that, following his mother's death, he began to feel unwell. Initially, he didn't seek medical attention, dismissing his symptoms as trivial. However, as time passed, more severe symptoms emerged, prompting him to consult a doctor. The tests ordered by this doctor revealed unexpected and life-altering results, which he struggled to share with Dennis.

He didn't want to worry her, especially since the wounds from his mother's death were fresh, and because they had already put so many of their plans on. He thought it best to wait for a more opportune moment to break the news.

He knew Dennis was extremely anxious about illnesses and would likely blame herself, connecting the diagnosis to her visions. To spare her from thinking she was responsible for his health issues, he chose to keep silent.

Indeed, whenever Dennis mentioned the lights—their secret discussions about the orbs that always popped up before a death—she overthought it, internalizing the correlation between the two. But Mark felt certain that none of what Dennis feared about the lights was true. He believed that she would have mentioned if she had seen anything, and her silence had kept his secret safe.

Back in Mark's room

"What did the doctors tell you?" Dennis clipped, her patience growing thin.

"Acute lymphocytic leukemia!" Mark blurted out.

"What?" Dennis responded; her voice tinged with disbelief. "What did you say?"

"You heard me," Mark sighed. "I didn't know how to react either. I spent hours, days, weeks mulling over how to tell you. I could never find the right approach. Ultimately, looked for a way out—an escape."

"But..." Dennis's mind was reeling.

"I fled. That's what I did," he continued. "The tests came back; the doctor's prognosis wasn't promising. There was a slight possibility for recovery, but nothing was guaranteed. I wanted to wait until I had some positive news to share alongside the bad.

"But good news never came. I kept seeing you making so many plans, dreaming of our future together, all while knowing deep down that I wouldn't be there for our future. After much thought, I convinced myself I couldn't drag you down with me, force you to watch me die. I couldn't be just another person who died in your arms," Mark said, overwhelmed by the flood of emotions and memories his confession brought forth.

"And the money? What was it for? What did you do with it?" Dennis pressed, her voice laden with a mixture of distrust and pain.

"I thought the best thing I could do was make you hate me, to think of me as nothing more than a scoundrel and a thief," Mark explained, pausing to take a sip of water. Dennis, still processing, urged him to continue. "I took your money to rob you of your future so you would hate me. It was the worst thing I've ever done, and believe me, I've punished myself enough for it."

"I would have understood if you just told me!" Dennis pounded her chest, overcome by grief. "You should have never pushed me away; I never hated you, much less thought of you as a scoundrel. *I loved you!*"

A silence fell over them and Dennis, gradually regaining composure, found herself again in Mark's arms. She could feel his warmth, and it seemed as if all the memories were as vivid as ever, as if no time had passed. It felt almost like she might wake up and find this all to be a nightmare. Mark's voice brought her back to reality.

"Do you want me to continue?" He asked gently.

Dennis leaned back, wiping her eyes, nodding. "Yes, please, tell me everything."

"I left for Canada," Mark continued. "There, I got in touch with a doctor who offered an experimental treatment. Your money—I never touched it. All of it is still in the bank, stored in a safe deposit box along with a letter I wrote years ago. I hoped that if the treatment worked, I would come back to you and explain everything. But time moved slower than I expected.

Months turned into years. That was when I decided to tell you I was in the navy. It was the best excuse I could come up with to keep you from finding me, but every day was a struggle without you.

"The initial treatment failed after 18 months, but then another doctor offered a new study, which I accepted. This doctor later discovered that my condition was chronic, not acute, and that I might live for years, though the implied outcome was inevitable. It was a glimmer of hope, a light on the horizon, a reason to keep fighting, hoping someday I might recover and return to you.

"Complications kept me hospitalized for long periods, alone, with no one to visit. I don't know how I survived, let alone without any news of you. But in my darkest moments, it was the memory of you that pulled me through, always brightening my day," Mark concluded, his energy spent from the emotional recounting.

"Did you really think so little of me?" Dennis said, her gaze falling. "How could you think that abandoning me was the most logical thing to do? Did it never occur to you that it would make me suffer more, thinking you abandoned me in cold blood rather than knowing the truth? I'm trying to wrap my head around it, but I can't understand it, Mark."

"I know," Mark replied. "And I'm not trying to make you understand. Even I don't understand it myself. I just ask you to let me come clean. I can't carry this burden any longer."

Dennis bowed her head. Mark continued.

"After four years, I got a skin infection. Thanks to my weakened immune system, they weren't able to save my leg. Ultimately, the doctors decided the best course of action to be amputation in order to keep me alive, as the treatment was showing positive effects—not curing, but slowing the cancer's progression, giving me more time.

"As time passed, I wanted to see you one last time before I died. I felt like a dead man from the day I was diagnosed with leukemia, so I wondered, why keep living? I had nothing left to offer you but suffering, maybe a year at most, so I decided to end my life after seeing you one last time," His voice cracked, and he struggled to continue.

"How can you say that? Why would you do that after fighting so hard to stay alive? I don't understand," Dennis interjected.

"You don't need to understand, because I don't either. But I didn't want to delay the inevitable any longer, I wanted to forget about everything once and for all," Mark paused, his emotions raw.

"And what happened? I couldn't reach you after seeing you back then. The phone number you gave me didn't work; I tried calling, over and over. You never answered," Dennis added.

"I tried to take my own life, but I failed. Every attempt was a failure; I guess I was too weak to do it properly. Each time I tried, I envisioned your face, wanting it to be the last thing I saw. But instead, I saw something I couldn't have understood if it weren't for what you had told me," Mark explained.

"What do you mean?" Dennis asked.

"I mean, when I had taken those pills and was waiting death to take me, with my eyes closed, I saw not just your face but a flurry of white lights—or orbs as you called them—bright and varying in size. At first, I thought it was a hallucination from the overdose, but then I realized it wasn't."

"How?" Dennis's curiosity was piqued.

"Because I began to see them even with my eyes open, whenever I thought of you. It was incredible. I tried many times to explain what I saw to others, but no one believed me, and eventually, I ended up in a hospital, lifeless yet alive. Then, finally, someone came along who listened and understood me," Mark's expression softened as he recounted this turn in his story.

"Rona?" Dennis interrupted suddenly. "Rona Michaels? The psychiatrist?"

"Yes, she's my psychiatrist," Mark confirmed. "She brought me here; it's because of her that I'm still alive and breathing."

"I can't believe it! She's my therapist too. She knows that I can see orbs, too. This is incredible, but please, go on. I want to know everything," Dennis urged, her interest deepening.

"Dr. Michaels told me about this place, that I could live here and receive ongoing treatment to keep the cancer cells from growing too quickly, giving more time to live, which is all I want now," Mark said. "When I arrived, everything was different—the people, the doctors, the atmosphere, the way life is led here. My first days were spent getting to know the other residents—we're called 'residents' here, not patients—and soon, they became my family. Many of us were forgotten by society or abandoned by our families because they couldn't accept our differences. Not all doctors are like Rona or the ones here who understand us."

"I know all about that," Dennis laughed. "If you tell them something that doesn't have scientific backing, they think you're crazy. Remember what happened with my parents after the accident?" They both laughed, the shared humor a brief respite from their heavy conversation.

Holding hands, the tension between them eased, and they began to feel better, not yet realizing they had been joined by someone else.

"Look who it is!" Mark exclaimed, his voice tinged with happiness despite its brokenness.

"Huh?" Dennis asked, her confusion evident in her tone.

"Look out the window, you'll see it. It's not very bright, but it's out there, watching us. I think it's waiting for me to tell you all about it, who it is to me."

Dennis turned and saw it—an orb, large but dimly lit, seemingly motionless in the corner of the window. She stood and walked over for a closer look. She felt compelled to speak, grappling with new perspectives and the sense that the light was waiting for something she was on the verge of understanding.

"What do you want?" Dennis demanded, looking up at the light with a mix of anger and past resentments in her voice. She wasn't sure what she felt or intended by speaking to it, but she yearned for some sign, something to quell the terrible unrest these lights stirred within her.

"Yes, I'm talking to you! Move, or better yet, leave! I know what you bring. I don't want you interfering; you've taken enough from me, leave us alone!" Dennis shouted with desperation. And to her surprise, Mark interrupted her.

"No, no, you're wrong. It's not a bad thing; it never has been," Mark said. "You can see them because you're special. Because they're special. They saved my life. Three times they came to my aid. They were the ones who lit up my dark skies. They are the reason I am still alive, and you are the connection. You brought them to me, every time I thought of you. Dennis, we were always wrong. You are a being of light; there's no doubt about that. I've done a lot of research about these lights and what they mean. You're here with a clear mission to help others. You have to listen to me; these orbs are beings of light here to assist us, those who need their light. Here are two more people who see the lights just like you and me— you need to hear their stories. While we aren't beings of light like you, we've received their light, which aids not just in healing our diseases but our souls as well. Once I understood this, everything became much clearer. In the end, I realized, it was always you. You've been helping people without knowing it; every time you approached someone in need, those orbs appeared, not to bring harm but to bring good. You are that therapy for the soul we so desperately need."

Dennis looked at him, stunned—it sounded as if someone else were speaking through the man in front of her. It couldn't be Mark. His face was pale, his words almost too surreal for her brain to accept. She walked to the chair near the window and steadied herself before sitting down.

"I don't understand," she protested. "Those lights took my parents from me and have caused me so much pain; they always take those I love. You're lying. You must be."

Mark walked over and took her hands again, reassuring her. "No, it is true. They never took anyone away. On the day of that terrible accident, they were here, taking care of you. They are part of you, and they go wherever you go, helping those around you because that was your mission even before you were born—to deliver love and light. Think, Dennis. Think for a moment about all the events that have happened, try to remember, and you will see it. You will be able to see it as I have."

Mark's eyes sparkled with hope as he watched for Dennis' reaction, but Dennis still had much to ponder. She was never easy to convince, and today, all of her beliefs were challenged.

Dennis tried to gather her thoughts amid the whirlwind of revelations. It was too much to process all at once. Gradually, memories of positive experiences associated with the lights, the energy she felt from them began to make sense. Were they preparing her for this revelation all along? How could she have been so oblivious to the true nature of these lights for so many years?

"I need to tell you something," Dennis said, her voice heavy with emotion.

"Anything," Mark responded, his tone inviting.

"A while before you abandoned me—because that's what you did— the lights were at your house," she said. "I kept seeing them and didn't want tell you. I thought it might worry you, as you've only heard me talk about these lights as a precursor to death. I decided to keep quiet. But I feared for you. At one point, I even thought you had left me because of them. I felt like they had taken you from me, just as they did with my parents." Her voice broke into a sob, preventing her from continuing.

"No, of course not," Mark reassured. "Don't you see? If you saw them, it was because I was already ill. You gave me the time to realize something was wrong and to seek medical help. Though my diagnosis was severe, it could have been worse. I might never have had the chance to reach this point in my life, where I've come to understand things, I never could have otherwise.

"You don't know how they've changed me. My very being is altered, though I deeply regret the way things happened, and more so for making you suffer. I'm sorry, and I would do anything to have spared you that pain, but I know now that was unavoidable; things always happen as they should. Time and light always find their way. You have no idea how much I missed you! I've wanted to tell you all this so badly, but I knew I had to wait. Though I knew you would come, I didn't know when. I waited for you every day, hoping for the time to pass quickly until the day you would be here with me again so I could explain and unburden my heart."

As their hands met, the warmth of the love they still harbored for each other surfaced spontaneously. Dennis and Mark reconnected through tears and shared grief, the product of a cruel twist of fate. To her, everything she had just heard seemed overwhelming, almost too much to grasp. Everything that had caused her such suffering now framed the story of why she existed. For Mark, it was a realization of his deepest yearnings—to see Dennis again and tell her everything that had oppressed his heart and shackled his soul.

In that moment, as they embraced, it seemed a bridge of light was built between them, mending what was broken, closing the distance that had grown, reconnecting them fully as they had been in the beginning, when they first met and dreamed together of a promising future, only to have it sinisterly interrupted by life's inexplicable turns.

Was anyone to blame for what had happened? Were Mark's actions justified? Was his request for forgiveness enough? What was left unsaid? Numerous questions lingered, yet Dennis felt a part of herself restored, though the hardest part was still ahead.

The room's ceiling seemed to crowd as more orbs gathered, moving smoothly, not wanting to interrupt or attract attention, yet their presence was overwhelming. The energy Dennis released was like a magnet for these lights; the deeper her emotions, the more orbs appeared around her.

This was something she had never fully understood, or perhaps, had never wanted to. Now, she faced the challenge of accepting and embracing this incredible gift. It was like starting over, revisiting the immense pain and isolation she felt after losing her parents. Maybe now she could begin to comprehend what she hadn't before and release the dark feelings that had led her astray.

Mark made a subtle gesture, encouraging Dennis to look up at the ceiling. The room was awash with the orbs, their slight, semi-transparent whitewash barely distinguishable against the surface, but their golden glow outlined their auras as they rotated throughout the room.

Dennis observed the numerous orbs, each emanating distinct energies, despite their similar appearance. She knew the feeling well—the sense of losing consciousness and slipping into a trance whenever the lights were present. That was why she had long tried to suppress this feeling, avoiding or even ignoring the lights, but they had never truly left her.

As tears welled up in her eyes, Dennis met Mark's gaze. Still holding her hands, he said, "I know I don't deserve your forgiveness, and I don't expect it. You were the first and best gift life gave me, and all I've ever hoped for was another chance to see you again. This moment, your presence here, is my second-best gift. You have always been the light that brightened my life, and you are the peace I need to continue my journey."

Tears streamed down Mark's cheeks, his expression one of joy. Dennis, overwhelmed by a surge of emotions she hadn't felt in years, struggled to find words. Finally, she spoke, "No more lies, no more separation. From today, we start fresh."

She sealed her promise with a kiss, reuniting their paths once again.

CHAPTER 19

The Message

Things could not have changed more dramatically, and all within a single day. After hours of conversation with Mark, Dennis resolved that things could not continue as they had been. It was inevitable that she would need to confront the new challenges that life was presenting her.

Days began to pass quickly, and Dennis found herself struggling to cope. She had been sleepless for days, contemplating how to navigate the new meaning her existence had thrust upon her. Her first thought was to seek advice from her therapist, who had helped her accept and understand her past. This seemed like a sensible strategy, especially considering the therapist was also Mark's doctor, which made it even more pertinent for her to discuss these new developments with someone who might understand the complexities of the situation.

Dennis had numerous concerns about Mark and his health. She wanted to be better informed and decided to talk to his doctors to understand his condition more clearly. Though she knew the prognosis was not promising, she needed to know where he stood and how much time they might have left together.

Meanwhile, her relationship with Lucas was in turmoil. That day, Lucas had been unusually quiet, painfully aware that he was losing her. He had grown to care deeply for her and felt he was falling in love, but he also knew this situation was beyond his control. And so, he chose to give Dennis the space she needed, resigning himself to whatever outcome the future held, even if it meant stepping back.

Dennis's daily life became increasingly hectic. She worked relentlessly each day to finish her tasks early, not only because she needed time for almost daily visits to Tammy but also because Mark was back in her life, and she wanted to spend as much time with him as possible.

Despite the new stresses, Dennis felt a sense of recovery, a retrieval of something she thought she had lost. She hadn't had the time—or perhaps hadn't allowed herself the time—to sit and think through everything that was happening. Part of her didn't want to face certain truths because it would mean dealing with deep-seated issues she wasn't ready to confront.

Her personal narrative was evolving. The burden she had carried for so long no longer felt like a burden but a gift. However, it was clear that she needed time to fully understand it. Memories of those lights, which she had long blamed for taking her parents, might not have been as dark as she thought. Dennis had spent so much time alone, resenting those orbs of light, never considering that things could have been different. No one was there to challenge her misconceptions, not even the lights themselves.

There were moments when just the thought of what might have been brought tears to her eyes. She regretted not visiting Mark's mother when she was ill, thinking now that perhaps she could have done more if only, she had learned the truth about her abilities sooner.

Dennis avoided dwelling on these thoughts. Whenever she found herself reflecting, she would shake her head and busy herself with something else, unwilling to face a reality that felt too overwhelming. The apparent truth about her powers was a lot to accept. How was she supposed to know what to do to help those in need? The responsibility of being a being of light felt immense.

It was a regular Tuesday, and her day was going smoothly, though Dennis wasn't able to book an earlier appointment with Dr. Michaels; her scheduled appointment was still three weeks away. That afternoon, she called several times without success. The receptionist told her that an appointment slot would only open up in the event of a cancellation, so nothing was guaranteed. Although Dennis understood, she was itching to talk to the one person who could possibly begin to understand her situation—after all, Dr. Michaels knew about the lights, her crises, and always listened without judgment.

When the receptionist didn't call back that afternoon, Dennis decided to visit Tammy as planned. It had been a while since Tammy was sent home, and she was in much better health now. Her demeanor had brightened and her familial relationships greatly improved, especially now with her mother's presence and support.

Arriving at Tammy's house, Dennis saw Mrs. Harrison's car parked outside. It wasn't unusual now, after their reconciliation. When Dennis knocked on the door, Tammy's daughter opened it.

The girl was serious and silent, simply opening the door and walking away, leaving Dennis with an unspoken greeting hanging in the air.

With quick steps, Dennis headed to Tammy's room, where she found both Mary and Tammy with pale, somber expressions. Without any of her usual pleasantries, Dennis blurted out, "What's going on? Is everything okay?"

"Hi, Dennis, I'm glad you came," Mary said, standing up and making her way over to her. "I was actually about to call you."

"What's wrong, Mary?" Dennis asked again. "Please say something. You know I can't handle suspense like this."

"It's nothing too serious," Tammy interjected. "It's just that the doctor wants to see ASAP tomorrow. My last MRI showed something… unexpected."

Dennis's expression darkened, and she slumped into a chair next to Tammy's bed, overcome by a wave of concern. She remained silent, her head bowed, lost in thought.

"Are you okay?" Mary inquired, looking at Dennis with concern.

Dennis looked up and nodded, her throat tight. She struggled to hold back a flood of emotions, determined to appear strong. But as soon as she left Tammy's house and got into her car, she broke down into tears. She drove aimlessly, her vision blurred by tears, until she found herself at *The Stay*. She parked far from the entrance to avoid drawing attention. It was after eight o'clock at night—too late for visitors.

Looking at the facility from her car, Dennis thought of Mark and the time they might have left together. An overwhelming feeling of loss, similar to the pain she felt after losing her parents, gripped her. Her tears flowed freely, her heart aching with each thought of Mark and Tammy. How could she have this gift and yet feel so powerless to help them?

Hours passed as she sat by her car, staring up at the starry sky, wrestling with her guilt over Lucas and her inability to reciprocate his feelings. She wanted to call him up, to lean on him for support. But she knew it wouldn't be fair to him.

As she stared at the stars, one in particular caught her attention. It seemed to glow brighter and move towards her. Initially mistaking it for a shooting star, she made a wish but stopped short as she realized it was not a star but a bright orb of light, hovering directly in front of her. Frustrated and overwhelmed, Dennis confronted the orb.

"Why should I believe you're a good thing when all you do is take away those I love?" She demanded, waiting for a response that never came.

Her desperation grew as the silent light offered no answers, and in a fit of anguish, she shouted, "I don't want you here! You only bring me pain!"

Then she collapsed to the ground, overwhelmed by grief. Suddenly, she felt strange and light. Looking up, she saw two orbs of light on either side of her, gently raising her off the ground. Terrified, she screamed, "No, don't take me! Let me go!" But then a faint voice from the larger light reached her, calming her fears.

"You've been our mission from the beginning. We were told to protect and care for you but not to interfere in your life," the light explained, its voice soft but clear.

"Why me? What makes me so special?" Dennis asked, her voice tinged with a mixture of despair and curiosity.

The main orb continued its gentle, circular motion, its light flickering slightly as it spoke.

"Dennis, you may not remember, but you were sent back to this by your own choice."

"What?" Dennis replied with an incredulous tone.

"Yes, Dennis. The accident that took your parents took you as well. You three were supposed to return home that day."

"What? Home? Like, my house? What are you talking about?" Dennis was getting more confused with each passing second.

"It may be hard to understand, but that accident wasn't fated. Consequently, you—as you humans say—died. To us, you began your journey home."

Dennis felt like she was being spoken to in a foreign language. She had to process each word twice, struggling to grasp what the Light was trying to communicate.

"Dennis, don't strain yourself to understand everything right now," the Light continued. "Just listen, and in time, you'll get it."

Gently, the orbs brought Dennis to the ground. Standing on solid ground once again, she leaned against her car for support, slowly gaining her bearings.

"You possess the gift of aiding others, a gift bestowed upon you when you entered this world. It was meant to be nurtured over time with your parents' guidance. However, when the accident happened, things changed. Not everything is set is stone, life can be unpredictable. And so, when you were coming back home, they asked if you would consider staying behind. You knew your job was far from done, and so you agreed. While your parents moved on, we were assigned to watch over you."

"What do you mean 'they'? Who are 'they'?" Dennis asked her tone softer but still unbelieving.

"'They' are our most exalted spiritual guides. Beyond this earthly plane, we all exist as energy, aiding those on Earth. We channel energy to humans and help maintain nature's balance. We greet those returning home after completing their earthly missions."

Dennis accepted the Light's explanations. A wave of calm enveloped her, easing her anxiety.

"But why me? Why was I sent back alone? What's so special about me?" Dennis inquired.

"No, Dennis! You still don't understand. This isn't about you, it's about the others. You are meant to bring energy to many around you, providing the necessary support for their souls to complete their earthly missions. Your journey is just beginning, soon you'll understand what we mean. Know that we will always be with you, even if unseen. You are never truly alone. This mission is challenging, but it is yours, and you have been chosen for it because you are a formidable lightworker. You've been engaged in this work for a long time. Soon, you will find inner harmony and gain understanding."

As Dennis opened her mouth to ask another question, the Light cut her off.

"Don't overwhelm yourself with questions today, Dennis," it said, gently. "That's enough for now. Go forth and open yourself to the Light, there you will find the understanding needed to move forward. When you need us, just call out to us."

"But I still have so many questions…" Dennis started, but there was no more time. The lights began to spin rapidly. The three orbs aligned before her, with the two that had arrived last ascending quickly. Then, an overwhelming emotion washed over Dennis.

It was difficult to describe precisely what she felt, but it was akin to an immense love. She watched as the Lights left her, their brilliance intensifying with distance. The three lights paused one last time, then vanished at incredible speed into the night, leaving only the twinkling stars above.

Dennis remained, gazing into the vast sky, pondering the significance of the words spoken by the Light. Her reverie was broken by the sound of an approaching vehicle. As she watched it pass, Dennis decided it was time to return home.

She drove slowly, the streets quiet and empty. As she parked, she noticed a number of orbs floating in the corner of her vision. Uncertain if they were following her, she calmly walked in the opposite direction from her building's entrance. Reaching the corner, she thought she had lost sight of them, but realized they were still there.

Deciding that she was unlikely to lose them, Dennis returned to her building. As she opened her apartment door, orbs greeted her by dancing in the middle of her living room, pausing for a moment to acknowledge her entry. It was then that Dennis resigned herself to the fact that no matter where she was, they would always be there—they always had been.

She walked into her room, threw herself onto her bed, and succumbed to a deep sleep, enveloped by a newfound peace.

The next morning, she woke feeling surprisingly refreshed. Dennis prepared for the day with a lightness she hadn't felt in a long time. As usual, she made her coffee and headed to the office, but today, the weight that had burdened her shoulders seemed lifted. She greeted her colleagues warmly as she walked down the hallway to her office. Once there, she placed her belongings on her desk, then drew back the curtain to let the bright morning light flood the room. Finishing her coffee by the window, she felt a moment of serenity.

And then the phone rang.

"Yes?" Dennis said, answering the phone.

"Good morning, Dennis. Mrs. Harrison would like to speak with you. She's waiting in her office," said Mrs. Harrison's assistant.

Dennis made her way to Mary's office, feeling unsure about what the interaction may hold. "Good morning, Mary. How are you today?" Dennis greeted her upon entering.

"Good morning, Dennis. Honestly, I'm quite worried. There's something important you need to know," Mary confessed.

"What's going on?" Dennis urged, worried that there may be bad news about Tammy.

"Well, as you know, Eileen has been away receiving treatment to manage her diabetes, but there's been a complication—she's come down with a lung infection that has weakened her significantly. I need to go be with her, so I'll be away for a few days. With everything we have going on here, I'll need your help."

"Of course, whatever you need," Dennis assured her.

"Firstly, I'm most worried about Tammy. The doctors found cancer cells in another part of her body. But they're optimistic about catching it early. We'll know in a few weeks if we need to extend her chemotherapy."

"That's a relief," Dennis responded, releasing a breath. "The doctors know what they're doing, I'm sure she will pull through."

"Thank you, Dennis. Honestly, I've been up all-night waiting to hear from her doctor. Now, the second thing is that I'll need you to oversee the office while I'm away. I have no concerns about the team to handle themselves, but I need you to be here if any decisions need to be made. You've been indispensable since Tammy's absence."

"You don't even have to ask, Mary. I'm here for you," Dennis said warmly.

"It'll only be for four or five days," Mary concluded.

"Take your time. Everything here will be fine. And please send my best wishes to Eileen. I hope to see her when she returns," Dennis said.

"Absolutely, we'll have you over for dinner once we're back," Mary smiled.

Returning to her office, Dennis noticed a man in the hallway who seemed to be looking for someone.

"Can I help you?" she called out.

"I'm looking for Miss Russell. I have a delivery for her," the man responded, holding a medium-sized white box.

"That would be me," Dennis replied with a smile.

"Then this is for you," he said, handing her the box. Inside was a beautiful arrangement of flowers.

"Thank you so much!" Dennis said as she signed for her package and placed the flowers on her desk. As the delivery guy left, she checked the flowers for a card or note and, finding none, hurried after him before he could take the elevator.

"Excuse me, was there supposed to be a note with this?" she asked.

"Oh, yes," he said, sheepishly. "I almost forgot, sorry about that."

Dennis received a small, white envelope from the man and eagerly opened it to find a note from Lucas.

I don't need any explanation. I just want to know if we can still have coffee together, like before?

Her heart fluttered. Back in her office, Dennis placed the flowers by the window and pulled out her phone. Initially, she thought to call Lucas but opted for a text instead: *I'd like that coffee too, but I'm not ready to explain everything just yet.* She finished her message with a single heart.

Almost instantly, Lucas texted back. *I don't need to know everything now, just that I haven't lost you completely. Do I still have a place in your life?*

Dennis took a moment to put together a response that would read more candid than if she said it in person. *You are very important to me, but I need time to figure things out. I'm sorry if this is too much for you, but I'd really like a shoulder to lean on.*

Same time, same place? Lucas texted.

Same time and place. Dennis confirmed.

As she pocketed her phone, a sense of security washed over her. The thought of seeing Lucas again brought out an unmistakable feeling of comfort.

CHAPTER 20

True Love

Even after calling repeatedly, Dennis was still unable to secure an earlier appointment with Dr. Michaels. With no other option, she was forced to wait until her original scheduled time. Thankfully, time passed quickly. Her appointment had been for five in the afternoon, the last slot of the day. Dennis knew that this session would take longer than usual; she felt she had a great deal to discuss with Rona.

Her day went by smoothly. Mary was still out of the office. Between visits to Eileen and Tammy, it was difficult for Dennis to spend full time at the agency. Nevertheless, things at the office were under control and projects were progressing as expected. Dennis had visited Mark the day before and had a wonderful time. There were no tears. Instead, they had laughed together and managed to have a long and calm conversation. He told her all about the other patients he was friends with, and Dennis shared how she had landed her current job, which she loved.

She also had the opportunity to meet some other residents of *The Stay* during her last few visits, but she was particularly interested in learning more about a person Mark brought up multiple times over past several weeks. Her name was Sarah, and she had been bed-bound in her room for some time. Dennis wasn't exactly sure why she was there, but she had seemed pretty normal when he introduced the two of them. Looking at her physically, Dennis couldn't discern any obvious medical issues. However, there was something about Sarah's expression that lingered in her mind.

Dennis threw a few things into her purse and left for her appointment. She parked across the street and walked over to the office. Once inside, she checked in with the receptionist and then went to the waiting room. She waited a few minutes before being called and she entered the consultation room without delay. She settled in a chair in Dr. Michaels' office while waiting for her to come in. About five minutes she finally entered the room.

"Hi Dennis, how have you been?" Rona greeted. "I'm happy to see you."

" I've been fine, well..." Dennis said with a nervous smile. "I don't really know. A lot has happened these last few weeks. I've been really eager to see you, actually. I even tried to call in for an earlier appointment, but apparently, you're very busy."

"I have had a full schedule, which is good, isn't it? I can't complain— not everyone has a stable job," she smiled before continuing. "But actually, I've been working on a personal project.

Getting my house in order, so to speak. I'll tell you all about it when the time is right. For now, let's focus on you."

"Hm," Dennis started. "There's so much to talk about, I don't know where to start."

She straightened up a bit, scooting to the edge of her chair. She bent over for her purse and rummaged through her bag. She fished out a piece of paper where she'd listed some of the concerns she wanted to discuss with her psychiatrist.

"What have you got there, Dennis?" Rona asked.

"My notes! I didn't want to come here and forget everything I needed to tell you," she replied.

"Ah, I see. Of course," Dr. Michaels said. "Please, go ahead."

Dennis looked down at her list. "I think we should talk about Mark Wilson."

"Mark? Mark Wilson? One of the residents at *The Stay*?"

"Yes! Precisely," Dennis replied. "That Mark Wilson."

"What do you want to say about Mark?" The doctor had pulled out her pen, ready to take notes. This was something new.

"Do you remember when I told you that the love of my life had abandoned me?" Dennis asked. "Well, it turns out that I've found him again."

"Really? And what happened? Have you been able to talk? Did he explain himself?" Dr. Michaels asked several questions following Dennis' remark about that.

"That's the thing," Dennis interjected. "It's Mark, Mark Wilson— your patient at *The Stay*

"Mark Wilson!" Dr. Michaels called out in disbelief. "Who would have thought! How did I miss that? I should've been able to connect the dots. I just have so many patients, too many cases to juggle.

"But yes, now that you mention it, he has consistently brought up a significant other he had in the past. Not exactly his girlfriend, but he's referred to her as the light of his life," the doctor paused. "Tell me, Dennis, how did you find each other?"

"Remember when I had mentioned going to volunteer at *The Stay* with Lucas?"

"Of course. I volunteered there, too."

"Right," Dennis said. "That was the day I saw him. Honestly, I couldn't believe it. He was there! And after so much pain and so much time, I managed to stumble upon him where I least expected it. I learned a lot that day."

"He told you about his illness, I imagine," Dr. Michaels chimed in.

"Yes," Dennis replied. "He came clean, told me everything. And while that alone has been very difficult to process, there's more."

"That must've been a lot for you to go through, Dennis," Rona commented. "You must have been under a lot of stress. Why didn't you call me? You know I am always here for you. More than just your doctor, I want you to see me as your friend. After all, I think we've gotten to know each other well, don't you think?"

"Actually, I tried," Dennis said. "I called your office multiple times to try and see you, but your schedule was completely full. But that doesn't matter, I'm here now."

"Tell me, Dennis," the doctor asked. "What do you want to talk about now? What concerns you the most?"

Dennis peered at her list.

"Well," she started. "The first issue that came up regarded my feelings. I feel that Mark is still the most important person in my life, even after all the hurt and confusion he's caused me. When he opened up to me, I learned so much about his side of the story. That he didn't leave me because he didn't care about me, but to spare my feelings, knowing that he was dying. That nearly killed me. I felt my soul being torn apart.

"That's really hard to sit with, Rona. He's going to die. There's nothing I can do to help him. He's going to leave me again, this time forever and I don't know how to accept it. I'm starting to think it would have been better for him to have remained silent."

Dennis' eyes welled up with tears.

"I understand," Dr. Michaels said. "Do you think that after finding out about his situation, learning about why he left you, he deserves a chance to be understood?"

"Of course I do!" Dennis replied. "The problem is that I still love him, and I don't want to lose him. I feel like I failed him. If only I had told him…"

"Told him what, Dennis?" The doctor asked.

"I mean—" Dennis hesitated. "Do you remember when I told you that I could see lights? Those lights that seemed only to appear before a tragedy would affect someone I loved?"

"Yes, I remember," the doctor nodded. "But I also recall that we came to an agreement about trying to understand those lights. We agreed that life is full of wonderful things that not all of us are meant to understand, but that doesn't mean these things are bad. Do you remember when I shared my own experience with you?"

"Yes, of course," Dennis said. "But there's more."

Dr. Michaels motioned for her to continue.

"It's Mark," she started. "He told me that my lights saved his life in the past. He says—okay, I know this sounds silly, but he says I'm something called a 'Lightworker.'"

Upon hearing Dennis say this, Rona stood up from her seat and walked to her desk.

"Dennis," she said. "Wait here for a few minutes, please."

"Okay," Dennis replied.

The doctor returned shortly to continue their conversation.

"Dennis," said Dr. Michaels, drawing a tight breath. "I'm going to do something that's not typically allowed, but I think it's necessary. I want you to know that Mark has been diagnosed with schizophrenia. While even with that diagnosis, I find that some of the things he has told me sound very compelling. But I want you to understand something, and this is between us, person-to-person, not doctor-to-patient. I can't go against what science says. I can't say that science is inadequate, nor can I say that all of what my patients have experienced is real—I would be out of line, negligent, compromising my role as a psychiatrist and medical professional.

"But this doesn't mean that I don't believe you, or Mark, or the others who see me as someone they can trust and confide in about things they can't understand. I can only tell you this: Mark has his own journey; he has suffered because of it and learned from it. His mistakes are the same as anyone else would make, especially without the knowledge that you have now, or without the experiences you've had.

"Trust me, the experience I had shared with you could not have been shared with another professional. It would have discredited me and possibly cost me my license. Do you understand? Remember when we talked about nothing happening by coincidence? That's still true. Look at things as they are falling into place and you will see what I mean."

"But, Rona," Dennis said. "There's still more."

"By all means," Dr. Michaels said. "Continue."

"Well," Dennis began. "When Mark and I met up to talk, he told me how these lights had saved him, and how they appeared whenever he thought of me. He also told me that he had met others who also saw these lights. He told me that these people taught him about 'Lightworkers'—people who have the gift of channeling some kind of pure, healing energy. And he told me that I was one of them."

"What about this worries you?" Dr. Michaels asked. "Is it that you very well could be one of these people, or could it be that Mark may be losing his mind or just looking for an excuse for you to forgive him?"

"I think I might have an answer for that," Dennis responded. "I don't really think it was an excuse from Mark. I can't after having one of the most crazy and inexplicable experiences of my life."

"What happened, Dennis?" This piqued the doctor's curiosity.

"It's…complicated," Dennis answered, wary of telling the truth.

"Nothing is too complicated for me," Rona encouraged. "It was hard for me, losing my son. Even more so to see him reappear and not being able to tell anyone. After catching a glimpse of what his afterlife was like, I had to accept that I wouldn't ever see him again until it is my time to go."

Dennis hesitated.

"A few nights ago," she started. "The lights came to me. I had been having a very bad night. Everything seemed to be falling apart, and during a moment of deep pain, one of the lights approached me and actually spoke to me.

"I want to preface with this: I hadn't been drinking, in case you were wondering. I was highly skeptical myself. But I finally realized I was receiving an important message. I think it could've been my despair that brought them to reveal themselves."

"A message?" Rona asked.

"One of them," Dennis continued. "The biggest and brightest of the bunch, came up to me and told me about my purpose as a Lightworker. Almost verbatim what Mark had said, perhaps with even more detail. What's more, was that the Light said that I had been 'sent back.' Naturally, I asked what they meant, and the Light explained that there are these greater energies guiding us, watching over me and many other people like me, and that those guides had sent me back here to continue my mission. Obviously, I asked them what mission they were talking about, and it told me that I was here to help people, to bring them the energy and healing so that they can continue their destinies here, on this plane. Do I sound crazy?"

"Dennis," the doctor responded. "This is something very serious, and I can imagine it has confronted all of the ideas and beliefs that you've held."

"You're not wrong," Dennis sighed. "But what's really bothering me is, what kind of help am I supposed to give if those I think I can help will leave anyway? How can I help, if I don't know how?"

"Do you think it's something you can accept? Or would you rather refuse to acknowledge this message?"

"I don't think I'm refusing to accept what has happened, but I don't know how I can help. Look at Mark, there's no cure for his disease. How could I possibly help him? I'm just so confused."

"Dennis, perhaps it's time to consider things from another perspective. Is this life the only possible way of existence? Is making sure that we all stay alive for as long as we can really the most important priority we should have? Should I refuse to believe that my son is now living another life, a happier life?" Rona posed these questions as a way of encouraging a broader view for Dennis. "There are so many things that are virtually impossible to understand, but I've learned that it's easier to take experiences and events as they come."

"No," Dennis replied quickly. "I'm not saying that all isn't true."

"Consider that perhaps this life we know isn't the only one we have, and certainly isn't the last. Dennis, I saw him with my own eyes. My son. Alive. And I know he is here with me when I need him. I can feel his presence."

"I'm trying to understand," Dennis said, tears sliding down her cheeks. "That's what I'm working on. But that doesn't mean I won't want to keep people alive. Why do they have to leave me? It hurts. It hurts so much to think that I will never see a loved one again."

"I know," Rona said in a comforting voice. "But it's all about how you perceive things. No one really leaves completely, it's more like a transition. My son told me that we would see each other again, and I believe him. I'm sure of that. Reconsider what it means to live. Don't give up. I told you in the beginning: you are special. And now as you're saying this, you've confirmed what I've always thought. You must believe in what you are and cultivate that which is inside you."

"But I don't know what I am!" Dennis protested. "I don't know how I can help someone when I feel like I can't even help myself."

"I know it's difficult, but with determination, you'll reach understanding," Rona said.

Dennis managed a slight smile, seeing Dr. Michaels so passionately engaged in their discussion.

"Thank you for your support," she said. "I knew I could trust you with this. At least I know you believe me. I really needed to know that I'm not crazy."

Both women smiled.

"I think that in some way," Rona said. "This has allowed me to carry on the message that my son left me—that of believing in life as a cycle of endless growth and learning. Our souls will return to that place from which they once left. We will return home, I know."

"Do you think that we'll see each other in the next life?"

"I'm absolutely certain we will meet again."

"How do you think I'm supposed to help others?" Dennis asked after a beat.

"You'll figure it out, I'm sure," Dr. Michaels said. "Just like when I finally understood that I had to share my son's wisdom with those whose experiences were similar to mine. It has become my job to give them confidence and help them understand that they are not alone."

Dennis looked up at Dr. Michaels.

"Dennis," she continued. "You will always find others like you and those who need you. Those who need to be heard and perhaps those who need to return home and of course those who will remain here."

"I know it's late and we're going over time," Dennis said. "But I have something else to ask you."

"For discussions like these," Dr. Michaels responded. "Time is irrelevant. It's my job and my pleasure to help you as much as I can. Please, go ahead."

"Even though I know Mark's time is short," Dennis continued, her voice carrying a deeply conflicted tone. "I still love him as much as I'd loved him before. I'd like to help him, even pick up where we let off, but I don't know how. Besides, there's Lucas. What would I tell him?"

"That's certainly a tough situation you're in," Rona said, thoughtfully. "On one hand, Mark has been thinking of you to push himself through his battle. It's clear his love for you is still immense. You two finding each other now will certainly put a lot of his own guilt at ease as well as bring him great comfort. And I'm not surprised that you're experiencing a revival of the past feelings you held for him. The situation you're in has come on very suddenly, so it's only natural to experience a lot of confusing and conflicting feelings. I think, however, that deep down, your heart knows perfectly well what you need. On the other hand, with Lucas, I think he's a very wise and mature person. He will know how to handle himself if you choose Mark. He is very special, and you know it. Just remember to approach the situation calmly and the stress will soon pass. Remember, nothing happens by coincidence in this life; everything has a purpose, don't forget that."

"You're right," Dennis said. "I think I'll talk to Lucas and be honest with him about what I need right now."

"I think that's very wise," the doctor responded. "Dennis, Can I ask you a favor?"

She nodded.

"I would like to use you for something." "I'm sorry, I'm not sure I know what you mean," Dennis said with a nervous smile, her cheeks flushing. "What do you want from me?"

"I want you to ask your lights if they can carry a message to my son," Dr. Michaels clarified. "It's not that I don't try and talk to him on my own, he just hasn't shown himself to me since that day. I want to make sure he's hearing me, for him to know that I look forward to the day when I am with him again."

"What, you're not planning on leaving soon, are you?" Dennis asked. "Who will I talk to about my problems without you?"

"No, no," Dr. Michaels laughed. "It's just that I miss him. I want him to know that I want to be with him."

Dennis and Dr. Michaels both leaned in for a comforting hug. Before Dennis left her office, she turned to Rona and said, "I'll see what I can do," with a wink.

When Dennis left her appointment, it was already dark. As she quickly crossed the parking lot to get to her car, she stopped at the door and looked over at the scenery. Bay Park—a favorite place of hers since she started dating Lucas. Memories of Lucas flooded her mind. They had shared so many good moments, joys, so much laughter. Tender moments of peace and rest. Everything that Lucas had given her was pure and sincere. Her heart was pounding.

She got into her car, started the engine, and the radio came on in the middle of a song. "I'm waiting for your call," the voice sang. Dennis couldn't shake the gut feeling that this was a message meant for her. Suddenly, she was overcome with the need to talk to him, the need to hear his voice.

Dennis drove back home as quickly as she could and hurried inside. As soon as she got inside, she threw down her things and pulled out her phone, dialing Lucas' number. The phone rang, but no one answered. She hung up, waited a few seconds, and dialed again. The phone echoed its rings into the silence until, just when it seemed she'd go to voicemail again, she heard Lucas's voice.

"Hello?"

"Lucas?"

"This is he," Lucas answered, trying hard to sound like he didn't know who was calling. "With whom am I speaking?"

"Oh, come on," she chided. "You know it's me. What are you playing at?"

"Sorry," he laughed. "I just wanted to see how badly you needed to talk to me. That's why I didn't pick up the first time. Had to make sure. Are you okay?"

"Well...kind of," she admitted.

"What's wrong? Is there a problem? Do you need me?" he probed.

"No, don't worry, it's nothing like that," she explained. "But I did want to talk. You haven't called for days. I haven't heard from you since we met up for coffee. What happened?"

"Nothing. I was just trying to give you the space you needed. I know you've been busy and a lot has changed in your life."

"Yeah, that's actually what I wanted to talk about—" Dennis paused, suddenly aware of her deep feelings for him.

"Dennis? You there?"

"Yes, sorry," she said, snapping back to reality. "I just don't know how to say this..."

"What is it?" Lucas said, laughing nervously. "Whatever it is, just say it. I'll do my part and try to understand."

"It's nothing bad, I just...miss you," she confessed. "I miss you and I don't know how to handle it. It's eating me alive."

"Dennis," he said, his tone soft. "You don't need to explain yourself; I know it's been a tough time for you. But I'm glad to hear you miss me. I miss you too. I think about you all day, but I'm trying not to interfere with your life or your decisions. I would never want to pressure you, you know that."

"I just feel like I don't understand anything anymore," Dennis confessed. "I'm so confused, and I really just need you by my side. I want to see you."

"Really? Right now?" he teased, feigning reluctance.

"Seriously," Dennis insisted. "I'm not in the mood for jokes."

"But I need to know if you're worth clearing my schedule for," he teased further. "I'm not leaving the house for a simple hi-and-bye."

"Are you seriously playing hard to get right now?" Dennis couldn't help but smile.

"Well, everyone gets their kicks somehow. Come on, tell me, how badly do you want to see me? On a scale from one to ten, would it be a five? Or closer to ten?"

"You're being ridiculous!" Dennis chided again. "Keep this up and it'll drop to zero. Don't test me."

"No, Dennis, please don't get upset," Lucas begged. "I just wanted to lighten the mood."

"It's okay," she sighed.

"But really, how much do you miss me?" he asked again, this time earnestly.

"Okay," Dennis relented. "I'll say it just this once and no more—and don't take it too seriously because I'm not playing your little game anymore."

"Alright," he persisted. "How much?"

"Ten. I guess ten," she said, her voice strained.

The next sound Dennis heard was the hangup tone. Confused, she quickly redialed. But there was no answer. A wave of anxiety swept over her. What happened? Maybe she should've indulged Lucas' playful behavior.

Just as she was about to dial again, she heard a knock at the door. She approached and peered through the peephole cautiously. To her surprise, she saw Lucas standing on the other side. He was making silly faces, knowing she was watching him through the peephole.

Her heart raced and her cheeks flushed with warmth. Dennis opened the door and Lucas stepped inside before she could utter a word. He acted swiftly, knowing he had only one chance to make it right.

As soon as he entered, Lucas pulled Dennis into a tight embrace, wrapping her in his arms. Pulling away slightly, he looked tenderly into her eyes. "Do you really miss me that much?"

"Yes," she whispered.

Without another thought, Lucas kissed her passionately, expressing with fervor how much she meant to him. He didn't let go, continuing his kisses and caresses, emboldened by his passion. Lucas was capturing her heart, and she surrendered to his embrace in earnest, forgetting all of her worries. The indescribable, overwhelming need she felt for Lucas made her forget everything in that moment.

As they broke apart, Dennis rested her head on his chest.

"You don't have to decide anything now," Lucas spoke gently. "I'd never want to rush you. I just need to know that I have your heart."

Dennis smiled up at him and leaned in to kiss him tenderly. She knew no further explanations were necessary. She finally understood that she loved him, deeply and truly. A miracle had unfolded, and she had fallen in love with Lucas.

CHAPTER 21

Some leave... Others stay

Dennis' life had done a full 180 since that fateful night when Lucas stole her heart. Everything was different. She had surrendered herself to him fully and felt immensely happy, not just because of the joy he brought her, but because she had also come to realize that their relationship had slowly permeated every aspect of her being. It was as if she had been given a new lease on life; she felt loved and supported, and life seemed to smile at her despite the array of challenges she continued to face. She was aware that there would still be difficulties ahead of her, but she felt more optimistic than ever, resolved to open herself up more and take on any challenge that she faced. She had fully embraced the philosophy that nothing happens by chance, and everything holds a purpose—a mantra taught to her by her friend Rona.

Dennis and Lucas didn't see each other every day, but he still made it a priority to make her happy every day. He sent her texts, emails, flowers, and other small tokens that brightened her day. She did her best to return the favor, except she didn't typically send flowers back as she found it somewhat unorthodox, although occasionally when they were together, she would pluck a flower and present it to him as a gesture of her affection—a gesture he cherished deeply and held close to his heart.

Dennis had meticulously organized her schedule to make time for the most important people in her life. On Mondays, Wednesdays, and Fridays, she met with Tammy after work. On Tuesdays and Thursdays, she drove to *The Stay* to spend time with Mark and the other residents. She usually arrived there at about six in the evening after finishing at the office and wouldn't leave until about ten at night. Saturdays were reserved for her personal errands in the morning because she still needed to do her shopping and take care of household tasks, but the afternoons were devoted completely to Lucas. They did a lot of different things—going out, watching movies, shopping, or simply taking a stroll. Their dates often extended late into the evenings, either at her place or his. Sometimes, Dennis would have flashbacks of her previous relationship with Mark, and it stirred a sense of fear within her. However, she would quickly remind herself that this relationship was her present, not her past, which brought a smile to her face, reinforcing her belief that things would unfold differently this time.

On Sundays, Lucas would make Dennis breakfast, albeit very early, since they both liked to make the most of their day. After breakfast, Dennis and Lucas would visit Tammy. Dennis wanted her friend to see her happiness firsthand; she wanted to share her joy and show off that she had found someone who made her feel loved and cherished. Tammy had always told her that life wasn't just about work, though she still praised Dennis for her determination and efforts to succeed.

After visiting Tammy's house, they decided to spend their day sightseeing. They loved driving around and discovering hidden gems and meeting new people. Together, each day strengthened their bond a little more.

Recently, Dennis had noticed a decline in Mark's mood. Though she often found herself crying in secret—unsure of how to cope with still harboring deep affection for him—she had come to accept that he would eventually leave her. This time, however, things were different; he wasn't running away this time. Mark had come to terms with the fact that Dennis loved another man. Truthfully, he was fine not picking up with her. For Mark, it was good enough that Dennis was still in his life and, perhaps most importantly, that she had forgiven him and understood the truths he had shared with her.

The visits were always delightful. They laughed, talked, and even played board games whenever feasible, often with the other residents. Dennis couldn't add more time to Mark's life, but the moments they spent together were immensely fulfilling for her. She knew that her efforts stemmed from a heartfelt, sincere desire to help and care for others.

From time to time, Dennis would be seen talking to herself, particularly when she was about to enter a room. She would pause at the door, attempting to forge a connection with the lights. She closed her eyes tightly, then lifted her gaze to the sky, and began to pray, as though she were speaking to God. Although it was difficult for her to express her feelings, she managed to always pray for strength for others.

Dennis wasn't quite sure how to address or interact with the orbs of light, or even how to speak to them. It felt odd to her to think of communicating with them without being able to see them, though gradually, she was getting used to saying things like, "Well, here we go, I hope you're all ready to work." Sometimes, when she felt more confident in her abilities, she would cast aside her shyness and command her orbs: "I want everyone to give energy to these people who need it so much."

Dennis had developed a routine for whenever she saw Mark or Tammy: she would embrace them and hold them close for a few seconds longer if the opportunity arose. This was the only way she had discovered to channel some of her energy to them. This method appeared to be quite effective as Tammy often remarked that every time Dennis visited, she felt great, and every time Dennis hugged her, she felt energized. Tammy didn't know what Dennis was capable of, and perhaps she never would, as Dennis had never thought to tell her or explain it to her. She could barely grasp it herself, let alone explain it to others.

Mark knew. He was aware that Dennis gave him energy every time she visited, not only did he feel it, but he also saw the beautiful lights that filled the room every time she arrived. These lights had clung to Dennis for many years, which, ironically, was the reason he had distanced himself from her in the first place. If he had understood their significance at the time, he would never have left Dennis. He loved her as he would never love another person again; in fact, he still loved her, even more than before.

Meanwhile, Dennis had gotten to know Sarah, a woman in her fifties who was quite friendly and easy to get along with. She was always kind, laughed frequently, and actively participated in group activities. However, Sarah had a past that she kept entirely to herself. Not even her doctor could pry any details from her. Sarah looked forward to every Tuesday and Thursday in hopes that Mark would encourage Dennis to mingle with the other residents. Sometimes, they just stayed in Mark's room and Dennis didn't interact with anyone else. Other times, they would both venture into the large common room to hang out with everyone, which was what Sarah eagerly anticipated.

Sarah's excitement was evident whenever she saw Dennis. She would practically run to greet her, always ready to help, offering her juice, coffee, or whatever else was available, all to make Dennis feel comfortable. She was attentive to everyone but showed special attention to Dennis.

As time passed, Mark's health continued to decline. Despite this, he more frequently insisted on going to the living room to spend time with the other residents even though he now relied on a motorized wheelchair to move around. Dennis often suggested staying put where she could just take care of him, but he always declined, preferring instead to be with everyone else.

Deep down, Dennis sensed that Mark wanted the energy that seemed to manifest with her presence to be shared with all the residents so that everyone could benefit from this incredible gift. Though, something was telling her that he was nearing the end of his days.

On one of the many days when Mark and Dennis planned to join the others in the large room, Dennis noticed the absence of Sarah. Most of the other residents were usually present, Sarah among them, but she was missing that day. Puzzled by her absence, she couldn't help but feel concerned, so she approached the nurses' station to inquire about her.

The nurse informed her that Sarah had been feeling very down since last Friday and had lost her appetite, which was worrying because this change had come out of nowhere. When Mark was occupied with his treatment around eight o'clock that night, Dennis slipped away to look for her. She walked down the hallway of bedrooms, searching for the door marked with Sarah's initials, and finally found it. The door was slightly ajar; Dennis rapped lightly to announce her presence and waited.

When no response came, she decided to enter. Inside, Sarah was sitting on the edge of her bed, absorbed in reading a book with headphones on. Dennis walked slowly towards her, making hand gestures to catch her attention without startling her. Sarah saw and put down her book and taking off her headphones.

"Sorry, Sarah, I didn't want to scare you," Dennis started. "I noticed you weren't with the others today and when I asked about you, they told me you haven't been feeling well. Is that true?"

"And you thought you could lift my spirits by dropping in with your buddies? Is that it?" Sarah responded, her tone suggesting annoyance.

"Excuse me?" Dennis replied, her voice tinged with shock. "I just wanted to check on you. I didn't mean to bother you, sorry."

As she turned to leave the room, Sarah stopped her and exclaimed, "No, I'm sorry, was being a jerk. Forgive me."

Sarah got up from her bed and walked closer to Dennis. When she got near, she jumped forward and gave her a big hug.

"I know," Sarah said. "I know about the energy you bring."

"What do you mean?" Dennis asked.

"The lights, girl!" Sarah explained, her voice uncharacteristically shy. "Those glowing orbs that Mark keeps talking about."

"Can you see them?" Dennis asked, her voice trembling slightly.

"Not like Mark," Sarah confessed, looking somewhat mystified. "He sees them with his naked eye. I, on the other hand, can only feel them. I know they're there, but to really 'see' them, I have to close my eyes."

Dennis, still puzzled, opened her mouth to ask another question, but Sarah cut her off.

"But don't worry about me anymore—I'm fine," she asked, changing the subject. "How are you?"

Dennis wanted to press the topic further, but Sarah made it clear that she had moved on. They left the room together, Sarah clinging to Dennis's arm, and walked back to the common room where the other residents, including Mark, were gathered.

As time passed and it came time to leave, Dennis found herself dwelling on Sarah's initial outburst. Her harsh words kept replaying in her mind, which convinced her that she needed to sit down and talk with her. Dennis was determined to learn more about Sarah, her reasons for being there, and what Mark might have known about her but hadn't shared.

When Dennis returned the following Thursday, she intended to ask Mark directly about Sarah. However, when she arrived at his room, she walked in and was shocked to see Sarah there, watching over a sleeping

Mark. After recovering from her surprise, Sarah spoke before Dennis could say anything.

"I know," Sarah exclaimed suddenly.

"You know what?" Dennis asked, surprised.

"I know what you want to ask," Sarah stated cryptically. "And the answer is complicated."

"What are you talking about?" Dennis pressed for clarity.

"You want to know what's wrong with me, don't you?" Sarah responded.

"Yes," Dennis said. "But how did you know that?"

"Nobody had to tell me. I just knew," Sarah explained. "Just as I knew you and Mark would meet again. I was the one who told him you would come, although he didn't believe me until you actually showed up."

"And how do you know this?" Dennis asked, growing increasingly more surprised. "More importantly, how did you Mark and I would find each other again?"

"That's the problem," Sarah sighed. "First, that's personal, and second, it's complicated."

"I don't think it could be any more complicated than anything I've been through," Dennis responded, her expression one of someone who had seen it all.

"Don't believe that, Dennis. You still have much to learn, much to understand," Sarah sighed, approaching her.

"I don't want to pressure you, but I feel like I need to get to know you. I can't explain it, but that's how I feel. Do you think there might be any specific reason why?" Dennis inquired.

"To be honest, I don't think so. No one can help me!" Sarah exclaimed.

"Well, I can't change your mind, but I want you to know that I'm here and you can tell me whatever you want," Dennis offered earnestly. "I don't intend to criticize or judge you; I just know that sometimes we need someone to listen, someone who understands that life isn't always all it's cut out to be."

After saying that, Dennis sat down near Mark just as he was starting to wake up. Sarah looked at her and reached out to touch her shoulder as a sign of gratitude.

"I want to know what your situation is," Dennis said, capturing Sarah's hand in her own. "I want to know your story. Please give me that chance."

"Dennis, we'll have a chance to talk very soon, I assure you," Sarah said as she left the room, seeing Mark open his eyes and try to settle into bed.

"Hi, Mark. You were sleeping when I got here and I didn't want to wake you," Dennis said.

"That's okay, Dennis," Mark responded. "I'm just happy that you keep coming to see me and after everything I put you through. What more could I ask for?"

"We don't need to dwell on those things, they're in the past. But you know, Mark, I'd love to know what you know about Sarah. I feel drawn to her, but I can't figure out why," Dennis asked, a hint of concern in her voice.

"I don't really know much," Mark explained calmly. "But when met her, she told me that you would come back into my life. That I would have the opportunity to see you again before I die. And that's exactly what happened. Other than that, she's been very sweet and is a good listener."

"Do you know if anyone comes to visit her?"

"No, not that I know of."

"How long has she been here?"

"She was already here when I arrived, and it's been about two years since then, right?" Mark said, sounding a bit uncertain of the exact time.

Dennis merely nodded but said nothing more. The rest of their time was spent between sipping tea and reading, which had become a comforting routine for both. After a couple of hours, Dennis saw Mark fall asleep and quietly left.

In the following weeks, Dennis had another session with Dr. Michaels, whom she also asked about Sarah. Unfortunately, she had little luck, as Rona was not Sarah's doctor. On top of that, Sarah's doctor was a very traditional, older man who did not discuss his patients' conditions with anyone. During their meeting, Dr. Michaels told Dennis "By the way, it worked. I've felt my son's presence much more strongly over the past few weeks." Dennis just smiled in response.

Their session had been straightforward, discussing only a few things, nothing in-depth. Dennis felt confident she was doing her best, and only time would tell if she was right.

Things changed when Dennis woke up that next Monday with a feeling of unease, sensing that something was amiss. The first thing she did was call and check that Tammy was okay, having left her in seemingly perfect condition the day before. Knowing how quickly conditions things could change, she'd rather be safe than sorry. Fortunately, everything was fine with Tammy.

Next, she called *The Stay* to check on Mark. The nurse informed her that Mark was in a delicate state and suggested it would be a good idea for Dennis to visit him that morning instead of waiting until Tuesday. Terrified at the thought that it might be their last moments together, Dennis knew no amount of preparation would ease the pain of watching him leave.

Dennis made a few calls to alert her office and Mrs. Harrison that she would not be able to come in to work and that she would be at *The Stay* in case anything urgent came up. Shortly after, she received a call from

Mary, asking if she needed help or anything else, assuring her to count on her support if needed.

Over the past few months, Mary and Dennis' relationship had grown significantly. It had started through their mutual connection with Tammy and later through shared workplace responsibilities. As time passed, their professional relationship blossomed into a friendship that strengthened with each shared meal, coffee, or casual encounter—precious moments for discussing things they didn't talk about with anyone else.

How can one describe the feeling of knowing that the person you love most might leave at any moment? They both understood that silent language; they looked at each other, no need for words or questions. They both knew the pain but also the strength that bonded them even closer.

In the moments before arriving at Mark's room, Dennis noticed she was accompanied by several orbs of light. When she arrived at the property, she saw them swirling around her. Then, as she stepped out of her car, she noticed another group by the front door, as if waiting for her to enter. A lump formed in her throat as she realized what she had feared for months might be happening.

"Good morning," Dennis said to the nurse at the front desk.

"Hi Dennis," the nurse replied. "It's nice to see you, Mark is in the intensive care room, you can head directly there. Do you know how to get there?"

"Yes, thank you."

Without further conversation, Dennis hurried to Mark. As she turned down the hallway, she saw Sarah sitting outside the room.

"Hi, Dennis," Sarah said.

"Hey, how's Mark?" Dennis asked.

"He's okay."

"How is he holding up?"

"Dennis, he's fine," Sarah reassured. "He's ready for the next step in his journey. He has seen it; I have shown him."

"Excuse me?" Dennis asked, confused. "What do you mean by that? What the hell is going on?"

Dennis was upset, feeling once again that everyone was keeping her in the dark, making her feel ignorant.

"Come, sit down, and I'll explain," Sarah said in a calm voice. She took Dennis's hand and pulled her closer.

When they were close enough, Sarah took both of Dennis's hands, placing her own hands-on top of them. Suddenly, Dennis felt relaxed, as if enveloped by a soft and cozy sensation. She let herself be carried away by this pleasant feeling, not thinking about what or why Sarah was doing this.

With her eyes closed, Dennis visualized a dense fog beginning to dissipate, revealing a clear path. It was a dirt road with grass growing on the edges under a blue sky, immaculate and cloudless. She began to hear birds singing nearby and the sound of a babbling brook. Dennis felt immersed in what she was seeing, as if she were more inside the scene than not. It all felt very real.

Suddenly, she saw a small house with a beautiful front garden, well-cared for and tidy. At the small gate stood a woman holding a little girl in her arms. Dennis felt a chill down her spine, and then the fog returned, allowing her to open her eyes.

"What was that? What was I seeing? I don't understand," Dennis said, confused?

"That's what's in store for Mark," Sarah said.

"What? What do you mean?" Dennis asked, looking directly at Sarah.

"For a long time, I have been able to see what others cannot, and I can also feel what others cannot."

"Like a seer?" Dennis asked, a bit incredulously.

"Not exactly. Let me explain: I can see what is to come, but I can also see beyond, on other planes. I can see how our lives change when we leave this plane. I know it's not easy to understand, but eventually, you will, just as you've understood other things," Sarah said as she sat down by the door. Dennis, who had been standing, eventually sat next to her.

"Sarah, be honest with me. Why are you here? Why did you appear in my life? Is there anything I should be doing for you? Can you see or know what's coming in my life?" Dennis had many questions and craved answers.

"Dennis, it doesn't exactly work like that. Some things I can influence over time, but this skill has come after many years of rejecting my gift. I lost my family because of it. No one believed or understood what was happening to me. After many doctors and wrong diagnoses, I realized that the best thing I could do was keep quiet. And for keeping quiet, I ended up in a psychiatric hospital. Eventually, some of the doctors thought I might benefit from this new institution. I fit the requirements for the new program."

"Requirements?" Dennis asked.

"The ability to be alone, unattended, no violent history, and no recent signs of recovery."

"Why not recovery? I don't understand."

"Didn't you know? This place is a hospice. The therapies and treatments are experimental. It's all privately funded, which allows them to offer these treatments as studies, searching for new treatments that might work and improve the lives of patients here."

"Sarah," Dennis started. "Has your condition improved since you've been here?"

"It's hard to explain," she responded. "But I started talking again. I still can't talk about personal things, but I've finally begun to speak with others without all the fear I used to feel, fearing I'd someone's future or past that they didn't want to know about."

"What happened to your family?"

"My spouse decided I was too much. We got divorced many years ago. I haven't heard from him since," Sarah replied with a sad expression, as she had never stopped loving him.

"Did you have children?"

"Yes. Two," Sarah said, her gaze distant.

"And they don't visit you?"

"At first, I didn't care," Sarah explained. "I thought it was better that way. When I was first hospitalized, I didn't want to see them. After I began to feel better, I missed them terribly. I asked for them, but my husband had just petitioned for full custody of our children, arguing that my condition prevented me from being able to care for my children.

"The judge agreed. I would have to prove I'd been stable for a long time before I'd be able to see them again. This made me angry with everything and everyone. I spent months in a bad state, so they put me on medications. Depression overwhelmed me, and I couldn't fight it. I grew lonely and silent.

"About eight years ago, a new doctor took my case and wanted to contact my family, believing family contact could help my condition. Their response was not what he expected; they didn't want anything to do with me. It took me even longer to understand why they didn't want to see me. Over the years, I realized I caused them a lot of pain. I was the one who abandoned them first. They were very young when I left, and I didn't see how it affected them. I left when they needed me the most, and that caused me to lose them."

"What was so serious that you ended up in a psychiatric hospital?" Dennis asked, hesitating a little. But she knew she had to ask, otherwise she would never know why Sarah had ended up at *The Stay*.

"They thought I was in danger of killing my husband."

"What?"

"You heard me," Sarah confirmed. "We'd been having problems for a long time at that point; we argued a lot. Then, I began to see things in my dreams and tried to talk to him about them. He told me I was going crazy. Our biggest problem arose because he did not want to acknowledge that something big was happening to me. I visited many doctors and all they thought to do was change my medication. Over the years, I've been on so many antidepressants and antipsychotics, and they all produced awful side effects. My misery to the point where I was no longer the myself. I cried all the time and no one understood me. I would see people and feel their approaching deaths. Sometimes I'd see souls lingering around people, waiting for the opportunity to pass on a message. And I tried to help by delivering those messages, but it was not the wisest thing to do. Quite the opposite, actually. Every time I tried, I made people think I was crazier than I was before. Eventually, I learned to hide within myself. Then, one day, I saw that my husband was going to get into a big accident. Naturally, I wanted to prevent it. I called him and searched for him to tell him to be careful, that what was going to happen could cause him serious harm. That was my misfortune."

"How come?" Dennis asked.

"Because, at the end of the day, my husband still got into that accident," Sarah answered. "And it was awful. It almost cost him his life."

"But what did you have to do with him having that accident?"

"He accused me of orchestrating the whole thing."

"Did you have something to do with it?"

"No! Of course not, haven't you been listening? I *saw* it. I saw the accident before it happened. All I wanted was to protect him, but he didn't believe me. On the contrary, he used it to get away from me. They said that I was a danger if I was not under supervision. After that, I just decided to shut up."

Although Sarah had tried to avoid it, tears rolled down her cheeks. When she finished telling Dennis the story, she broke out into sobs.

"In the vision you showed me," Dennis said, changing the subject. "I saw a woman and a little girl. You said that that's what's waiting for Mark. What did you mean by that?"

"Mark will go to another plane, just as we all will once we leave this one. Some go back to other planes where they used to live before they came here, others go to new places and take on new missions."

"Missions?"

"Yes, missions! We all have missions. We are beings of light in search of constant learning, always open to new knowledge, on this plane and in any of the others."

"Why are you so sure?"

"I've seen it," Sarah said, standing up with a confident tone in her voice. "And I've managed to understand it. But there are actually very few of us who can understand what we really are, where we come from, or what comes after this life as humans."

"How long have you been by yourself now, Sarah?" Dennis asked, still curious.

"Oh, a long time," she answered. "I don't remember the exact day, but it's probably been about twenty years now."

"And after all this time, after that doctor's last attempt, haven't you tried to contact your children again? They must be adults. If you want, I could try to find them and tell them about you, explain to them that you are better." Dennis's gaze was hopeful. She believed it was possible. Dennis always wanted to help others.

"No! Really, that's not necessary. From time to time, I see them in my dreams, and I know how they are."

"But don't you feel the need to see them and feel them next to you?" Dennis replied.

"Of course I do! All the time! But I know it's not time for that yet. I still know that one day we will be together again; we just have to wait."

Dennis looked at her, surprised at what Sarah was saying. What must've it been like, to see the future? How did she have the patience to wait around? Sarah's situation was unbelievable, Dennis thought.

"Sarah," Dennis said, standing in front of the window, looking at the green fields that were the courtyards of *The Stay*. "Is Mark dying? Is it true? Will he really go to that place you showed me?"

"Yes," she admitted. "He's going to leave us very soon. The others have been waiting for him for a long time. Of course, time doesn't pass like it does here in other planes—it's different. Mark was a being from another plane when he was given the mission to come into this world. There was something important he had to do."

"What was so important that he had to come into this world?"

"Dennis, we all, in one way or another, have missions to accomplish. We work together in search of universal peace. Of course, we do not know exactly how it will happen or when. We only have to think that everything we do is previously thought out and that our steps here, on this plane, are based on a universal plan."

Sarah took both of Dennis's hands and continued. "Dennis, Mark came to this plane to be your partner. Specifically for you. He was sent here to be your friend and support you while you grew up and became an adult. He was meant to be by your side and protect you so that you could continue on your path. I know it must be difficult to understand. I hope this information doesn't make you feel bad. I know that you have gone through many things that are very difficult to overcome and accept.

"I know, but I have also seen everything you have done for people who needed the light to keep living. The kindness you have developed, your attitude, and your great strength to overcome difficulties have been the results of the life you have lived. Every event in your life has been carefully planned, and, although that sounds crazy, it's true. You would not have been the person you are today if it were not for everything you've gone through. Life on this existential plane is a bit complicated, don't you think?"

Dennis was stunned trying to process all this new information. She turned and walked to the window again, looking at the ground outside. Nothing felt real. It was like a nightmare from which she couldn't wake up.

"It's true," Dennis said, eyes fixed on the horses outside. "Mark came into my life shortly after I lost my parents in that accident. Ever since we met, he was everything to me. We grew up together, made plans, and then everything fell apart. That's when the suffering returned. I don't need to relive it."

"Dennis, human life is not planned the way you think," Sarah said. "No one plans to harm others; no one wants you to suffer. Our missions within this plane are limited by the natural course of our own existence. Our souls will always be free and will go in search of the greatest knowledge, always! Don't forget that."

"So Mark will be going back to where he lived before he came to this plane?"

"Yes, Dennis, he's finished his mission here, and he must go back to where he came from."

"But," Dennis started. "The woman I saw in the vision looked as real as you and me. Why die then?"

"Deep down, we are different. What we call the soul is something incredibly beautiful and complex, composed of an energy that we do not yet understand. We evolve on every plane in which we exist. Wherever we go, it doesn't matter if it is the future or the past. Our soul shares the body of the person it has chosen before undertaking its mission.

"In other words, it's possible that the soul that inhabits our bodies today will go to other planes and coexist with other kinds of life that are not exactly like ours here. And it is also possible that, as a way of helping us to understand situations, our soul, or the soul that shares our existence, shows us other lives in a slightly more familiar way. This way, we can understand better. For that reason, I believe that what we see is somehow an image or likeness, which can help us understand what or how it will happen. But who really knows what follows?"

Dennis was worried that her life had never been what she thought it was. Instead, an infinite world presented itself in front of her—other lives, other beings, other places, many things that were difficult to understand. But when thought through carefully, they began to give a new color to what she knew as her own life.

"You know I see orbs, bright lights?" Dennis asked Sarah.

"Of course I know," Sarah said.

"Why can you feel them but not see them?"

"I don't know. I think seeing them in my dreams has helped me feel their presence when you're here or when Mark sees them."

"Was it Mark who told you that I could see these lights?"

"Yes. From the beginning, when he was able to open up, the first thing he told me was about the first light he saw. Then he didn't stop talking about them, especially after he met you again. Now he's ready to go; he just needed to leave you in good hands, and I think you already are, or am I wrong?"

"You mean Lucas?" Dennis asked, though it was obvious that Sarah was referring to him, after all, she'd seen him in her visions.

"Yes, I mean who will be your partner for a long time," Sarah replied.

"Does Mark know that he has a wife and daughter elsewhere?"

"Not specifically in that way, but soon he will see them, and he will be able to recognize them and remember his life and those who live in it. You don't have to worry about that; he'll be fine. He's going back home."

"Are you leaving, too?"

"Yes, soon."

CHAPTER 22

New Hopes

"Dennis," Mary said. "Do you want cream in your coffee?"

"No thanks," Dennis responded.

"It's good to see you less sad."

"I feel much better."

"How long has it been now?"

"Six months."

"Six months! How time flies. Anyway, I wanted to talk to you about organizing a meeting for Tammy. Her treatment has shown great results. The doctor says this month should have the last rounds of the second stage of her chemo treatment. Then we'll have to wait and see what happens. They have high expectations, though. So do I. I think we're looking at remission. Tammy's a fighter, don't you think?"

"Oh, absolutely. Tammy will get through this, I'm sure. And, of course, I'd love to help you. What do you have in mind?"

"Not much, really. With Eileen's being sick and feeling down and all the work around the office, it's been hard to find time for anything else. But I'd definitely like to do something to celebrate Tammy's last treatment. I know it may sound silly, but I feel the strength and determination my daughter has shown is admirable and deserves to be celebrated. Honestly, the whole family deserves to be celebrated—everyone has contributed a little to this battle."

"I completely understand. Don't worry, leave all the planning to me."

"Oh, Dennis, I don't know how to thank you," Mary said, pausing for a moment. "Actually, there's also something else. Tammy has finally decided to take my last name. So, I'd like to also give her a stake in this company."

"That's a wonderful idea. I know she'll appreciate that," Dennis replied, taking a moment to think about her next words. "Mary, I actually have something I'd like to tell you."

"Sure, what is it?"

"Well, I really just wanted to tell you that I'd like to keep Eileen company for a few days if wouldn't mind."

"Really? Are you serious?"

"Of course. You know that I still volunteer at *The Stay* even after Mark's passing. I quite enjoy spending time with the residents there, but I'd really like to spend some time with Eileen for a change. I think that do her some good, and it would also free up your schedule to take care of some other things. What do you think?"

"Honestly, Dennis, Eileen has been very depressed. She's locked herself in her room and has no desire to live her life. She's dwelling on death, nothing else matters to her right now."

"Then we'll need to help her feel better, don't you think?"

Dennis and Mary continued their pleasant conversation, tucked away in a corner of Mary's office. They sat at a table in front of a large window that looked out onto the small garden the groundskeepers tended at the back of the property. From there, Mary would spend time taking in the view—a beautiful landscape that always helped her to think or clear her mind whenever she needed inspiration. Most of the time, it where she sat to think about her daughter Tammy and everything concerning her. Her schedule was always so packed, so it felt nice having a place to escape and relax.

Dennis's offer was a gift. Mary felt very good about Dennis. It was something she didn't quite know how to explain, but she *felt* it. She had a feeling that Dennis had something to do with Tammy's recovery, but she just couldn't figure out how or why. The important thing was that Mary felt good about Dennis' involvement in their lives, and that was enough. She was convinced that Dennis was more than just a positive influence, not only on the people she interacted with, but in general. Even at work, every project Dennis worked on turned out well.

As for Dennis, her life right now could only be described as a roller coaster. First, everything was looking up—dreams and hopes, a promising future, and pure and innocent love. Then, everything changed. Her life suddenly went downhill, sufferings and disappointments flooded her day-to-day. Her life had become complicated, almost to a sinister extent, and although it seemed she would never get through it, things finally began to change. Life then became a little better, kinder, and more bearable. Everything began to look up again, but this time she knew there would probably be new challenges she would have to face. It would no longer be like before; she was more prepared and would not be caught off guard. But there were things left for one day in her future. Not everything new in Dennis's life was bad—incredible things were happening, and she knew it.

Dennis kept going to *The Stay*, visiting Sarah as often as she could. She made a promise to herself to keep doing it. Sarah had been her missing link, showing and explaining all the things Dennis didn't yet fully understand but was definitely willing to try to comprehend. Sarah also seemed to appreciate Dennis's presence and looked very excited every time she came to visit her.

They never really talked about what they had discussed that one morning. Instead, they spent time their doing activities together, going outside and walking, sometimes even just sitting in the garden and weeding. Incredibly enough, they even enjoyed just sitting in silence together.

Her relationship with Lucas had gotten more serious, too. Dennis felt loved again and, even more importantly, she had loved again. Knowing that Lucas wasn't going anywhere was a comfort to her. It only reaffirmed what she felt. He had had the patience to wait for her and, in the end, had managed to captivate her. Now it was time for them to grow and make plans together. But he also didn't want to pressure her; he always wanted to wait for the right moment and let things happen naturally.

Dennis had also decided to get to know herself better. She had become interested in meditation classes and had even begun following a Reiki master. This was something entirely new to her, but she was willing to give it a try. She had thought a lot about the things Sarah had said and the message the Light had given her. All signs were pointing at a certain energy within her that she could channel to help others.

For this reason, Dennis thought the best way to start was by learning to concentrate and control her anxiety. She wasn't wrong—this was the right path, and she would soon realize that this decision had been for the best. Just as before, it was a new step forward.

Three months later, preparations for the celebration finally began to take shape as Tammy's doctors had declared her to officially be in remission. Everyone was ecstatic about the news, Dennis especially. Knowing that somehow her energy had helped Tammy recover was a feeling she couldn't explain. Sure, the medicine had done its part, but, without a doubt, the energy Dennis was channeled to Tammy had made a significant impact.

Dennis felt compelled to make a real effort for Tammy's celebration. It wasn't just a family celebration; it was something much bigger than that. Mary had planned on promoting Tammy to a management position at the company. Eileen had decided it was time for her retire, leaving an open spot. In light of this, Mary thought it best to have her daughter by her side. This was just the right time for Tammy to start incorporating work back into her life, too, even if little by little. She was excited to feel busy again. Tammy had always demonstrated great potential for the Harrison company. Mary couldn't wait to see Tammy's reaction when she made her the offer.

The classes that Dennis was taking were yielding great results. She had never imagined being able to relax to such an extent that she could finally meditate. This revitalized her. It also helped her channel energy better. Her first few classes were spaced out a couple of times a month, but by her second month, she had signed up for weekly classes. She was learning a lot and really loved what she was doing. Her teacher even seemed to notice an innate energy within her. Of course, Dennis hadn't shared the details of her life with her teacher. Instead, she focused on internalizing what she was taught, and she was doing very well. She liked it and had decided to stick with it. Eventually, after breezing through the basic classes, she set her sights on the more complicated classes. She liked the idea of becoming a Reiki master.

She practiced with everyone, giving everyone a bit of her energy. Tammy was always laughing about Dennis, but she was also the one who had benefited the most from her energy. She felt like Dennis' hands were magical.

"I don't know what I would have done if you hadn't been in my life," she said to her one day.

"What do you mean?" Dennis asked.

"Well," Tammy replied. "You've been very important throughout this stage of my life. You've been like an anchor, keeping me grounded. I don't think I've had the opportunity to tell you how much I love you, Dennis."

Tammy hugged Dennis tightly, and Dennis squeezed back if not tighter.

Dennis' schedule had now become extremely congested, filled with events, projects, and meetings. But she always found a way to take time for herself. She had started reading and journaling. She didn't write anything significant, her journal was purely an outlet for her emotions and was also a good place to keep lists and reminders. She had also rekindled her love for reading after spending so much time reading to Mark, and she continued doing so with Eileen a couple of times a week.

Spending time with Dennis really helped Eileen to balance her advanced diabetes and her murky emotions. As an older woman, she had very little energy to fight, which had caused her to sink into a depression. Had it not been for Dennis' company, her situation would have been much, much worse. Dennis visited her during the week and really whenever else she could, determined to share her healing energy. She spent time reading to her and talking with her. Eileen seemed to respond well, and they even began to spend time outside, gardening together—not always for very long, but something was better than nothing.

The time Dennis spent with Eileen allowed Mary to visit her daughter. Mary was very grateful to Dennis, but she was still careful not to leave Eileen alone for too long. After all, they only had each other; Eileen was Mary's only family outside of Tammy. They had always been each other's rock, so it was a priority for Mary to be there with her.

For Dennis, sharing her time with people who needed it made her feel good. She still didn't know what the best course of action was—whether she was supposed to go out on the streets to look for people who needed her help or something like that. Sometimes, she even thought about putting up signs to advertise herself. But that was silly. Whenever she was stressed about this, she reminded herself that things would happen when the time was right. This encouraged her, and she tried not to overthink it. It was better to act and give her best every day than to waste her time trying to think up a better way to do it. After all, she still liked the volunteering she did.

Her ability to meditate was getting better. Dennis always looked forward to coming home, closing her eyes, and letting herself fly. Yes, she would close her eyes and let go. She could easily envision a clear blue sky, feel the wonderful breeze in the trees, and hear the sound of the sea if she thought about it. She often got so relaxed that she'd put herself right to sleep. One night, however, something different happened. During meditation, she decided to stop and get up. But, as she did, she ended up turning around and seeing herself. Her body was still there, on the bed, in the same position where she had settled to start the practice.

Dennis was struck with fear which quickly faded into curiosity. She raised her hands and noticed they were almost transparent. She floated close to her body, at least four feet off the ground. It was the first time she had ever truly seen herself, and it was *very* strange. She looked different from how she pictured herself, foreign. Just a body lay there motionless, unprotected, as if almost lifeless. But that body was hers!

After a moment, she realized she could move at will. It was as if processes of thinking and acting had been cut out entirely. When she felt herself thinking about Lucas, she ended up floating in the room where Lucas was, many miles away from where she physically was. She thought it was incredible that she was there, and it hadn't taken her a single second—all it had taken was a thought.

Lucas was engrossed in his paperwork, sitting at his desk. Dennis wanted to talk to him, but couldn't find her voice. So instead, she thought of his name. *Lucas, Lucas,* she called out with her mind. He turned his head immediately, sensing her presence. He could hear her voice and feel her, but something was off. When he heard her, he turned to look and saw nothing. He had to think again about whether or not he really heard her voice.

The feeling of having heard Dennis' voice distracted him from his work, and he decided to get up from his chair. He began to walk around his apartment, from corner to corner, but found nothing. Meanwhile, Dennis was still floating in the air, watching from above. Lucas was beginning to grow nervous. He knew he heard something, but not being able to see Dennis made him feel as if something bad might have happened. So he pulled out his phone from his pocket and dialed her number.

The phone rang, which jolted Dennis' from her trance. At first, she couldn't remember everything that had happened, but after a few minutes, while talking on the phone with Lucas, the images began to reappear in her mind little by little. She felt a chill run down her spine as she realized what had happened. She told Lucas she would call him later, saying something had come up, but the truth was she needed to put her thoughts in order.

After calling Lucas, Dennis sat down with her hands on her head. "What the heck was that?" She felt confused, but admittedly the experience wasn't been unpleasant.

After a while, Dennis came to the conclusion that she must've had an out-of-body experience. She'd heard people talk about this before and, after thinking about it, realized that their descriptions lined up pretty well. Dennis sat down at her computer to look up more information on the internet. She spent hours scrolling through pages and pages of experiencing before realizing it was late—very late—and she hadn't slept at all. She had spent her whole night researching, entirely too invested in the topic. Like many other things in her peculiar life, she had to learn to handle this without fear.

As soon as she saw her Reiki master again, she asked him what he knew about out-of-body experiences, describing the strange sensation she had felt. She didn't tell him the full story, though. Yes, Dennis had been learning to trust people, but she still had reservations. Her teacher told her that for some, it was a common practice involving mastery of the mind and total relaxation of the body. He admitted that he himself had never had such an experience, however.

"Dennis," he added. "These practices can be guided, but it's not good to do them alone when you don't know what you're doing."

"Guided?" Dennis asked.

"Yes, indeed," he continued. "It is done with dedicated meditation and practice. An individual can learn to control their time spent outside and learn how to return to their body without the danger of getting lost this way."

"Would you be able to help me with this?" Dennis asked, looking him in the eye. "I would like to try it. I feel something inside calling me to it."

"Of course," he said. "But it would require more personalized one-on-one time, so it would have to happen outside of class. Although I would only be able to guide you to start. After a while, you will have the skills to practice by yourself. But it is essential that you meditate for this at least twice a day. With practice and time, you will get to where you need to be."

"Twice a day, isn't that too much?" Dennis thought about being able to leave her body at will.

"I know, Dennis," her teacher said. "Typically, people who practice this type of meditation do it at sunrise and sunset every day."

Dennis seemed a little concerned as she already had little time to herself thanks to her busy schedule. However, she resolved to take it one day at a time, finding time when possible.

She was still a few weeks away from finishing her Reiki classes, and then it would be another year before she could take on the most advanced course. All these new activities, she felt, would strongly reinforce her skills and help better channel the energy she transferred to those who needed it.

She was unsure whether to tell Dr. Michaels about this. She still saw her, though less often than before. Should she keep this from her? The same question arose when she thought about Lucas. Should she tell him or not? Would she tell anyone or keep to herself? Dennis was never good at opening up to others, perhaps because she always tended towards solitude. What she wanted most at that moment was to follow Sarah's advice. She would wait for the moment to come. She was sure something would let her know whether or not to tell someone, and for the moment, she would continue learning what she could.

Dennis meditated every night and felt happy. She could close her eyes and visualize many things in her mind, seeing orbs of light with different colors and intensities, some even with beautiful golden glows. She felt she was finally getting to see the real energy behind those beings, which made her very happy. When she felt comfortable, she let her mind go, and if the conditions were right, she felt herself slipping away. Although she didn't have much practice yet and still felt a little scared, she seemed to be getting better at it. Just by thinking about someone, she could travel and be in the same place as that person. Of course, they couldn't see her, but that was okay. She was happy to be doing it at all.

Although Dennis made an effort to learn and read about this, she sometimes felt very discouraged. Some of these trips that occurred had no control at all. She traveled to places where she saw people she had never seen before, sometimes seeing people sleeping, other times awake. She saw children and adults, animals and places. Every time, she was only an observer.

"Dennis suggested that we could use the company garden and let the agency employees participate," Mary said, trying to come up with a series of excuses, attempting to hide the fact that they were planning a party to celebrate Tammy's recovery.

"Mom, I think it's excellent," Tammy said. "What a great idea. Of course, we should invite everyone. What do you think?"

Mary, back in the living room, scrutinized Tammy. That's when Tammy extended her arms toward her. Mary put her tea down on the coffee table and embraced her daughter. Just then, Dennis walked into the living room holding her own cup of tea.

"I take it this means you like the idea, Tammy?" She asked. "So you won't mind if I tell you that everything is already set?"

The three women stayed for a long time to talk about how all the preparations had been made to give Tammy her surprise. Things were going very well. Tammy felt renewed and full of life, and this gathering would be an opportunity to finally breathe deeply and just enjoy the moment. She always felt if it weren't for the support of everyone who had been with her along this hard road, she wouldn't have had the courage to go through everything she had been through.

Tammy was a brilliant woman, and despite everything she had been through lately, she felt very lucky. She had learned to love her mother deeply, her relationship with her loved ones was better than ever, and she had come to see Dennis as the sister she never had. Although life didn't end for her, she still came away from her illness with a valuable lesson: to cherish life for what it is.

As she practiced, Dennis had promised herself not to say a word, knowing she should not interfere with the course of the lives she observed during her meditations. Still, she wondered what the purpose of traveling and seeing those people or places was. That intrigued her a lot.

As expected, Dennis did the best she could with everything that came her way. She was determined to overcome any obstacle she encountered, so she constantly reminded herself to be patient, that the answers would come. And so, the days went by, and she willed herself to move on with her life.

Preparations were already complete for the party Mary had organized to celebrate Tammy's recovery. Now all that was left was to tell Tammy. Additionally, Dennis had been making arrangements for Sarah to attend the event. The friendship that had formed between them was very nice. Sarah was very easy to get along with and, having been alone for so long, was grateful for a friend. She was very enthusiastic about the idea of leaving *The Stay*, and it was evident that her recovery was in full swing. She was talking and laughing again, sharing her thoughts, and working with others very well. Going out and facing society would be one more step toward her final recovery.

Mary knew that Dennis had invited Sarah. They had the opportunity to talk about it at one of the many lunches that Mary and Dennis often shared. But in any case, it was still necessary to wait for the director of *The Stay* to sign the permission. This would only be the beginning; Dennis hoped that if this turned out well, she would be able to continue taking Sarah outside the facility.

Their newfound friendship was developing into something beautiful. Dennis, who unfortunately didn't know what it was like to have a mother or a sister, saw a mentor in Sarah. Sarah, for her part, felt that Dennis's friendship kept the hope alive that her children would forgive her and see her as a mother again one day. Many times, she wondered why she didn't have visions of her own children. Normally, she saw the lives of people she did not know, which often angered her, making her feel like something was blocking her ability.

Despite the friendship and trust that grew stronger every day, Sarah had not commented on her visions or dreams about Dennis's life. Sarah had decided to keep this information to herself. Dennis, who never asked but understood Sarah's effort, thought that this was for the best.

Mary and Dennis had decided to go together that afternoon to Tammy's house. They were excited to give her the news and hoped that she would take it well and be excited about her party. As Tammy was not in a position to get upset, they had decided to do it this way—a surprise but less shocking. They would tell her beforehand so that Tammy could prepare for it, as her life didn't need any more stress.

"Hi, Tammy," Dennis asked. "How are you feeling today?"

"I'm doing fine," Tammy said, showing her surprise at seeing her mother and friend together. "I feel very good, thank you. Did I miss something? How come both of you are here?"

"Actually, Mary and I just bumped into each other in the driveway. A total coincidence," Dennis said. But she wasn't good at lying, and Tammy immediately became very suspicious that the two women were up to something.

"Hmm" Tammy said. "What a funny coincidence. Could I offer either of you something to drink?"

"I'd love another cup of that raspberry green tea," Dennis responded. "I loved it last time."

"Mom, what are you up to?" Tammy asked, searching Mary's face for a reaction. "I wasn't born yesterday! I can tell something is up."

"It's nothing, really," Mary said. "It's just that Dennis and I had an idea and wanted to ask you to see what you thought."

"An idea? What kind of idea?" Tammy asked curiously.

"We thought it would be nice to get together for a small celebration. Nothing big, of course, just something with the family as a way to celebrate the latest good news," Mary said, walking to the kitchen. "You know, a lot of people have been following your journey, asking for you and how your progress is going."

"Of course, I know that. And believe me, I am very grateful," said Tammy. "But what exactly do you mean by 'celebration'?"

CHAPTER 23

Dennis and Sarah

The company's gardens had been transformed with large, beautiful white tents, designed with windows and access doors. Inside, the tents were all connected, with three in total. The middle one was the largest, featuring a beautiful crystal chandelier, hung at least four stories high. The lighting was spectacular, with colors ranging from deep blues to soft pinks. Flowers adorned every visible space, while tables and chairs were arranged in the side tents. In the center, a small platform was set up—not very large, but sufficient for the musicians, leaving the rest of the space open. The catering company handling the event had conveniently set up in one of the offices on the first floor of the building, just steps away from the tents.

Everything was ready, and now they only awaited the arrival of the guests. Among them were the agency's employees, some personal friends of the owners, as well as Tammy and her entire family, who were now closer than ever. Dennis had invited Dr. Michaels, her new friend Sarah, and, of course, Lucas. Although it was still early, Dennis felt restless. She always liked to maintain control over every situation, and this occasion was no different. She had worked tirelessly for days to ensure everything was perfect as planned. This event was shaping up to be a magnificent and memorable gathering, hopefully leaving everyone with pleasant memories.

Dennis sat in one of the chairs at the entrance of the main tent, observing every detail to ensure that nothing was out of place. She had invested too much time, as always, in seeking perfection. Feeling the need to occupy herself while waiting for Lucas, who had gone to pick up Sarah, Dennis glanced at her watch. It was still a long time before four in the afternoon, the set time for the other guests to arrive.

It wasn't yet noon, and Dennis hoped Sarah would have the chance to spend some time in a less crowded setting to ease into the environment. She also looked forward to sharing some quality time alone with Sarah and Lucas and anticipated striking up a conversation with Tammy, Mary, and others. After all, it had been quite a while since Sarah had been with people outside of *The Stay*.

At exactly noon, Lucas's car pulled into the parking lot of the Harrison Advertising Agency. Dennis spotted them from a distance and quickly ran to greet them. She kissed Lucas warmly before he even had a chance to finish closing his car door, then walked to the other side and opened the door for Sarah.

"Hi Sarah," Dennis said. "It's so nice to see you. Welcome!"

Sarah, looking as lovely as ever, smiled broadly and replied, "Thank you, Dennis."

"Come! Let me show you around. I hope you like it," Dennis added proudly, eager to showcase her hard work. She had poured her heart into this event, and her knack for decoration was on full display.

"Dennis, everything is beautiful! I love it," Sarah said, her eyes scanning the entire area, taking in every detail.

Dennis hooked her arm through Sarah's and led her around, pointing out various features and chatting about everything. Then she asked,

"Sarah, would you like to see my office? I'd like to show you where I work."

"Of course, take me there! Let's see your creative space," Sarah responded happily.

Dennis extended the invitation to Lucas, not wanting to leave him alone, but he had already settled under the shade of one of the beautiful willows in the garden.

"Not this time, my love," Lucas replied with a smile. "I'll wait here, and when you're done, we can grab a bite. I'm already hungry."

Dennis nodded and left with Sarah. As they headed to the top floor where Dennis's office was, Lucas sat back, watching some of the caterers begin their preparations in the kitchen. Occasionally, he glanced up at the highest floor, as if expecting to see Dennis looking down at him through the window. But she probably hadn't reached the top yet—the elevator wasn't the fastest. Besides, she was likely more focused on showing Sarah her office than looking out the window.

Lucas's thoughts were many and deep. He knew he had fallen in love with Dennis and couldn't imagine life without her. He had so many plans, but they never discussed them in detail. Something always interrupted the conversation, forcing him to change the subject. However, he had resolved to find the right moment to talk to her and share what something hadn't yet managed to say—his future with her depended on it.

Meanwhile, in her office, Dennis and Sarah were enjoying a rich conversation. Dennis spoke about her projects, and although Sarah was well-acquainted with what Dennis was passionate about and her future aspirations, she listened attentively, showing genuine interest in everything Dennis shared. Dennis was showing her some models of one of her most recent projects when Sarah suddenly wandered over to the window and stood there, gazing down for a while.

"Are you okay?" Dennis asked, puzzled. "Did I say something that made you uncomfortable? I swear it wasn't intentional."

"No, not at all. It's just…" Sarah paused, watching the people moving around on the first floor. "I was just thinking about what my life might have been like if I hadn't been so weak. Maybe I could have accomplished things like you have. Dennis, you should be proud of who you are and all that you've achieved."

"Don't say that, Sarah. You are an amazing woman, and I'm sure that if you set your mind to it, you can see how fulfilling your life has been. We all face challenges, and it's true that not everyone knows how to overcome them. Those who do are rare, believe me. We all need good advice, a helping hand, the unconditional support of someone close. Without that, it's hard to fight back."

Dennis' threatened to well up with tears.

"Don't worry, Dennis," Sarah laughed, and Dennis joined in. "I understand that very well. It's just that, for a moment, I wondered what my life would have been like if I didn't have this gift. I often question its purpose. Sometimes I get confused and think about things that have no answer. But it's okay, believe me. Sometimes, though, I can't help but wish I were just ordinary and normal." Sarah paused.

"Have you noticed?" She said, pointing out the window. "Lucas hasn't stopped watching us—he's looking for you."

"Oh, yeah! There he is," Dennis waved to greet Lucas, who smiled in return, finally catching her attention, which made him very happy.

"Are you in love with Lucas?" Sarah asked, waving to him as well.

"In love? I think so," Dennis replied with a deep breath. "I feel I've finally found the perfect person. He's been so patient with me and has shown me so much love. He's made me believe in love again. He's everything to me—if this is what being in love feels like, then yes, I am."

"And how do you feel about Mark now?"

"Mark..." Dennis began. "I still miss him a lot, and I would like to see him again. It's something entirely different, though. I can't really explain it. Even though I feel much calmer now, it will never be the same. He was... well, I don't really know what he was. What I do know is that when I lost him, it felt like losing a part of myself. And when I found him again, that part of me was still missing. It's as if that piece of me died, disappeared when he left. And even though I've come to terms with everything that happened, I never regained what I lost.

"When Mark died, I found the strength not to grieve for him anymore, especially with Lucas by my side through everything. It wouldn't have been fair for Lucas to see me suffer over Mark."

Tears began streaming down her face.

As Dennis wiped her tears and adjusted her hair, Sarah looked at her as if she wanted to say something. But she knew she couldn't speak yet—it wasn't the right time or place. It was difficult to keep a secret, but she reminded herself that all would be revealed in due time.

Sarah had the gift of seeing things others couldn't, and sometimes she had visions when meeting people. However, she never knew anything about them in advance—these visions occurred randomly and in person. Dennis had shared so much about everyone who mattered to her, allowing Sarah to feel as if she knew them too. But this was merely a feeling, as Sarah had no idea what she would feel when she finally met the Harrison sisters in person. She hadn't had any visions or premonitions that could give her more insight into them. This wasn't unusual for her, as there were other people close to her for whom she'd never had visions about either.

While Dennis was away, Lucas had decided to lend a hand to those setting up the flowers and other decorations. Time passed and, without him realizing it, it was already after 2 in the afternoon. And he still hadn't eaten anything yet—even his hunger had been forgotten!

Dennis and Sarah had returned by then. Dennis began searching for Lucas and quickly spotted him.

"I was looking for you—I got worried when I couldn't find you. I'm sorry I took so long; we lost track of time," Dennis smiled as she approached her boyfriend and kissed his cheek.

"Really? I thought you'd just forgotten about me. I was here, sad and alone, just wondering when someone would bring me something to eat," Lucas replied, smiling as he teased Dennis with sarcastic humor.

"Don't say things like that—it makes me feel awful!" Dennis said, defensively, not realizing he was only teasing. "You know that's not true! I care a lot about you. It's just that time got away from me, y'know?"

"Don't worry about it, I was just joking," Lucas hugged her tightly and kissed her to stop her from apologizing. "You don't need to be so serious. Now, shall we eat something? Before the guests arrive and leave us with nothing?"

They both laughed.

The three of them walked to the kitchen area, filled their plates with snacks, and sat at the entrance of the first room. The breeze was pleasant, and so was the company. They talked and reminisced about old times, creating one of those moments where nothing seemed more important than simply being there, enjoying the moment. Sarah knew this—she had to savor this time, as she had seen it before in her visions.

While they were still seated at the table, Dennis spotted Mary's car and ran to greet her. When she opened the door, she was surprised to see Eileen accompanying her.

"How wonderful to see you here, Eileen!" Dennis exclaimed. "I'm so happy you decided to come. You've been missed."

"Thank you, Dennis," Eileen replied with a smile, a rare but welcome sight. "I think being here today is important for me—after all, my family will be here."

Dennis chose to celebrate the moment rather than ask too many questions—everyone had been hoping Eileen would return to the person she had always been.

"Of course it is, and we're all very happy," Dennis said as she helped Eileen out of the car. Lucas and Sarah had come over to say hello as well.

Sarah knew Mary mostly from everything Dennis had told her, but she had never seen her before, the same going for Eileen. When Dennis introduced Sarah to Eileen, she shook her hand and felt as if a wave of immense sadness fell over her. At that moment, Sarah realized she was sensing the sadness that Eileen carried with her. It was difficult to understand what was causing this deep sorrow without knowing anything about Eileen's life.

Sarah squeezed Eileen's hand a little more firmly, which made Eileen look directly into her eyes. Whatever she saw in Sarah's gaze was something she couldn't comprehend at the time—it was a different feeling, something hard to explain. Sarah, in turn, experienced a similar sensation, feeling both confused and surprised. It was as if they had known each other for a long time, despite this being their first meeting.

They all ended up sitting at the same table, waiting for the other guests to start arriving. Mary was anxious to see Tammy, with whom she had spoken just a few minutes ago, and who was expected to arrive soon. Mary hoped Tammy would arrive before the other guests, as she wanted some time alone with her daughter and family.

It was a delightful sight to see them all talking and smiling. Lucas held Dennis's hand on his lap, while Eileen found Sarah to be a pleasant conversational partner. Mary entertained them, all the while keeping an eye on the doorway, waiting for Tammy. The banquet service had already set the tables with rich platters of sandwiches and antipasti. The bar was ready for guests to order cocktails.

This evening was shaping up to be one of the most enjoyable moments for these people. Tammy would arrive soon, and the celebration would begin a beautiful evening filled with laughter, conversations, and good times that would be cherished in their memories. However, this didn't mean everything would be perfect forever. Some would have to learn to appreciate the meaning of the here and now, which is often more important as it forms the basis of future memories.

Tammy's car finally arrived, and Mary jumped up from her chair to greet her.

"Hello, my dear girl, how are you today? I'm so glad to see you—I've been anxiously waiting for you!" Mary's happiness was evident on her face. Tammy's husband and children got out of the car, all very happy to be there together as a big family.

After greeting Eileen and Dennis, it was Sarah's turn, who had stood back, hoping to be the last to greet them. After all, she was the only one who wasn't family. Dennis was the common bond among all these people, but Sarah? She knew she was an outsider.

"Tammy, let me introduce you to my friend Sarah," Dennis said cheerfully, reaching out to invite Sarah over.

Tammy listened to Dennis and extended her hand warmly to greet Sarah. "Hi Sarah," Tammy said, shaking Sarah's hand. "Dennis has told me a lot about you. I'm glad to see you here."

Sarah remained silent, managing only a small smile before lowering her gaze. Dennis immediately sensed that something was off but chose to diffuse the situation by inviting everyone to move on.

Mary took her daughter by the hand and led her to one of the central tables, telling her she had something important to share.

"Attention, attention, please. Everyone, I'd like to have your attention for a moment. I have something I want to say now that we're all here with family," Mary said, tapping a fork against the glass she held, signaling for quiet.

"I want to thank all of you, especially God, for allowing us all to be here today. I also want to express my gratitude for all the good wishes and support you've given my daughter, whom I proudly invite to join me here by my side.

"Tammy, dear, life has given me the chance to be by your side again and, most importantly, the chance to be your mother. You've also allowed me to be part of your family, and for that, I'm deeply grateful. But in addition to everything, I preface that this isn't meant to pressure you, but I won't accept a no."

Mary laughed.

"So don't think too much—just say yes. From this moment on, you'll be part of the Harrison Agency, not as another collaborator, but as one of the owners. I've given you part of my shares and rights, and I want you to accept them because what we've built is both mine and yours."

Mary looked at her daughter with deep affection, silently praying she wouldn't refuse the offer.

"Oh, Mom, you didn't have to do this—you really didn't," Tammy replied, pausing before continuing. "Yes, it's true we've all worked hard—not just you and I, but also Eileen, whom I can finally call my 'aunt.'

"I also want to include Dennis, who has been incredibly important throughout this entire process, not to mention everyone else who's been close to us. In short, we've all worked hard, and I can proudly say that I will continue to work here for the rest of my life. This will be the place where my children will find their roots, and the children of others who join us in the future. Mom, thank you. I know how much this means to you. And for my part, what's important to you, I want to be important to me too. Cheers!" Tammy exclaimed, smiling as she and the others toasted to the health of the occasion. Tammy was now officially one of the owners of the Harrison Agency.

As Tammy smiled and hugged her mother, Dennis couldn't help but glance at Sarah. She knew something was wrong because Sarah wasn't as happy as the others—she was only pretending. Dennis wondered if Sarah felt something was out of place or if something was about to happen. She looked for the right moment to pull her aside.

"I'm going to get something I need, will you come with me, Sarah?" Dennis asked.

"I can go," Lucas offered, surprised that Dennis was asking Sarah instead of him.

"No, that's okay. I'd rather go with Sarah so she doesn't feel alone," Dennis replied.

"Oh, I see! Sarah can't feel alone, but I can? Do I not matter? I get it," Lucas said, teasing Dennis with mock indignation.

"Don't start. I'll make it up to you later," Dennis responded with a smile. But Sarah had already stood up, knowing exactly what Dennis would ask her. The real question now was whether she should tell Dennis the reason for her sadness or keep it to herself.

There were no situations more distressing for Sarah than these. Not knowing what to do when she felt such overwhelming sadness was the worst. Since shaking Eileen's hand, Sarah had been grappling with that strange sensation she couldn't comprehend or shake from her mind.

She felt an immense sadness, leading her to believe something might be wrong with Eileen or someone in her family. But she couldn't see beyond the surface—there was nothing to help her understand the source of the great anxiety she was feeling.

This feeling was unlike anything she had experienced before. She thought back to when she met Mark and was overwhelmed with a sadness that seemed insurmountable. But after a short time, she had seen what was coming for Mark, and things had changed. She considered other situations but found nothing that resembled what she was feeling now.

It was difficult for her to tell her friend, who was only trying to help, that she felt something unsettling with Eileen. How could she burden Dennis by confessing that she sensed a deep agony and sadness coming from Eileen? No, that was out of the question—especially now, during a family celebration. She couldn't be the one to bring additional worries. No, it was clear that she had to keep quiet.

"So, are you going to tell me why you're so sad?" Dennis asked as they walked hand in hand toward the main building.

"It's nothing serious, really. It's just that seeing everyone together made me a bit nostalgic. I thought of my husband, my children... Just that. I'm sorry if I've caused you any concern," Sarah replied, lowering her head.

"Are you sure? Look, I don't want you to feel bad. You know I wanted you to be here so you could relax and share this time with us. You're very important to me, Sarah.

"Really, what does that guy matter anymore? He's in your past, and now we're working on making your future much brighter. I'm sure we'll get you reunited with your children soon." Dennis managed to captivate Sarah's attention, making her feel a bit better, though deep down, she had a sense that something significant was on the horizon.

That evening, everyone laughed and enjoyed themselves in a way that hadn't happened in a long time. Many of the agency's employees were there, taking turns talking with Tammy and her family. Tammy had always maintained a very good relationship with her colleagues, being not only a great boss but also someone who always made time for anyone in need. That's how Dennis had known her since the first day she attended her class at the university. How could she not? Tammy had become her mentor from that moment on, now a close friend.

Dennis took comfort in what Sarah had told her—after all, there was nothing to indicate that something was wrong. They returned to the table and, seated with the others, enjoyed the dinner that was being served. The music played beautifully—one of Mozart's symphonies, perfectly complementing the elegant decoration with its floral arrangements and soft lighting.

As dessert was served, Sarah noticed that Eileen wasn't taking her eyes off her. She wondered if she had done or said something that caused Eileen to stare so intently. It made her feel self-conscious, especially when she saw Eileen walking toward her. Sarah felt that something was wrong but couldn't pinpoint what it was.

"Would you mind if I sit with you for a while? I feel quite alone at the other table," Eileen asked.

"No, of course not," Sarah replied, pulling out a chair for Eileen to sit on. As she offered her hand to steady Eileen, she felt something very strange—something she hadn't felt in a long time. It was a sensation that flooded her being, something buried deep in her memory, but she couldn't quite place it.

She quickly withdrew her hand, feeling a bit uncomfortable with the sensation but also curious about why she felt it. It wasn't accompanied by any vision of Eileen's life—not even a glimpse. She couldn't see anything about her. Eileen didn't notice what Sarah was feeling because she didn't know anything about Sarah's abilities. But there was a reason, something very important, why Eileen had made the effort to sit with her.

Eileen started a conversation with Sarah, and although Sarah wasn't the most talkative, she answered Eileen's questions. Eileen knew she couldn't be too direct, so she stuck to easy topics. She commented on the place, the music, and the food. As the conversation went on, Sarah began to feel more comfortable talking with Eileen, and later with Mary. Both women had always seemed very serious and distant, not easily approachable. But, after some time, they were actually very pleasant and easy to talk to. The situation no longer felt strange, at least in Sarah's mind.

Suddenly, Rona passed by the table, greeting everyone with a cheerful demeanor. She was pleased to see Sarah sharing time with new faces. When she saw Dennis, she couldn't help but give her a hug.

"Hi Dennis, how are you? You look very happy," Rona said, hugging her tightly.

"I'm doing very well. You look great, too—I'm glad you're here," Dennis replied warmly. She had grown to love Rona very much, as she had been a crucial support throughout this entire process. Dennis had come to understand something essential: Rona Michaels, despite her career and devotion to science, was also a human being who believed in her and in the inexplicable things that sometimes happen.

Rona had many reasons to be happy that day. Not only was she enjoying the celebration, but she had also made a very important decision in her life—one that would finally bring her inner peace.

"Dennis, I want you to be the first to know," she said with overwhelming happiness. "It's important for you to understand that, despite everything, my doors will always be open to you."

"Rona, what's this about?" Dennis replied, her tone filled with concern.

"It's nothing to worry about, but I'm leaving medical practice next month," Rona said calmly.

"Oh no! Don't scare me like that—what do you mean? You hadn't mentioned anything!" Dennis stood up from the table and moved closer to Rona.

"Has something happened? Do you need help?" The questions poured out of Dennis faster than Rona could answer, while the others at the table watched with growing curiosity.

"No, it's not like that, but I'm happy to share the news," Rona continued. "I've decided to open my own holistic center and retire from psychiatry."

Voices around the table erupted in comments and congratulations on Rona's decision, including Dennis'.

"That's wonderful! But you nearly gave me a heart attack! I can't believe you kept it so quiet. You know how much your help has meant to me—don't even think about going somewhere far away, because I'm not letting you go," Dennis smiled, joining in with the others.

"Thank you, Dennis. Don't worry—I'll stay in touch, and I'd love for you to visit the center. There's still a lot to do, but I'm full of plans, and I could really use some suggestions from you."

Suddenly, the sound of metal clinking against a crystal goblet echoed through the room. Mary was standing in the center, ready to give a speech. Everyone turned their attention to her, ready to listen. She began by thanking everyone for being there to share such an important moment for the Harrison family—Eileen, Mary, and now Tammy—without forgetting Dennis, who was already considered part of the family. Mary expressed her gratitude for the support she and her daughter had received from all those who worked at the agency, emphasizing that the Harrison Agency was what it was thanks to everyone's collective efforts.

The speech continued for a few more minutes before Mary called Tammy to join her. Once Tammy was by her side, Mary addressed everyone again:

"I know many of you already know this, but I want to officially announce that Tammy has decided to take my last name. From this moment on, she is and will be Tammy Harrison, part of this agency not only as an employee of high qualifications and experience but as my daughter. Welcome, Tammy Harrison!"

The room buzzed with excitement after the news was announced. Everyone raised their glasses and toasted, celebrating what felt like the beginning of a new, joyous chapter. But not everyone shared in the happiness. Sarah, forced to keep her feelings to herself, couldn't bring herself to tell anyone—not even Dennis, with whom she had a strong friendship. Fear of causing unnecessary worry kept her silent.

CHAPTER 24

The Truth Hurts

"Don't you find it strange that everything went so well?" Dennis asked.

"What do you mean?" Lucas responded; a bit confused.

"The party went so smoothly. Everything was so calm."

"Calm? What do you mean?"

"Well, you know, nothing out of the ordinary happened. Everything was just... calm."

"Ah! You mean because your lights didn't appear?" Lucas replied with a teasing tone.

"Don't be funny—you know what I mean. Sometimes it's hard for me to understand. Sometimes I want to see them, and sometimes I don't. But yes, I guess that's what I meant. Wasn't that strange?" Dennis insisted.

"Strange?"

"Yes, strange!" Dennis exclaimed with a shaky tone. "There wasn't a single light the entire day. In fact, I think I haven't seen them for several days now. Have I stopped seeing them? Did they leave me? Did they leave all of us?"

"My love, why are you so worried about the lights? I think, deep down, you miss them and can't live without them." Lucas got out of bed and walked to the bathroom, where Dennis was getting ready for work, looking at herself in the mirror.

"Don't joke about this—I'm being serious."

"So am I," Lucas said, hugging Dennis from behind, trying to make her smile with his playful expressions. He loved her deeply, but he was afraid that something distract. from the relationship they were building. Even though Dennis had freed herself from the pressures of her past, and Mark was no longer getting between them, he still worried. He couldn't help it—he knew everything could change in a second, and it tormented him.

Their relationship had reached new milestones. Things had progressed naturally. Before they knew it, they were practically living together, planning their futures together, just as Dennis had once done with Mark. But Lucas was always afraid of doing or saying something that might make her change her mind, causing everything they were building to suddenly fall apart. The thought of that was terrifying for Lucas, especially since he kept avoiding a small but significant detail that he hadn't brought up yet in their time together. He was certain that once Dennis found out, she might reject him and hate him forever.

For weeks, Lucas had been haunted by the same thought. He didn't want to break the promise he had made to Dennis—not to read her mind without permission. They had both agreed it was best for them, a way to try to live as normally as possible and deal with the inexplicable only when necessary.

Lucas understood this very well and respected with Dennis' boundaries, but it was difficult for him. What bothered him the most was the secret he'd been keeping from her. He knew he'd have to tell her eventually, one way or another, and he prayed for the strength to do so.

Dennis finally left the apartment that morning, still a bit unsettled by her worries. It didn't bring down the happiness she felt in her relationship, though. She was finally certain that she was in love again and that she was completely loved in return. Lucas had become her other half, and he complemented her perfectly. Although life was unfolding in unexpected ways for her, she understood there would always be surprises—she knew that well. What she didn't quite understand was why her lights had suddenly disappeared.

As Dennis drove to work, she found herself lost in thought. Her eyes were fixed on the horizon, where she could almost see the bay and the park where she gone on her first date with Lucas, a place they still visited often. They both loved the scenery there. Today, everything was eerily quiet—she didn't even have to wait for a single boat to cross. The drive was smooth and uneventful.

When Dennis usually arrived at the office, she would greet everyone she passed. But that day, she didn't see many familiar faces. Only a couple of people were in the building. As she walked into her office, she felt something was off, but she couldn't quite pinpoint what it. She paused, took a sip of her coffee, and stood by the window, gazing down at the garden.

Dennis looked back on Tammy's party—from the moment Sarah arrived to when Mary announced that Tammy would officially join the leadership of the company. She mentally replayed the day's events step by step, and without realizing it, she drifted into a trance, her mind wandering without her even noticing.

When she became aware again, she found herself floating in Tammy's room. She looked down at her, noticing Tammy sitting there, seemingly lost in thought. Then she shifted to Sarah, and she saw her from afar, walking outside the room. Next was Lucas—she could see him driving his car, listening to music with a smile on his face, which made her smile too.

Then she saw herself sitting in her office, and a flood of images began to play like a slow-motion movie. She saw Sarah sitting at the table on the day of the party, and across from her, Eileen, who hadn't taken her eyes off Sarah. *Why was Eileen so curious about Sarah?* Dennis wondered. She then watched as Eileen suddenly got up from her seat and walked over to Sarah, sitting down next to her.

Eileen's look toward Sarah was very intense. Then, she saw Tammy sitting next to her husband, wiping tears. He held her hand tightly, clearly overcome with emotion, grateful to have Tammy by his side, alive and well after enduring the horrible nightmare of almost losing the love of his life.

It was just at that moment that Mary called Tammy to accompany her to share the news with the others. Dennis realized that she was observing all the things she hadn't noticed that day—the details she couldn't have seen with her own eyes. Suddenly, she saw herself sitting next to Lucas. While she was talking, Lucas, who was beside her, kept his hand in the pocket of his jacket. Inside, he held a small box, turning it over and over. But Dennis' mind had been elsewhere, and it seemed he had felt that too. Something in her heart told Dennis she knew what that little box contained. She felt a pang of regret, realizing how many opportunities Lucas had suggested—moments for them to be alone—that she had completely ignored.

She didn't have much time to dwell on it, though, as she suddenly noticed two small lights discreetly peeking out from behind Tammy and Mary. There they were! Those blessed lights she was so worried about. Did they appear as part of her trance? Or was she just not meant to see them that day? A strange feeling, almost happiness, washed over her as she realized that her lights hadn't left her. They were still there, and she began to understand that this was important for her—perhaps part of a final realization where everything converged. Perhaps that was exactly her life: a collection of situations and experiences that could only be lived as an observer, letting go of the need for answers and accepting that each moment had special meaning for the people who made up her social circle.

Not far away, she saw her psychiatrist friend, Rona, at another table talking happily with some other guests. The new project and the changes she was working on were definitely the path that would lead her to feel happy and satisfied with her life. Surely her son had received the message, and it was he who was helping her feel better in this new chapter of her life. Dennis felt glad that Rona had made that decision.

It became clear to Dennis that everyone at the party had their own personal takeaways, bringing her to reflect on what hers had been. She concluded that it wasn't just one moment, but all of them. Everyone there was part of her life, and they were all very important to her. This is what had transformed her existence—from the beginning with Mark, then Tammy, Mary, and Eileen, and of course, Sarah, her dear friend. And she couldn't leave out Rona, who had helped her immensely in understanding herself. And, of course, Lucas, who had restored her hope in love. They were all significant parts of her life.

The phone rang suddenly, snapping Dennis out of her trance. She felt a little groggy, but after a couple of minutes, she remembered everything—each of those images she had seen in her mind. This made her feel very good, especially when she remembered that her lights hadn't left.

After collecting herself and trying to get back to normal life and work, her thoughts wandered, bringing with them intrigue. She thought about Eileen and Sarah—what was the connection between them? Why was Eileen so interested in Sarah? She also thought about Tammy and her husband—were those tears of happiness that she had seen? And Lucas—what was in that little box? Dennis smiled. The butterflies in her stomach told her that maybe she did know what was in there.

Her workday went smoothly. That day, she planned to go straight home and take some time for herself. After all, it felt like she'd been observing her friends all day. She grabbed her bag and left her office around 6 o'clock. As she drove away, her phone rang—it was Lucas. Dennis turned on the speaker and answered.

"Hello?"

"Hey! I was on my way home and was wondering if you'd like to have dinner with me tonight."

"Hmm," Dennis murmured. "I'm already on the highway. But I can turn around, it's not too much trouble. I can meet you at our place in a little while."

"Magnificent, I'll wait for you. Ah, if you don't see me in the parking lot, I'll be inside the restaurant. I think might need some water for my ibuprofen—I've had this annoying headache since noon. I just hope it's not the start of a cold or something."

"Oh, I didn't know you weren't feeling well. Why didn't you say anything?"

"I don't think it's anything serious. Maybe I just need to eat?"

"Are you sure you don't want to rest instead? I could cook something for you if you'd like."

"No, honestly, I feel like the fresh air by the bay will do me some good."

"Okay, I'll see you there in about fifteen-twenty minutes."

Dennis looked for the first exit off the highway to turn back toward the city and meet Lucas. This distracted her from all other thoughts, and at that moment, the only thing on her mind was the man who stole her heart.

Every time she talked to him, it was as if something magical happened inside her—all her worries disappeared, and she focused entirely on seeing and hearing him. Sometimes Dennis realized that she had fallen deeply in love with Lucas and felt a little afraid that something might separate them. But other times, a smile would appear on her face, and a sigh would escape from within, making her feel like she was floating on air.

It wasn't long before Dennis was crossing the bay, parking at the park. It wasn't too late, but the crowd had thinned out—there weren't many cars left. When she entered the parking lot, she immediately spotted Lucas's car and parked hers right beside his.

Dennis got out of the car and headed to the restaurant. Just as Lucas had said, he was already inside, waiting for her. She took a few more steps and saw him—there he was, sitting on one of the benches by the water's edge.

"Hello, love," Dennis said as she approached Lucas. "What are you doing out here? I thought you'd be inside. How's that headache?"

"Hi. I thought the fresh air might help. I've taken a couple ibuprofen already. I hope they start working soon." Lucas replied. "You got here quickly. Weren't you far away?"

"No, thankfully, I was only a few miles out when you called."

"Do you want to head inside now?" Lucas suggested.

"Do you think we could stay out here a bit longer? We can eat in a little while."

"Of course, I don't mind," Lucas agreed.

They sat down next to each other. Lucas took Dennis's hands and began to caress them nervously. "Is everything okay?" Dennis asked, sensing something was troubling him.

"What do you mean?" Lucas responded, trying to play it off.

"You seem nervous—I could see it from a mile away."

"Nervous? Me?" Lucas said, trying to deflect.

"Yes, don't pretend you don't know what I'm talking about—you know exactly what I mean."

"Oh, Dennis," Lucas said, his voice filled with hesitation. "I really don't want to talk about it."

"What do you mean you don't want to talk? If something's bothering you, don't bottle it up. Tell me what's going on."

Dennis became more serious, turning to look at him, waiting for an explanation.

"Well," she persisted. "Here I am, sitting and waiting for you to say something. What's wrong? Don't make me start guessing, because I can jump to some crazy conclusions."

"No, Dennis," Lucas said. "I just... I don't know where to start."

"Well, start at the beginning. You're making me nervous now."

"I only ask that you listen and don't interrupt me. It's taken a lot for me to gather the courage to tell you this," Lucas said, his voice heavy with emotion.

"Lucas, please don't tell me you're breaking up with me," Dennis said, her worry growing. "If something's wrong, we can talk about it. I don't understand what could be so serious."

"Please, let me speak," Lucas pleaded. Dennis leaned back, her expression serious.

"Okay, then. Speak."

"Well, I've been lying to you," Lucas admitted. "You heard me. From the very first day—right here on this bench, the day we met—I didn't tell you the whole truth."

Dennis's confusion and intrigue grew, but she remained silent, just staring at him.

"I told you about myself—about my abilities, things no one else knows. I shared details about my personal life, but there was something I didn't tell you, something that's haunted me all these months. I've fallen madly in love with you, Dennis. I can't live without you, but every day,

I've been terrified that this secret would come out and you'd judge me for not telling you sooner.

"Do you remember when we first met? When I told you about my ability to hear other people's thoughts? I ended up discovering something a bit later—something about your parents' accident and everything you went through after losing them."

"Of course I remember, but, please, get to the point," Dennis insisted. "I don't know what you're trying to tell me, but whatever it is, say it now."

"It was a couple of days later, in the middle of the night. I woke up with a clear vision of something I hadn't remembered well. When I woke up from my coma years ago, I'd been left to die—until that very second when I was disconnected from the machine. The truth is, the soul that belonged to the boy in the coma had left this plane long ago. Lucas Verdi was the teenager who, under the influence of alcohol, caused the accident that took your parents' lives. Lucas Verdi is partly to blame for the suffering you've endured and for why your life has been so complicated. But before you say anything or judge me, please just hear me out."

Dennis's face went pale, her expression frozen. She couldn't quite process what she was hearing.

"Lucas Verdi died that day, too, and his soul returned to where it came from. I know this might sound crazy. But, in life, we all play the parts assigned to us, like actors in a play, and we're only in the scenes we're meant to be in," Lucas explained, watching her closely.

"I know you must have a lot of questions," he continued. "And I can probably only answer a few. Like, if Lucas Verdi died, who am I? I'll tell you this straight up, though I think you'll start to understand things that weren't clear before.

"Dennis, I'm your soulmate. This isn't some silly joke—it's the truth. I would never knowingly do anything to make you suffer, but life on this plane is strange and complicated. While we're here, we can only accept the conditions imposed on us and try to survive how we must," Lucas continued, searching for any reaction from Dennis, who remained almost motionless.

She didn't react.

"I know this sounds like a betrayal on my part, but believe me, it's not. I would never do anything to hurt you. I live for you. I waited so long to find you. I knew when I came that I would have to abide by destiny, and I waited... and waited... until one day, I saw you.

"You were supposed to come home with me that day. We've been together since the beginning of our lives, and though we sometimes separate while fulfilling our roles, we always come back to each other. But this time was different. That day in the accident, you were left behind. You were the only survivor, although you weren't supposed to be.

"I don't know what happened, but I had to be by your side. I searched for a thousand ways to bring you back to me, but it was impossible. This time, you had to walk your path alone, without me. When we come to this plane, we can't remember where we're from or who we really are. That's why it's been so difficult for you to overcome all these challenges—because they weren't part of your mission. I don't know why you didn't come home. I don't know why you stayed here."

Lucas took a deep breath and continued his story. "I had just barely regained consciousness and began to make my own memories, when you started coming to the cafe. I know it sounds hard to believe, but your light woke me up. The day I was disconnected from the machine, it was you who gave me the confidence I needed to move forward with my plan. Time passed, and when I saw you for the first time in the café, I didn't remember you right away. But eventually, I realized I had seen you before. There was something special connecting us—more than just a memory. It was like an invisible bond between you and me."

Dennis, pale and unable to speak, got up from the bench and tried to leave, but Lucas took her hand.

"Dennis," he pleaded. "If there's anything—any small feeling you have for me—please let me finish. Don't shut me out; you need to hear this. I don't know how else to ask you to stay and let me finish, except to beg you, for the love I feel for you, for the love we have for each other."

Dennis turned to look him in the face and said, "I don't know why you've told me all this. Can't you see I'm hurt? How can I stay by your side? How can I believe what you're saying? I don't understand anything!"

Dennis cried inconsolably, overwhelmed by sadness.

"Dennis, please, let me continue. Don't go," Lucas pleaded, still holding her hand, not wanting to let go. She looked at him and reluctantly sat down on the bench again, but she couldn't stop crying.

"I know you don't understand. It was so difficult for me to know that this body—this person—caused the tragedy of your parents' deaths. I didn't expect that when I had decided to come to this plane, I'd accepted the condition of living in the body that was the source of your pain. I thought that somehow, I could get you to understand or believe in me. But even without fully understanding why you stayed here after the accident, I began to approach you and offer you my unconditional love, little by little. Then I realized that you had to be here—there were others who needed you, like Mark and Tammy. You've been so important to them; you've been the light they needed to move forward. After all, that's what we are. We're here to help souls find their way home—that's all."

Dennis stopped sobbing for a moment to ask Lucas a question.

"Lucas, what exactly do you mean by all this?"

"I mean that I begged for a way to return to this plane, and the only possible way was to take the body of Lucas Verdi. That's what I did. It took me time to come to terms with it. At first, I only knew that my coma was the result of a car accident in which two people lost their lives, but I didn't know it was your family until shortly after I met you. It was then that I had a vision in which you, as pure energy, came to see me once again. That's when I remembered what connected us and why I had come to this plane."

"And what did you say you've come here to do?" Dennis asked sarcastically.

"I've come to share your life and then bring you home—to the place where we are from, to the place where all those other souls who are always by your side come from, those lights you call orbs."

Dennis looked at him without blinking. There was something in his words that made her feel he was sincere, but her rational mind still resisted, making her feel that it was all a lie. How could this be real? She knew there were things that couldn't be explained. She knew that Lucas could hear her thoughts. She knew the lights she saw were real, and Rona's testimony had confirmed she wasn't crazy. But despite all this, and despite all the evidence Dennis could find, she felt she couldn't believe him. She felt that Lucas was simply trying to excuse his irresponsibility in killing her parents.

How could she forgive or even overlook the fact that her parents died because of that body? Dennis couldn't think clearly at that moment, and it was hard for her to imagine a time when she might even try to understand.

"Lucas, I think I should go. It would be better that way," Dennis said in a subdued voice, her tone conveying the depth of her devastation.

"I can't let you go. You have to believe me! *I* wasn't the one who caused that accident. What's more, you shouldn't know that there's life beyond this world. You have to understand that this is just a part of your journey. We've always understood this well—I don't know how else to make you see it. You have to find a way to remember, to go beyond this human perspective. Please, try."

"I can't, Lucas. I'm too confused. I don't know what to believe or what I should understand. Right now, all I know is that I'm sitting in front of a man who isn't who I thought he was," Dennis said, her voice trembling.

She pulled her hand away from his and walked off, leaving Lucas behind, consumed by the greatest pain he had ever felt. There were no words of comfort for Dennis, and none for Lucas either, who had risked everything—at least in this life—to make Dennis believe him. Only time would tell what would happen and whether she could cope with the immense pain in her heart.

CHAPTER 25

A Heart That Beats Again

Day after day, Dennis tried to keep going. She wore a smile as a shield, protecting herself from any questions that might arise. It had been almost two months since she last saw Lucas, but not a moment passed when she didn't think of him. Dennis wished she could stop feeling the way she did about Lucas. She longed to hate him, to unleash years of pent-up emotions, and finally declare that she had found the source of all her sorrows. But, on the other hand, she hadn't shed a single tear over what had happened. It was as if something deep inside her wouldn't let her feel that way. Most of the time, she refused to entertain anything Lucas had told her—all those confessions about their connection. It was something she didn't want to dwell on, but she knew, deep down, that at some point, she would have to.

Life moved quickly for everyone around her, and Dennis thought no one had noticed her separation from Lucas—or at least, that's what she hoped. She wasn't ready to explain herself to anyone, but there was one person she couldn't hide from, no matter how hard she tried. Sarah knew, maybe she had always known, but when Dennis asked if she knew what would happen next, Sarah simply replied, "It's your life, and you must live it. Everything will be fine, you'll see."

Dennis continued with her daily routine, keeping herself busy. The only thing she stopped doing was going to *The Ranch* on Saturdays to avoid crossing paths with Lucas, but everything else remained the same. However, when night fell and she went to her room, was saddened to not see him waiting for her in their bed. Those were the moments when everything hurt the most, when she couldn't help but feel an overwhelming need to find him because she couldn't live without him. Every night, Dennis felt like she was choking, struggling for breath, and she fell asleep praying for the strength to understand everything that had happened.

Visits to Eileen continued, and so did Sarah's, though Sarah never commented on the situation, despite her likely having seen something in her visions of Dennis's future. But both women remained silent, and that made things easier. Meanwhile, Eileen had become determined to grow closer to Sarah.

It all seemed a little strange, perhaps, but Sarah liked Eileen very much and didn't give it too much thought. Still, one thing did catch her attention: why couldn't she feel or have any visions about Eileen? Sarah had no visions, no intuitive feelings about her, even when they were together.

At first, Sarah thought the visions might come later, as time went on, but Eileen had been visiting her often—almost three times a week—and still nothing. It was as if she couldn't see or know anything about Eileen.

Everyone had noticed Sarah's recovery. She no longer felt like just another patient at *The Ranch*. She helped early in the kitchen, preparing breakfast, assisting the nurses' station, and ran around distributing books. She kept busy with countless small tasks, and the days flew by. She went to bed tired, but it was the good kind of exhaustion that came from being productive, from helping, from living in a normal way.

This brought a smile to her face and joy to her heart. Something particular had her feeling more alert and alive—feeling productive and in control of her actions without being burdened by the visions and sensations that had once forced her to withdraw from everyone and everything.

Similarly, Eileen hadn't felt this good in years—decades, even. She couldn't quite explain it, but she knew this surge of positive energy came from being around Sarah. From the first day she met her at Tammy's reception, Eileen felt a reflection of something very special and dear to her, something so private that even she couldn't fully understand why these feelings were emerging now, after meeting Sarah.

These past two months had stirred up deep emotions in Eileen, so much so that one day, while dining with Mary, Eileen dared to talk to her sister about things from the past that seemed to have been buried long ago.

"Mary, do you have time for us to talk?" Eileen asked her sister.

"Of course. I always have time for you. What's on your mind?" Mary replied.

"Something's been happening to me, and I don't know how to deal with it," Eileen began.

"If you're worried about not going to work anymore, don't be. You know you're my sister, and I'll do everything I can to support you. Besides, it's not that necessary—believe me, there's plenty of help there," Mary reassured her.

"No, it's not about that. I don't feel the need to go back to work, at least not that kind of work. I gave forty years of my life to the agency. I think it's time for new minds to take on those roles. I don't want to be the one holding the agency back with an old-fashioned mindset."

"Oh, Eileen! I didn't realize you didn't want to go back to the agency. You have every right to want a change of environment. Though it's hard to believe you want to retire and do nothing."

"Of course not. You know I'd wither away if I did nothing. But sometimes, I feel like my life has been so empty... especially after everything that happened. I never thought about myself again. I hid behind that big desk and just dedicated myself to work—it was the only thing that eased my pain for years."

"Yes, it's true. It was all very sad, and I think it's easier to lock those feelings away than to face them. I've seen how things have been with Tammy, but I'm happy that, somehow, relationships have been mended and we're more united than ever. So, I understand your suffering."

"Yes, I know, and I'm happy that Tammy was able to recover and overcome the horrible things that woman did to her because you were her real mother, and you can't deny it. I always thought her stance was absurd, but after a while, I didn't know what else to think. The only thing I can tell you is that my love for my niece is as great as yours is for her. But that's not really what I wanted to talk about—it's more about something else."

"Something else? What do you mean?" Mary asked.

"My...personal tragedy—that's what I mean."

"Oh, *that*," Mary replied, uneasily. "You know, I don't remember much about it. I was just a kid when it happened, and everything happened so quickly. I couldn't even be by your side until you finally decided to return. What happened? It's been so long...I never said anything or asked because I thought you had decided to leave it behind. Am I wrong?"

"No, you're not wrong," Eileen sighed. "In a way, that's true. You were about to turn eighteen when it happened—I remember because they wouldn't let you leave the country to come and be with me because of the legal documents needed. As your legal guardian, I couldn't authorize them since I was out of the country. It was a complicated situation. Everything happened so fast that I never fully understood what or how it all happened. I just felt like I had been broken in two."

"Yes, I remember you left me in charge of the agency in its early days. I hadn't started college yet, but you had already graduated, gotten married, and had your baby girl. I still remember her lovely eyes and curly hair. Peter was still in school, right? He hadn't graduated yet?"

"No, it was his last semester. He was France for an internship, which is why I left. I remember he met with people from his internship. They were offering him a job. It was a great offer. We were happy—we had made plans and were likely to end up living there. The place was beautiful, and we found a small house that could accommodate us. We had many hopes and dreams, and remember, we even talked about taking you with us?" Eileen's eyes filled with a special sparkle as she recalled those memories.

"Of course, I remember—I couldn't bear to be far from you or Andreas. You were my family."

"But that day, I felt something…weird. And I told him not to go to work. But he insisted and left in the car with Andreas while I stayed home. Hours passed, and I started to worry. I couldn't understand why it was taking so long when he had just gone to get something to eat. When I couldn't take it anymore, I went down to the reception, and that's when I found out. I wanted to die right there—I didn't understand anything. My mind just kept getting foggier with every second I stood there, listening to those people talk."

"How did you learn that Peter and Andreas were involved in the accident?" Mary asked gently.

"The man said that a truck had lost control, crashed through the barrier, and hit the car in front of it," Eileen replied, her voice trembling.

"Why are you remembering all this again, Eileen? What's happened to make you revisit these sad memories?"

"It's just that sometimes I think I didn't stay there long enough, that I shouldn't have given up the search. I could never understand how they found *nothing*—only the charred remains of the car after it fell into the ravine," Eileen said, tears rolling down her cheeks.

"But you did everything you could. Besides, it had been almost a year—there was nothing else to find. Don't blame yourself for something that's impossible to know. Do you remember how many others searched for weeks and months? If they had been alive, they would have been found, and they would be here with us today. But that's how life has been—very hard on us. That's why we've worked so hard to help and understand the pain of others, right?" Mary said, trying to comfort her sister.

"Yeah. But I have this feeling that I can't get rid of. Andreas would be a woman today—maybe married with children or who knows. I can't help but think that so many things could have been different. I felt Andreas was with me for a long time. I felt her close to me—I saw her in my dreams, I could feel her warmth next to me. But as time passed, one day, I stopped feeling her, and I thought maybe I was forgetting her. But no, I never forgot her—I just tried to keep those thoughts to myself. Even then, I never felt that connection with her again."

"Maybe that was the moment when you finally accepted that they were gone, don't you think?" Mary suggested, searching for a less painful explanation.

"No, I've never believed that Andreas was dead. Something told me she was alive. Even though the feeling never returned and I never felt that connection with her again, my heart always believed she hadn't died."

"And what has led you to think about all this now, Eileen? I don't mean that you don't think about it—I'm sure, like me, that it's never forgotten, only kept in the heart."

"It's Sarah."

"Sarah? What happened with Sarah? You mean Dennis's friend, Sarah?" Mary asked, sounding a little confused.

"Yes, her."

There was a silence before Eileen continued.

"It may seem crazy to you, but hear me out."

"Okay, you're making me anxious. Please, tell me."

"The day we went to the reception, and I got out of the car and saw Sarah for the first time, something incredible happened. My heart started pounding, and my hands began to sweat. I couldn't stop looking at her— I'm almost certain I must have made her uncomfortable." Eileen paused, her voice trembling with the weight of her confession.

Mary only hummed, clearly worried.

"I struck up a conversation with her, and we spent the rest of the evening together. It was amazing! That feeling I had for Andreas so many years ago came rushing back. My heart was pounding, and I felt a special warmth."

"Could it be that Sarah only *reminded* you of what Andreas might have looked like today? Maybe because of her age? Don't you think?"

"That's what I thought at first, but it's something deeper—something within that doesn't let me sleep anymore."

"What?" Mary asked eagerly.

"I've continued to spend time with Sarah. I visit her every other day at *The Ranch*. We talk, we walk—we have a wonderful time together. But she's very reserved. She doesn't like to talk about herself, and I haven't dared to share much about myself either. I think it wouldn't be appropriate—she might think I'm crazy or feel like she's being pursued, and I don't want that to happen. It would be horrible. But I can't understand why the connection is so strong, why the warmth she radiates feels exactly like what I felt when Andreas was with me. And there's more—the other day, we were walking in the gardens at *The Ranch*. We arrived at the stables and watched the people riding horses. When she leaned on the fence, she raised her left arm, and there on her forearm was a birthmark, just like the one Andreas had—a butterfly, in the exact same place. It even seemed to be the same size, though it may have grown with her. Can you believe it?"

"Are you serious?" Mary questioned. "Are you really thinking that Sarah might be Andreas? This is very serious, Eileen. Let's calm down a bit and take a step back. Apart from how you feel or what Sarah makes you feel—and beyond the birthmark on her arm—what else do you know about her?"

"That's the problem—nothing. I know nothing about her. It's impossible to have a deep conversation with her. She doesn't budge."

"Maybe we could do some research—ask some questions. What about Dennis? Don't you think we could learn something through her?"

"Well, yes, I've tried. On the occasions I see Dennis, I've tried to steer the conversation toward Sarah, but Dennis is very private about her, too. The only thing she always says is that she loves Sarah very much and believes she'll soon be fully recovered and back to a normal life."

"Maybe I can talk to her and ask some other questions," Mary offered. "But if you feel this is so important, I won't question your feelings. You know you can count on me, and I'm glad you came to me. Don't worry—we'll find the answers. But I must confess, just thinking that Sarah could be Andreas…I don't know how to describe it. I have so many questions, and I can't deny that I would be overjoyed. But I just want you not to harbor false hopes—not now, after so many years have passed."

The two sisters continued to talk for hours until the light of dawn reminded them that a new day was about to begin.

Mary felt the same urgency as Eileen, if not more. The need to know the truth created incredible anxiety in her, so she decided the first thing she would do was call Dennis and start investigating what was behind Sarah. There had to be something—her sister's feelings couldn't just be dismissed. Mary couldn't accept that Eileen was simply reaching a point in her life where past events were resurfacing without cause. Though it was possible that her brilliant and dedicated older sister was being overwhelmed by memories of the tragic accident in which Peter and Andreas lost their lives, Mary couldn't fully believe that.

Perhaps sadness, loneliness, and memories were taking over Eileen's mind—it was a possibility. But it was difficult to accept that a woman so sharp and devoted to her work was losing her mental stability. Mary wondered more than once, *Have I neglected her? Does she feel lonely?* This was also possible.

So many things had happened that nothing was planned anymore. Everything was handled day by day, especially after Tammy's illness had turned their lives upside down, forcing other priorities to the forefront.

The next day, when Dennis arrived at the office, she received a message from Mary asking to see her. She went to Mary's office almost immediately.

"Good morning, Mary," Dennis greeted her as usual.

"Good morning, Dennis."

"Has something happened? You sounded concerned in your message."

"No, don't worry. I just wanted to talk to you, but there's nothing to be alarmed about."

"Phew," she sighed in relief. "I thought something might be wrong with Tammy."

"No, God forbid! It's something different."

"Ah, if it's about the art festival and the presentation, don't worry. The staff team we have working on it is excellent. We have almost everything ready, and by the beginning of next week, we should have a clearer preview and can start preparing for the competition once again. You know I thrive on challenges, and participating in this is incredible. I'm also very grateful for all the opportunities I've had, especially the support the agency has given me."

Dennis clearly had no idea what Mary wanted to ask her.

"Oh, Dennis, don't worry about that. One of the best things that has happened to all of us is meeting you, starting with my daughter. She has received so much support from you. She even says that she couldn't have moved forward without your energy—her words. Tammy says you're her guardian angel here on earth."

"I just love her very much. She was my mentor. Anyways, Mary, why did you call me? What's on your mind?"

"Oh, I need to talk to you about Sarah."

"Sarah? What about Sarah?" Dennis asked, her tone tinged with concern.

"Nothing's wrong—it's just that Eileen has grown curious about her, and I know you're her friend too. I'm just being cautious. I don't want Eileen to get involved in something complicated, you know? I don't know much about Sarah, and I'm concerned for Eileen—that's all."

Mary struggled to find the right words without revealing the real reasons for her concern.

"Ah, well...I met Sarah a long time ago, before Mark died. For as long as I've known her, she's been at The Ranch. But if you're worried about what kind of problems she might have, I can assure you that you can rest easy. Her problems were circumstantial, and she eventually chose to stay there. But in these last few months, she's made a lot of progress.

It's as if she was never sick to begin with. She understands things and is ready to return to a normal life," Dennis said with confidence in her voice.

"I see you've become very attached to her."

"Oh yes, Sarah is amazing—a wonderful woman. Her soul is pure, but her feelings are very fragile, which is why she's been there. But she's full of life."

"What else do you know about her? How long has she been there? Where is she from?"

"It's hard for me to answer all those questions because, like Tammy and you, Sarah has become like a sister to me. But I get that you want to know everything about her. After all, there are a lot of people out there who might take advantage of Eileen's vulnerability and good heart."

"Sure, but I'll tell you what I'm really concerned about later. For now, I just want to know more about her, and I appreciate your trust. You're not obligated to share anything, so I'm really grateful for whatever you can tell me," Mary said, a little calmer.

"Well, I'll tell you what I know. You might be wondering if she has a family—yes, she was married and has two children, who are teenagers now, I think. But they don't have contact with her. When her husband divorced her, he took custody of the children and told them many things lies about her. The children grew up distant from her, and that's why she took long to recover; she retreated into a state of loneliness. She didn't talk to anyone, just stayed silent. But recently, things have started to improve. In fact, as soon as she was transferred to The Ranch, her recovery began. She's no longer taking anxiolytics or any other medications—just receiving weekly therapy sessions."

"How incredible! That she has a family but couldn't see her children grow up—how unfair," Mary said, clearly surprised.

"Yes. Unfortunately, her life has been quite traumatic. I don't want to go into more details because that's more personal, and I don't want to violate the trust she's placed in me."

"No, Dennis, not at all. I understand perfectly—this information is more than enough."

"I'm glad you see that Sarah isn't a bad person."

"Oh no! I never thought Sarah could be a bad person. I have full confidence in you, and knowing that she's your friend, even more so."

"I'm glad to hear that. If you have time for something else, I wanted to run something by you: I have an idea I'm thinking of proposing to Rona."

"Yes? What did you have in mind?"

"I'm going to ask Rona if it's possible for Sarah to work at her new practice. I believe it could be a great opportunity. Sarah has shown strong signs of being ready to reintegrate into society, but the hardest part for her is that she has no one. That's why I want to help her, and I'll let you in on something."

"Yes? What's that? I hope you're not planning on telling me you want to go work with Dr. Michaels, because I won't accept it."

The two women smiled.

"No, not at all. But I think they might call to verify my credentials because I've listed you as a reference," Dennis said.

"Yes? And what are my references good for? I won't give good references if it means you're leaving us for another job—no, no, and no," Mary joked, smiling.

"No, Mary, of course not. I wouldn't leave this job for anything in the world. But, I do actually need your references because I've applied for a mortgage loan. I want to buy a bigger apartment so I can offer Sarah a room and help her get back on her feet."

"You're so kind! Would you really do this for Sarah? Does she mean that much to you?" Mary asked, finally beginning to understand the depth of Dennis's feelings for Sarah.

"Yes, very much. She's someone very important to me."

"Well, consider it done. There's nothing more to say. Your judgment is worth a lot to me and to everyone here. And, Dennis? Could I ask you for a little discretion on this subject?"

"Oh, of course. You know I don't like to gossip. Although, I could tell Tammy—what do you think? Do you think she might think her mother is being too cautious?" Dennis teased, making a few playful expressions. Of course, she was confident—Mary wasn't just her boss but someone she deeply cared for, as well as being the mother of her friend and mentor.

Dennis didn't think for a second that there could be any other reason why Mary might be interested in knowing more about Sarah, but there was. There was an incredibly important reason, one that could change the lives of several people.

Everything Dennis had told Mary was important because it implied that Sarah wasn't crazy or someone with terrible problems—certainly not a criminal or anything like that. But where did this leave Mary in her quest to investigate Sarah's origins? It left her in the only possible place—she would have to seek help, and that pointed to a private investigator. She couldn't go around asking everyone what they knew about Sarah—that would be inappropriate. Mary Harrison didn't handle things that way. She was a woman who planned and executed her actions meticulously.

By the end of that week, Mary had already spoken to a private investigator that someone she trusted had recommended. She hadn't told Eileen anything, not wanting to raise her hopes. It was difficult for her to believe there could be any real connection between Sarah and Eileen's daughter. The police in France had exhausted all resources in searching for her brother-in-law and niece, extending the search for a long time. Mary thought it was impossible, but at the same time, something pushed her to seek more information.

Mary had talked to Tammy, and they decided to have dinner together that Sunday. It was a good opportunity to start a conversation with Sarah, so Mary called Eileen and suggested she invite Sarah to dinner. Eileen thought it was a great idea. Naturally, the invitation extended to Dennis, though she hesitated because no one knew about her separation from Lucas yet. Still, she said yes, figuring she'd come up with something to explain his absence. She'd figure it out, even if her heart wished none of this had happened.

Eileen visited The Ranch and told Sarah about the dinner. Sarah was touched that Eileen wanted to invite her but said she didn't want to intrude on their family plans. She assured Eileen she didn't feel bad about it, but Eileen insisted it wasn't just a family gathering. She considered Sarah a friend and enjoyed her company. She also mentioned that Dennis would be there, trying to make Sarah feel comfortable enough to accept without feeling pressured. But Sarah kept declining until, she saw Eileen was getting into her car.

"Eileen, wait!" Sarah shouted out, overcome with the compulsion to act.

Eileen stopped immediately.

"I don't want you to think I'm ungrateful, please, but I also don't want you to feel like you're responsible for me or anything like that. I appreciate your friendship more than you know, but I don't want to intrude."

"But you wouldn't be intruding at all. I've been very lonely, and now that I've made new friends, I want them to be part of my life, that's all."

"Really? You don't feel obligated because you see me here?"

"No, not at all. If you weren't the person you are, we wouldn't be spending time together, I guarantee that." They both smiled warmly.

"Then I'll ask for permission and let you know so your driver can come. It's still difficult for me to get out on my own—I wouldn't know how to get to places farther away than the stables," Sarah said with a small laugh.

"I know, don't worry. Just let me know, and the driver will be there at around 12 noon. Does that work for you?"

"Yes, of course, I'll let you know."

CHAPTER 26

Finally, Clarity

Dennis glanced at her watch impatiently, still sitting in her car a couple of blocks from the Harrison residence. She had mustered the courage to attend the dinner, but on the way, something made her feel very uncomfortable. She wasn't sure what to do—whether to go forward or come up with an excuse to avoid seeing the faces and expressions of everyone when they saw her arrive without Lucas.

The day was beautiful—clear skies and perfect temperatures for enjoying time with friends and good conversation. But Dennis felt terrible, almost sick. She was afraid they wouldn't believe her excuse that Lucas couldn't come because he had decided to cover a co-worker's shift. She didn't really know what else to say, and that was the first thing that came to mind.

Finally, she turned off the engine of her car and continued on her way. Within minutes, she arrived at Mary's house, where the first person she saw in the garden was Tammy, walking arm-in-arm with Rona. Rona? Dennis wondered what Dr. Michaels was doing there. She couldn't help but be surprised, thinking that everyone already knew about her situation or, even worse, that they would try to console her for what she was going through. But Dennis was very wrong, as she would soon realize.

"Hello, how are you? You both look great out here. Enjoying the weather, right?" Dennis said, trying to hide her nervousness, assuming everyone already knew about the turmoil she was experiencing.

"Hi, Dennis. Yes, you're right. If we don't take time to enjoy what's important now, who knows if we'll get the chance tomorrow, right, Rona?" Tammy replied.

"Yes, absolutely," Rona agreed.

Dennis had come over to greet them with a hug and a kiss on the cheek—Tammy, who was her friend and mentor, and Rona, who had been a source of strength in her life. Although she felt horrible inside at that moment, everything seemed upside down. But Dennis held her head high and continued her charade, preparing herself to face the situation if anyone discovered her secret and move on. After all, her life had been a constant battle with things incredibly difficult to explain.

"Dennis, guess what?" Rona said, her tone full of happiness.

"What?"

"I came today to share some wonderful news."

"Yes? What's the magnificent news?" Dennis asked.

"Well, everything is ready, and the center will open soon. Everything has gone wonderfully—the permits and legal procedures are complete. Now there are just a couple more details, and I'll be able to open. That's why I'm here today—to invite you all. I'll be having a small celebration, nothing big, but I want each of you to be there. I'm so happy!" Rona finished.

"I can't believe it—everything's ready? That's great! And you were expecting it to take several more months," Dennis responded.

"Yes, it's true, but when you have angels on your path, things definitely happen faster." The three women laughed, and then Tammy invited them to come into the house, where her mother and aunt were with Sarah, who had arrived an hour earlier.

Tammy's family were in the back of the house, already digging into a juicy piece of meat that was slowly cooking on the grill. Next to them was a table full of dishes with delicious fruits and vegetables. As Dennis walked in and saw them talking so enthusiastically, she felt good. There was Sarah, proving that her determination to start a new life was serious and real. Dennis cared for her deeply and couldn't hide the affection she felt.

"Oh, what a joy to see you all here, chatting pleasantly. How are you?" Dennis asked.

"Hi, Dennis! It's so good to see you—it feels like we haven't seen you in ages," Mary exclaimed, and they all laughed.

"Yes, I'd say it's been about twelve hours," Dennis replied sarcastically.

Sarah got up from the couch and went to hug Dennis. A little uneasy, Sarah asked Dennis almost in her ear, "Have you seen her?"

Dennis, perplexed, looked at her and answered, "No."

"What do you mean? But you came in with her." Dennis was confused. She had thought Sarah was referring to Lucas, but Sarah was actually referring to Rona.

"I'm talking about Rona—her," Sarah said, pointing to where Rona had sat.

"Oh, yes, of course," Dennis replied, and it was at that moment she remembered what she had promised Sarah before. She had told Sarah that the next time she saw Rona, she would talk to her about some work opportunities for Sarah.

"Don't worry, we'll find the right moment," Dennis reassured her.

Gradually, everyone gathered in the outdoor courtyard. Under a beautiful pergola was a well-decorated table, and the grill continued to give off delicious aromas, enticing the guests to sit down and enjoy the meal. Dennis was a little curious to see that, for some strange reason, no one had yet asked her about Lucas. How was that possible? Mary was very fond of him, and Rona hadn't mentioned anything either. Tammy and Sarah... well, Sarah probably knew the situation but hadn't dared to bring it up. Suddenly, she heard a voice that made her so pale she had to sit down.

"Okay, here I am with the richest Italian pastries you've ever eaten!" Lucas walked in carrying a tray of sweets, and after setting them on the table, he began greeting everyone. When he reached Dennis, Lucas hesitated for a moment but then continued.

"Hello, my love. I'm here. It didn't take me long, did it?" He leaned in and kissed Dennis quickly, too fast for her to react. She felt numb, frozen. After a moment, Lucas leaned in again, whispering in her ear, "I won't say anything if you don't."

"Okay, but eventually, we'll have to tell them. I understand today isn't the time," Dennis replied.

Lucas sat down next to Dennis but was careful not to crowd her, remaining attentive and courteous. He participated in conversations with the others, and at one point in the evening, he moved to sit next to Tammy's husband, with whom he chatted animatedly. Dennis took advantage of those moments to observe him from afar. Her heart was pounding so fast she didn't know how to control it.

Everyone gathered around the table to eat dessert. The pastries Lucas had brought were truly delicious, and everyone had something to say about them. Amidst the compliments, Lucas suddenly addressed Rona directly and asked, "Rona, what's your position on reincarnation?"

Lucas's question captivated everyone's attention, filling the air with a strange uneasiness. The reaction of those present was almost instantaneous—everyone wanted to hear Rona's response. Though she might have been a bit confused by the question, Rona answered immediately.

"Well, I can tell you that more and more people—both scientists and ordinary folks—are paying attention to this topic, especially with recent studies from prestigious universities and symposia around the world. From my own experiences, I believe in the idea of an infinite life, where our souls return as many times as necessary to live in the body of a human being. But what a strange question coming from you, Lucas. Where did this curiosity come from, if I may ask?"

"Just curious. I had an incredible dream where I learned about past lives," Lucas replied.

"Really? It would be very interesting to talk more about this later if you'd like. In my new practice, I'll have an expert in past life regressions. It could be very beneficial to learn from the past lives we've experienced, don't you think?"

"I would love to participate—count me in," Lucas said eagerly.

"Of course! But don't think it'll be free—maybe I'll give you a discount for being a first-timer," Rona teased, glancing at the other guests, who looked at her in amazement. "Don't look at me like that! I was just joking. But seriously, your support has been so important during this transition. I'm excited to get started, and I want you all to know that this practice is being opened with the goal of helping us address our daily problems. We need to learn that to heal physical issues, we must heal the soul, too. So, you know where to go!"

"Rona, what other services will there be?" Mary asked, intrigued.

"Well, we'll offer a range of services—from comprehensive lines of health supplements to rehabilitation programs based on new yoga techniques, as well as hypnosis, past-life regression therapy, and we'll hold symposia from time to time. There will also be a segment dedicated to universal therapy."

"What's that?" Dennis asked, now thoroughly intrigued.

"Universal therapy? Well, we'll have groups where people can share their experiences without fear of being criticized or judged by those who haven't yet crossed the threshold of ignorance, to put it politely. It will be voluntary, and I believe it will be beneficial for many. Plus, it will come with a surprise—a rather pleasant one."

"A pleasant surprise? Why?" Dennis pressed.

"Well, Dennis, many people go through experiences they think are unique, but they're not. More than one person can go through the same thing, and often the issue lies in a lack of knowledge and expression about what we experience and live through."

"Yes, I suppose that's true," Eileen added from the side of the table. "When I was younger, I had a special connection with only one person— my daughter."

Her words made everyone look at her in disbelief and curiosity.

"I know what you're thinking. But it's true—I was married and had a daughter. I lost them in an accident a long time ago, when I was very young. But it's true, the connection I had with my daughter was very strong—it was something inexplicable, even after the accident."

Eileen's revelation took everyone by surprise, including Dennis, who was starting to connect the dots and form a wild idea in her mind—an idea that, she feared, might eventually turn out to be real.

"But Mom, how come I never knew about this?" Tammy asked, her voice tinged with disbelief.

"This happened long before you came into my life, and we decided to leave it in the past because there wasn't much to salvage. You filled much of the void in your aunt's heart," Mary explained.

"My God! If I had known..." Tammy said, still incredulous. "I'm so sorry you had to go through that."

"Eileen, may I ask what you meant by 'after the accident'?" Rona inquired gently.

"Sure. My husband and daughter were killed in a car accident, but my daughter's body was never found—the car plunged off a large cliff. Even years later, I felt a strange connection with her soul, as if she were still alive. It was something inexplicable, and I never knew what to do or where to turn. Perhaps if today's theories had existed back then, everything might have been different."

There was a brief silence before Lucas, full of emotion, said, "Ms. Eileen, I'm so sorry. I didn't mean to bring this kind of conversation to the table. Please forgive me."

"Don't worry, Lucas. You weren't the one who brought these memories back to my mind," Eileen reassured him.

Mary looked at Eileen as if to ask if she was sure about what she was saying, but Eileen didn't continue the conversation, deciding to remain silent until the moment felt right again.

Lucas was deeply affected by what he had heard, realizing just how complicated life on this human plane was. It was like a labyrinth where everyone hopes to reach the other side, only to die along the way. He knew this in theory, but knowing it as a soul and living it as a human was entirely different.

Dennis saw him leaning against one of the pergola's corners, holding a cup of coffee, and she walked over to him.

"Are you okay?"

"Yes," he answered. "But I'm sorry I said what I said."

"But it's not your fault," Dennis said.

"Yes, it is. If I hadn't had the stupid idea of asking Rona about past lives, the conversation wouldn't have taken this turn."

"Well, I don't know. But why bring up the afterlife?"

"Something foolish on my part. I wanted to see if she could prove what I've told you is real."

"But why involve Rona?"

"Because she decided to help me, and she thinks that maybe if you agreed to a regression session, you could understand things better."

"Does Rona know? Does she also believe you? Have you told her?"

"Dennis, don't judge me," Lucas replied tersely. "You don't know how I feel. It has taken a lot of work to learn to live on this human plane without prior preparation or a clear purpose like we usually have. And even more so when I remembered—since then, it's been hell not being able to make you see what we are and what you mean to me. And of course, Rona knows—she knows everything about me. She has been a very strong support in my life. You must remember that I mentioned her to you from the beginning."

Lucas couldn't stop a few tears from escaping, which Dennis gently wiped away with her hand.

"Don't be like that—it's okay," she said softly.

Meanwhile, at the table, everyone was still discussing the same topic, but Sarah remained unusually quiet.

"Sarah, aren't you going to comment on these insanities these people are saying?" Tammy's daughter asked, almost laughing.

Sarah was taken by surprise. She hadn't expected anyone to ask her such a question, but what she said next was even more surprising.

"Well," Sarah started. "Believe it or not, what Dr. Michaels explained is true. You can go through life thinking that certain things only happen to you, but the truth is that more than one person experiences the same thing. It's like when you have the flu. The flu is common, and people get it, but if you don't see your neighbor for a couple of weeks, you don't know if they've had or are currently dealing with the flu. Do you understand? It sounds strange, but it's true. Life is very complex in that way—believing, seeing, and understanding. I think being more open-minded would give us the opportunity to share more."

It seemed like Sarah was closing her point of view, but then she added something that resonated deeply in Eileen's ears, shocking her.

"When I was a child, I used to hear a woman in my head, but I couldn't understand what she was saying or see her the voice came from— I only heard her in my mind. It was very strange," Sarah said.

"What was weird, Sarah? That you heard the voice?" Rona asked.

"No, it wasn't just hearing the voice. I could understand some things she said, but not everything. It was only on rare occasions that I managed to grasp what she was telling me. Many times, when I mentioned this to others, it led to the situation I ended up in—it was clear that it was more trouble than it was worth. I'm sure that at least a couple of times, what she said had to do with the spot on my arm. It was something like 'Where are you, little butterfly?' That's how I associated the spot with a butterfly," Sarah explained.

At that precise moment, a loud thud was heard as something hit the floor. It was Eileen, who had fainted. She lay unconscious on the tile, and everyone jumped up, alarmed, but no one immediately called for an ambulance. It was Tammy's husband who finally reacted, dialing the emergency number. Soon, an ambulance arrived, and Eileen was transferred to the clinic for emergency care. No one knew what had happened, nor could they associate what Sarah had said with Eileen's reaction. However, Mary already felt in her heart that they were facing something extraordinary—something incredible. Sarah was indeed Eileen's daughter; the mention of the butterfly spot on the arm confirmed it. Eileen had spoken of it many times since her daughter was born.

Hours passed, and Eileen was recovering in a room at the clinic. She had undergone several tests, and the doctors didn't find anything serious. They believed it could have been a drop in blood pressure, possibly related to her diabetes, and advised her to pay closer attention, but assured that there was nothing dangerous. In the waiting room were the family,

Dennis, Lucas, and, of course, Sarah, who didn't dare ask anyone to take her back to The Ranch. Rona had left a while earlier, asking Dennis to update her on Eileen's condition.

Mary emerged from the room and told everyone that Eileen okay, that it was just a drop in blood pressure. But Mary kept glancing at Sarah, now with a different intention. Mary wanted to see features of the niece she had never known, but it was difficult. She didn't remember her brother-in-law either, which was understandable after so many years had passed. As Mary said goodbye to Lucas, Dennis, and Sarah, she watched as Sarah put on her coat and let her hair down. No one had ever seen her with her hair down and without glasses. Seeing Sarah's figure from behind reminded Mary of Eileen many years ago when she was still in college. *How incredible*, Mary thought. *How did I not notice?* She watched them walk down the corridor, while she remained with her daughter, as they had always shared most of their time together, in both good and bad times. Mary could now imagine what Eileen had been feeling these past few weeks. All of this was incredible.

Lucas offered Sarah a ride back, but Dennis told him not to worry— she would take care of it. They couldn't quite agree until Sarah insisted that both of them take her back, and that was the end of the matter. They exchanged looks, and Lucas said he didn't mind, while Dennis nodded without putting up much of a fight. They left in Lucas's car, with Sarah and Dennis in the back so they could talk. But Sarah was especially worried that night.

"Sarah, are you okay? What's the matter?" Dennis asked.

"It's hard to explain. You know I can feel and see things, right?"

"Yes, of course, but I also know you don't like to talk about it."

"I know, but that's the problem. When I think I should see or feel something to help, I can't. Like now, I can't see anything—nothing in

Eileen's future or past—and it makes me uncomfortable because I feel something, and I don't know what it is."

"Oh, don't worry. What you're feeling is just worry. Believe me, I've felt the same thing thousands of times."

"No, Dennis, this is different. I don't know why I made that comment—I shouldn't have. But it was almost unintentional, spontaneous, as if something inside me compelled me to say it. You know I don't like talking about these things, right?"

"Of course, I know. But don't worry, I don't think it's a cause for anxiety."

Sarah was silent for the rest of the trip. When they arrived at The Ranch, Sarah said goodbye to them. "Thanks for bringing me, Dennis," she said. "Remember that time you asked me something specific?"

Dennis replied, "I think so."

"Well, the answer is yes. Good night and take care."

They watched her go inside, and Dennis moved into the front seat before they left. The drive was quiet, neither Dennis nor Lucas daring to say a word. As they neared Dennis's apartment, she wasn't sure what would happen next. When the car stopped, Dennis wanted to get out, but not before looking at Lucas and saying:

"Maybe we could go for coffee one of these days. What do you say?"

"You have no idea how much I'd love that," Lucas replied, his voice almost breaking. He barely held back his tears, nearly on the verge of an emotional outburst, but he restrained himself, managing to smile and say, "Rest well."

"Thank you," she replied, beginning to walk toward the entrance. As she turned to look back, she saw Lucas gesturing with his hand. Dennis asked what was going on, and he offered to pick her up the next day since she didn't have her car, having been dropped off at the clinic.

"So," Dennis said before she could think. "Did you want to stay here tonight?"

"Well, I don't want to pressure you. I can come back in the morning."

"No, it's not pressure. I want you to stay."

Lucas put the car in reverse and parked where he usually left the vehicle. He locked the car and followed Dennis inside. Once upstairs, Dennis went to the kitchen and started boiling water for tea.

"I'm making tea. Do you want some?" she asked.

"Of course. I could use some after this unusual afternoon."

"Yes, it's been pretty crazy," Dennis said, still talking from the kitchen. Lucas was afraid to even move a muscle—he didn't want Dennis to think badly of him. Everything that had happened was more than enough, and now he just had to trust that somehow things would start to change.

Dennis returned from the kitchen with two cups of tea and placed them on the living room table. She sat down in the armchair across from Lucas.

"Come, sit down," she beckoned. "I want you to tell me more about that life and that other person you say I am."

This took Lucas by surprise, but it was a welcome surprise. He couldn't believe that Dennis was finally opening up to learn more about their lives. *Does this mean things were finally on the right track?* Lucas wondered.

Lucas spoke to her for hours, describing where they came from. Dennis seemed increasingly interested and asked questions, which Lucas tried to answer as best he could. However, he made it clear that there were things he couldn't fully explain, and Dennis tried her best to understand. There were moments when Dennis seemed to recall something, but she would soon claim she couldn't remember.

Though frustration was present, she no longer got angry; instead, she pondered. She asked a lot about the lights she saw—the orbs—and her curiosity grew as Lucas explained that they were the same on the spiritual plane: bright and fast, able to cross an infinite number of planes and realities, something she could only fully understand in the world from which they came.

"And what are you and I over there? Where do we live? What kind of life do we lead?"

"I'll try to explain, though it's difficult to grasp as a human," Lucas answered. "But I can assure you that you love who you are, and you've always worked hard to learn and grow. We always do well, our missions are short, and we have time for ourselves. Life isn't like it is here, but in one way, both lives are similar, and even stronger and more powerful—that's love. Love is the greatest source of energy we possess, where the cure for all ailments is found. When the day comes that you finally say, 'I've found love,' you'll understand that you can no longer hate. Love is the light we radiate to the universe."

That night flew by, and while Dennis and Lucas's relationship wasn't fully restored, it was on the right path. Dennis went to sleep that night with new ideas in her head, trying to connect the dots. As she thought about everything, she fell into a deep sleep, letting herself be carried away by fatigue and new knowledge.

Without even realizing it, she had received the answers to all the questions she had asked herself throughout her existence. It was incredible to think that as souls, they would come to this plane and consider suffering as learning, but that was exactly what Lucas was trying to explain to her—that the stronger they became, the greater and more powerful love became.

With a sudden start, Dennis woke up. She had it all there, and she didn't want to lose it. She kept her eyes closed, trying to retain every moment of what she had seen in her dream—if it had been a dream, because she could no longer tell the difference...

This time, she was able to see him. She saw his face and wanted to hold onto that memory, to not lose it. She felt something she couldn't explain—something that put a lump in her throat. Even though she wanted to scream, she couldn't.

In that dream, Dennis saw that great orb of light again. She watched it approach from afar, drawing closer until it was almost in front of her, then she saw it take the physical form of a person. Her heart beat faster than ever, and she wanted to preserve every moment of that vision. Even in the dream, she repeated to herself over and over again, "You will not forget this face, you will not forget this face." All she wanted was to be conscious and to know who that golden light—who had visited her before—really was, and now was visiting her again.

She felt a special warmth, and her body felt lighter, so light that she felt as though she was floating. A feeling of relaxation took over her being, and she could only observe. She no longer felt anxious or exalted but rather calm, in a state of peace. No matter how hard she searched, there were no adequate words to describe the experience she was living.

She tried to look around and saw only bright flashes of light—white and gold—in an almost cotton-like environment. Everything was shining, and in the middle of the glow, she saw him, facing her. He was an almost transparent being, in white tones, wearing a long tunic that covered most of his body. No feet were visible, but his arms and hands were.

He moved with a smooth glide, almost effortlessly, as if at the will of his mind. His face was passive, with an elongated cranial structure and a similarly shaped chin. She couldn't say that his eyes or mouth were more noticeable than the rest of his body—they weren't; everything was uniform.

When this being approached Dennis and smiled at her, that's when she felt that strange sensation. Dennis looked down and saw herself beside him. She looked at her hands, and they were just like his. She, too, was wearing a robe, and she couldn't see her feet. Dennis didn't feel afraid. On the contrary, when he took her hands, that's when Dennis could finally remember. She remembered her life, remembered who she really was, and she couldn't help but feel a sense of clarity that completely enveloped her, revealing everything.

She remembered at that moment what this being of light had told her on a previous visit—something she had tried so hard to recall, and now it presented itself so clearly. His message was the same: this being repeated to her that everything would be fine, to trust him and trust herself, that she would soon find her way home.

Dennis knew that by opening her eyes, she ran the risk of waking up from that incredible dream, and that once again, she might not be able to remember anything at all—or perhaps she would completely forget what she had just experienced. But she had to wake up; she had to open her eyes. She could only trust that this time would be different, that she could feel free, even though she understood the risks of knowing everything and how complicated her life could become. She also knew that this was the reason she had been searching for so many years. This was what Lucas had tried to explain to her in so many ways—this was the truth, and the truth was showing her that Lucas had never lied to her.

This last thought gave Dennis the courage she needed to open her eyes. Knowing that Lucas hadn't lied to her made her infinitely happy. Now that she knew she could live this life as a human with him, it made her feel much more at peace, because she would be living it with the one who had always been her other half.

Dennis let go of the sheets she had been clutching so tightly, and at that moment, she opened her eyes without thinking any more. She stared at the ceiling in her room for a couple of minutes, waiting to see if everything would disappear—or if everything would stay instead. She felt how, little by little, she remembered less, and the images began to dissipate like the wind moving clouds in the sky. Dennis tried and tried to hold on to them, but then she realized that in a matter of seconds, she would lose everything. She jumped out of bed, ran to open the door, and there was Lucas, standing right in front of her.

"Don't force it," he said. "Take my hand, and you'll feel it again."

Dennis took his hand and then threw herself into his arms, hugging him with all her strength. At that moment, all her visions returned. She remembered and felt that she was in the presence of the one who loved her in a way that was beyond human comprehension. She clung to him, and he to her. Now, they had been granted the opportunity to be together again and to know who they truly were. After all, Lucas had found what he had spent so many years living as a human trying to find again.

Neither Lucas nor Dennis knew in that infinite moment what would happen tomorrow; they only knew that in that precise moment, they had found each other again and demonstrated that the love they had for each other was even greater than before they embarked on this journey. It was to be hoped that this realization would help complete Dennis's journey, for one day, just as Lucas had told her, they would return home together.

Life is strange, and it is different for each person who lives it. It is a personal and predestined path that must be lived according to the time in which one exists. It is not useful to harbor grudges or ailments, nor to cling to material goods, as they are only part of life on this plane. When you return home, you will only take what you have learned, and what you leave behind should be of some use for others to learn from your journey, but never to avoid the experiences that others must live.

CHAPTER 27

Connecting the Dots

Life, and its incredible walk never stops,
But sometimes we are the ones who decide to stop
To be able to appreciate what we are experiencing.

E ileen felt much better within hours of waking up at the clinic, but her primary care doctor decided to run some additional tests just to be safe, so Eileen spent a couple more days in the hospital. However, her health wasn't the only thing on her mind; she couldn't stop thinking about the fact that she had found her daughter. What kind of miracle was this? She didn't know, but she was certain it was her, and that made her feel extremely happy. Mary, on the other hand, kept thinking about how they would tell Sarah. It wasn't something easy to reveal—news of this magnitude required complete certainty. To prevent any problems, she continued her conversations with the private detective, who advised that a DNA test would be the most appropriate step.

At first, Mary had no idea how she could get Sarah to provide a sample without her knowing, but the detective assured her that he had contacts at the clinic who could help. They suggested requesting a blood donation for Eileen as the perfect excuse.

The first call was to Dennis. Being Sarah's closest friend, it might be easier for her to suggest it, framing it as an invitation to donate blood. Indeed, this is exactly what happened—there were not many questions, just a quick offer from Dennis, who said goodbye with, "I'll ask Lucas and Sarah."

The next day, they were all donating blood in Eileen's name, which made everything move quickly. That same morning, the three donors stopped by to see Eileen in her clinic room, and what a surprise they all got.

"May we come in?"

"Please!"

"What are you doing out of bed? I thought you'd be resting."

"No, I feel much better now."

"Yes, I can see that. When are they sending you home?" Dennis asked.

"I think this afternoon. Besides, I don't want to be here any longer—being locked in this room makes me feel short of breath."

"That's true. I feel that way sometimes, back at The Ranch," Sarah said softly. "Eileen, what a scare you gave us! I hope I wasn't the cause."

"I can imagine," Eileen said. "Don't worry, it wasn't your fault or anyone else's. My blood sugar just dropped, that's what the doctor said."

"Eileen, I'm so glad you're okay, but I'm sorry to leave you. I have to go back to work," Lucas said, holding Dennis's hand tighter than ever.

"Oh, don't worry. I'm just glad I got to see you, and thank you for donating blood. Sarah, you don't have to go back yet, do you?"

"Well, technically I should go back, but I'll have trouble getting there because if no one takes me, I won't be able to go back on my own," Sarah laughed.

"There's no problem with that. I'd love for you to keep me company, and when the doctor discharges me, you can accompany me home, and then the driver can take you back to The Ranch. How does that sound?"

"Oh, of course, I'd be happy to keep you company."

"I think it's great, so you'll be in good company," Dennis said.

"I'll be in excellent company. Thank you, Dennis, for bringing Sarah."

For a moment, Dennis stared at her as if she didn't quite understand what Eileen had just said, but everything moved on quickly. Dennis hurried to say goodbye to Sarah with a kiss on the cheek and was already on her way out with Lucas. Dennis didn't let go of that thought.

"Don't you think Eileen's interest in Sarah is strange?" She said, once in the car with Lucas.

"Honestly, I haven't noticed anything unusual. Eileen is a very kind person, and maybe she feels affection for Sarah—perhaps Sarah reminds her of her daughter, now that we know she had one. What a revelation, right?"

"Yes, you're right. That must be the connection she feels. I suppose they could be the same age. Maybe I just find it incredible that Eileen had a daughter and never mentioned her."

"Well, who can say? These are personal things, and it must be very painful for her. Once you've tried to survive something like that, it must be difficult to bring it up all the time. Don't worry anymore; you'll see that everything is fine. Sarah is in good hands; nothing will happen to her."

"Yes, I know. It's just that my nature doesn't let me be otherwise—I always tend to overthink things."

"Oh, yes, I won't argue with that," Lucas said with a laugh, and they both laughed together.

Meanwhile, the day wore on, and Mary had already spoken twice to the private investigator. She was eager to know when they would have the DNA test results, but it wouldn't be right away—unfortunately, they would still have to wait a couple of weeks at the very least.

On the other hand, Eileen spent hours entertaining Sarah with stories about the daughter she had lost, and Sarah listened with great interest. Everything Eileen told her seemed incredibly familiar to Sarah. At around noon, the doctor stopped by Eileen's room to check on her and discharge her. With a few instructions and orders to rest, the doctor sent her home.

Eileen called Mary to let her know she didn't need to pick her up since Sarah could accompany her home and that it would be enough to send the driver. The driver soon arrived, they packed up Eileen's things, and headed toward the exit. There, the old Rolls-Royce was waiting to take them to Eileen's house. The journey was enjoyable, and they continued to talk non-stop. Eileen told her stories, and Sarah listened— sometimes asking questions, other times staying silent. What mattered was that the time they spent together flew by, and they didn't even notice.

Evening fell, and Mary joined them for dinner. Amid conversations, Sarah noticed it was getting late, and she needed to return to avoid getting into trouble. After all, she only had permission to be away for the day. This was something Sarah had been thinking about—she knew she needed to find a job soon. It was the only way The Ranch would recognize that her reintegration program was working and finally allow her to move on. That was her urgency, and she had told Dennis, who was considering buying a bigger place so she could offer Sarah a room to help her start over. However, Dennis hadn't told Sarah this; it was something of a surprise she wanted to give her.

Everyone had something on their minds: Mary was anxious to find out whether Sarah was truly her niece, almost to the point of despair; Tammy was filled with ideas for herself and her family, determined to make the most of every minute of life she had left; Rona was happy, and the busier she was, the happier she felt—what she was living was a dream come true, and she finally felt she could truly help others. And of course, there was Lucas—now that Dennis had regained trust in him, he had certain questions lingering. But he was definitely more patient than Dennis. He would look for the right moment to complete what he hadn't been able to do before: ask Dennis to marry him. Now he was sure that the future they had was bright, and in that future, they were together and happy.

Eileen no longer doubted that Sarah could be her daughter, and she was bursting with anticipation, waiting for the moment when she could share the incredible news. With all the talking and spending time together, it was likely that Sarah already felt much closer to her. However, Sarah herself didn't think about Eileen being her mother or that she could be the daughter Eileen had lost. Instead, she thought about how lucky that daughter would be if she were alive.

Each day, Sarah's desire to leave The Ranch grew stronger. She saw and understood that there was still much to do, and she knew there were people who loved her and with whom she felt very comfortable, but under no circumstances did she want to feel like a burden. That's why she was counting down the minutes, waiting for Dennis to call and tell her that she had already spoken to Dr. Michaels.

Dennis, on her part, despite everything on her mind, found space to keep up with all her obligations. This included her Reiki instructions and active participation in the Agency's events, where she had dared to enter one of the last challenges for the Scholarship campaign proposals. This project touched her personally; without the Agency's help, she might never have been able to continue her studies and reach the position she held now. Dennis was determined to be involved in creating a permanent fund to help girls in the same position she had been in years before.

That following Friday, Dennis had an appointment with Dr. Michaels at about five in the afternoon, just after work. She would stop by the new office, which would open very soon.

"Hi, Dennis! How have you been? How's everything going?"

"I'm fine, everything is going well, which is really good. You know, sometimes I find it hard to believe that things are okay, but they are. I see everything is perfect here. The office is very nice—I love it. It all feels very cozy and relaxed."

"Thank you! I'm so glad you feel that way. I've put all my ideas into action, and I think I've finally achieved what I had envisioned. I love this place we've created."

"You've done a wonderful job. When does the center officially open?"

"You'll laugh, but there's just one thing missing that I hadn't thought of. I'll figure it out soon enough. But don't keep me waiting with baited breath—tell me what brings you here today. If it's to sign up for one of the workshops, you don't have to worry—I'll let you know as soon as they're available."

"No, it's not exactly that. But, sure, don't forget to let me know—I'll definitely sign up. Actually, I'm here to talk about Sarah."

"Sarah? What's wrong with Sarah?"

"There's nothing wrong with her—nothing bad. It's just that Sarah has already spoken to her doctor, and he recommended that she's ready to leave The Ranch and start a rehabilitation program. You know about those programs, right?"

"That's excellent news! Sarah needed time, and I knew she would eventually put her thoughts in order. I'm really happy for her. What's her plan? Will she return to her family?"

"No, that's the thing. She doesn't want to go back and look for her children until she has reorganized her life. She wants to get out of where she is and start over. Maybe later, she'll gather the courage to reconnect with them."

"I think that's a very wise idea."

"Yes, she's been preparing for this for months, and she's ready."

"And how can I help? I imagine you're looking for advice or something special, right?"

"Yes, the truth is that one day, when we were talking about you and the new practice you're opening, the idea came up that maybe…"

"Dennis, don't be coy—just tell me what you were going to say."

"Yes, I will. But I don't want you to feel pressured. It's just that I thought maybe Sarah could work here. Any position would be more than good for her. I've also offered her a place to live with me until she finds something better, which I'm sure she will do in a short time."

"Did you really offer her that?"

"Yes, I care about Sarah a lot. I know she's a good person and deserves a hand to start over."

"I didn't realize you two had grown so close. I'm really pleased. You're a good person, Dennis, and Sarah is like you. She's suffered, but with effort, she's managed to get back on her feet. This truly pleases me. You know, remember I told you there was just one little thing left to solve? Well, I think I've solved it."

"Oh, that's great! What was it?"

"Don't rush me! Now, when is Sarah moving into your house?"

"Well, we haven't discussed it yet. I promised to help her find a job first. She doesn't want to leave The Ranch without having a job, even though I offered for her to move in first and then look for one. She's very proud and insists on having a job so she won't be a burden to anyone. I think I would feel the same way."

"I completely understand. She's a wise woman, and she knows what she wants. It's fine—don't worry. You know, I'll be here all morning tomorrow. Do you think you could bring Sarah? I'd love to talk to her."

"Of course! I appreciate it."

"Don't thank me just yet—let me talk to her first."

"Now, I suppose we can have that coffee and talk a little about other things, right?"

"Of course! I wanted to tell you that I'm participating in a public campaign, which I hope will yield good results and maybe even lead to a great project."

"That's fantastic! And how are your Reiki studies going?"

"They're going well. I think I'll be ready to take the final course very soon."

"And what do you want to do once you've completed your classes?"

"Would you believe me if I said I haven't thought about it yet? I suppose I'll look for a way to put my teachings into practice."

"Absolutely, Dennis. I think that's an excellent idea. And you know what's an even better idea?"

"What?"

"Simple: Wouldn't you like to teach here?"

"What?"

"You heard me! You could lead a class and teach them what you've learned."

"Are you serious?" Dennis asked, almost incredulous.

"Sure! We can coordinate it for once a week. I'm certain there will be more than a few people eager to take classes and learn how to lead a better life."

"You've left me speechless. I hadn't thought about it, but it's an extraordinary idea! Though I'm not sure if I'm qualified to teach others.

It's taken me a lot of work to understand the essence of life myself, so I don't know if I would be the ideal teacher."

"What are you talking about, Dennis? That's exactly the point! You've lived it. You know what pain is, what effort is, and you understand many things that others don't. You'd be the perfect person to teach. Think about it—it could be very rewarding."

"You know, I think I love the idea. I'm not sure if I can do it, but it sounds amazing. I'll definitely think about it and let you know."

Dennis left Dr. Michaels' new clinic full of ideas and excitement. Realizing that she could share with others what she had learned over the years was something she had never imagined. She would have to think about it more carefully—she already had so many things on her agenda that she would soon need to borrow time. But that was Dennis, and it would surely be worth it, just like everything else she had put her effort into.

A car horn blared outside.

"Sarah, are you ready? I'm so sorry, I overslept today! And even though I tried to leave earlier, I couldn't. Rona is waiting for you—come on, I don't want you to be late!" Dennis called out; her voice tinged with urgency.

"Never mind, Dennis, don't worry. Everything will be fine, and we're not late, you'll see," Sarah replied, her kind smile easing the tension.

"I just don't want to get stuck at the Bay Bridge. Remember, it's Saturday, and if we hit the bridge during a boat crossing, we'll be late!"

Dennis and Sarah shared a laugh, the moment lightening their spirits.

They finally arrived at the new clinic, and Sarah stepped out of the car. Dennis leaned out the window. "I'll pick you up in an hour," she said. "I'll use the time to run some errands downtown. Afterward, I thought we could grab Lucas and spend the afternoon at Bay Park."

Meanwhile, Lucas had been carefully planning the perfect moment to propose to Dennis. He had enlisted the help of friends to secretly plan everything because he couldn't wait any longer. He also wanted to get ahead of Dennis' plan to buy a new apartment and had been looking for something suitable for them both. He fully supported Dennis' decision to offer Sarah a place to live; after all, who knew Dennis better than Lucas— a noble soul, full of love to give.

Lucas had already decided that during a dinner party, instead of presenting a ring, he would give Dennis the key to their new apartment. He had also arranged for their closest friends and family to be there to celebrate, assuming, of course, that Dennis would accept. Now, he could only hope that everything would go as planned.

Lucas had even spoken to Tammy, Dennis' closest friend. And she was overjoyed and immediately joined in the planning of his magnificent surprise. Tammy had told Mary, who then told Eileen, and Eileen had told Sarah, who was thrilled, though she had known about it for some time. Lucas also trusted Rona deeply, as she had guided him through the challenges of living a human life. She was one of the first to know about his feelings for Dennis and was now at the top of the list of those conspiring to make this surprise truly special.

"Hello, my love, how are you?" Dennis said to Lucas over the phone.

"I'm doing well, just working like a dog."

"Really? Are you very busy today?"

"As usual. Unfortunately, one of my coworkers called in sick, so I'm covering his shift."

"That's too bad. I was hoping we could have dinner and a walk in the park. Sarah was going to join us too."

"Sarah? That's great! At least you won't be alone. I'm sorry I can't make it, but I'll see you tonight."

"Yeah, Sarah is in an interview with Rona. It's okay, though. I'll spend the day with her once I pick her up."

"Okay, I'll leave you to it. I love you—today more than yesterday and less than tomorrow," Lucas said.

"Me too," Dennis replied.

Lucas didn't actually have to cover anyone's shift. He had lied to Dennis because that day, he was finalizing the purchase of a beautiful apartment. Everything was going according to plan.

After finishing her errands downtown, Dennis headed back to the clinic to pick up Sarah, but she didn't expect what happened next.

"Hello! Are you ready? How did everything go?" Dennis asked, curious about Sarah's interview, still standing in the doorway.

"Everything went really well. You can't imagine how happy I am. Rona is so kind—I just love her," Sarah said, her face beaming with joy.

"So, was it about the job? Did she offer you something?" Dennis asked eagerly.

"Yes! You're looking at the new receptionist of the clinic," Sarah announced, her happiness radiating.

"Really? That's amazing! Congratulations! I'm so happy for you," Dennis exclaimed.

"Thank you, Dennis. You know, you have a lot to do with this. Your friendship has restored my confidence in myself, and I owe that to you. And to Mark, too. If it weren't for him, I would never have met you. Life is amazing, isn't it? It's like a circle—everything connects at some point. You just have to be patient and wait."

"Oh, Mark," Dennis sighed and the memory. "I still think about him sometimes, but it doesn't feel the same as before. My soul is at peace now."

"Yes, I know. You just had to understand."

"Understand?" Dennis asked, looking a little confused.

"Yes, understand your purpose and understand what you are and where you come from."

"Sarah, you... you've always known more than you've told me. Why couldn't you have been more honest with me before?"

"Dennis, I just told you—you have to be patient and wait. Things don't just happen; everything has a reason. There is always a goal you're working towards. I've learned that, and you... you almost fully understand it now."

"Yes, you're right. How can you know things and keep them to yourself without telling anyone? You're amazing."

"It wasn't easy. I had to learn that there are many things I'll never understand, but at the same time, I had to open myself up to believe in the most incredible things. That's how I understood that I wasn't crazy— that I was just different, just like you. We are different, but we have something in common: we're both here on this plane, living an earthly life."

"Yes, it's true. Sometimes I let my mind wander, and I think I don't understand. Other times, I think about all the things that have happened and what I've been able to see, and I realize this is my place—here and now. It makes my heart happy now that I know who I am and where I come from."

"I'm so glad. Remember when you asked me if I could clarify all those doubts and questions you had?"

"Yes, I remember."

"I felt terrible not being able to tell you that I had seen your future, but I knew I had to keep quiet. The only reason behind the ability to see what others cannot is what remains—in this case, our friendship. This relationship has restored my confidence."

"Yes, I understand... I wonder how Mark is. Is he at peace? With his family? In another world or another dimension?"

"Maybe we shouldn't dwell too much."

"You're right. Let's get going, then?"

"Actually, Dennis, I've already been working for an hour," Sarah said with a smile.

"What?!"

"Yes, Rona asked me to start immediately. There are so many things to do before the official opening."

"Oh, no! Will you be working all day? I thought we would have the rest of the day to go out and spend some time together."

"Oh, Dennis, I'm sorry—I just couldn't say no."

"No, don't worry—I understand perfectly. I'll take advantage of the day to get some things done. I'll pick you up later—just give me a call."

"Thank you, Dennis."

Dennis was genuinely happy for Sarah, but her plans for a pleasant afternoon had evaporated. First Lucas, and now Sarah—what would be next? She shook her head and thought, *what nonsense am I thinking? Everything is fine—in fact, everything is better than ever. I just need to figure out what to do this afternoon, and that's that.*

Dennis had plenty of things she could focus on, but none of them felt right at that moment. Instead, she decided to stick to her original plan for the day. She got ready to head to the park by the Bay, take a long walk among the towering redwoods, and maybe treat herself to dinner afterward. It had been a long time since she had done something like this alone, as she used to.

After parking her car, Dennis set off on her walk, enjoying the gentle breeze coming in from the Bay. The feeling was incredible, revitalizing her from the inside out. She hadn't walked far when her phone rang.

"Hi, Dennis, how are you?" Mary's voice came through.

"I'm good, Mary. What about you?"

"Well, I didn't want to bother you, knowing you do a lot of other things on Saturdays, but I was hoping to see if you could spare a few minutes," Mary asked.

"Of course. Is everything okay? Is it about Tammy?" Dennis's voice carried a note of concern.

"No, don't worry, everything is fine. It's something different."

"Oh, that's good to hear. You know how worried I get. But sure, tell me, how can I help?"

"Where are you now? Maybe I could meet up with you, and we can talk more calmly?"

"This sounds very mysterious. Please tell me it's nothing bad."

"No, Dennis, it's really nothing to worry about. You'll see, but I don't want to start talking on the phone—it's a bit long, and it would be better in person," Mary said, hoping Dennis would agree.

"Of course, no problem. I just hope you're not going to fire me." Dennis laughed, trying to lighten the mood.

"I would never! Where are you?"

"I'm at the park by the bay. I had plans with Lucas and Sarah, but they both canceled. I'll tell you about it later."

"Perfect. I'll see you in about 30 minutes or less. I'm still in the office, you know—Saturdays are for tidying up my desk."

"I'll wait for you, no rush."

Dennis couldn't stop worrying, her mind racing with possibilities. She couldn't help but think something was wrong with Tammy, and the anxiety pressed against her chest. The minutes seemed to stretch endlessly as she tried to distract herself by watching people pass by, but it didn't help.

Mary arrived at the park and called Dennis to find out where she was.

"Yes, I'm near the shore. I'll walk there now," Mary said after Dennis gave her directions.

A few minutes later, Mary spotted Dennis sitting on one of the benches near the water's edge.

"Hello, Mary."

"Hi, Dennis. What a wonderful breeze! You really should make the most of your time outside, don't you think?"

"Yes, of course. I used to have much more time for walks and excursions, but well... Don't leave me in suspense anymore. Tell me what's going on. It must be important if you decided to come all the way out here."

"Yes, it's important."

"You see, I was right. What's wrong with Tammy?"

"No, it's not about Tammy. It's about Sarah."

"Sarah? What about Sarah? You're not worried about me bringing her to live with me, are you?"

"No, Dennis, it's not that. I'll explain. Remember that Sunday when Eileen fainted?"

"Yes, I remember."

"Do you recall what Eileen was talking about that day?"

"Oh, I do. It was a surprise to learn that Eileen had a daughter. Believe me, I was shocked. I could tell it must be very painful for her to talk about it, and that's probably why it's been kept quiet. But what does Sarah have to do with all this?"

"Eileen came to me months ago, telling me about a strange feeling she had towards Sarah. She thought Sarah might be her daughter—yes, her daughter who was presumed dead. You can imagine how shocked I was. I didn't know whether to think Eileen was losing her sanity or something."

"Did this really happen? I can't believe it. I never thought introducing Sarah to my loved ones would cause a problem. I promise you that was never my intention," Dennis said, clearly embarrassed.

"No, Dennis, let me finish."

"Okay, sorry."

"Eileen couldn't shake the feeling, and it grew stronger day by day, so I felt obliged to investigate further. Even though I knew my brother-in-law and niece had died many years ago, something told me I had to dig deeper. That's why I asked you so many questions and wanted Sarah to visit more often."

"I hired a private detective. Eileen had shared something very personal with me—something no one else knew—about the special connection she felt with her daughter for years. It was real, but no one believed her. My niece's body was never found, which left Eileen clinging to the hope that she was still alive. At first, I thought Eileen was just seeing in Sarah the daughter she lost, but I was wrong."

"How? What happened? Why do you say that?"

"Well, the day Eileen fainted, she saw Sarah's mark—the butterfly on her arm. That was the last piece of the puzzle. My niece was born with that mark, and I couldn't ignore it. So, I did what I had to do. I needed irrefutable proof, so I had a DNA test done for Sarah."

"I know what you're going to ask—whether I can help," Dennis said.

"No, Dennis, it's already done. Remember when you and Sarah donated blood for Eileen? That's when the test was done, and it was sent to the lab. We were supposed to wait two weeks for the results, but they came in early."

"And what happened?"

"The investigator called me—the DNA results confirm that Sarah is Eileen's biological daughter. Eileen knew in her heart, but she needed this confirmation. For me, it was both a relief and a torment. I felt like I had failed them both by not supporting Eileen enough when she needed it most."

"Goodness, Mary, what you're telling me is incredible," Dennis beamed. "I can't even begin to imagine how... or what to think."

"I haven't been able to sleep, thinking about what Sarah's life must have been like. If we had just kept looking for her..." Mary's voice broke as she sobbed, unable to control her regret.

"You can't torment yourself with that now. You have to make the best of this and move forward. The important thing is that Sarah is Eileen's daughter. It's incredible. I can't believe it. Am I dreaming?"

"Yes, I know, but I let my sister and niece down. I should have supported Eileen more. I shouldn't have let us forget them so easily. I feel so guilty," Mary confessed, tears streaming down her face.

"Does Eileen know?"

"Yes and no. She knows we're waiting for the results, but I haven't told her they've already come in."

"You're worried, aren't you?"

"Yes. I'm afraid she'll rush to tell Sarah, and I'm terrified that Sarah might reject her or that Eileen might have another health scare, or both."

"Oh my God, that's awful. But don't worry. Ugh, we need to think carefully about how to break the news without anyone getting hurt. Let me think—I'm sure we can figure something out, even though it's complicated this time."

"Thank you, Dennis. I didn't know who else to turn to. You always seem to know what to do."

"Come on, let's walk for a while. Maybe with a clear head, we can find a solution to how to share this news without anyone having a heart attack or running away."

"Thank you again, Dennis," Mary said, taking Dennis's arm as they began to walk along the path by the bay.

"Don't even mention it," Dennis replied, determined to help in any way she could.

CHAPTER 28

The Best News

"You've been acting really strange these last few days. I don't know what you're up to."

"Me? Really? Why would you think that about me?"

"Of course, you! Who else? You're working all the time, hardly spending any time with me, and whenever I call, you're always busy."

"No, what are you talking about? But, okay, I can't lie to you—it's true."

"Really? Maybe I should find another boyfriend. It feels like you don't love me anymore." Dennis teased Lucas, though her suspicions that something was off were well-founded, even if she didn't fully realize it.

"Don't joke, Dennis. You know you're my life, and I'd never do anything to hurt you."

"Well, you'd better not see me angry, then."

"No, who would want to see you angry? Certainly not me."

Their laughter echoed as they said goodbye at the apartment door, heading off to work.

Dennis watched Lucas leave. She still had a bit of time before meeting Rona at ten in the morning. After finishing getting ready, Dennis grabbed her keys and bag and left. That particular morning, she drove more cautiously, at a slower pace than usual, and before she knew it, she found herself on the Bay Bridge. As she waited without hurry, she let herself be carried away by the smells the breeze brought in, recalling how many times she had lost track of time, letting her mind drift away.

If only you could remember where your mind wanders off to, Dennis thought. But it didn't matter so much anymore. Now that she had discovered her true self, all those situations that used to torment her seemed less important. Everything had taken a backseat; life was calmer now, as if the hunger for answers she had long sought had finally been satisfied.

Still, in certain moments, Dennis couldn't help but ponder the mysteries in her life, some of which were still hard to grasp. How was it possible that the roles we play in life could be so painful and difficult to fulfill? It was still a struggle, but she had begun to sense that the answers to all her concerns would undoubtedly come—and today was one of those days when some surprises would bring those long-awaited answers.

Dennis would have to be part of the significant news they were about to share with Sarah, knowing that it would clarify many of the questions Sarah had pondered for so long. Dennis wondered whether Sarah would believe them or if her reaction would be adverse, unexpected, perhaps even hostile. She couldn't help but feel worried and anxious about such a challenging and incredible situation.

Lucas had reacted similarly when Dennis had told him. But Lucas, more than anyone, understood that their purpose here on earth wasn't something easily comprehensible at first. Besides, it had taken a lot to finally convince Dennis, and that was just a glimpse of what lay ahead. At least they could take comfort in the fact that Sarah already had some understanding of the inexplicable, which made Dennis think that perhaps she wouldn't take the news too badly.

Dennis arrived at Dr. Michaels' clinic, which had opened two weeks ago. Sarah had been working there as a receptionist from very early in the morning until late at night, every day of the week. Sarah didn't mind; on the contrary, she wanted to be there as much as possible.

"Hello, good morning." Dennis walked over to Sarah's desk to hug and greet her.

"Hi, Dennis! How are you? It's good to see you. I don't see you on the schedule this morning—is everything okay?"

"No, nothing's wrong. I came to talk to Rona about something personal; she mentioned she'd have time today."

"Oh, I see. Let me check for you."

Dr. Michaels had provided Sarah with a car, which, though a bit old, still ran well and got her to work. It made things much easier for her. Dennis had already mentioned to her that she could consider moving in with him soon since he was looking for a bigger apartment. Sarah had taken this as great news, especially since she had already informed La Estancia that she was searching for a new place. Things were going well— very well. Sarah was happy, always smiling, and she loved her job. But now, they would have to wait and see what impact this new information would have on her life.

Dennis waited nervously to speak with Dr. Michaels. Although they had discussed this several times, today was the day they would finally tell Sarah what they had discovered. They had debated the best way to break the news and had decided against having Eileen tell her directly, fearing rejection. Now, all they could do was hope they had made the right decision.

"Dennis, you can come in. The doctor is waiting for you."

This brought back memories for Dennis, recalling the first time she had an appointment with Dr. Michaels. How incredible! So much had happened since then; time had certainly flown by—of that, she had no doubt.

"Thank you. I'll be out shortly," Dennis said.

"Yes, of course, I'll be here."

Dennis entered the office, greeted Rona, and they chatted for a while. Rona, knowing there wouldn't be much activity that morning, opened the door and called out to Sarah.

"Sarah, do you have a moment?"

"Yes, of course. What do you need?" Sarah asked.

"Nothing much, but I'd like to tell you something," Rona said.

Sarah stood up from her desk, walked into the office, and sat down next to Dennis.

"What's going on? Don't tell me I've lost my job!" she joked.

"No, silly, don't joke about that."

"Seriously, Rona, what's this about? What did you want to tell me?"

"You know, Sarah, there's something important we need to talk about."

"Yes, you've said that already, and I'm waiting for you to tell me what's so important. Please, I can't stand the curiosity and suspense any longer!"

"Well, I understand. It's just that we're unsure how this news will affect you—or how much it will affect you," Dr. Michaels said nervously, trying to find the best way to proceed.

"What news? Is it about my children? Please, just tell me!"

"No, it's not about your kids or your ex. It's about your past—or rather, your family. You've never shared much about them with us," she said, trying to ease the tension that was starting to build.

"My family?" Sarah asked, surprised. "I thought everyone knew. Didn't they read my hospital record?"

"No, I'm sorry. I never inquired or sought any other information about you except what you provided me," Rona explained.

"Ah, well, is that everything? Was that the important thing?" Sarah asked, a bit confused.

"Would it be too much to ask you to tell us a little about your life as a child? What happened to your family?" Rona added gently.

"There's not much to tell, really."

"How so? Your mother or father—where are they from? Where did you grow up?"

"Ah, I don't have parents. I never did."

"You don't have parents? How did you grow up, then? Who raised you?"

"I was born in France, in a very rural place far from everything. I think my mother died when I was born, and from there, I was passed from home to home. I remember that by the time I was six or seven, they left me in a home, where I spent many years. I grew up there until I became an adult and was able to work. Eventually, I met the man who would become my spouse, and he brought me to this country." As Sarah spoke, her expression slowly changed; the smile that had been there before subtly faded away.

"But I didn't know you spoke French. That's incredible!"

"Well, I don't speak it because I've never needed to."

"You really surprise me. But I'm so sorry for what you've gone through. It must have been so painful—I can only imagine." As the conversation progressed, Rona began to feel less confident about delivering the news she had been dreading.

Dennis didn't dare to utter a word. The realization that she knew so little about Sarah, whom she already considered a friend, made her question what kind of friend she really was. At the same time, Dennis thought that if Sarah had wanted her to know more about her life, she would have told her. Suddenly, a thought came to Dennis' mind, and she remembered the words Sarah used to say when the opportunity arose: *Everything eventually connects; you just have to be patient and wait.* Dennis understood that what was happening had to happen and that somehow, things would take a positive turn. After all, Sarah had made her believe that everything would be okay. It was a comforting thought in that moment.

"Can I ask why there are so many questions about my family right now?" Sarah inquired.

"Well, I don't think you know everything about your family," Rona said carefully.

"How? What do you know? What are you trying to tell me? It would be incredible if you told me I have relatives and that they're millionaires," Sarah laughed sarcastically, but she was in good spirits. She couldn't imagine what was coming next.

"Yes!" Dennis blurted out. "Something a little like that."

"What kind of joke is this, Dennis? It isn't very funny." Sarah had started to get up from her seat, ready to return to the front desk. She felt a little confused.

"No, you're right. I'm sorry, and I wouldn't make a joke like that. It's true—you don't know everything about your family." Dennis stood up to stop Sarah from leaving the room.

"What are you talking about? A while ago, it seemed like you didn't know anything about me, and now you're telling me this. I don't understand."

"I know, believe me. We've been trying to give you some news, and we don't know how. But this is the truth," Dennis said, wiping away a tear that slid down her cheek.

Sarah's expression changed. Her face grew serious and pale as she looked at Dennis with a distrust she had never felt before.

318

"Sarah, come, sit here. I'll tell you everything," Rona said.

Sarah sat down again without saying a word, her hands trembling, her body cold. Something was happening, and she didn't know what.

"Well, you weren't born in France, but here in this country. Your mother and father were traveling in France when the unexpected happened. Your father and you were involved in an accident—one that unfortunately brought misery to your mother. The car fell off a cliff, and no matter how hard the rescuers tried, they couldn't find you. Your mother..."

As Rona told the story, Sarah quickly connected each word to the story Eileen had shared, as if she were reliving that Sunday when Eileen spoke of her deceased daughter. The same chill ran through her body from head to toe. The details of how Eileen had searched for her daughter for years echoed in Sarah's mind. It felt as if her head might explode. She couldn't comprehend that all those visions and thoughts she had as a child were real, after all. She had fought so hard to push them out of her mind, to ignore the woman's voice, to not feel what she felt, that now, when she tried to understand it, it seemed impossible.

Little by little, a nearly unfamiliar feeling began to surface within Sarah. She couldn't help it—her eyes clouded with the accumulation of tears that began to flow from the depths of her being. One by one, memories of those nights when she was still a child returned. In those moments, the only thing that eased the desperation inside her was the voice of that woman she heard in her head, never knowing that it was her mother. The bond between that mother and child, far from ordinary, was deep and almost indestructible. When the accident happened, it made that connection even stronger. The only thing that mother wanted and asked for was to find her daughter.

But Sarah had never known that the voice was her mother's. In fact, she never knew her mother was alive—quite the opposite. All those moments of anguish and uneasiness that Sarah had endured had caused her to suffer greatly, not realizing that what she heard in her head wasn't the loss of sanity but a wonderful gift cultivated by the love of a desperate mother. It was an incredible ability, one that few possessed, but it had also led to her being labeled as "crazy," nearly driving her to lose her mind completely.

Now, it turned out that it hadn't been her imagination, but something much bigger—something that no one could explain, since there was still no science that could comprehend it. But that didn't mean everything Sarah experienced in the past and now in the present wasn't real; it just meant that not everyone could understand it.

Dennis slowly reached over to put his arms around Sarah's shoulders, offering her comfort. No one knew how she would ultimately react, but from what Dennis could see, this had touched her deeply, bringing up the same anxiety she had felt so many times when life had placed her in situations that defied explanation.

"Sarah, for whatever it's worth, don't close yourself off. You have all of us here to help you, and you'll see that things will look different," Dennis said. Rona added, "Dennis is right. We can talk about this as many times as you need, and we'll find a way to help you feel better."

"And remember, you don't have to do or say anything until you're ready. Everyone will understand," Dennis assured her.

Sarah didn't say anything. The only sounds were her sobs and deep breaths as she sat there, nearly motionless. Rona looked at Dennis, and Dennis returned her gaze, both wondering what would happen next. But no one knew anything at that moment—they just had to give Sarah time and let her emerge from the trance she was in on her own.

Minutes passed, and Sarah finally reacted. She sat up in her chair and began to wipe away her tears with her hands. Then, she raised her head, searching for her friend's gaze, and said, "My dear Dennis, you have been something very special to me. I dreamed of you from a very young age, without clearly knowing why. But I knew I would meet you, just as I met Mark. It's all been part of this labyrinth where we're prisoners, unable to escape, no matter our intentions, because we're here to live this life. And although many of us cannot understand and find it repulsive to think that suffering can be a part of learning, you should know that it is. I begged and prayed with all my heart never to hear that voice again, not knowing that it was my only connection to my mother—the only strength that helped me survive those endless moments of loneliness when I was just a child, aimless and homeless, unable to understand anything. That voice was my mother's!" Sarah threw herself into Dennis's arms, who listened to the painful words she spoke.

"I don't know what to say to ease your pain. I don't want to sound redundant, but you know you'll feel better, right?"

"Sarah, Dennis is right. How you feel now won't last forever, I can assure you. Just trust that you'll feel better," Rona added, trying to comfort her. Both Rona and Dennis feared that Sarah was devastated by the news, but in reality, Sarah didn't feel afflicted at all—quite the opposite.

"I'm not sad. I know I'm crying, but this is the most incredible news I could have received—don't you see? I've never been crazy! Everything I thought I imagined actually happened." Sarah's expression began to change again.

Dennis and Rona didn't know whether to laugh or remain silent as they watched Sarah's reaction. It was definitely a surprise. They never could have imagined how important and traumatic it had been for Sarah to keep quiet and hide the abilities she possessed just to survive in a world where no one understood her.

Dennis understood this very well. She knew that no one would believe her if she went around saying she saw lights moving at incredible speeds—and that these lights were actually our original forms outside the human body. Everyone would have called her crazy, and she knew it. But fortunately, she had found Rona, who not only believed her but also made her feel comfortable with the situation. More than that, the same doctor had experienced situations and events that she couldn't discuss openly without risking her psychiatrist's license.

Sarah turned to look at Dr. Michaels. "Thank you—thank you a thousand times," she said. "You are a compassionate soul. You extended your hand to me, and today you've also given me back something I thought was dead forever. I'll be the best receptionist you've ever had; I can guarantee it."

Sarah, Rona, and Dennis, all holding hands, shared a good laugh. It was clear from their faces that normality was returning.

As things began to settle back into place, Dennis felt the urge to ask something. It was impulsive, but she needed to know what Sarah would do now that she knew her mother was alive—and that her mother was none other than Eileen, the same person she had been interacting with for the past few months.

"Sarah, can I ask you something? I don't want to pressure you or make you uncomfortable," Dennis asked, her tone curious.

"Of course you can. But I think I know what you'll ask—you want to know what I'm going to do now, don't you?"

"Yes, exactly. But I don't want to pressure you or seem nosy."

"Oh, you and your concerns! You're not intruding at all. In fact, I think I've been the one who's intruded the most in your life, considering all I've known about you for so long." Sarah smiled.

"Well, if you say so. I'm intrigued by what you'll do next. Your reaction has been different from what I imagined. Nothing strange, but I didn't have a clear picture of what your life had been like. Now, it's more than clear to me," Dennis said, holding Sarah's hand tightly.

"What I'll do is, of course, go see Eileen. Does she know?" Sarah asked, pausing before continuing. "Although I think I'm being silly—of course, she knows. She must have known since that Sunday when she told us the story. She wouldn't have told anyone else except those who really needed to hear it, right?"

"I think you're right. But don't assume everyone knows. Mary has been very cautious about this, and indeed, this has been one of those events she describes as 'the best news anyone could get,'" Dennis said.

"Yes, I agree. You can't imagine what this means to me," Sarah added.

"Then go! Get out of here and run to see that woman!" Rona urged; her voice filled with emotion as she thought about what it would mean to see her son after he had died. She knew a mother would give anything to see her children again, no matter how or when.

Rona and Dennis exchanged glances as Sarah left the office. She was finally going to see her mother. A moment of happiness had finally arrived for Sarah. When she was completely out of sight, Dennis called Mary.

"Mary?"

"Yes, hello, Dennis. How did it all go?" Mary asked, her voice filled with impatience. She had been counting down the minutes.

"Everything went better than we expected. You can't imagine—Sarah is on her way to see you."

"Are you serious?"

"No, I'm not joking. She's on her way to your house right now to see Eileen."

"But how did she take it? What did she say? How did it go?" Mary asked, her voice a mix of curiosity and concern.

"Don't worry, everything's fine. Sarah took it very well. Of course, it was emotional for her, but she handled it. You don't have to worry about seeing her cry like that again," Dennis reassured.

"So, was it hard for her to believe?"

"Not exactly. It wasn't that she didn't believe it; it was more about understanding it. What hurt her the most was realizing that all those things that happened to her, and are still happening to her, weren't just in her head. But let me tell you, she was actually happy—happy to finally be able to say she was never crazy."

"Oh, my God, I can't imagine what she must be thinking. Do you think she blames me?" Mary asked, her voice tinged with guilt.

"No, I can assure you, Sarah has a very different perspective on life. She believes that everything happens for a reason, that it's predestined. Don't torture yourself. Now be strong and let Eileen know," Dennis said, trying to calm Mary, who hadn't slept well for weeks.

Mary hung up the phone and went to the living room, where Eileen was sitting, reading an article in one of the magazines they always kept on the coffee table.

"How are you feeling?" Mary asked gently.

"I'm fine, although I have a strange feeling in my chest, but otherwise, I'm okay. I've taken the medicine as the doctor prescribed," Eileen replied.

"It might be something else," Mary said, trying to ease into the news she was about to share.

"Something else? Like what?" Eileen asked, her curiosity piqued.

"Something else, like Andreas," Mary hinted.

"Andreas? What do you mean? Be clear and stop beating around the bush," Eileen urged, a little uneasy.

"Well, don't get too excited—you know it's not good for you," Mary said as she moved closer to where Eileen was sitting.

"But go on, what about Andreas? Why are you bringing him up now? You never talk about her, so what's different today?"

"Are you not the one who felt a strange connection with Sarah, believing she could be Andreas? Or are you changing your mind now?"

"Of course not! I couldn't change my mind. My heart tells me I'm right, and you'll see that the truth will come out sooner than you think. I've been thinking about talking directly to Sarah. I'm done with beating around the bush—I'll tell her what I believe."

"Are you sure that's a good idea?" Mary asked cautiously.

"Absolutely. I don't think I'll wait beyond this weekend—I'll tell her everything."

"And why wait until the weekend? You can do it today. Sarah's on her way here to see you."

"She called you? And why didn't you tell me sooner?"

"I'm telling you now—I just got the call. Are you sure you'll be okay telling Sarah this?"

"Yes, I think it's the best thing to do," Eileen replied, her voice firm.

"Then I'll be around in case you need help," Mary said with a reassuring smile as she sat down next to Eileen. "But there's something I need to tell you before you see Sarah, just so you'll be calmer when you talk to her."

"What is it?" Eileen asked, her curiosity deepening.

"You have the green light to proceed without fear of making a mistake, sister. You were right—Sarah is Andreas!"

"Oh, my God, I knew it! I knew it from the moment I saw her that day. But how can you be so sure now?"

"Simply because it's the truth. It's a long story, but it doesn't matter now. What matters is that she's your daughter, she's my niece, and somehow, she's come back into our lives," Mary said, holding Eileen's hands, trying to convey how glad she was to know it, too.

Time passed as they continued talking, sharing memories, and reveling in the joy the news brought them. The doorbell rang, and the housekeeper went to answer it. It was Sarah.

"Hello, Miss Sarah. How have you been?" the housekeeper asked.

"Actually, I could say I've been very well," Sarah replied, looking happy. "I came to see Eileen—is she at home?"

"Yes, Miss Sarah, she's in the living room with Mrs. Mary. Please come in; you know the way."

"Thank you very much."

Sarah handed her bag and jacket to the housekeeper and walked into the living room without wasting any time. Once there, she found both women sitting opposite each other. Their eyes met, and Sarah's eyes began to fill with pent-up tears, but she held them back just a little longer. She tried to keep her composure and continued walking until she reached them.

"I'm here—you were waiting for me, weren't you?" Sarah said with a trembling voice, trying to maintain her composure. But as she stood in front of them, she dropped to her mother's feet. "You don't know how I feel. I should never have pushed you out of my mind. I would have known you were my mother eventually. I'm so sorry." Sarah's voice broke as she wept, releasing the sorrow she had kept in her heart for so many years.

"Oh, no, don't say that. I'm the one who should apologize. I was your mother, and I should never have stopped searching for you. You don't know how I cried for you for years, unable to find comfort, until one day I just stopped feeling. It was like dying inside. But that day, the day I saw you for the first time, that day my life came back to me, my daughter!" Eileen exclaimed as she embraced Sarah.

Mother and daughter held each other tightly, trying to make up for all the lost time in that single moment. The hugs and kisses they had missed out on seemed to find their perfect moment. Mary, still sitting in the chair next to them, waited for her turn to hug her niece and tell her how sorry she was for not listening to her sister all those years ago and for not supporting her in continuing the search.

But at this point, there was no use in asking for forgiveness or assigning blame. The reality was that, somehow—believable or not—Andreas had returned to the lives of the Harrison sisters. Life is a roller coaster, full of emotions and experiences, trivial and unexpected events, sometimes happy and sometimes sad. It was all part of a plan—a divine plan—that both Mary and Eileen were likely fulfilling.

For Mary, having Tammy close again and watching her battle and overcome the cancer that had plagued her was incredible. Understanding that Tammy had fought and won because she wanted to stay here for her family, and for the love she deeply held for her mother, was a tremendous realization for Mary. Having Tammy's love again was something she couldn't fully explain—it filled her with life and energy. On the other hand, Eileen was just beginning a new chapter in her life, one that was unexpected but was already bringing her the best moments of her life.

Both sisters took deep breaths that day, from the depths of their beings, filled with love and dreams of a future that would bring them a better life, even if they didn't know how long that future would last. What was clear was that they would cherish every minute of it.

"I can't believe I'm here with my mother," Sarah said. "But it's real this time. You don't know how I dreamed of this moment—so many times that I eventually stopped thinking it would ever happen."

"My dear daughter, how much time I've wasted, but now nothing and no one will ever separate us again. You'll see that we'll get through this," Eileen said, holding her daughter in her arms.

"You'll see that from now on, everything will change. We'll be the family we were always meant to be," Mary added as she embraced them both—her sister and her niece. "What happiness," she thought.

"My family!" Sarah exclaimed with a laugh. "It sounds incredible. I can't believe a family appeared in my life overnight."

"Well, you see, not only have you found your mother—who, by the way, couldn't be a better one—you also have an aunt who's going to love you like another daughter. And you have a cousin, and with her, her whole family," Mary said.

"It will take time to process, but what won't take time at all is loving you, Mom. I've had all this love stored up for so many years that I've lost count. From this moment on, you have all my love," Sarah said, her heart swelling with emotion.

Eileen's heart couldn't beat any faster—it was pure, healthy happiness. "I feel the same, my daughter. Nothing and no one, neither time nor distance, ever managed to extinguish the love I felt for you. It was only kept safe in my heart, and now that I've found you again, nothing can prevent me from living only for you. I love you, my little butterfly—you've finally come back to me!"

CHAPTER 29

Specifying Plans

"Alicia, are you ready? We're just waiting on you," Tammy called out. "Hurry up, we're already late."

"Yes, I'm coming, Mom. Don't worry, we still have more than two hours," Alicia replied, trying to reassure her mother. But Tammy was eager to get to the restaurant as soon as possible.

"It doesn't matter—just hurry up. I have things to take care of there, and I don't want Lucas thinking I won't follow through on what he asked of me."

"Yes, I'm ready. Let's go."

"And you have the little box, right?" Tammy asked.

"Yes, Mom, I have it right here, and it's well hidden. Stop worrying—everything will be fine," Alicia reassured her.

The rest of Tammy's family was already waiting in the car. Getting Alicia out of the bathroom had been the last hurdle, though they still had plenty of time to get to the location where the surprise would unfold. Finally, Lucas was going to propose to Dennis. Though practically everyone already knew, the excitement of the moment remained palpable. After waiting so long, today was the day.

They had planned everything meticulously. Tammy and her mother had conspired to keep Dennis busy all week with various tasks. Mary had put her in charge of organizing the company's participation in a pageant, while Tammy—who had recently taken on a new position at the agency—had asked Dennis to help her get back into the swing of work after a long health-related hiatus.

Dennis had been so preoccupied in recent weeks that by the time she saw Lucas each night, all she could do was apologize for being exhausted, promising that tomorrow would be better. But Lucas, who had orchestrated this entire distraction, understood perfectly why she was so tired. His goal was to ensure she had no clue about the grand surprise planned for this special day.

Meanwhile, Eileen, after much discussion with her daughter, had convinced her that the most logical step was to move into the house. Of course, this made Eileen the happiest, though she worried Sarah might feel pressured. On the contrary, Sarah was eager to move in but feared overwhelming Eileen. Both women had reservations after everything that had happened in recent weeks, but one thing was certain—they had found a balance in their lives that had seemed lost for years.

Sarah was more determined than ever to excel at her new job. She felt happy and fulfilled, both inside and out. Strangely, the pain of losing her children no longer felt as sharp. She knew she would have to face that sorrow eventually, but she was no longer running from the weight of her past. She waited patiently, much like Lucas had waited for everything to align so that his relationship with Dennis could finally stabilize. Now, he knew it was time to move forward and solidify their future together.

"Hi, Eileen, how are you? Sorry, Mom, this is just difficult for me, but give me time..."

"Don't worry, my dear. Nothing matters more than knowing you're alive and that soon you'll be by my side. Or have you changed your mind?"

"No, Mom, I haven't changed my mind. I just don't want you to feel pressured. You know we can be together without living under the same roof," Sarah said, ensuring she was making the right decision.

"Of course, I know that. But I can't imagine you feeling more at home anywhere else than in your own home. You know everything I have is yours, right?" Eileen reassured her, reminding Sarah once again that she was her sole heir. It wasn't an enormous fortune, but it was enough for Sarah to live comfortably—and, if her children ever returned to her life, for them as well.

"Yes, Mom, you've told me several times, and I'm grateful. But I just want to focus on the time we have together and make up for the years we've lost."

"I feel the same way. But I don't want you second-guessing yourself—you'll be happy here, and we'll be together."

"I know, and I haven't changed my mind. I've already told La Estancia that I'll be moving my things this Sunday. There's just one thing left, which is why I called you early."

"Well, tell me what's missing. I've already arranged for the movers, and everything is set for Sunday," Eileen said, her tone carrying a hint of worry.

"Nothing major, Mom—it's just the letter I need."

"The letter? Oh, right! It's ready. I'll give it to you this afternoon when you pick me up. You are still coming, right?"

"Of course. Dennis thinks I'll be busy with moving preparations this afternoon, just as we planned. That way, I could get out of the dinner invitation she made."

"Another cancellation—she must be wondering what's going on," Eileen noted.

"Poor Dennis. Yes, I've canceled on her three times in the past few weeks, but I promised Lucas I'd help with the restaurant decorations.

Everything is nearly set, but Lucas wanted those little lights—the ones I showed you. And when else could I have done it if not after work? The good thing is that everything turned out beautifully. I just hope Dennis doesn't feel too lonely or upset when she realizes we've all been conspiring for this surprise."

"I doubt it. You'll see—Dennis is a special woman. She'll understand that we all played a part in making this moment even more meaningful. How could she be upset that we were helping Lucas create something unforgettable? No, I don't believe it for a second," Eileen said with confidence.

"You're right. I won't worry anymore. Everything is ready, and I'll pick you up around five. Does that work? That way, we'll have time to grab a coffee before everyone arrives at the restaurant."

"That sounds perfect. I'll be waiting for you, sweetheart," Eileen said.

Among all the emotions Sarah was experiencing, finding her mother again was the most profound. It stirred deep reflections and memories of childhood, when she had listened to that soft, reassuring voice. Though she knew she might never fully recover those moments, she longed for even a fragment of them. But Sarah understood better than anyone that life was complicated, often impossible to decipher.

She was truly happy for Dennis, knowing this proposal would bring her joy. Dennis loved Lucas, and he loved her. But Sarah couldn't see beyond that—she didn't know what the future held for them. Though she sometimes wished she could glimpse more, she trusted that whatever came next would be filled with happiness. After all, Dennis had already endured her fair share of hardship—the kind of suffering life demands from everyone.

But Sarah had learned that life was about more than just enduring pain. There had been moments of love and normalcy too. The births of her children had been among the most unforgettable experiences of her life, memories tucked away in a corner of her mind, waiting to resurface. Returning to a sense of normalcy was allowing her to reconnect with those feelings, gradually restoring her confidence and self-worth. And why not believe that within this new normal, she might even reconnect with her children? She didn't know how or when, but the hope remained.

At Dr. Michaels' Holistic Center, things were improving every day. Sarah wasn't just a receptionist—she played an essential role. Highly organized and deeply trusted by Rona, she managed nearly everything. As Rona often said, Sarah had become Dr. Michaels' right hand.

Rona had long dreamed of opening this center. She knew that stepping away from psychiatry meant risking everything she had built over the years. But after losing her son and meeting people like Dennis, Lucas, Sarah, and so many others who had entrusted her with their deepest emotions, she realized traditional psychiatry couldn't always help. That realization had led her to open the center—to explore and support the things conventional science had yet to explain.

The holistic center was thriving. More people registered every day, and the services expanded in kind. Rona hoped that within a year, her center would be operating at full capacity, just as she had dreamed when the idea was born. This included regression sessions, which she had a particular interest in. After having been a therapist to incredible people, some with extraordinary abilities, she realized that the science she practiced couldn't help them.

Rona believed that perhaps the secret to understanding and helping people with such abilities lay in learning more about our own lives, in a deeper sense—like exploring our past lives. Perhaps in this way, we could begin to understand more about what we call the soul. These new convictions had driven Rona to take a chance on a different path, but with the same goal—to help others find existential balance.

Rona had offered to teach Dennis Reiki, but the truth was, Dennis hadn't brought up the subject again. So Rona decided to let it be until Dennis expressed some interest. After all, Reiki is a teaching that must be pursued because it is deeply felt, not out of pressure. Learning to manipulate and channel energy to those in need must be an act of giving from the depths of one's being. For this reason, Rona believed that if Dennis felt that call, she would be the first to know, because she would come to her, while Rona continued to oversee the other activities the center offered.

Rona had also been part of the surprise Lucas planned for Dennis, assisting him with everything related to the beautiful place Lucas had bought, which would soon be their home. It was different from what he initially wanted, as he ended up buying something a bit larger on the outskirts of the city, not far from where they worked, but far enough to offer a restful retreat on weekends.

The place was lovely—not immense, but after the renovations completed over the past month, it had an incredible view of the sea. The little house sat at the end of a cul-de-sac, much higher than sea level, which was important to Lucas, who didn't want to worry about losing his home in a storm.

At the same time, the property had a direct path to a nearly private beach, not open to the public. He was sure Dennis would love the place, as the seaside was one of the landscapes she adored. The sea breeze made her feel renewed and connected her to her own nature, helping her to replenish her energy daily.

Lucas had spent many days searching for the perfect place. Although his salary wasn't large, he had started saving early and had enough to make the investment. Over the past six months, he had been given two more stores to manage, which made him feel very good. After all, he had put his best effort into his work, and this was the reward for his dedication.

Rona had connected Lucas with some people who helped expedite the purchase of the house, giving him the time he needed for the necessary renovations. The plans had changed a bit since Sarah would no longer be living with them, something they learned after the purchase. But Lucas was sure that an extra bedroom would be good for them, and why not think about it—maybe in the future, their family could grow.

Dennis had called the property office and canceled the search for a new apartment. It had felt like divine intervention—every time she found a potential place, something would happen, and the opportunity would slip away. She was a bit exhausted from the search, and when Sarah told her that Eileen, her mother, had offered to let her move in, Dennis felt a little sad but understood completely. Although she had mixed feelings, Dennis had a clear view of the situation. It made perfect sense—Sarah had reunited with her mother, the most wonderful thing that could happen to her. It would have been illogical for her not to choose to live with her, especially since Eileen was such a lovely person, as was Mary.

Dennis couldn't be happier for Sarah, even if it meant she wouldn't be buying a bigger house for the time being. She was already exhausted from looking at properties and not finding anything suitable. But Dennis rarely thought about living with Lucas full-time, perhaps because she didn't want to disrupt their relationship or make plans like the ones she had made with Mark—plans that, although in the past, still instilled fear in her. She preferred simply not to think about it.

From time to time, Dennis would let her imagination run wild, envisioning a future where she and Lucas lived together happily. But the fear and anxiety these thoughts provoked were stronger, forcing her to push them aside. Besides, Lucas had never hinted at anything like that, and she didn't want to be the one to bring it up. Dennis preferred things to stay as they were rather than risk losing him. She loved him too much to put any pressure on him.

When Lucas decided to propose to Dennis, he originally planned to give her the keys to the place where they would build their home together instead of a ring. However, in recent weeks, he changed his mind and decided to buy a ring for Dennis, enlisting Tammy's help. Who better than her? Of course, Tammy offered her unconditional support.

They visited several jewelry stores searching for that "special" ring until they found what Lucas considered "the perfect ring." It wasn't a traditional ring, because nothing about his relationship with Dennis was traditional. The ring had a wide band made of white gold, with the words "NA-WEER-TIS" carved around it and small white and bluish diamonds set into the band. Inside, the date of the proposal would be engraved. Tammy found the words Lucas wanted to engrave on the ring strange, but she didn't dare ask what they meant, assuming it was something private— and it was.

Tammy took on the task of getting Dennis' ring size, which wasn't easy since Dennis didn't wear rings. This meant they had no way of knowing her size, so Tammy had to come up with a series of creative excuses to get Dennis to accompany her to a jewelry store. Tammy used the excuse that she needed to have her wedding ring repaired because it had become too loose due to her illness, which was true and made the story believable. However, this still didn't create a situation where Dennis needed to try on a ring, so Tammy had to think of something else to get Dennis to agree to wear a ring.

Tammy's first attempt failed because Dennis didn't want to try on a ring for no reason when they took the ring to the jewelry store. Tammy didn't want to push her, wanting to keep her from realizing the true intention behind the visit. But the second attempt was more successful. Tammy decided to talk to the jewelry store owner and ask for help. They devised a plan, and when Tammy called Dennis to ask her to come pick up her ring, which was ready, Dennis didn't object.

Once at the store, the owner immediately told them the ring was ready, but she had a small concern, which Dennis didn't find strange at all. On the contrary, Dennis was eager to help. When Dennis asked what the concern was, the owner said, "I think they made it too small."

"How so? Didn't you measure it?" Dennis asked.

"Yes, I did, but sometimes the measurements I send don't come back right," the owner replied, starting the conversation that would eventually lead to Dennis trying on the ring.

"What a hassle. I think it's best for Tammy to come and try it on herself. That way, if the size is wrong, they can send it back immediately. That's probably the best option," Dennis said, preparing to leave.

"Couldn't you try it on yourself? What size are you?" the owner asked.

"Me? I'm not really sure—I think I might be a size eight, but I'm not certain," Dennis replied with uncertainty.

But this was exactly the response the owner was hoping for, and she continued without hesitation. She approached the counter, already holding the metal key ring used for sizing, and said, "Let's see what size you are. If you're a seven, you can try it on, and we'll know right away if the size that arrived is correct." She moved quickly, not giving Dennis time to think twice, and gently took her hand, looking for the ring finger to try the size 7 sizer.

The jewelry store owner had vast experience and had already estimated that Dennis was likely a size seven based on the shape of her hands. But, of course, she couldn't rely on that alone—she needed to try the size to be sure.

As the owner measured her finger, which turned out to be a perfect fit for a size 7, Dennis looked up at the ceiling and noticed a glowing orb in the corner of the room, motionless but shining brightly.

Dennis had learned to appreciate the lights—they were a part of her life now, and whenever she saw them, she understood that they were a good sign. Although they had sometimes caused her sorrow or anxiety, they had never brought her harm, and Dennis now understood that. She wondered inwardly what that light was observing—was it her? Or perhaps the jewelry store owner?

The owner's voice brought Dennis back to reality when she said, "I knew you were a seven—your hands are slender and graceful." She smiled, pleased to have guessed correctly. "Now, if you wouldn't mind trying on Tammy's ring, we can see if it fits correctly."

"Sure, I think it's good to know my size. I've never really needed to know it since I don't wear rings," Dennis said.

"Any special reason? It's rare to find someone who doesn't wear any jewelry on their hands," the owner of the jewelry store commented.

"I'm not really sure. I don't remember ever buying anything for my hands—not rings or bracelets. Now that you mention it, it seems strange to me too. I guess I just never gave myself the opportunity," Dennis said, looking at Tammy's ring on her hand. It was a simple band, with no decoration or anything special, just a traditional wedding band.

"I think it will look good on Tammy, since it fits me perfectly," she commented.

"I'm glad to hear that—so we won't have to send this ring back to the company," the owner of the jewelry store smiled.

Thanks to Tammy's idea and the help of the jewelry store owner, they managed to get the perfect size for the ring Lucas would give Dennis that afternoon, the day that seemed like it would never come but had finally arrived. That night, he would propose to her as he had planned for so long, marking the beginning of what he called "the way home."

Alicia, Tammy's eldest daughter, finally came out of the house, and the family piled into the car to head to the restaurant in Bay Park, where they would join the others. Tammy wasn't nervous; instead, she was eager to see Dennis's reaction when she discovered the beautiful surprise that Lucas, with everyone's help, had prepared for her.

"It'll be like a fairy tale," Tammy thought to herself, so exciting—the place divinely decorated with flowers, lights, food, and all the people who loved them both. What more could she ask for?

Although Tammy was certainly right, when they arrived at the venue, she realized that her expectations of how the room would be decorated had fallen far short. When they entered the restaurant, one of the coordinators approached them to guide them to the next room. As soon as she opened the door, the sight that greeted them was so stunning that Tammy had to sit down to take it all in.

The room, always intended for parties and events, was beautiful on its own, but this time, it had been embellished even more. The walls were covered in antique gold brocade wallpaper, which looked especially stunning adorned with garlands of tiny lights from which glass beads hung, shimmering like pure crystal.

A three-tier chandelier hung in the center of the room, with multiple lights on each tier. The glow from the chandelier reflected off the small crystals hanging throughout the room, producing a multicolored radiance that filled the space, covering everything within it.

The tables were draped in cream-colored tablecloths, and each centerpiece was a floral arrangement of white and yellow roses surrounding a small candle in the middle. The flickering light from the candles, combined with the sparkle of the crystals, seemed to create intricate patterns on the tablecloths. The entire environment had been prepared with great dedication—the flowers, the lights, the candles, and every detail had been placed with the deepest affection that those close to Dennis felt for her.

Although the celebration wasn't large, Lucas hoped it would be something very special for Dennis, the woman he loved, the woman who was his companion in body and soul, and whom he could finally have by his side forever.

Dennis, for her part, had been so consumed by work and the sudden influx of extra activities that she hadn't noticed how almost everyone, except for Sarah, had been avoiding her. When Sarah canceled their last dinner together, Dennis felt a strange unease. After all, they had grown very close over the past few months, sharing time and personal moments like two good sisters. But that last-minute cancellation made her briefly wonder if something was wrong that she hadn't noticed.

However, Dennis quickly dismissed the thought, reminding herself of everything Sarah had been through in the last month—from finding her mother to the point of now moving in with her. "Sarah definitely has a good reason to be short on time," Dennis thought.

What Dennis didn't know was that Sarah had spent hours and hours decorating the venue, from finding those tiny garlands of lights to arranging the flowers and everything in between. Everyone had pitched in, taking turns to help make everything perfect, but without a doubt, Sarah had coordinated everything with Lucas.

The days had passed quickly, with Dennis barely stopping until she lay her head on the pillow each night. The last few weeks had been the most demanding. She had a lot of work and obligations she had committed to. It seemed that everyone and everything required her presence.

But deep down, Dennis had learned to thrive in such situations because staying busy had helped her survive the worst stages of her life. Being occupied was the best therapy for her. Of course, this time she didn't feel depressed; quite the opposite. Dennis felt that life was smiling on her, making her feel the need to spend a little more time with herself and Lucas, to enjoy more moments with him. But the truth was, Dennis was so accustomed to working non-stop that longing for free time was something new to her.

Soon, more new things would enter her life—sensations she hadn't felt before would make their presence known, ultimately leading her to remember where she came from and who she had left behind.

CHAPTER 30

The Expected Moment

"Hello, my love, how are you? I haven't heard from you all day. I hope nothing's wrong," Lucas said as he called Dennis.

"Hello, no, my love, nothing's wrong. I've just been so busy I haven't even had time to eat. I think my stomach is about to stage a rebellion," Dennis replied.

"Wait, you haven't eaten at all? Dennis, you're going to make yourself sick if you keep this up."

"No, don't worry. It's just today. I lost track of time, but I'll grab something soon."

"Alright, I'll try not to worry if you promise me that. But how about having dinner together tonight? It's been a long week," Lucas suggested. "Oh, but now that I think about it, wasn't tonight your dinner with Sarah?" he added, keeping up the act so Dennis wouldn't suspect a thing.

"Yeah, that's true, but Sarah had to cancel. She's still dealing with the move and insisted she didn't need my help. So we won't be having dinner together. Honestly, I think I'd rather just go home and rest."

"That's a shame. But really, wouldn't you like to have dinner with me instead? It's been a while since we enjoyed a meal out. We could go to

Bay Park—great food, beautiful view, and maybe even grab some ice cream afterward. Doesn't that sound nice? Come on, say yes. It would be good for us to spend some time together, don't you think?" Lucas made his case carefully, needing her to say yes so his plans could move forward.

"You know what? Even though I feel exhausted, I think you're right. We need to take a break and enjoy some time together. So yes, let's do it. Thank you for the invitation, my love. See you there?" Dennis said, sounding enthusiastic about the plan.

"Of course! What time do you think we should meet? I'll be free after six, so I can probably get there around six-thirty," Lucas replied, nudging her toward the time they had already arranged with the restaurant coordinator.

"You don't need to rush for me. I think seven sounds perfect. I'll probably be leaving the office around six."

"Perfect. Seven it is. See you at the restaurant. I love you," Lucas said, feeling relieved that everything was now in motion.

He hung up quickly, not wanting to give Dennis a chance to change her mind. Everything was in place. Dennis had agreed without much questioning, which was a relief. Lately, she had been worrying about whether she was neglecting their relationship due to work. It was a thought that weighed on her from time to time, and Lucas knew she would have agreed to anything to make it up to him. What Dennis didn't know was that tonight was not just about their relationship—it was about their future together.

Meanwhile, Sarah picked up her mother, and they arrived at the restaurant around half-past five. They had time for the coffee they had planned and went over the last details of her move. Sarah showed Eileen the decorations in the reception room, which had turned out beautifully.

Eileen was visibly impressed. "Sarah, you are amazing. This is truly beautiful."

"Mom, what are you talking about? Of course, it is! I must be your daughter after all. You've always been brilliant," Sarah replied with a laugh.

Eileen smiled, knowing Sarah was right. She and Mary had always been women with grand ideas, and the company they built together had grown into something strong and reputable. Sarah felt proud to be part of something founded by her mother.

A little while later, Tammy arrived with her family. Sarah and Eileen got up from their seats to greet them, and in the middle of their conversation, Tammy asked about her mother.

"Don't worry, dear, I think she'll be here soon. She went to Villanueva's Bakery to pick up the cake. You know how traffic gets in that part of the city," Eileen said reassuringly.

"It's okay, Aunt, don't worry. I just didn't get a chance to call her before we left. You know how it is—getting everyone out the door one by one was a challenge, but we made it!" Tammy said with a laugh.

By six-thirty, other guests began to arrive, including some of Lucas's friends and Dennis's coworkers. Rona arrived with Lucas, and right behind them, Mary came in, carefully carrying the cake box. There was still time before Dennis arrived, but Lucas kept his phone close, just in case she showed up early. His nerves were starting to get the best of him. Everything was ready—except for the most crucial part: waiting for Dennis to say yes.

Lucas had planned every detail—the house, the ring, the reception— but only now, in these last few minutes before she arrived, did a terrifying thought creep into his mind: What if she said no?

He had never considered the possibility. Of course, it could happen. And now, just minutes before she walked through the doors, fear gripped him, making it feel like a very real outcome.

From across the room, Rona noticed him shifting anxiously and walked over. "Lucas, what's going on? You look worried. Can I help?"

"No, I think it's nothing," he replied, forcing a smile.

"Are you sure? Has Dennis called?"

"No, it's not that. I just realized something I hadn't thought about before."

"Like what? Did you forget something?"

"No, I didn't forget anything. It's just... what if she says no?"

Tammy, who had overheard, immediately stepped in. "Lucas, you have nothing to worry about. Dennis loves you. This will make her happy."

At that moment, Lucas's phone rang.

"Hello?"

"Hello, my love, I just arrived. I'm parking the car. Are you already inside the restaurant?" Dennis asked.

"Yes, I just got here. I already have a table for us. You'll see me on the left as soon as you enter."

"Everything okay? You sound a little off."

"No, everything's fine. I'll wait for you."

Lucas hung up and turned to the others. "Okay, this is it. Wish me luck."

He stepped out of the reception room and headed toward the table he had reserved in the main dining area. Just as he was leaving, Alicia ran up to him, nearly out of breath.

"Lucas! Here—it's the ring. You almost forgot!" she said, pressing the small velvet box into his palm.

Lucas's eyes widened in surprise. He had been so consumed by nerves that he had nearly left without it. Taking a deep breath, he pocketed the ring and walked toward the moment that would change everything.

Sitting at the table, he tried to calm himself. His mind raced through everything that had led him to this moment—the memories, the challenges, the journey back to Dennis. The human experience was unpredictable and difficult, but he had fought for this love. Now, all he had to do was ask the question.

Dennis arrived moments later, placing her bag on the chair beside her. "There you are! Finally, I made it."

Lucas smiled. "Hello, my love. Yes, it's true—it's been a long day. How was the traffic?"

"Surprisingly light. I thought I'd get stuck, but it was smooth."

"That's good," Lucas said, his nerves tightening. He poured water for both of them, drinking his down in one gulp.

Dennis narrowed her eyes. "Something's off. You're acting weird. What's going on?"

Lucas exhaled sharply. "You know I love you, right? You are my everything."

"Then what exactly is all this? You're torturing me; I can't possibly understand what's happening if you don't clearly explain it to me," Dennis spoke, her nerves utterly frayed—a rare occurrence for someone who generally held her composure impeccably.

Lucas paused briefly, observing Dennis closely, before slowly withdrawing his left hand from hers. With deliberate calmness, he reached into the pocket of his jacket and carefully extracted a small velvet-covered box. With gentle precision, he placed it into Dennis's trembling hands, his own heart beating rapidly from anticipation and apprehension.

Immediately, Dennis's expression changed dramatically. Her heartbeat accelerated noticeably, signaling the intense emotions swirling within her upon seeing the small black box. It felt like an eternity as she stared down at it, questions and confusion tangling in her mind, her breathing growing increasingly shallow.

"Dennis, my love, please understand that I'm not trying to pressure you," Lucas began cautiously, sensing her overwhelming emotions. "But I genuinely need to know..." With extraordinary care, Lucas slowly opened the box, revealing a delicately crafted ring he had designed specifically for this important moment. He looked tenderly into Dennis's eyes, his voice steady yet filled with vulnerability. "Would you officially become my other half?"

Tears quickly filled Dennis's eyes, streaming down her cheeks uncontrollably, blurring her vision as she stared fixedly at the exquisite ring. Overwhelmed by a wave of deep emotion, she felt her heart pounding wildly, lodged seemingly within her throat, leaving her unable to speak. Her limbs felt heavy and frozen, completely stunned by the sudden intensity of Lucas's heartfelt proposal. The moment had been completely unexpected, catching her off guard and filling her with a profound joy unlike anything she had felt in many years. Time stretched painfully long, each second seeming to last a lifetime as she continued silently staring at the ring, emotions roiling within her.

Misinterpreting her silence, Lucas grew increasingly anxious, his heart sinking as worry and doubt seeped in. He reached toward her carefully, his voice gentle and deeply concerned. "Dennis, my love, please don't cry. If you aren't ready, you don't have to answer now. I never intended to cause you any distress. Perhaps my approach was wrong—I probably should have discussed it with you beforehand." Lucas's voice trembled slightly with uncertainty and regret as he watched Dennis closely, desperately hoping he hadn't ruined everything. "Maybe it would be best to set this aside and discuss it later."

As Lucas cautiously began to retract the box, Dennis reacted instinctively and swiftly, grabbing hold of it urgently. "No, no, wait! I'm so sorry!" she exclaimed with earnest apology and immediate regret. "I'm such a fool—I'm sorry! Don't take it away from me; it's mine! You bought it specifically for me, so you can't take it back now." Her tears continued falling freely, yet through them, a radiant smile illuminated her features, her eyes sparkling brightly with pure happiness. "Of course I will marry you! I love you so deeply—I will always be at your side. You can't imagine how profoundly this means to me."

Lucas released a profound sigh of relief, visibly relaxing as he saw Dennis's intense emotional state gradually subside into calm acceptance. "My love, you truly gave me such a scare. I thought I might have a heart attack—I genuinely worried I had hurt you or upset you."

"Everything was just so unexpected," Dennis confessed softly, her eyes locked onto the beautiful ring again.

"Would you like to see how it looks on your finger?" Lucas gently suggested, hoping to lighten the mood further.

"Oh, of course! How silly of me not to have tried it immediately," Dennis said, feeling a bit embarrassed yet overjoyed. Carefully, Lucas slid the ring onto her finger. As he did, Dennis was suddenly overwhelmed with vivid memories flashing through her mind, images of a life she had somehow forgotten.

"Do you like it?" Lucas asked softly, noticing the distant look in her eyes.

"Wait..." Dennis swiftly removed the ring, closely examining its delicate engraved inscription. "NA-WEER-TIS?" she murmured, trying to decipher its hidden meaning.

"Yes, I can explain the meaning—" Lucas began gently.

"No, wait, I think I already understand," Dennis interrupted, bringing the ring lovingly to her lips, then pressing it close to her heart. Gazing intently into Lucas's eyes, she unknowingly communicated with him telepathically, her voice flowing directly into his mind. "This is my name, isn't it? The surname is yours? And the middle name—is that our daughter's? Why didn't you tell me we had a daughter? Where is she now?

Why can't I see her?" Her excitement and emotion were tangible as she rapidly voiced her thoughts.

"Calm down, my love," Lucas replied tenderly, also speaking mind-to-mind. "You're right; our daughter is safe at our real home. You can see her whenever you want once we return. It has always been this way. Do you remember now?"

"Yes, memories are returning, but I can't bear the thought of waiting to see her again," Dennis expressed anxiously. "Knowing she's alone—what can I do?"

"Everything will be alright," Lucas assured her gently. "Do you recall why we came to this plane without our full memories? Precisely because we couldn't fulfill our mission burdened by memories of what we left behind. Everything will be resolved. Perhaps we should continue this conversation aloud now?"

"What do you mean?" Dennis asked, slightly confused.

"I mean we should speak aloud again to avoid raising suspicion by staying silent for so long," Lucas suggested with a gentle smile.

"Oh goodness, I didn't even realize," Dennis replied softly, breaking into gentle laughter as she resumed speaking aloud. Both smiled warmly, amused at how deeply Dennis had been absorbed in her inner reflections. After a quiet pause, she slid the ring back onto her finger, smiling joyously.

"Love, I have to tell you something else, but please don't cry. It's not a tearful moment," Lucas said gently, trying to keep the mood light.

"Oh, don't tell me there's more? Honestly, you're going to kill me with these surprises."

"I promise, just one more."

"Another one? What is it now? Don't make me guess; you'll have to tell me," Dennis said, her smile unwavering.

"Okay, this one is simpler. You just have to come with me."

"Where to?"

"Just over here, don't rush." Lucas stood, winking subtly at the coordinator standing by the door. Dennis rose to follow him.

"And what is it now?"

"You'll see. Nothing will impress you as much as the ring did," Lucas replied with a nervous chuckle.

Together, they approached the living room, and as the coordinator opened the door, everyone inside shouted joyfully, "Surprise!" Dennis barely had a moment to breathe as people eagerly approached to congratulate her with hugs, laughter, and well-wishes. The overwhelming scene left her feeling as though she might burst into tears or wake from a beautiful dream.

As Dennis greeted everyone, she paused to admire her surroundings. The room was beautifully decorated, adorned with delicate strings of lights, fresh floral arrangements on the tables, and thoughtful details everywhere she looked. Her favorite dessert—a Black Forest cake—caught her eye, sitting invitingly next to a white envelope.

Sarah approached, embracing Dennis tightly, their mutual emotion evident. Pulling back slightly, Sarah asked, "Do you like it? I hope you're not mad at me; this was the real reason we didn't have dinner together." Dennis immediately understood the recent distance wasn't estrangement but preparation for this joyful moment.

"Oh, no, don't even say that. I'll probably spend forever thanking you and everyone here. You can't know how much this means to me; it's not just a wonderful surprise—it's everything," Dennis responded emotionally. Both friends laughed gently, sharing in the warmth.

Dennis took time to move from table to table, expressing heartfelt thanks to each guest individually. She spoke with Eileen, who joyfully shared news about her daughter moving in, warmly expressing gratitude for Dennis's unwavering support. Next, Dennis joined Mary, who was seated alongside Tammy and her family. It was heartwarming to see Mary fully recovered and surrounded by her family, visibly happy and energetic. Tammy's husband tenderly held her hand, their children playfully laughing, enjoying their moment of family bliss.

At another table, Dr. Michaels sat with colleagues from the Holistic Center and friends of Lucas. Dennis immediately reached for Rona's hand, speaking softly and earnestly. "I genuinely don't know how to thank you enough—for everything you've done. Meeting you changed my life entirely. I had no future before, but because you were there for me, today feels like an incredible gift."

"Don't say that," Dr. Michaels replied warmly, rising to hug Dennis affectionately. "You always had a future; you just needed help seeing it. You're an extraordinary person, always there for everyone. Actually, I'm the lucky one—my life changed the moment you came into it." With a teasing smile, he added, "I think you'll like the other surprise Lucas has in store."

Dennis's eyes widened in playful disbelief. "Another surprise? I can't believe it."

"Oh no, I shouldn't have said that," Rona laughed lightly, clearly amused by Dennis's reaction.

"Well, now you have to tell me," Dennis insisted, grinning. "Lucas told me there were no more surprises. I can't stand the suspense."

After spending more time mingling, Dennis eventually returned to Lucas, who had also been enjoying the company. Relieved that his anxiety had passed, he now appeared completely relaxed and content.

Feeling slightly surreal, Dennis still hadn't entirely absorbed the events unfolding around her. She was confident, though, that eventually everything would settle, and she would fully grasp and cherish these incredible memories.

The dinner atmosphere was intimate and warm, with just the most meaningful people present. It perfectly reflected the life Dennis and Lucas shared. She ate quietly, driven more by the desire to savor each moment than by hunger. Occasionally glancing at Lucas, she noticed his glowing happiness, which deepened her contentment further.

During the meal, Dennis's attention was captured by several playful, glowing orbs dancing across the walls. They moved unpredictably, radiating a captivating energy. Nobody else seemed to notice, yet Dennis felt their presence strongly, sensing they shared her profound happiness. Deciding to trust her instincts, she imagined they were celebrating alongside her.

Seeing Lucas rise from the table, Dennis asked, "My love, where are you going?"

"I'm going for the cake," Lucas replied. Instead, he picked up a crystal glass, gently tapping it to draw everyone's attention. "Forgive my interruption. Dessert will arrive shortly, but first, I need to express my gratitude. Thank you all, especially those who are integral parts of the life of the woman who will soon become my wife. Your presence and support mean the world to us." He took a breath, smiling. "My love, I know I said no more surprises, but today I admit I've been the greatest liar. There's one more, but it's absolutely the last, I promise."

"Alright, what is it?" Dennis approached him, wrapping her arms lovingly around his neck. "I know you'd never make me suffer, so this must be something wonderful."

Lucas handed her the white envelope beside the cake. "Open it. I sincerely hope you like it; changing it would be rather complicated." Amused laughter filled the room.

Dennis playfully remarked, "Clearly everyone but me knows what's inside," her curiosity piqued. She opened the envelope, spilling documents and photos onto the table. Initially puzzled by the unfamiliar yet beautiful places, realization suddenly dawned. "Oh, I see—it's our honeymoon location!" she declared excitedly, prompting amused anticipation among guests.

"Dennis, check the address," someone suggested. Carefully examining the documents, she realized she was holding a property deed. "This can't be..." she whispered in astonishment. Examining the photos again, she finally recognized their new beachfront house.

"Lucas! I can't believe this," Dennis exclaimed joyfully, her eyes wide with happy disbelief. "Is this truly our new home?"

Lucas nodded warmly, confirming the extraordinary gift. Without hesitation, Dennis leaped into his arms, kissing him passionately amid joyful applause and laughter.

Their joyful tears mingled as the celebration continued late into the evening, the orbs seemingly joining in the festivities. Dennis knew she'd need considerable time to process fully the profound changes in her life. Lucas, meanwhile, felt no such need—he simply felt profoundly grateful, reaffirming the deep and enduring love he shared with Dennis, a love unaffected by circumstance or place.

He loved her, and she loved him, profoundly and unconditionally.

CHAPTER 31

A Special Gift

The days passed as expected, slowly resuming a comforting semblance of normalcy, somewhat calmer yet still gently highlighted by events from the preceding days. On the day of the reception, everything unfolded so rapidly that Dennis feared she might forget some precious details. She desperately wanted to preserve each moment—from Lucas's first call inviting her to dinner, to the final minute when the decorations were cleared away. Each instant was precious to her, but life had an undeniable way of rushing forward, often too quickly to grasp fully those fleeting moments.

The next morning, Dennis woke up exceptionally early, determined not to lose a single second, eager to embark on her new life in their new home. Lucas, on the other hand, appeared more exhausted than usual, as if the cumulative stress of the previous weeks had finally caught up with him. As Dennis paced excitedly around their apartment, she spotted an empty box meant for recycling. Inspired, she swiftly began filling it with personal items. Once the box was full, she approached Lucas, gently but insistently urging him out of bed, announcing she was ready to see their new home. Although it was merely six o'clock on a Saturday morning, Dennis, who had already been awake for hours, felt the timing was perfect.

Realizing sleep was impossible amidst Dennis's bubbling enthusiasm, Lucas got up, surrendering to her infectious excitement. They quickly left, skipping breakfast and agreeing they would grab something to eat in route to the house. The journey was relatively short—about forty to forty-five minutes—yet for Dennis, the travel duration was insignificant compared to the happiness she felt.

As they neared their destination, Lucas intentionally slowed the car, allowing Dennis to take in the charming surroundings. Gradually, he pointed out their new house, nestled at the end of a quiet street. He finally parked in front of the cozy, single-story bungalow, outwardly modest yet clearly renovated, featuring a freshly updated entrance and a newly installed front door. Lucas handed the keys to Dennis, who eagerly rushed to unlock the front door, her excitement visible and palpable, reminiscent of a child experiencing Christmas morning.

Upon stepping inside, Dennis was utterly stunned. Lucas had completely renovated the interior, designing the exterior wall facing the ocean to be entirely composed of windows. Every room—bedrooms, kitchen, and living area—opened onto an exterior corridor, ensuring breathtaking ocean views from almost every corner. The corridor, elevated slightly above the beach, was furnished with a charming patio table and chairs, and decorated with vibrant flowers, immediately making the place feel like home. Lucas hadn't done all this alone; Rona had offered invaluable decoration ideas, and the contractor had skillfully maximized the home's beauty and functionality. In witnessing Dennis's overwhelming joy, Lucas profoundly understood the significance of his efforts.

Carrying the box Dennis had packed, Lucas watched as she excitedly explored the space. "Don't you have anything to say, my love?" he asked gently.

"I don't know what to say. I feel like crying; I'm completely overwhelmed," Dennis replied, eyes shining with intense emotion. "Everything is so incredibly beautiful."

"Please don't cry," Lucas urged softly. "All I ever wanted was to make you happy."

"They aren't sad tears," Dennis assured him. "It's just... I never imagined something so wonderful could exist."

"I'm glad," Lucas smiled warmly, taking her hand gently. "Let me show you the rest. No more tears today, alright?"

They walked together, thoroughly exploring every room and the lovely exterior corridor, which provided a panoramic view of the sea and coastline. They descended a short staircase leading directly onto the sand, taking a leisurely walk along the beach. The remainder of the day was spent exploring the quaint coastal town, its streets filled with inviting shops, charming restaurants, and cozy antique stores characteristic of small towns in the region. They bought lunch at a local establishment before returning home. Dennis wanted nothing more than to enjoy the meal in the comfort and intimacy of their new home, basking in unparalleled joy.

During their peaceful meal, Lucas gently raised the topic of marriage. "My love, I've been thinking we could get married in a month. What do you think?"

"A month?" Dennis replied, momentarily taken aback. She hesitated, realizing she had never truly envisioned what she desired for her wedding.

"Do you think it's too soon?" Lucas noticed her hesitation. "I believe we can manage it, but…"

"What? Tell me," Dennis prompted curiously.

"Well," Lucas began with a warm smile, "I thought it would be wonderful to host our reception right here, at our new home. It's beautiful and spacious enough."

"That sounds absolutely perfect," Dennis agreed immediately, excitement filling her voice.

"Fantastic! We're in agreement, then. We'll plan the reception here as soon as possible. How does that sound?" Lucas asked enthusiastically.

"Yes, why not? Everything seems to be falling into place perfectly. I'm sure I'll find a dress that suits me," Dennis laughed joyously, running into Lucas's arms for a heartfelt embrace.

That afternoon was extraordinary, marked by deep emotional intimacy and profound love. Dennis and Lucas shared a connection beyond mere affection—they were soulmates reunited. At that moment, they embraced not just each other but their truest selves, unafraid and full of light, as if this were simply one of countless memories held dearly within them.

As the wedding day drew near, Dennis sought help from Sarah and Tammy to select her wedding dress, both friends eagerly offering their assistance. Meanwhile, Lucas contacted the restaurant where he had proposed, arranging catering for their celebration at home. Remarkably, all preparations—including catering, floral arrangements, and other important details—were swiftly completed in less than a week. Dennis found a gorgeous wedding dress, and soon everything fell effortlessly into place, sometimes making it difficult for her to believe this wasn't merely an exquisite dream. Despite her happiness, a subtle worry lingered—a vague fear that something might disrupt their joy.

Finally, Dennis's moving day arrived, just two weeks before the wedding. Packing was an exhausting process, despite Lucas having completed his move the previous week. Dennis meticulously sorted through years' worth of belongings, carefully deciding what to keep, donate, or discard. She came across items evoking powerful memories: treasured childhood keepsakes, photographs of her parents, old clothes, and her mother's jewelry box. Holding these tender memories, Dennis softly declared, "These won't remain hidden away any longer. They'll finally have a place at home. Mom, Dad, you'll always have an important place because I know you're with me, guiding and protecting me." As she spoke these heartfelt words, a few gentle orbs of light lingered quietly nearby, as if respectfully listening.

"If only... how I wish I could see them!" Dennis whispered yearningly. The orbs stayed briefly, silent and comforting, drifting away softly afterward. She wasn't disappointed, understanding now that things had changed profoundly. She accepted the gentle silence, understanding it was part of her new reality.

Among her possessions, there was one particular item Dennis couldn't bear to discard. Ever since learning about her daughter from her previous existence, her thoughts frequently drifted toward her child—wondering when she might learn more or even see her. Although curiosity consumed her, Dennis had not discussed this with Lucas, worried he might dismiss her hopes. Instead, she decided to seek comfort in Sarah's friendship.

"Are you nervous?" Sarah asked warmly as the wedding approached.

"Yes, I'm nervous," Dennis admitted, "but I suppose that's normal. It's like there's something fluttering inside me."

"The famous 'butterflies,'" Sarah reassured with a gentle laugh. "Don't worry, everything will be fine."

"Thanks, Sarah. You're probably right. Lucas and I have already shared a life together, but I still feel nervous. Bridal jitters, I suppose." They shared a comforting laugh.

"Sarah, I wanted to ask you a favor," Dennis began cautiously. "With everything that's happened lately, I don't want to burden you, but..."

"Please, Dennis, you know you can ask me anything," Sarah encouraged earnestly.

Dennis hesitated briefly, then spoke. "Remember that conversation we had a long time ago, when Mark was ill?"

"We've had countless talks back then," Sarah gently prompted.

"The one where you showed me where Mark would go after this life," Dennis clarified softly.

"Ah, that conversation. What exactly do you want to know?"

"It's something I've been hesitant to ask... I know I should be patient, but I can't help wanting to know."

"Know what? What's troubling you, Dennis?" Sarah inquired softly.

"Do you still have visions? Can you still see into people's lives?" Dennis asked tentatively.

"Yes and no," Sarah replied thoughtfully. "It's not something I can control; it's quite rare now, but yes, occasionally it still happens. Why do you ask?"

"I'll be direct," Dennis said, taking a deep breath. "Can you see anything about my future?"

"What specifically do you want to know about your future, Dennis?"

"I'm not completely sure," Dennis admitted, hesitating. "I just feel like I should know if there's something important waiting for me."

"If you're wondering whether I've already had visions about you," Sarah began gently, "then no, I haven't had any recent ones, only those from long ago. But give me your hands; perhaps I can try again now," she offered earnestly.

Dennis extended her hands toward Sarah, who grasped them firmly yet gently, closing her eyes to focus intently. After several quiet moments, Sarah slowly opened her eyes, gazing directly at Dennis.

"I think I understand what you're truly asking," Sarah began with compassionate care, "and I'm sorry, my friend."

"What did you see?" Dennis asked anxiously.

"I saw your life in your other home."

"Did you see him? And Lucas? Was he there?" Dennis questioned urgently.

"Yes, I saw Lucas. He was there with you, looking slightly different, just as you did."

"And her?" Dennis asked, her voice trembling slightly. "Did you see her?"

"Yes, I saw her," Sarah replied gently. "She's very beautiful."

"Then you know," Dennis said, a wave of emotion overcoming her. "You know I have a daughter, and I don't know when I'll finally see her."

"Yes, Dennis. I've always known," Sarah said softly. "But please don't be upset with me. Understand, some things we're not meant to fully know until the right moment arrives. Life is intricately designed this way, for our growth and understanding. Do you understand what I'm saying?"

"Yes, I do," Dennis said quietly. "But ever since I discovered her existence, I can't stop thinking of her—so small, and me not being there with her."

"But you will be, eventually," Sarah reassured her tenderly. "Time here isn't the same as there. A lifetime here might only be a brief moment there. You'll see her soon enough, and I truly believe you'll gain more clarity before long. Trust, and please be patient; peace will come to you."

Dennis knew Sarah was trying to comfort her, and although Lucas had explained these matters before, truly accepting it remained difficult. Dennis longed deeply for a greater understanding, unsure how to find it.

Time passed quickly, and soon enough the wedding day arrived. From the early hours, Dennis and Lucas busied themselves finalizing the arrangements they had begun the previous night. Mary had generously provided numerous floral arrangements, filling the house with the delightful fragrance of white roses and vividly colored lilies. Catering staff arrived early to set up, planning to return later around three for the final touches. The ceremony was scheduled for five in the afternoon, leaving ample time to spend with friends and loved ones.

Their guest list was modest, closely mirroring the attendees from Lucas's proposal, with the addition of a few relatives who traveled from afar and a couple of Dennis's acquaintances who had yet to confirm attendance, creating an intimate, familial atmosphere.

Dennis consciously avoided traditional wedding customs, neither borrowing nor incorporating anything old into her attire. She had even decided to keep Lucas from seeing her wedding dress before the ceremony, preserving a special moment of surprise.

Wanting simplicity, Dennis chose to forgo a traditional walk down the aisle. They had arranged for a gentle, elderly officiant, recommended by a friend—an experienced woman known for only agreeing to marry couples she genuinely believed would last. Upon meeting Dennis and Lucas, she immediately consented, as though she had been waiting specifically for them.

Their home transformed beautifully for the occasion, becoming almost magical. Flowers elegantly adorned every space, indoors and out. Small white-covered tables lined the exterior corridor, complemented by sun umbrellas decorated with delicate silver garlands shimmering softly in the sunlight. Chairs were carefully arranged on the sand, precisely where Dennis had envisioned the ceremony—with the serene sea as their backdrop.

Guests began arriving around four-thirty, though Sarah and Tammy arrived much earlier, at two, enthusiastically assisting with preparations. They shared drinks and enjoyed quiet moments together, while Lucas diligently checked every detail, ensuring everything was perfect.

Outside, Sarah, Tammy, and Dennis shared laughter and fond memories. Dennis cherished their friendship, never feeling the age difference, deeply loving both women. Eventually, they helped Dennis into her wedding gown, emotions rising despite their efforts to maintain composure.

"You can't start crying now; your makeup will be ruined!" Sarah gently teased.

"Dennis, please don't be sad; you'll have us crying too," Tammy added warmly, attempting to lighten the mood.

"I know," Dennis admitted softly, "but these feelings are overwhelming; something inexplicable is happening inside me."

"Everything will move quickly, and soon we'll all be celebrating," Sarah reassured with a comforting smile.

"Exactly! And look at this perfect weather—not even a hint of wind, just a lovely warm breeze. What more could you possibly want?" Tammy chimed in cheerfully.

Inside, Dennis felt a profound longing, wishing her parents could witness and bless this new chapter of her life. However, she didn't anticipate what happened next.

"Everything is ready," Sarah praised warmly. "Your hair is perfect. You should really consider doing this professionally—hairstyling, makeup, event decorating; you're naturally gifted."

"I do this out of love," Sarah responded, gently wiping a tear away. "Remember, I'm always here whenever you need me."

"Now, my task is to keep you both from starting to cry!" Tammy laughed, trying to lighten the mood. "Dennis, are you ready? You look gorgeous—stand right here."

"The dress really is lovely," Dennis admired herself thoughtfully in the mirror.

After heartfelt embraces, Dennis requested a few minutes alone, needing a quiet moment to herself. Sarah and Tammy obliged, reminding her to remain composed and to check on Lucas.

In solitude, Dennis gazed at her reflection, acknowledging the woman she had become—strong, independent, mature. Memories of Mark surfaced without sadness, simply peaceful acceptance. Remembering the bright orbs she once feared, she now understood their benevolence.

"Come to me," Dennis spoke softly yet firmly, symbolically embracing peace with her past. "Everyone is welcome; today is my big day."

Instantly, luminous orbs began gently filling the room, drifting in gracefully from all directions, forming an enchanting whirlwind of light around her. Unexpected tranquility washed over Dennis, deeply soothing her. The orbs gathered at the back wall, forming a glowing, expanding circle.

As the radiant circle grew larger, Dennis noticed something materializing within it—a strange opening forming slowly. Soon, it expanded enough to reveal a silhouette approaching from within. Unable to clearly see the figure, Dennis felt irresistibly drawn toward the mysterious opening, stepping forward instinctively, filled with anticipation and wonder.

Dennis felt no fear; an overwhelming tranquility prevented any sense of alarm. Instead, she experienced a sensation of increasing weightlessness, as if she were gently floating forward, drawn toward the luminous opening in the wall.

Her gaze remained fixed on the heart of the brilliant glow, and slowly, the figure within the brightness became clearer, moving steadily closer. It reminded her vividly of the night she had truly seen Lucas for who he was—the night she realized his soul belonged to another plane of existence. That revelation had confirmed for Dennis that the spiritual plane was real and that life did not truly end with the physical body.

Dennis's eyes pierced through the shimmering haze, eager to discern the shapes more distinctly, and she felt her heartbeat quicken with anticipation. Gradually, the silhouettes clarified, revealing two distinct figures moving toward her. Without consciously realizing it, Dennis stretched out her hands, instinctively yearning to touch them, to connect physically. She understood instinctively that she was receiving an extraordinary gift.

As the silhouettes drew nearer, they solidified into recognizable human forms surrounded by radiant, soft light. Dennis's outstretched hands finally met theirs, and in that moment, she understood who they were. They were her parents, appearing to her on this profoundly meaningful day—her wedding day.

"Is it really you?" Dennis asked, establishing a mental connection with the figures standing before her.

"Yes, my beloved child. It is indeed us, and we've come to be with you," spoke the gentle female voice.

"Dad? Is it truly you? Am I dreaming or imagining this?" Dennis questioned, seeking certainty that this moment wasn't merely a creation of her longing.

"Yes, sweetheart, it's us. We're truly here. We don't want you to ever feel alone—we've always been near you, always," her father's reassuring voice answered softly.

"I can't believe it! You're right here, but I can't even hug you. You can't know how deeply I've missed you," Dennis expressed emotionally, reaching instinctively toward them.

"We do know, my dear daughter," her mother gently comforted her. "We have always been by your side, every moment. You've always mattered immensely to us, and we've never ceased watching over you."

"But why couldn't I see you sooner? Why didn't you appear before now?" Dennis asked, longing and confusion mingling in her voice.

"Dennis, we cannot alter what was meant to be," her mother explained patiently. "This is the life each of us has chosen. Even if it feels challenging, it's the journey we decided to take, for our own growth and learning."

"Mom, you really are my mother, aren't you?" Dennis asked again, seeking absolute certainty.

"Of course, my darling girl. Of course, I am."

"Why did you both have to leave me? I've missed you more than words could ever describe."

"We understand, Dennis. Believe us; we wish things could have been different, too. You were meant to come home with us that day, but things unfolded differently," her mother gently explained.

"What happened that day?" Dennis asked urgently.

"Something we cannot fully comprehend," her mother answered gently. "These decisions were made between you and the Creator before your arrival here. It's beyond what we fully grasp from our current perspective."

"I don't understand," Dennis confessed softly.

"It's difficult to fully comprehend, living as you are on a lower astral plane than the one you originally belong to. But eventually, you will return home, to your true home," her father added reassuringly.

"When? I want to go home now," Dennis pleaded with a sense of longing.

"We understand," her mother said compassionately.

"And do you know about my daughter?" Dennis asked hesitantly.

"Yes, my dear," her mother comforted her. "Your daughter is well. You have nothing to worry about."

"But when can I finally see her? I don't want to wait anymore—I need to return home now," Dennis insisted emotionally.

"Patience, my love. All will happen in due course. Everything will unfold as it should," her mother gently reassured.

"But what about Lucas? Won't he return with me?" Dennis's voice carried concern.

"Dennis, Lucas chose to come back specifically to be with you. Something occurred, preventing you from returning home as you normally would. He won't return until his time here is complete," her father explained softly.

"What about our daughter, Mom? What will happen to her?" Dennis's voice trembled.

"Don't worry, Dennis," her mother gently assured her. "Everything ahead is something you've already chosen. You'll soon understand and won't feel so alone from now on."

"What do you mean by that?" Dennis questioned, seeking clarity.

"Try not to be so anxious, daughter," her mother gently advised. "Enjoy this moment, embrace this reunion with your true love—one who has been with you since the dawn of time."

"Mom means your bond with Tis has always existed. You've always been soulmates," her father added softly.

"Dad, are you saying Lucas's true name is Tis?"

"Yes, my child," her father confirmed tenderly.

Dennis recalled the engraving on her ring, 'NA-WEER-TIS,' and suddenly understood.

"Is my true name NA?" Dennis asked, her voice filled with newfound wonder.

"Yes, my dear one. You are NA, and you've come here to aid those in need. Your energy will be vital for many during your earthly journey," her father explained affectionately.

"And the name WEER—is that my daughter's name?" Dennis asked, now clearly understanding.

"Yes, Dennis," her mother gently replied. "Your daughter will also be an angel of light and healing, traveling far to bring necessary energy and healing to many worlds."

"Mom, Dad, do all souls have similar purposes?" Dennis asked earnestly.

"No, Dennis," her father clarified. "Every soul's mission is unique. We are all beings of light, but each of us has different tasks. We return to correct errors, learn new lessons, experience new emotions, and explore various planes of existence. There are countless reasons for our journeys. But at our essence, we all remain Light."

"I have so many more questions," Dennis said wistfully.

"We know, daughter, but you'll gain understanding in time. Remember, we will always be beside you, even if you can't always see us clearly."

"But will I see you again?" Dennis asked with hope.

"Yes, Dennis," her father replied gently. "Perhaps not in the way you'd prefer, but we'll always be close by until it's finally your time to return home."

"Don't go now, please!" Dennis pleaded softly.

"It's time," her mother whispered tenderly. "Trust that all will unfold perfectly. Now, enjoy your life, and remember your purpose: help those in need."

As their figures slowly receded, Dennis stood silently, processing the extraordinary encounter she had just experienced. Deep within, she knew her heartfelt wish had come true. She had seen her parents, confirming they were always near, watching over her. It may not have been exactly as she'd envisioned, but it was profoundly meaningful.

Still contemplating this profound moment, Dennis heard Tammy knocking at the door, gently calling her, signaling it was time. Taking a deep breath, Dennis looked around, realizing she was still standing before the mirror as if nothing had transpired.

Tammy entered cautiously, smiling warmly. "Everyone is waiting, Dennis. Are you ready?"

"Yes," Dennis responded, a radiant smile gracing her face. "I'm ready."

Filled with joy from seeing her parents and the certainty that she was taking a momentous step, Dennis left her room and entered the living room. She walked with her head held high and a broad smile on her face. All the people Dennis knew were there, everyone who was part of her circle—a somewhat unique circle she called her family. And there, too, was the man, the being, who had loved her the most and had done the impossible to make her happy in this earthly life.

That was finally the day when everything ended and, at the same time, everything began. That day, Dennis married Lucas. When the woman, officiating the ceremony asked Dennis if she would accept Lucas as her spouse, she replied:

"Yes, I accept! Again today, as before, I want to share this life and all others, as well as eternity."

CHAPTER 32

At Last Together

The memories of the past few months wrapped around Dennis like a gentle blanket as she sipped her coffee in the outer corridor, enjoying the crisp winter morning. She nestled deeper into the warmth of her blanket, warding off the chill brought by the changing season.

Her thoughts drifted aimlessly, difficult to organize as memories surged into her mind like gentle raindrops at the beginning of a soft shower, each one bringing back emotions and sensations etched permanently in her heart.

Tammy's recovery had marked a significant turning point for Dennis. Tammy wasn't just her mentor but had evolved into a friend—almost like a sister—teaching Dennis nearly everything she knew about their work. From the moment Tammy had entered Dennis's life as her teacher, she had been a steady and supportive presence, always pushing her forward and encouraging her through every challenge. In return, Dennis had naturally stepped up to support Tammy through her struggles, unaware at the time that these actions were part of a greater purpose within her earthly journey.

Her professional life had long served as Dennis's primary source of stability and support. Since joining the Harrison Agency, Dennis had dedicated herself completely, her enthusiasm and relentless effort significantly contributing to the company's growth. Her unique personality and unwavering willingness to do whatever was needed quickly made her an indispensable member of the agency. The Harrison sisters, Mary and Eileen, recognized Dennis's profound impact, deepening the bond they shared with her.

Mary was particularly touched, profoundly grateful for the immeasurable support Dennis had given her daughter, Tammy. She found it nearly impossible to express her gratitude adequately. Similarly, Eileen often struggled to put Dennis's dedication into words, frequently describing her as angelic—a sentiment that, despite occasional laughter from others, rang undeniably true.

Other individuals had become equally significant in Dennis's life, like Dr. Michaels, who had steadfastly believed in her without judgment. Rona's presence in Dennis's life was equally important, confirming through shared experiences that Dennis's inexplicable visions and emotional journeys were genuine and significant. This validation had inspired Rona profoundly, leading her to create the Holistic Center—a place designed to offer others the understanding and comfort Dennis had found in her.

Dennis's reunion with Lucas—or rather, the rediscovery of one another—occurred during a more settled period of her life. Although she still grappled occasionally with accepting the nature of her gift, she was calmer and more at peace. Unknowingly, Rona had played a crucial role in reconnecting Dennis and Lucas. Moreover, through Rona, Dennis was able to revisit her past relationship with Mark. It had been a painful chapter, leaving emotional scars that almost prevented Dennis from opening her heart again. Yet time had proven a gentle healer, and Lucas's profound love ultimately mended those deep emotional wounds.

Meeting Mark once more allowed Dennis to finally gain closure, answering lingering questions that had haunted her after their abrupt separation. She was able to forgive Mark fully, acknowledging openly that despite the pain, a part of her heart had always held love for him. It had been an innocent, childlike love, pure and genuine, rooted deeply in gratitude for the solace he had offered after losing her parents.

Sarah's entry into Dennis's life had been another of Mark's lasting contributions—a friendship that blossomed naturally, bringing healing and companionship. Through their friendship, Dennis found herself a bridge, reconnecting Sarah with Eileen Harrison and facilitating Sarah's healing journey. Dennis's unwavering support helped Sarah gradually reclaim her true self, restoring emotional balance and eventually allowing Sarah to re-enter society, beginning a new chapter as a resident at La Estancia.

Dennis cherished these relationships, each uniquely valuable and profoundly meaningful. They were the family she'd never known—a circle of unconditional love and support that defined her life.

That morning, as the brisk air swirled gently around her, Dennis embraced the preciousness of these memories, fully aware of the privilege inherent in each moment she lived. Her world was special, not limited to the life she experienced now, but embracing the other realms she had glimpsed. She felt deep gratitude for being precisely where she was.

Recently, Dennis had been feeling unwell, prompting a visit to the doctor a few days earlier. Following medical advice, she'd taken some time off to rest, waiting anxiously for the results of routine tests conducted to ensure nothing unusual was happening.

The ringing of the phone interrupted her contemplation, and Dennis answered immediately.

"Hello?"

"Hi, Dennis. This is Dr. Cortez's office," the woman on the other end greeted warmly. "Mrs. Dennis, your results are in."

"Already? That was fast—I expected them on Tuesday. I'll pick them up soon," Dennis responded.

"That's fine, but the doctor specifically wanted me to reassure you that there's nothing to worry about."

"So everything's okay?" Dennis inquired, her voice filled with relief.

"Yes, perfectly normal for your condition," the woman casually replied, unaware that her words were about to ignite a whirlwind of emotions within Dennis.

"My condition? Could you clarify exactly what you mean by 'condition'?" Dennis asked urgently, confusion and excitement intertwining.

"Yes, Dennis, your pregnancy," the woman replied matter-of-factly, not realizing Dennis was hearing this news for the first time.

"Oh my goodness!" Dennis exclaimed loudly, barely able to comprehend the magnitude of what she'd just heard, emotions oscillating between laughter and tears.

"Dennis, I'm sorry, I didn't realize you didn't know..." the woman apologized hurriedly.

"No, no, it's perfectly fine," Dennis quickly reassured, unable to hold back her joy. "I'll speak to the doctor later—I need to call my spouse right away."

"Please promise me you'll stay calm, Mrs. Dennis," the woman urged, sensing Dennis's excitement.

"I will, absolutely. Thank you," Dennis replied quickly, ending the call.

Unable to contain her excitement, Dennis immediately tried reaching Lucas, dialing his number insistently. Finally, after several attempts, Lucas picked up the phone.

"Lucas! For God's sake, you finally answered!"

"What's going on? Are you okay?" Lucas asked, clearly alarmed by the urgency in Dennis's voice.

"I got a call from the doctor's office. The results are in."

"Oh no, please tell me what's happening." Lucas sounded increasingly tense, dreading what might come next.

"Well, don't you want to guess?" Dennis replied teasingly, though there was a note of seriousness in her tone.

"No, I don't want to guess. What's wrong, Dennis? Is it something serious? Should we go back to the doctor? What is it? Tell me!" Lucas was on the verge of losing his composure, worry gnawing at him.

"Okay, I wish you were here so I could tell you in person, but I don't think I can wait any longer."

"All right, Dennis, it's fine, but please just tell me what's happening!"

"It's just that soon... we'll have a visitor!" Dennis exclaimed.

"A visitor? Who's coming?"

"No, my love, can't you guess?"

"Dennis? Is it what I'm thinking? Please, just say it plainly—my nerves are shot, and I feel like I'm going to be sick."

"Yes, my love, yes! We're pregnant!" Dennis's excitement was unmistakable, and Lucas, on the other end of the line, felt the same rush of emotion.

"My love, you don't know how happy I am. Give me a few minutes, and I'll head home. We need to celebrate!"

"Yes, my love, I'll wait for you."

That afternoon, Dennis and Lucas sat on the sand, hand in hand, gazing at the horizon as they tried to comprehend the immense joy filling them. Although Lucas had regained much of his memory from his existence on another plane, he couldn't foresee how the rest of his life would play out in human form. This wonderful news was an unexpectedly gratifying surprise, and all they could do was wait for time to pass.

The word spread quickly—Dennis practically called Tammy first, and almost immediately afterwards, she called Sarah. That alone was enough for everyone else to find out. Dennis's phone rang nonstop that morning, and though she was pleased, by afternoon she was worn out from so much emotion. Sitting on the sand, watching the horizon, both souls considered the future. Was this an extraordinary gift, or simply part of the life they were meant to live? Whichever it was, Dennis and Lucas felt certain they would welcome it wholeheartedly. Sitting shoulder to shoulder, hands interlaced, they watched as the future grew brighter. A few orbs of light gathered, twinkling and intensifying in radiance as evening approached. They, too, wished to share that special moment.

Months passed, one after another, and Dennis gradually adapted to the idea of impending motherhood. Lucas, for his part, enjoyed spending more time at home, looking after the little one who had yet to arrive, as well as caring for Dennis. She was far from complaining—she loved how Lucas tended to her every need. It was a wonderful time, and even though Dennis wanted it to hurry by, the nine months went exactly as they should—no more, no less. Dennis felt well throughout and decided she didn't need to stop working. Yet she and Lucas had already agreed that she would take a break to devote herself to their baby. Nothing was more important to her than spending as much time as possible with the people she loved.

They weren't sure what name to choose, mainly because they hadn't wanted to find out if it was a girl or a boy. As a result, the room they prepared for the newest member of the Verdi-Russell family was decorated with white and yellow gifts. "It has such a lovely ring to it," Dennis thought, though she was often visited by doubts and questions. She chose not to burden Lucas with these worries, but they still lingered. She frequently remembered the daughter she had in that other place, the one she, Lucas, and the others came from. She could almost see the little girl's face and felt a pang of sorrow that she couldn't know more or be with her. Occasionally, she would sigh and speak to the orbs that always appeared, asking:

SESSIONS, THERAPY FOR THE SOUL

"Will you really never tell me anything about my daughter? I just want to know that she's okay.

Couldn't you at least let me learn something about her?"

But the orbs never answered. It was as though Dennis heard only the deepest silence each time she asked, always met by that same, unwavering stillness. Around her sixth month, she decided to stop asking. She resolved that this life belonged to Dennis Russell on the earthly plane, and all she could do was make the most of it, nothing more.

Entering her seventh month of pregnancy, Dennis stopped working, officially starting her prenatal leave. She devoted more time to Sarah, who herself was only working three days a week so she could spend extra hours with her mother. Eileen's health was good, and she had countless plans to enjoy with Sarah, ensuring they were never bored. One afternoon, after shopping together, Sarah turned to Dennis and said, "I have something to tell you."

"Oh, yes? Tell me—nothing's wrong, is it?"

"Don't worry, it's nothing bad," Sarah replied, hesitating momentarily before continuing. "I've decided to contact my children. I'm done waiting for one of them to come looking for me."

"Really? That's wonderful—absolutely amazing." Dennis's eyes shone with excitement.

"Yes, I think it's time. It's been a year since I moved back in with my mother, and she's given me the strength to try. So much time has passed; I can't keep putting it off."

"You're right. I'm so happy for you, and of course, you can count on us. I also think you should give yourself that chance."

"Mom says we'll get help from the same professional Aunt Mary used when she confirmed I was her niece. It's the best approach; at least we already trust him."

"Absolutely. That sounds like the perfect plan. Do you remember anything about your kids?"

"Honestly, I only recall bits and pieces, but it's something. My medical records mention a last known address, and although the phone number is out of service, it's a start."

"I'm sure it'll all work out. Don't worry—everything will be fine. You have no idea how excited I am for you."

They finished their shopping spree with a delicious ice cream at the parlor in Parque de La Bahía—Lucas and Dennis's favorite spot. Everything seemed to be going well: Dennis had already stopped working a couple of weeks earlier, so she had ample time for rest, outings, and leisurely walks, basically doing whatever she felt like. Her checkups were all fine, but that evening Dennis felt oddly uneasy—something didn't seem right. During dinner, she admitted to Lucas that she was worried, although she couldn't explain why. Lucas suggested they go to the hospital just to be safe, but Dennis insisted it wasn't necessary.

"It's more like I'm sensing something, but I'm not sure what," she confessed, and they decided to drop the subject. However, the feeling persisted in Dennis's mind over the next couple of days.

Two days later, on an otherwise ordinary night, Dennis went to bed slightly later than usual. She'd spent some time in the baby's room, tidying up scattered toys and items. Exhausted, she soon fell into a deep sleep.

In her dreams, she perceived random images at first—nothing distinct. She felt incredibly light, reminiscent of that time when she managed to leave her body and find Lucas. Attempting to look down, she realized she couldn't see anything. Then she heard whispers, gradually becoming more audible. It sounded like a woman speaking to someone nearby.

As the scene clarified, Dennis found herself in a vast, flower-filled garden. She was seated on a wooden bench, watching a group of people wearing long robes that concealed their feet, though their faces were visible. Apart from a faint glow tracing their forms, they appeared almost ordinary. The group was composed of about ten figures.

Dennis glanced around, seeking any clue about where she might be or whether she was dreaming. Suddenly, she noticed one figure moving toward her—a woman, approaching slowly. When she reached Dennis, she stopped in front of her and said, "You won't have to wait much longer—she's on her way." The woman's voice resonated in Dennis's mind, though Dennis seemed to be seated or so she thought.

"Who am I waiting for?" Dennis asked, unsure who she was about to meet or even where she was.

"Please follow me," the woman replied, again speaking directly into Dennis's mind. Yet Dennis understood her perfectly. She rose and followed the woman, who added, "She's coming."

Dennis found herself alone inside a wooden pergola in the center of the garden, beneath a clear, vivid sky. She watched as the woman retraced her steps along a path of stepping stones bordered by tall trees and vibrant flowers, forming a breathtaking view.

Seeing no one else approaching from that direction, Dennis was startled to hear a melodic voice behind her. Turning to see who was speaking, she instantly recognized this person by the joy in her own heart. The woman was robed like the others—tall, fair-skinned, delicate features, a porcelain-like complexion, deep blue eyes, and white hair swept to one side in a long braid. She opened her arms, inviting Dennis closer, and Dennis moved forward, embracing her warmly.

The woman spoke directly into Dennis's mind, though Dennis couldn't quite grasp why none of her words seemed to connect with anything familiar. A moment passed—or at least Dennis believed it did—and she realized that the woman appeared to be saying goodbye. She stroked Dennis's face, gently moving her hair aside. Leaning in close, the woman spoke, and Dennis nodded in response, unable to fully comprehend. It felt as though Dennis were split in two: one part of her understood every word, and the other—the version of herself simply standing there—felt lost, uncertain what to do or how to speak.

It was a strange feeling, and it only grew stronger when Dennis spotted a bright light approaching, radiating flashes of colorful brilliance like a crystal catching the sun. The sight of the light wasn't surprising; the sensation inside her, however, was something else altogether. It was a warmth coursing through her body, like a gentle electric current. Dennis recognized the essence of that light immediately. The woman still standing near her received the light in her hands, then gently offered it to Dennis. Instinctively, Dennis opened her palms to accept it.

What happened next was beyond words. Dennis felt warmth in her hands, and suddenly, the orb expanded, its glow spreading until it completely encompassed her. It was as though she were encased in a shimmering, luminous bubble. She watched as the woman walked away, and everything around her lost its color. A dense whiteness surrounded her, and in an instant, everything disappeared.

In the distance, she could vaguely hear a soft melody—instrumental music, her favorite—but she kept sleeping, undisturbed by Lucas rising or by the music itself. Not until Lucas came to wake her for breakfast did Dennis truly awaken—and with a sense that something was stuck in her mind.

She jumped out of bed, nearly running to the bathroom to look at herself in the mirror. She needed confirmation that she was no longer dreaming. Gazing at her reflection, Dennis immediately placed her hands on her stomach, needing to feel her baby, and at that precise moment, everything became clear.

"Lucas! Lucas! You won't believe this..." Dennis yelled from the bathroom.

"What's wrong, Dennis? Are you okay?" Lucas called back, alarmed by the urgency in her voice.

"Yes, I'm fine." Dennis emerged, nearly sprinting, eager to hug him. "I had the most incredible experience. At first, I thought I was dreaming, but then none of it made sense, and things grew more complicated."

"Take a breath, Dennis. Slow down. Better yet, let's have breakfast—it's ready, and you can explain everything then." Lucas smiled, gently wrapping her in a dressing gown.

"It's amazing! I can't wait to tell you," Dennis said excitedly.

"All right, start from the beginning—what happened in this dream?" Lucas asked, leading her to the table.

"I know our baby's true identity!" Dennis exclaimed.

"Did you see the doctor?" Lucas asked, startled.

"No, of course not. It was the encounter I had last night."

"What encounter?"

"At first, I had no idea what was going on. I just knew it wasn't an ordinary dream. I found myself in another place and saw a woman—tall, fair-skinned, with deep blue eyes and white hair styled to one side in a long braid." Lucas's eyes widened; he recognized that description. There was only one being who looked like that.

"And did she say anything to you? Do you know who she is?" Lucas pressed.

"I'm not entirely sure," Dennis confessed, beaming with happiness, "but I do know what she gave me."

"What did she give you?"

"It wasn't an object," Dennis said. "She placed something into my hands—our daughter!"

"Dennis, I don't understand," Lucas replied. "What do you mean?"

"I'm telling you, our daughter Weer is inside me. I recognized her the instant she arrived—so bright, so radiant. The woman set her in my hands, and I understood everything. I can't recall all the details, but I know she's here with us, and she's not leaving."

As Dennis continued to describe her extraordinary vision, Lucas knew there was no denying it. He understood exactly who that mysterious woman was: the spiritual guide of the group to which both he and Dennis belonged. She was the one Lucas had appealed to, begging for permission to follow Dennis to this earthly plane. She was also the one who facilitated Weer's arrival in this life.

Lucas laid his hands on Dennis's belly, and they both felt the baby move more strongly than ever before, tears welling in his eyes. Once again, the three of them—Dennis, Lucas, and Weer—were reunited, ready to remain together far longer this time.

The weeks flew by, and at last Dennis gave birth to a beautiful baby girl, Sofia Weer. Healthy and radiant, she became the joy of both Dennis and Lucas. Welcomed by many loving friends and relatives, Sofia Weer had arrived into a family as large as it was devoted. In the days before her birth, Dennis had written several letters to her unborn daughter. One read:

Oh, my dear child, how can I explain what I feel...
Your sweet little face, the one I saw months before you arrived,
Made me realize you were my daughter, my little girl,
my purpose— If such a thing exists,
a drive that keeps me moving forward.
I wanted to hold you, hug you, and share so many things,
My heart speaks softly, whispering words of hope.
The wait is short; soon, I'll see you with my own eyes.
My spirit cries out with joy for everyone to know—
How happy I am to hold you in my arms,
Overflowing with pride and brimming with life...
At last, my little angel, you are here!

Life went on

Life continued for all those who, in some way, had become part of this new family—united by the circumstances that life itself had placed before them, perhaps with the sole purpose of crossing paths. For a long time, all the events and experiences were joyful and full of life for each member of this family, but when difficult situations arose, they all came together to support one another. They often gathered on Sunday afternoons to share their experiences. The conversations flowed easily, and the dialogue was always pleasant. Each of them had a bond that tied them to this group of people, who, almost without realizing it, had formed connections stronger than those forged by blood.

Sarah finally reconnected with her children, who soon joined this new family that had been formed by life's coincidences—or, as Sarah once said, as part of the Divine Plan. Both of her children were married with families of their own, and her former spouse had died many years earlier in a drunk driving accident, taking all the information about Sarah with him. The man had taken to drinking because of his own demons, which had haunted him ever since he decided to leave Sarah and practically erase her from his life and, in turn, from the lives of his children.

Sarah's spouse had done his best to erase her memory from their children's minds, and it seemed he had succeeded. But seeing Sarah again was like something opening up in their minds and hearts, unlocking memories buried deep inside. Sarah had always loved them, and they came to understand this. Although there was no way to reclaim the lost time, there was plenty of time ahead to create new memories and strengthen their bonds of love.

As in all things, the day of truth arrived when Sarah's daughter received a phone call. On the other end of the line, someone was telling her an almost unbelievable story. Though difficult to accept at first, the words of the person on the phone managed to reopen a heart sealed by the pain of her mother's supposed departure. The detective who had been in charge of Sarah's case had successfully located both of her children, much to the joy of Sarah and her mother. Sarah's eldest son had always kept memories of his mother alive within him. Although he could have forgotten them due to his age, he never let them go. He cherished those memories, and reuniting with his mother was like living anew, but now without the pain he had carried inside.

Eileen was overjoyed by everything that had happened in recent times. It was almost unbelievable to her—not only was her daughter alive, but she now had grandchildren and great-grandchildren to love and pamper after all the years of absence. What more could she ask for? Now, she just needed time and good health to fully enjoy the blessings life had given her. After all, fate, in its ironic way, was finally smiling at her.

Mary continued as usual, at the helm of the Harrison Agency alongside her daughter Tammy, with whom she faced new projects every day. Tammy's eldest daughter graduated as a publicist and joined the agency in a new department that Dennis had created. The Harrison Scholarship had become a vital socioeconomic initiative in their community, making its preservation and growth essential. As part of that development, new minds like Alicia's were invaluable.

The Harrison Scholarship offered opportunities ranging from temporary internships at the agency to full college scholarships for the winners. Initially, it was funded solely by the company, but over time, many other companies joined the effort, seeing it as a way to cultivate new, talented professionals, thereby contributing to the city's economic development.

Alicia, who had grown into a beautiful woman inside and out, loved her new job. She was the perfect person for the position, as Dennis often said, Alicia had the guts, and that was all that mattered. But there was something else, something special that everyone noticed about Alicia—she was the spitting image of her grandmother, Mary Harrison, making it easy to imagine whose hands the future of the Harrison Agency would one day rest in.

Tammy's son, on the other hand, stayed closer to his father, who had started his own business, something related to computer science and home automation. It was a place where the boy's knowledge could grow, allowing him to perfect what he had studied at university. He was still very young and didn't have a serious relationship, but time would guide him on the right path, and eventually, he would find someone with whom to share his life. For now, his focus was on personal growth and strengthening his relationship with his parents, which had significantly improved.

Tammy's spouse's business quickly prospered, offering them the financial stability they had worked so hard for. The relationship between them had finally found a perfect balance after the highs and lows they had endured. They understood each other better, and their communication was clear and reciprocal. It seemed as though they had all grown as a result of Tammy's illness. In a way, they were grateful for the second chance to reconfigure their family and values, and that she was still with them.

Rona had stabilized the Holistic Center, offering a range of services that benefited many people. She had even convinced Dennis to join them and teach Reiki, now as a Master. While it's true that Rona, or Dr. Michaels as everyone knew her, felt satisfied with what she had achieved, she never saw her son again. However, she was certain that he would be waiting for her when her time to leave this world came. She had been ready for that day for a long time.

Lucas had been presented with good opportunities, and he had seized them. He now managed several other businesses, allowing him to provide a comfortable life for his family—Dennis and their daughter, whom he adored. Family life was undoubtedly the best thing that could have happened to him. He no longer thought much about what his afterlife would be like. Both Dennis and Lucas had decided to give their best in this earthly life for as long as they remained on this plane. But this didn't change the fact that they both possessed certain gifts, known only to them, Sarah, and Dr. Michaels. It was better that way—they had to learn to live naturally and normally, like any other human being. Although there were times when they found themselves having a mental conversation, they quickly reminded themselves to keep it private. It was something very personal, a remnant of that other life they both shared.

Life again gave them a reason to be happy and experience fulfillment on this plane with the arrival of their daughter, Sofia Weer. It felt like a gift or a concession from the spiritual plane—perhaps because wishes are granted, or perhaps because it was written that way as part of the Divine Plan. What mattered most was that they had the opportunity to live and feel what people call happiness. As Sofia Weer grew, she gradually revealed herself to be a noble soul, full of sensitivity and compassion for all living things.

Over the years, Dennis and Lucas realized that little Sofia Weer could also see the presence of bright lights—something they had suspected but that did not surprise them. They guided her gently, helping her understand that there was nothing to fear and that it was not a bad thing. By the age of five, Sofia Weer not only saw the orbs of light but also spoke to them naturally, as if this were the most normal thing in the world. By the time she was seven, she had come to understand on her own that others might not understand, so she reserved these conversations for when she was with her parents. It was as if she had always known, never needing to ask for explanations.

And Dennis... She decided to leave the agency when Sofia Weer turned four, understanding that her daughter needed more of her time, and she was ready to give it. During this period, Dennis completed her Reiki studies, becoming a Master, and began teaching free classes at Dr. Michaels' Holistic Center. Despite her many activities, Dennis embarked on a personal project—creating and publishing a line of children's books.

Dennis had developed a passion for drawing, so she dedicated herself to illustrating her own books. This creativity would eventually shape the future of little Sofia Weer, who, in time, would become a children's book publisher herself. It was a career that allowed her, like her mother, to nurture and support the creativity of children—those innocent and vulnerable souls who need the most love.

Sofia Weer carried with her not only the teachings and love her parents had given her, but also the light within her, which she would use for good. She would go on to have a family of her own, with many descendants who would remember Dennis and Lucas as the most important pillars of their family. Dennis imbued her books with a unique vision, blending the magical with the real, creating a world where children could believe in the incredible without fear of judgment. Her stories reinforced the values of a child's heart.

Dennis and Lucas's life continued for many years, marked by an intense love and a shared commitment to giving their best. Dennis continued to quietly bring healing light to anyone in need, always accompanied by the orbs of light. This had been the commitment communicated to her by the spiritual guide that day—a responsibility Dennis gradually discovered and deeply respected. There were no more questions about the afterlife; she knew the day would come, but she chose not to dwell on it. She had learned to love her life on the earthly plane and, if it were up to her, she would stay here for a long time.

She accepted that her life had been complicated, but she also understood that the lives of all human beings are equally complex and difficult to comprehend. Some people might assimilate it better than others, but in the end, everyone carries with them only the essence of the good things.

There was no longer any difference between Dennis's life and the lives of others—she had become just another person within the system, and that was how she felt most at peace. She was content with herself, and yes, sometimes she would shed a tear when remembering the past. But she would quickly wipe it away, knowing that one day, not too far off, she would see those who were no longer here.

Dennis understood that after everything one experiences, only the essence of those experiences remains. That essence is the only thing we take with us when we leave this world. The rest is lived in the moment, in the instant when everything happens—that is the essence; the rest is left behind. The memories of lived experiences may fade, but the essence, the part that is felt within, is what lasts and nourishes the soul.

Our soul is the universal energy that lives within each of us. It is that power centered in what we call the heart, the force that gives us strength when we feel we can't go on, or the determination to move forward when everything seems to say no. It is what makes us smile even when we are very sad—that is our soul, the greatest and most powerful thing we have, here and anywhere else. The soul cannot be hurt, damaged, or destroyed, for it is the life-giving energy force. Let us always remember that. The answer to what you seek is within yourself—the light has always been and will always be in you.

Dennis finally returned home when she was 78 years old. That night, after celebrating her birthday with all the beautiful people who had been part of her family circle for so many years—a circle that had grown and strengthened over time—Dennis went to bed with a deep sense of happiness. She felt joy for the wonderful essence her soul had captured that night, sharing with everyone one last time. As she did every night, she kissed the photograph of her spouse, who had passed away two years earlier, and went to sleep. That night, Dennis ended a life—but it had not been in vain. Quite the opposite.

Dennis left behind the beautiful family they had formed, but she knew that Tis was waiting for her when she crossed the portal—a moment she had awaited day by day since the last time she kissed Lucas, her partner, her friend, her eternal love.

"How are you, my love?" Tis asked.

"Now, I'm much better, my love. I missed you!" Na replied.

"I missed you too, but here we are again."

"Shall we go home?"

"Yes, let's go home!"

THE END

Get To Know The Author

www.ingramcontent.com/pod-product-compliance
Lightning Source LLC
Chambersburg PA
CBHW071148020726
47502CB00002B/329